REGENCY DECADENCE

Ruby-red chiffon flowed to the floor from a circular ring on the ceiling. She could see every detail of the bed through the gossamer fabric. It would hold four people easily, and it was covered in opulent satin pillows.

"What do you think of this room?" the duke questioned lazily.

All she could do was look, her eyes glazed. Then, for no reason, her eyes lifted again to the ring securing the poor excuse for a bed curtain. It wasn't a ring. It was a large mirror.

When she didn't answer, he added, "If there is anything you don't like, feel free to tell me. It will be changed immediately."

Was he laughing at her? "No, everything is perfect," she said faintly. So this is where he makes love to his mistresses, she thought. No wonder he has such a reputation as a rake.

His eyes never wavered from her face. "I have a proposition to present to you, Amalie," he stated bluntly, "and now seems as good a time as any to discuss it."

Lady of the Night

BY GEORGINA DEVON

ZEBRA BOOKS
KENSINGTON PUBLISHING CORP.

ZEBRA BOOKS

are published by

Kensington Publishing Corp.
475 Park Avenue South
New York, NY 10016

Second printing: June, 1991

Printed in the United States of America

Chapter One

"Damn!" The soft explosion came from lips normally formed in an impassive half smile or curled in derision, their owner finding the world at large either amusing or contemptuous. That wasn't the case today.

His Grace, Julian Ambrose St. John, ninth duke of Camber, was sprawled in a cushioned wing chair in front of a raging fire. It didn't help his mood that the chair was covered in rose chintz, or that the private parlor he occupied was in The Swan at Cheltenham and not his London apartments. His grey eyes, shadowed by thick auburn lashes and heavy brows, stared angrily into the orange flames. To his jaundiced mind they mocked him for a fool. Soon to be a leg-shackled one, at that.

"Damn." The half-empty bottle of brandy, a drink he particularly favored, sat on the table next to him. However, having shot the cat didn't affect his appearance. A dark blue coat of Bath superfine, covering a sedate tan waistcoat, and a pair of tight buff breeches tucked into Hessians blackened with a mixture of champagne proclaimed him a Corinthian. The only mar to this sartorial elegance was his hair. The thick auburn locks, once brushed in an immaculate Brutus, curled in disarray around his broad forehead.

A heavy sheet of paper hung from one motionless white hand. This untimely missive was the cause of his anger. "Why that young whelp had to go and stick his spoon in the wall now, I wish I knew!"

His heir, a distant cousin, had died several weeks ago. The cause had been malaria, brought on by a prolonged stay in India. With his heir's death, Julian was forced to marry and beget an heir of his body, or see his dukedom and all it entailed revert back to the Crown upon his own death. It was rare for a title to go back to the Crown, with the decrease in infant mortality, but the St. Johns had been unlucky in their children. All were females, with the exception of Julian and his now deceased relative. With no males to take the title, primogeniture decreed that it revert to whence it came. His solicitor had been very specific on that point.

Julian flung his empty glass into the fire. The sound of shattering crystal was very satisfying. He imperiously rang the bell for another glass. Mine landlord, being cognizant of the great personage he housed, would answer promptly. Of that, Julian had no doubts.

Julian was there for a prize fight between the great Cribb and the savage Shelton. The fight had been worth the discomfort of the inn. His pleasure in it had even been intensified by the satisfaction of winning a monkey on the mill's outcome from his old rival, the earl of Perth. But it hadn't been sufficient to alleviate Julian's disgust and fury at returning to the inn and finding this letter.

He jerked the bell again before gaining command over his emotions. He was known the length and breadth of England for the superb rein he kept on himself. This same control made him an outstanding shot, a swordsman of renown, an amateur pugilist who could boast of having planted a facer on Gentleman Jackson, and a whip whom some called the best in the land. These were all qualities that would not help him now. Namely, to meet eligible females.

His habit of avoiding the functions of the beau monde insured that he now knew no lady of good breeding to become his duchess. This was made worse by his openly avowed preference for the haunts of the fashionable impures. Consequently, his conquests in the arena of the demimonde were well known to the matchmaking mamas. Some of them even went so far as to say he shouldn't be accepted into polite society for fear he would take advantage of their innocent darlings.

However, after they remembered he was as rich as Golden Ball and held one of the oldest dukedoms in the country, they always sent an invitation. He always declined. Insipid young misses and old dragons didn't interest him.

"Landlord, you try my patience." His voice was low and rich as he reached once again for the bell. Just as he grasped the copper noisemaker the door opened. Julian narrowed his eyes to sparkling slits in a face of immobile hauteur. The vision surprised him, at an inn such as this, but he gave no sign. His cool regard insolently traveled the length of the female walking

7

across the threshold as she turned to close the door.

What he saw was pleasing. She was slightly above average height, and slim, with a deep bosom and supple waist that flared into willowy hips. Her movements were graceful and kept to a minimum. As she turned and saw him for the first time, he was caught by the contrast between her dark eyes and her fair hair and complexion. Her large brown eyes were fringed by heavy dark lashes and topped by equally dark flaring eyebrows. Her hair was white in its blondness and fell in thick waves around her face and down her back. Her full lips were so darkly coral that Julian knew they were painted. At the moment, they formed an 'O' of surprise.

"I beg your pardon, I didn't know this room was occupied," she said in a deep voice. Much too deep and husky to belong to a lady of quality, Julian assured himself as he continued to take in the lady's ample charms. That he was dangerously drunk wasn't apparent to the lady or acknowledged by himself.

"Come in and make yourself at home, sweetings." He got up and swept her an elegant leg, showing the muscles of his calf to advantage. "You are a fair nymph come to succor me in this, my moment of darkest despair." His anger at the recent information evaporated in the heat of pursuit. She was but another outlet for his ferocious rebellion against the fate he saw in store for himself.

"I beg your pardon," she began before he interrupted her.

"Sweetings, you are becoming repetitious. Come, take a seat and close that delectable mouth of yours. It's been my experience that women of your stamp shouldn't talk: only sit, or lie, and look inviting." On these words, spoken with an arrogance ingrained in him, he advanced toward the woman.

Her gown was outmoded, with a high neckline and made of dull brown wool, but it didn't hide her full curves or deter him in his progress. In several swift strides, he was in front of her and tangling his long fingers in the windswept waves of her hair. "Such unusual hair you have, sweetings. It must come from a bottle to be so fair. What large eyes you have," he said, losing himself in their depths.

"All the better to see your ungentlemanly behavior," she retorted in that unladylike voice. Her body went stiff when he thrust his hand into her locks, but her eyes shot flames at him as her lips compressed into a tight line.

"A little tiger. That only makes the chase that much more enjoyable," he drawled, lowering his lips to hers. He felt her start, and his half-closed eyes watched her pupils dilate with anticipation . . . or fear? He cared not which. It was obvious to him that she was a woman of less than virtuous morals, otherwise she would never have intruded in his reserved parlor.

He was used to women trying to catch his attention, but this one was definitely an improvement over the general run of loose females who strove to make his acquaintance. Even to his jaded tastes her high cheekbones and determined chin, covered by skin so translucent he was sure it was made so by artifice, were seductive. She was an ethereal beauty worth keeping for a while.

He released her lips enough to whisper against them, "Perhaps my continued stay in this godforsaken

9

inn will be relieved of the tedium I had first envisioned, my fair charmer."

His brandy-scented breath wafted across her lips as she licked them with a nervous tongue. The glistening imparted to their coral softness was irresistible to the disreputable duke. With one hawklike motion, he again fastened his firm mouth over hers. His free hand reached out and encircled her small waist while the one wrapped in her curls pulled her head forcefully back. He could feel her whole body trembling against his. For a second, no more, her delicate hands pushed against his chest.

A low rumble of laughter escaped him to come between their entwined lips as a muffle of sound. "Don't fight it, sweetings. Enjoy it. I'm sure it's nothing you haven't experienced before." He was verified when her arms crept around his neck and pulled him closer than he already was.

With an exultation he wasn't used to feeling when kissing a woman, he met her ardor. Their bodies fused together. He could feel the dampness of her gown as it penetrated the cloth of his shirt and buckskins. Her warm lips clung to his, returning passion for passion. Caught in the feelings of the moment, Julian allowed his hands to roam down her back and cup her hips to his. With an expertise born of practice, one nimble hand applied itself to the brass hooks and eyes at the top of her gown. He was thus pleasurably occupied when the parlor door opened and the landlord entered.

Interrupted at a most crucial moment, Julian raised his head and eyed the reluctant man with a gleam that promised retribution. With a curse, he put the woman slightly from him. That her hands flew to pull up the shoulders of her gown he had just managed to loosen, he cared naught.

"What do you mean entering my apartment without knocking first?" he demanded. Engrossed in his berating of the man, he didn't notice the woman edging furtively toward the door.

"Pardon me, Your Grace, but I did. Knock that is, but no one answered. Seeing that you'd rung the bell, I thought it best to open the door and see what I could do for you, Your Grace. I'm sorry to interrupt you." The landlord's tones were subservient, but there was a look of slyness in the glance he cast the woman. His Grace was known for his ladybirds, and this one appeared a rare one indeed.

"Well, as you can see, you're *de trop*. Bring me another glass. The last one has somehow found itself in the fireplace. Now get out." Julian watched the man bow himself out and added, "Be sure you wait for an answer next time before you open that door."

In the fracas, the woman slipped out the open door. Without a backward glance, she fled down the hall. Too late to stop her, Julian watched her disappearing figure in frustration. With a grunt of disgust, he turned his back on the door closing behind the landlord and flung his slender frame into the much abused chintz chair. So much for a dalliance to take his mind off the problem caused by his cursed relative.

There's nothing for it, he thought irritably, but to return to town immediately and find a bride. A small pang of regret for the lost beauty was all the thought he gave the woman as he stomped out of the room

11

heading for his bedroom and his valet.

He didn't recognize me. The litany ran through her mind as Lady Damaris Amalie FitzHubert, Dami to her intimates, rushed from the room without a backward glance. In an attempt to bring some order to her person, she worked hastily at the fastenings to her bodice, never slackening in her pace. Gasping for breath, she paused at the top of the stairs leading down to the entryway. The backlash of emotion caused by her recent encounter with the duke made her sag against the wall. Taking three deep breaths — her brother Simon, sixth marquis of Cleve, said three careful breaths always helped to restore a measure of lost aplomb — she finished hooking her gown together.

It was too late now to find the retiring room she'd been searching for when she had inadvertently stumbled into the duke's lair. She would have to return to the carriage as she was. There wasn't time to correct the havoc wreaked on her hair by traveling with her head stuck undecorously out the carriage window the better part of the day.

Dami looked carefully down the deserted stairs before descending. Reaching the bottom unmolested, she squared her shoulders and walked out into the warm afternoon sun. Its golden rays haloed the bustling activity of the popular posting house and lent a feeling of unreality to her recent encounter. She was thankful for the activity, as it masked her approach to the elegant black coach emblazoned with the crest of the marquis of Cleve. Not waiting for the coachman to help her up, Dami scrambled in the door. She collapsed against the plush blue velvet squabs with a sigh of relief.

"Damaris," a foreboding voice said, "just what do you think you are doing coming back here looking the same ragamuffin you were when you left? I thought I sent you into The Swan with the express purpose of tidying yourself before we reach Rose Arbor in London?"

Opening one eye, Dami looked at her mama seated across from her in the coach. Of course, the dowager marchioness of Cleve was facing the horses, a much more comfortable position than Dami's, which was facing away. Mama complained of getting sick otherwise. The dowager's lavender watered silk round gown proclaimed to the world that while not in deep mourning, she was still honoring the passing of a dear one. It was a most becoming shade to the lady's fair complexion, not to mention setting off her still elegant figure. Right now, her lorgnette was raised to sharp blue eyes as she perused her errant daughter.

"Mama, you must believe me that I tried, but the girl in the tap room gave me the wrong directions." Dami's husky voice was calm as she determined not to tell her mother the true nature of her attempt at beautification. "By the time I had wandered around the first floor at least twice, I judged it to be too late to continue looking. I know how you long to reach London, and feared that any more time wasted here would only make the remainder of the journey that much harder on you. Believe me," her eyes twinkled, "I appreciate your effort to present me to society and how hard this trip is on your always delicate health."

"Hummph." Dropping the subject, the dowager said, "I daresay that scamp of a brother of yours is having one last mug of ale before he presents himself for departure." With an imperious stomp of her walking stick, she summoned the coachman. "Jem, go roust Lord John from the tap room. It's past time we were on our way if we plan to make London before dark."

Within minutes, Lord Jonathan Lewis FitzHubert, youngest son of the deceased fifth marquis of Cleve and twin to Damaris, was heard shouting for his horse. They were off in a cloud of dust.

Grateful to be moving away from that fateful inn, Dami closed her eyes and leaned back, hoping to simulate sleep while she endeavored to put her thoughts in some semblance of order. Seeing Camber had shocked her. For a fleeting moment his eyes had been warm with emotion, and she had thought he remembered her. But he hadn't. Not that she'd really expected he would when they finally met again, but she hadn't expected his lack of recognition to hurt this much either.

No. Instead of the brief, violent encounter they'd just had, she'd cherished a foolishly romantic dream of remeeting him at her come-out ball. In her fantasy, she was dressed in white, her hair piled high on her head with one curl resting against her bosom. Around her neck a choker of pearls gleamed in the light from hundreds of candles, and matching earrings dangled provocatively against her cheeks. Strains of the first waltz filled the perfumed air as Camber claimed her. Her whole being flooded with love as his arms circled her possessively.

Dami shook her head to clear it. How unlike reality. It wasn't surprising that he'd treated her like a demi-rep, since that was the type of female he frequented. A rueful smile curved her lips. She, in her ill-fitting drab dress and stringy hair, to be mistaken for a woman of easy virtue was really very amusing. Too, she was quite certain she had reinforced his first impression by returning his kiss in such an abandoned manner. Well, she couldn't help that. He always did that to her. At least the two times he'd kissed her, which were the only two times she'd been in his company, had been that way. A pleasurable warmth engulfed her as she remembered the first time.

It was a fine day in late autumn, the fields full of ripe corn, and the sky a clear blue with not a cloud in sight. She was playing truant from her father's rigorous schedule of estate management. That this kind of education was unusual for a girl made her no fonder of it.

She was on her way to a large oak tree that hung over the stream flowing between her father's property and that of their closest neighbor. Her horse was doing a fine trot; she had no time to lose if she wanted to enjoy the privacy of her tree.

Never an avid horsewoman, she was barely in control of her mount. If the truth be known, she was afraid of the large beasts. They always knew it, too, and took shameful advantage of her when she least expected it. This morning she was having trouble controlling the animal, a feisty stallion who resented her presence on his back. In a blatant attempt to unseat her, the demon reared high on his hind legs. Too scared of losing her seat to think, Dami dropped the reins and grabbed the pommel. The long skirts of her riding habit didn't help. Feeling the release of control, the creature bolted.

In a state of panic, she clung blindly to her precarious perch. Tears started to run down her cheeks. The wind wrenched off her hat. Her long white hair came down and streamed behind her like a beacon. Certain that her end was near, she closed her eyes and prayed that it wouldn't be painful.

Just as she convinced herself to let go of her stranglehold and fall to the ground, she heard the sound of another horse approaching at breakneck speed. Opening her eyes, now wide with fright and red-rimmed from crying, she saw a centaur. To her bemused mind, he was the most magnificent man she'd ever seen as he drew his horse skillfully next to hers and reached for the flying reins. A quick move of his wrists, and he pulled her recalcitrant animal to a stop.

Shaken beyond enduring, she sat frozen in the saddle. The young man, for she saw he wasn't any older than her older brother Simon, got off his horse and was at her side before she could fall. With a gentleness at contrast to the strength he'd just demonstrated, he grabbed her about the waist and lifted her to the ground. Her legs shook so badly, she would have fallen if he hadn't kept his hands around her.

His voice was deep with concern. "Do you think you can stand by yourself if I release you?" A worried frown pulled his eyebrows together as he continued to support her.

16

Her hands pressed against his broad chest, and she noticed that he was tall, very tall. The sun sparkled in his grey eyes and turned his hair to bronze as he looked down at her. His thin, aristocratic nose, wide forehead, and square jaw convinced her he must be of noble character. To her young mind, he was her knight in shining armor. That he was dressed in a tight fitting coat of bottle-green superfine and pale yellow pantaloons tucked into glossy Hessians was superfluous.

"You aren't going to faint on me?" He started sounding exasperated as she continued to gaze up at him with a look smacking of imbecility. "Come, let me help you to the shade of this tree. It should help." He slipped one arm completely around her as he drew her to his side, thus effectively removing her clutching hands from the lapels of his immaculate coat. "Sit here," he ordered her, helping her to the grass. Taking a large lawn handkerchief from his pocket, he said, "Wait here while I go to the creek and wet this. It should help you feel more the thing." A mischievous grin curved his sensual lips. "I'm not in the habit of carrying hartshorn for expiring damsels."

She watched his retreating back. He had been gently flirting with her. Unknown to her, she looked older than her thirteen years. Her normally pale face, still flushed from the wind and fear, and her hair falling in tangled waves down her back gave her a wild look. Her body ripening toward womanhood and her habit, a little too tight, added to the illusion.

She was starting to regain some of her composure, as much as a young girl could when confronted with her first heartthrob, when he returned with the now damp piece of cloth. He handed it to her and sank down next to her in one graceful movement. The wet material in her hand, she attempted to wipe her forehead in as mature a manner as that action could be done. The enormity of the situation had impressed itself on her while he'd been gone. She didn't know him. They hadn't even been properly introduced, and here she was sitting in the woods with him — alone.

He must have seen her deepening color, for he said, "Don't turn missish on me now, sweetings." His warm tones teased her. One long brown finger reached for her chin and turned her to face him. Little sparks, possibly from the sun, fired his grey eyes as he gazed at her face. With her eyes cast demurely down and her lashes lying with tantalizing softness on her clear skin, she didn't see his careful perusal.

He kissed her. It was a slow, tender kiss, renewing the tremors she'd felt from her ride. But these tremors weren't from fear. She didn't understand why she had them, only that she wanted him to keep pressing his lips to hers. When he finally released her, she kept her eyes screwed shut, afraid that if she opened them he'd disappear.

A soft sigh escaped her lips. "Will you please do that again?" Her voice was filled with wonder. Receiving no immediate response, she opened her eyes to take in the full look of his now hooded ones. "If you please, that was so very nice."

Enlightenment was beginning to dawn on his features. He carefully unpried her fingers from his ruined cravat and put her from him gently. "You're very young aren't you?"

She didn't know what to say. If she told him her real age, he very likely wouldn't kiss her again, and she wanted him to very much. "Not so young that I can't enjoy life, milord." The saucy answer was accompanied by a roguish dimple in her right cheek. Perhaps if she brazened it out he would ask her name. Maybe even call. It never occurred to her that she was much too young to receive attention from any man. All she wanted at the moment was to be assured that she would see her knight again.

He chuckled as he raised himself up and dusted his dirty pantaloons. Reaching out a hand, he said, "Let me help you mount your horse again. He's getting restless and it's past time you were at home with your nanny." The words were softened by a smile, but he was implacable in his actions as he threw her up into the saddle.

Safely mounted, she waited for him to say more; asked him with her eyes to say more. "Don't you wish to know my name?" She was lost to all propriety.

"You're a very attractive little girl, and I apologize for the kiss. You see," he confided with a charm many an experienced woman found irresistible, "I thought you were older. Otherwise, I would never have been so ungentlemanly as to take advantage of you in that fashion."

"Were you taking advantage of me? I always thought that must be a most unpleasant activity, or so Mama is always saying." She paused before adding thoughtfully, "But it wasn't." He wasn't going to ask her name. She'd settle for finding out who he was. "Will you tell me your name, milord?"

"No, I don't think I will, minx. It's obvious, you're much too forward a young lady for me, not to mention much too young. When you leave the nursery behind, then look me up. Who knows, perhaps by then we will find much in common. For now, so long." He slapped her horse gently on the flank, sending her off in a canter. Her neck was craned around to see him till the very last.

Coming back to the present, Dami had trouble suppressing the laugh that threatened to issue from her trembling lips. She'd been very young and naive. He'd been very tender with her, though. Quite out of character for a rake of his stamp. Even at that age, he had already garnered a reputation as a buck who took his pleasure where he willed. That he'd stopped from going further with her, she'd always held to his credit.

The days following their brief encounter had seen her making indiscreet inquiries into who he might be. She found out he was the only child of the duke of Camber, with lands adjoining her family's, but she never saw her hero again.

That had been ten years prior, but the memory stayed with Dami. It was strengthened when Camber went off to the Peninsular Wars and wound up in the same regiment with her older brother, Simon Alistair FitzHubert. Simon's letters home were full of his mate and great-gun, Camber. Through those letters Dami's childhood infatuation deepened into something more binding than a fleeting sensation.

She had awaited each of Simon's letters with an eagerness she was unable to hide. Her parents thought she was an unnatural girl, interested in the details of war described by Simon. Not so. She was only too natural in her interest about Camber. But this she kept to herself as she read about his heroism and concern for his men. He became more than a man who stirred her blood. He became a man she could respect and love.

This happy source of communication finally ended when Camber sold out and returned home where he began to cut a dash through London's less reputable salons and theaters. It was well known that he mounted only the most sought-after women, and played and drank deep. None of this stopped Dami. Simon approved of him and her heart yearned for him. That he was very ineligible for an untried chit, she refused to admit. The same stubborn streak that had led her into scrapes a more careful damsel would have avoided kept her sights centered on Camber. She meant to find him and prove that they had everything in common. Just as he'd teased her to do ten years before.

To that end, she allowed her mother finally to persuade her to go to London for the Season. Prior to this, while Camber had been at war, she had centered all her energies on remaining in the country at Green Leaf. There was no sense in parading around town, which she wasn't sure she would enjoy, when the man she intended to marry wasn't there. Better to stay home and marshal her forces for her campaign.

It had been easy to cajole her doting father into keeping her with him in the country. She had been his favorite child. Unfortunately, to her way of thinking, he had also decided that she should be independent. He didn't want to see his daughter at the mercy of some man, possibly a fortune hunter, for the management of her inheritance. When he died, she would be able to take care of herself. His methods of protecting her had seemed eccentric to their neighbors and his wife, but they had borne fruit. By the time of his death in 1812, Dami could manage his estate by herself, read and write Greek and Latin fluently, speak French and Italian like a native, and speculate knowledgeably on the Exchange.

None of these talents endeared her to the few men she managed to meet at Green Leaf. It was increasingly borne upon her that gentlemen did not appreciate their ladies' being smarter than they. Figuring all men were this way, she vowed silently not to let Camber know she was a bluestocking. That revelation could wait until after she had his heart. By then, she hoped, it wouldn't matter to him what irregularities characterized his beloved.

"Damaris, I know you aren't sleeping," her mama said in tones designed effectively to dispel Dami's reverie. "Now, pay attention to me." This was punctuated by a piercing look from her lorgnette, once more raised to her eye. "You are going to make your debut this Season and I expect you to behave accordingly. I'll have none of your hoydenish ways. Your father, bless his soul, spoiled you beyond managing. Worse than that, he kept you from my side where you should have learned to run a house as large as Green Leaf without dong more than lifting a questioning eyebrow. As it is, you can't keep house, watercolor, sew, or play the pianoforte. All of which are indispensable accomplishments for a lady of quality."

"I know, Mama," Dami answered contritely. Her mother would never know, and Dami intended it that way, how much it affected her not to know those

22

things she had just been rebuked for not knowing. There had been moments when not being able to play the pianoforte during a musical evening with friends had brought her excruciating embarrassment. The other girls always tittered behind their fans as she declined to play or sing. And when she went for afternoon tea the others kept their fingers active with embroidery and delicate mending, while she ignored their sly glances at her hands resting quietly in her lap. Telling herself that they were just jealous of her rank and fortune hadn't helped.

Worse still was her inability to manage Green Leaf. It was a gap in her education that she felt severely. She knew that of all the womanly skills considered necessary in a gently reared young lady, this was considered one of the most important to a man choosing his bride. Since people in her class rarely married for love, men expected to be made comfortable at home. To do this a woman needed training. She had none.

"Damaris, I want you to pay attention to what I'm about to say." Lady Cleve shook an admonitory finger, covered by violet kid gloves, at her daughter. "I expect you to find a husband before the end of July. As you know, the Season will be over by then and we will return to Green Leaf. You are all of three and twenty. Already on the shelf, as my many friends have so kindly informed me these many years. However," she added kindly, for she did indeed love her only daughter, "I don't expect you to marry where you have no regard. I might even be inclined to accept an alliance not as advantageous as one might expect to see you make—if you are sincerely attached."

"Yes, Mama," Dami answered meekly.

" 'Yes, Mama.' Don't try to bamboozle me, my girl. I know you too well to be taken in by that air of 'butter wouldn't melt in my mouth.' You're an attractive girl, with one of the largest fortunes in England. Not to mention perfect breeding. Why, a Cleve came over with William in 1066." On this, her ladyship collapsed against the soft cushions and fanned herself with a delicate lace handkerchief. "As you know, my constitution has never been robust, so I shan't be accompanying you to all the functions. I leave your twin, Johnny, to squire you to those I can't make. As long as Kit's mother goes, too," she added. "But that don't mean I expect to hear tales of your behavior. Is that understood? No matter what else you have to recommend you, once you've lost your good reputation, no man will have you. Damaged goods aren't looked upon with relish by a man who's seeking his future helpmate." Her eyes softened as she watched Dami. "Perhaps that's a little harsh, but I've seen your high spirits get you into many a scrape that won't bear repeating in the drawing rooms of some of the sticklers you are about to meet." Another look at her daughter's chastened appearance caused her to add, "Don't forget."

"Yes, Mama." Secretly, Dami decided to do everything in her power to attract the duke to her.

Chapter Two

"How elegant," Dami said, looking around the room she and Kit had just entered. Chairs, settees, walls, thick carpets: all were done in muted shades of green. Dami turned to her bosom beau, Lady Christine Julie St. John, also known as Kit. "Your modiste has impeccable taste, if this room and your own clothes are any indicators. This promises to be an interesting afternoon."

"I'm glad Lady Cleve allowed you to come with me. For a minute I was afraid she would insist on coming herself, and if the jewelry she wears is any sign of her taste, we are better off without her." An engaging smile lit Kit's catlike green eyes, which were complimented by her flame-red hair, done à la titus. The style, a holdover from her first season, became her gamin face and sylphlike figure so perfectly one forgot it was no longer *comme il faut*. She added, "Pardon me for saying so, but her taste is positively Gothic."

Dami grinned at Kit's grimace of distaste. "No, Kit, that's too harsh. Besides, it was Papa who picked all of Mama's jewelry. We used to cringe whenever there was occasion for her to receive another piece."

With Kit's superior knowledge of current fashions, and her own innate sense of what was right for her, Dami knew that by the end of the day she would be turned out perfectly. Luckily, Kit was free to help get together a wardrobe on the spur of the moment. Their arrival in London late the night before had left Lady Cleve too exhausted to deal with Dami's immediate clothing needs.

Dami watched the trim woman dressed in dove grey who was approaching them, before gracefully extending her hand.

"Dami, this is Madame Eugénie. Madame, Lady Damaris FitzHubert. My friend here has just come to town and needs a complete wardrobe."

"How do you do, Madame." Dami smiled engagingly at the older woman. "I know I can trust you to do what's proper, and to take into account that while this is my first Season, I am not fresh from the schoolroom." Her eyes lit up when she saw that Madame understood her unspoken request to refrain from the white colors and frills thought becoming to a young lady just making her curtsy.

"Of course, Lady Damaris. I have some colors that should enhance your already striking coloring." Moving quickly, Madame indicated that they sit and look at copies of *La Belle Assemblée* while they waited for the material.

Sinking into the comfortable moss-green chair, Dami's attention was caught by a flurry of activity outside the front window. "Kit, isn't that your cousin Camber's coach?" Looking closer, she added, "Yes, it is. It has his crest." Air whistled between her parted lips.

A beauty stepped out of the black landau. Her ebony hair was pulled into a knot and topped by a dashing scarlet bonnet done in satin and trimmed with ostrich feathers. Her figure was equally magnificent, being full in all the approved areas and slim in the rest, and shown to advantage by a scarlet walking dress trimmed in black seal. Her toilet was completed by a black seal muff, tan sandals, and French gloves. The beauty quite took Dami's breath away.

"Dami, quit staring," hissed Kit. This was punctuated by a severe pinch on the arm. "It's not considered proper to stare."

"But she's so lovely," Dami answered as her eyes narrowed in comprehension. "However, were I to say it, I would have said, 'It's not polite to stare', rather than it's not proper."

"In this case, as you well know from the look in your eye, proper is the right word," Kit answered. Dami could be irritating at times.

"She's Camber's current mistress, isn't she?" There was a hollow feeling in Dami's stomach. Reading about the dashers Camber kept was one thing. That she could intellectualize. Seeing one, and a very beautiful one at that, was something quite different. She wished it didn't hurt so much. The thought of his kissing this scarlet vision as he'd kissed her made her feel sick with jealousy.

"Dami, if you insist on talking about a subject that no lady of breeding admits exists, then at least stop looking at the object of your conversation. It's not done, you know." Kit, watching her friend closely, noticed that Dami's face was blanched and her eyes and mouth pinched. "You aren't sick are you?" Concern for her friend overcame her annoyance at Dami's blatant regard of the woman.

"No. At least, not in any way that can be cured."

"Oh no," Kit said softly. "Don't tell me you've developed a *tendre* for Camber. It won't do, if you have. He won't associate with respectable women. And how can we," she added for good measure with a nod of her head in the lady's direction, "in our demure fashions and colors, compete with a bird of paradise like her? Come, Dami, Madame's assistant is bringing the tea tray to refresh us while we browse. Take your eyes off that woman and make yourself busy pouring out tea."

Dami pulled herself together and did as she was told. But she kept the object of her affliction in sight as the beauty conferred with Madame for several minutes. Finally the beauty left and Dami relaxed perceptibly.

"She is so exotic. Is that the type of woman Camber prefers?" If that were indeed true, then she was lost before she'd begun.

"Are you still on that subject? It won't do, Dami. All you're doing is hurting yourself. I know," Kit answered. "Hasn't Lady Cleve explained to you that gentlemen have these diversions regularly and that you are to turn your indulgent eyes elsewhere?"

"No, she hasn't. But that's neither here nor there. We're talking about your cousin, who is renowned for the number of mistresses he's had in keeping. Why, it's always in the gossip column of the *Gazette* when he changes charmers." She had to talk to Kit about it. It was the only way to find out what her chances were.

She couldn't bear the thought that she had no chance because of something so trivial as coloring. Though, to be honest, she certainly wasn't as buxom as the current holder of His Grace's affections, either. But he had kissed her at the inn, even though she was fair and slim and not dressed so enticingly. Surely that was a good sign.

"Julian doesn't care whether his friends are fair, dark, or in between. From gossip, all he requires is that they be beautiful and much sought after. Rumor has it that his latest was stolen out from under the nose of the earl of Perth. He and Julian are old adversaries." Kit took a sip of her tea. "Mind, this isn't from Julian, so probably quite a bit of what I'm telling you is exaggerated."

"I didn't think it was from Julian," Dami replied. "I may be a little open in my manner from time to time, Kit, but even I would never expect a gentleman to talk about his mistress with a female of breeding."

"Actually, it's the one subject Julian won't discuss with me. Usually, he's quite good at talking to me about whatever it is that's bothering me, but he draws the line at his entertainments."

"Are you trying to tell me that you are on good terms with your cousin?" The beginning of an idea was forming in Dami's brain. She would get Kit to have her over for afternoon tea and could meet the elusive duke that way.

Kit saw the gleam in her eye and put herself to disabusing her friend of any idea she might be forming. "Julian is my guardian and one of the trustees of my estate. However lenient he may be in many ways, he draws the line at being importuned by any friend of mine who wants to make his acquaintance through me. He's also made sure it's hard to do by moving to bachelor quarters and leaving St. Johns House to Mama and me. Furthermore, the last time I tried to take a young lady to his rooms, he cut off my allowance for a quarter. He was very adamant. One, he was not interested in any female I might present to him, and two, his were bachelor quarters and no respectable woman would visit him in them. That included me. Julian's funny about that. He does as he wants, regardless of his own reputation. Not that it damages a man as it would a woman, but he expects the females of his family to be like Caesar's wife— above reproach. I'm convinced that his duchess, if he ever takes one, will be the same." Kit gave Dami a piercing look. "Have I satisfied your curiosity now? If so, we had best make some decisions on your clothes or this trip will be wasted."

Dami let the subject drop, commenting on one of the day dresses pictured in the lady's magazine. The rest of the visit was outwardly spent picking colors, materials, and styles. By the time they left, Madame had promised several walking dresses and one evening gown for the next day.

Dami's mind cogitated on her recently gained information. It would be more difficult to get near the duke than she'd ever envisioned. She shook her head ruefully. That only made it more imperative for her to get started. How to do it was the problem. He didn't attend the events she would be going to, unless they were the opera or theater, and he wasn't interested in untried girls. She would think of something. Mama didn't wail about her ability to get into a bramblebush for nothing.

Dami leaned back in her chair with a sign of satisfaction and surveyed the audience at the Drury Theater. Everyone and his cousin seemed packed into the elegant boxes for the evening's entertainment. Even the demi-reps had their boxes, which they used as showcases for their talents.

Leaning forward, she had a perfect view of Camber and his mistress in their box just below hers. She dragged her eyes from the scene and commented to her twin, "Kean has done it again. No one is better than he when it comes to Shakespeare." What she didn't say out loud was that she had managed, for the duration of the first act, to put Camber and his mistress from her mind. It hadn't been easy when they were so near she could almost see the whites of his eyes. Definitely not easy when he leaned over to listen to something the exquisite woman by his side said.

It wasn't fair. Particularly when she seemed destined to run into Camber's light-o-love everywhere she went today. Earlier at the modiste's, and now at the theater. It was as though the impossibility of her goal was being flung in her face to convince her of its stupidity.

As it was, her stomach was tied into knots, and her hands felt as if she'd been holding tight to the reins of an unwieldy horse most of the day, a result of her having clenched them whenever her thoughts dwelt on Camber's current *divertissement*. Somewhere she had to find the strength of character to get through an evening of watching the duke cater to the woman.

31

It would be nice if Camber glanced in her direction at least once. But he didn't, which didn't improve her disposition. Dami's common sense said this was all to the good, since her evening gown wouldn't arrive till the next day. The dull brown she had on wasn't flattering. Still, her contrary heart hurt at his lack of interest.

Dami shook herself and turned to her companion determinedly. Perhaps teasing Johnny would ease some of the depression she was feeling. Her twin was too busy watching the enchanting Harriette Wilson, queen of the demimonde, to pay attention to his sister, or her comment.

"Johnny, you should at least appear to take an interest in my conversation." Her deep brown eyes were glowing with mirth mingled with chagrin, as she noticed the object of her besotted brother's attentions. "Who is that lady? And why is her gown cut so low and her face so made up? She isn't a cyprian, is she?" Dami knew she was.

"That lady is Harriette Wilson, the queen of the demimonde," he replied without thinking. His head snapped around as he realized his indiscretion. "Dash it, Dami, you shouldn't catch me unawares like that. I wouldn't have told you otherwise." He shook an accusing finger at her. "It isn't proper for a lady to be aware of a bit-o-muslin. You'll put me to the blush."

"You gentlemen are all alike, my dear brother. You expect us to sit back and placidly let you ogle our rivals right in front of our eyes. Really, Johnny, surely you know me better than that by now."

Johnny peered at her through an exquisite red enamel quizzing glass. "You know you shouldn't talk like that. Not becoming. People will think you're a hoyden. Not but what you are."

His last comment was beneath her notice, but Dami couldn't pass the chance to tease him further. "Do I pass muster, Johnny? I'll admit I'm not so dashingly dressed as your Miss Wilson, but surely my fortune and lineage must be thought adequate compensation."

She fanned herself languidly and checked out the occupants of the other boxes while she waited for Johnny's reply. The gentlemen were all in evening dress and the ladies were in clinging muslins and silks draped with jewels. The order of the moment seemed to be to flirt with anyone and everyone.

"Wasn't your looks. I was wondering when you were going to put your foot in your mouth one time too many and be sent home in disgrace." He continued to look at her as though she were some unusual specimen he'd caught. "Your free ways were okay in the country. That is, they were acceptable. But only because everyone knew you. They'll only get you in trouble here. Mark my word."

"Pot calling the kettle black, wouldn't you say, twin?" she responded to his somber comments. Keeping her voice carefully casual, she added, "Johnny, be a dear and tell me who the lady is sitting with the duke of Camber."

"Not supposed to notice her, Dami. Not good ton."

Her voice hinted at exasperation. "Johnny, I know she's a barque of frailty, as you would so inaptly put it, and in Camber's keeping. I want to know her name."

"Cutting up at me won't get you the answer, my

girl. Why do you want to know?"

Determined to get the answer, she turned her piercing gaze on him. "Because I intend to marry His Grace, Julian Ambrose St. John, the ninth duke of Camber. Any more questions?" She eyed him sternly before adding, "And don't you dare tell Mama, or anyone else for that matter. If I'd wanted Mama to know, I wouldn't have waited until she left the box to visit friends before starting this conversation."

"You're let in the attic, sister." He subjected the woman gracing Camber's arm to a thorough scrutiny. "She's a high flier all right. That's Mrs. Jones. The most sought-after lady of the demimonde. After Harriette Wilson, that is. I'll wager she's costing His Grace a pretty penny," he muttered.

Dami's dry "He can afford it" brought him back to a belated sense of propriety.

"Don't want to see you make a fool of yourself by chasing Camber. He ain't interested in debutantes." Her full lips parted to interject, but Johnny pushed roughly ahead. "I know you're all of three and twenty, am myself, but to the duke you're a green girl. Green ain't what he looks for in a woman."

"What you mean is that he isn't interested in virgins."

Her flat statement shocked him. He had thought he was immune to her blunt statements, even enjoyed them, but this was too much. "Not to wrap it in clean linen, that's exactly what I mean."

"It doesn't matter. I know the duke's reputation. He's a Corinthian and a libertine." A soft sigh, made almost harsh by the depth of her voice, escaped her. "But I also know he served in the Peninsular War with

34

Wellington, he takes his seat in the House of Lords regularly, and his estates are among the best managed in the land. And Simon likes him." The last was said as though it made everything else before it a mere bagatelle. "Surely, a man like that is worth fighting for, even if it's against my 'fallen' sisters. Just because they can play the game by his rules doesn't mean they should win."

Johnny put his large, well-manicured hand on her long, slender one, compassion evident in each measured word. "Dami, more than anything, I don't want to see you hurt. Luckily, the duke never attends ton functions. And even if he did, he wouldn't be interested in an untried chit." At her look of indignation, he continued diplomatically. "Not that you ain't good-looking. He just doesn't seem interested in the married state, and he has all the female, um . . . consolation a man could handle." He added ingenuously, "Why, every woman, respectable and otherwise, just flings herself at him. Daresay it becomes embarrassing."

"Yes. Well, I imagine the poor man must be fagged to death with all the female demands put on his aging body." A look of pure mischief lightened her delicate features. "Look at it this way, Johnny, I will be doing the duke a favor by taking him off the marriage mart and out of the muslin company. Undoubtedly, he will grow to appreciate what I intend to do for him."

"You're funning, and this ain't a funning matter. No woman chases after the disreputable duke unless she's stupid or ready to lay out her charms. All of 'em!"

"I will find a way. Wait and see." The look of

determination in her eyes was belied by the slight trembling of her chin. Poor Johnny, he didn't understand. She'd never told him about the first time she'd seen Camber, and she definitely had no intention of telling him about the kiss at the inn.

That kiss had confirmed her feelings. Before that there'd been moments when she doubted her sanity. No woman fell in love with a man she'd only seen once, and that ten years before. But she had, and she had followed him through a campaign against Napoleon that had left him a war hero, gritted her teeth and girded her heart as she read of his mistresses, and prayed that soon he would tire of sowing his wild oats.

It appeared he was still sowing. She saw Mrs. Jones tap him on the wrist. Dami felt like a mouse must when it becomes mesmerized by a snake. She knew she should turn away before she was consumed, but was unable to do so.

While Dami came to grips with her emotions, Julian Ambrose St. John gazed speculatively into the limpid jade eyes of his current mistress, Alicia Jones. His slate-grey eyes were decidedly cool.

"Julian, dearest, do let's leave. I vow I can think of much more entertaining ways to spend an evening than listening to this morbid play. I know you like Shakespeare, but this Macbeth fellow is positively depressing." Her uncultured voice was accompanied by her soft, plump hand on his knee.

"Of course, my love. Your wish is mine." The sarcasm was lost on his ladybird.

With a flick of her wrist, she hit him lightly on his muscular forearm. "La, Your Grace, you make me feel like a duchess," a sly look from lowered lashes, "your duchess."

A hard look entered his eyes, and the muscle in his jaw twitched. Mrs. Jones wasn't familiar enough with the duke to know she'd made a strategic error. Taking her dimpled elbow, the one he'd kissed erotically the night before, Julian raised her abruptly from her seat. "Come, Alicia. As you say, there are better things to do with one's time."

Guiding Alicia out of the box Julian was aware of the small stir they were causing by leaving just as the curtain for the second act was raised. He shrugged his broad shoulders. It didn't bother him that people talked. He also knew the woman on his arm relished being the topic of discussion under any circumstances. The thought caused him to grin sardonically. A lady didn't single herself out for attention, nor did she allow the man she was with to do so.

The grip he had on her elbow tightened in his annoyance before he caught himself. Why did all his inamoratas bore him to distraction within months? Particularly recently. Alicia was the fourth one to grace his small, pleasant house in Kensington in the last three months. What had been a pleasant diversion when he was twenty-four, seemed a dead bore now, at thirty.

Having his hand forced by the loss of his heir might not be all bad. As soon as he'd returned from Cheltenham he'd contacted his man of business and told him to draw up a marriage settlement, as he intended to find his bride quickly. He'd further ordered the man to keep mum. This was not a matter he wanted the ton to be privy to. Thank goodness the distance of India from England would keep the knowledge of his heir's death secret for several months to come. He could hunt for his future wife without having all the matchmaking mamas swarming over him, like bees to honey. He grinned at the simile. Sweet was something he had never been likened to.

A comprehensive glance around the crowded theater as he escorted Alicia out of his private box showed him a young man in full evening dress. The dandy's shirt points were so high he couldn't turn his head without moving his whole torso, and his waistcoat was a vivid purple heavily embroidered with silver thread. Julian shuddered at the sight.

A movement next to the man caught his attention. It was made by a girl in an outmoded brown gown. For a moment his gaze lingered, and a smile of pleasure transformed his harsh features. He was sure she was his charmer from The Swan. There didn't appear to be anyone else in the box with them. When the chit momentarily flicked him a glance, he bowed slightly in her direction.

"Julian, you haven't heard a word I've said." Full red lips pouted provocatively in Mrs. Jones's heavily made-up face.

He put the ethereal paramour from his mind and set himself to charm his current mistress. Time enough to pursue that avenue after he was rid of Alicia. He knew without a doubt that she expected him to stay the night. Well, he would do his duty by her, then pension her off. Perhaps the diamond and ruby necklace she'd admired so blatantly the other day. Whatever it was, he would be generous. It wasn't her fault she had ceased to amuse him.

From her vantage point, Damaris saw the duke passionately kiss the tender under portion of his mistress's wrist. And right after he had bowed to her in such an arrogant, mocking way. She was sure he still thought of her as a lightskirt. A wry smile accompanied the sharp pain in her heart. He probably thought she was Johnny's mistress. With her light hair and Johnny's dark, it would be hard to tell they were brother and sister at this distance.

She watched Camber disappear into the lobby. His black evening clothes enhanced his haughty bearing. She wanted him so badly. A fancy started by a stolen kiss in the woods had deepened into a fixation. In her dreams, he was everything she wanted in a man. She would settle for no one else . . . no matter what it took to make him hers.

She pulled her eyes away from the door to the lobby. The duke, *her* duke, was leaving with his current mistress. She might not have spent much time in society, but she wasn't naive enough to think they were going to get refreshments, at least not the liquid kind. Camber's strong arm had been holding Mrs. Jones's voluptuous waist too intimately for that.

It wasn't easy being in love with a rake. When he'd taken her heart, she'd been unaware of his real nature. Having since learned it hadn't changed her feelings. She consoled herself with the thought that a reformed rake was said to make the best husband.

But first she must bring herself to his attention. She had the entre into all the polite drawing rooms and her vouchers for Almack's had arrived yesterday in the post. However, she didn't have entrance into the circles His Grace favored. Her mind ran over all the encounters of the day. She could see no way to meet Camber by going to the society outings.

Seriously contemplating the standstill her plan had reached, she sought out her brother with her eyes. He was paying his addresses to Harriette Wilson. Watching him bow elegantly over her raised hand gave Damaris the glimmer of an idea.

Before she could follow it up in her mind, Lady Cleve returned to their box and started discussing the latest on dits she'd gleaned from her old friends. Dami set herself to listen to her mama, but her thoughts were on a way to make Camber's acquaintance by attending an activity normally barred to women of her station.

It was four o'clock in the morning. Julian was sprawled in a large, comfortable leather wing back chair in his library. His heavy-lidded eyes were a deep grey, almost black in the faint light, while the large ruby stick pin in his cravat seemed to blaze with a life of its own where the light from the fire hit it. The same glow played off the angles of his face, giving a ruddy color to his strong cheekbones and chin. In his right hand, he held a tumbler half full of imported French brandy. The rich amber color sparkled like a faceted jewel. His long, elegant fingers twirled the crystal glass.

A small candelabra, consisting of four burning candles, was positioned on the marble-topped mantel that crowned the fireplace. On his left was a small Hepplewhite table with a half-empty decanter, and the walls were filled with books that floated in and out of shadow with the flickering of the flames.

Deep in thought, he didn't hear the sounds of the storm outside. It had come up suddenly, just after he'd returned from Alicia's. The heavy winds whistled around the corners of his rooms, sweeping into the depressions caused by the windows and rattling the shutters in its wake. Thick, solid drops of water pelted the glass with a vengeance, the sound muffled by the opulent silk curtains.

It had been a very unpleasant night. Alicia hadn't taken to his idea that they part ways. In fact, she had been excessively vulgar about the whole thing. He sighed heavily. All these women from the lower orders were the same. Sexually exciting, with their heavily made-up faces and painted toenails, unbearable to listen to, with their uncultured voices and hackneyed English. Still, they were ripe and willing in bed.

The women of his station were insipid misses who flirted outrageously or simpered and stammered, not knowing exactly what they were trying to achieve when they set out to beguile a man's senses. More than that, they would have been shocked into a fainting heap if a man tried to reap some benefit from the interlude. His face became a mask of derision. Or they were faithless wives and merry widows. He had a strong aversion to being cuckolded himself and had no intentions of doing it to another. As for the widows, they bartered themselves, hoping to achieve his name and rank.

But with all their faults they offered respectability. At least the young misses and certain widows did. And thanks to that young fool who had insisted he make his own way instead of waiting for Julian to give him his title, he had to marry. He had no choice. That more than anything irritated him. But, perhaps it was time to take a wife and set up his nursery. Nothing could bore him as his last four mistresses had.

He would look on marriage as a new adventure. He slapped his elegantly clad knee decisively with a determined hand. Yes, that was what he would do.

Goodness knew he needed something to occupy his time more fully. There was only so much time he could devote to Parliament and the management of his already well-run estates. Plus, he didn't particularly care to become entangled in Lord Liverpool's network of spies, regardless of the Prime Minister's constantly badgering him and telling him that his talents would be indispensable. Subterfuge wasn't his way of conducting business.

Holding up the now empty tumbler, he stared at the leaping flames through the prism of cut glass. A rainbow of colors leaped out at his eyes. With a shake of his head, he turned, unstoppered the crystal decanter, and poured himself another shot of brandy.

If he intended to carry out his latest decision successfully, he must first reconnoiter the area. Forced to find a duchess he might be, but that still didn't allow him to settle on a female unsuitable for the station. He must find out what the newest batch of schoolroom chits had to offer. Possibly there would be someone worth considering. Even a young widow would be acceptable. It would mean attending Almack's and the other insipid diversions the ton considered appropriate, but it was necessary. His wife must come from a family as well-connected as his own. She didn't have to be rich, he had enough for both of them, and she didn't have to be pretty. Well, at least she couldn't be ugly if he were to perform his marital duties to beget an heir. He couldn't abide a totally unattractive woman.

With a jolt, he remembered the letter he'd received last week from Simon FitzHubert. Unless his memory failed him, there was mention of a sister who was on the catch for a husband. Getting to his feet, Julian went to his desk and rummaged until he found the now creased letter. Scanning it quickly, his gaze stopped at the line: "Damaris is all of three and twenty, so I guess it is past time for her to enter the beau monde and secure a husband." Julian read no farther.

Already on the shelf. But her antecedents were beyond reproach, her connections superior, and, if she looked anything like Simon, she might be a striking woman. Probably even pretty. Her fortune, he remembered Simon's mentioning once while in his cups, was one of the largest in England at the moment, and in many a long day too. Strange she wasn't married yet. This momentary flash of concern was quickly put aside. He liked the idea too much to let some niggling suspicion of trouble prick his bubble.

Julian set the untouched glass on the table next to him, and a knowing smile curved his full lower lip. That wasn't a bad idea. It would also save him the tiresome exercise of looking over all the marriageable chits and then having to make a tedious decision. The extra time saved also left him room to pursue his Corinthian interests. Not to mention other pleasurable enterprises.

No—he stopped that line of thought. He'd decided long ago that when he took a wife he would be faithful. His parents' marriage had been a love match, strange as that seemed when one considered their rank. The happiness that had permeated everything they did and everywhere they were had left him with a decided belief in fidelity.

Leaning his elegant head to one side, he tapped his chin with one long white finger. But then, his wasn't to be a love match. In all his thirty years, he'd never met a woman who could hold his jaded interest for long, let alone one he could love to the exclusion of all others. Perhaps complete fidelity was a little too much to ask of himself under the circumstances. He would just have to wait and see.

The fire was dying down, and the room was taking on the chill of outside. One last gulp of liquor and he snuffed out the candles and banked the fire. He was totally satisfied with his decision to marry the sister of the marquis of Cleve. A marriage of convenience wasn't unusual. It was expected of a duke.

Leaving the now dark room, he climbed the staircase to his rooms. His firm lips curved momentarily down. He was no romantic, of that he was certain. For a long time now, he'd felt disillusioned about that elusive thing poets called love. Surely, if such an emotion existed he would have felt it by now. Still, he was confident he and his future bride would be able to work out a reasonably complacent relationship. He wouldn't be a demanding husband after the heir was born.

He entered his private chambers quietly.

Smithfield, his valet, had gone to bed long before.

A large yawn and he pulled his clothes off and tumbled into bed. A satisfied smile curled his firm lips, giving his otherwise harsh face a look of innocent sweetness. He would write Simon first thing in the morning offering for his sister's hand. Satisfied, he closed his weary eyes for what he felt to be a much deserved sleep.

Chapter Three

"No, dammit, Damaris. I say no! I won't have my sister making a cake of herself over the duke of Camber. What's more, I won't help."

Oblivious of the beauty of the surrounding room, Damaris watched Johnny pace the floor, waving his hands all the time he berated her. Straw-colored watered silk hung elegantly on the clean lines of the windows, setting off the coordinating striped material covering the handsome Louis XV chairs and settee grouped intimately around the fireplace. The high walls rose up to an ornate, but tastefully done, plaster ceiling. It was a cool and aristocratic room, not the kind a heated argument should be taking place in.

Damaris tried to maintain her facade of detached interest, but it was getting harder by the second. She'd stayed awake most of the previous night thinking up this plan. It was the only way she knew of to make contact with the man she intended to marry. It would be taking a big risk, but there were times when one had to accept the dangerous: the frowned upon. She drew herself up and took a deep breath, watching Johnny all the while. After he had had his say and calmed down he would give in. He always did.

He'd been in such a good mood when she'd waylaid him in the hallway. Whistling a jaunty tune, he'd just picked up his kid gloves when she'd called to him, but she had had no other chance.

Since returning from the theater a week ago, she'd been to every activity. Sometimes five in a day. Venetian breakfasts, morning calls, driving in Hyde Park, routs, balls, Almack's, the opera, the theater, all of it . . . and no duke. She'd begun to despair, until she'd remembered her fleeting thought as she'd watched Johnny bowing over Harriette Wilson's hand at the theater.

She knew it was risking everything, but she would masquerade as a member of the demimonde anyway. The execution of her plan was still hazy, since she had no real idea of how to go about posing as the kind of woman she'd been sheltered from since birth, but it was now firmly lodged in her mind as the only way to meet Camber. It was her presentation of this idea to Johnny that had set him frantically circling the drawing room.

"You must be crazy, Dami. That's it, you've succumbed. The shame of it." He flung his right arm across his forehead, and bowed his head. "I must commit you to Bedlam. It's the only explanation for how you could concoct such an outrageous proposal. No young lady of good family could even conceive of such a plot otherwise, let alone ask her brother to help her bring it off." At her snort of derision, he raised his eyes to meet hers, and both pairs were filled

47

with an appreciation of his ridiculous threat to commit her to a mental institution.

Her lips smiled in acknowledgment of the farce he'd just enacted, but her large eyes turned serious. They implored him to understand the situation she was in. "Johnny, it's the only way. You know it is. The duke will never notice me otherwise. You know his reputation as well as I do. I must do something drastic."

"Like as not, Dami, the duke will seduce you," he stated bluntly, hoping to shock her into some semblance of propriety. "And you know that if he does, he will be perfectly in the right of it. That's what cyprians are for. Only, with your luck, you will become in the family way, but Camber won't be looking for a family. With his reputation, it wouldn't surprise me if he refused to marry you, even when he found out who you really are. He would undoubtedly feel it was your just desserts." A ferocious scowl marred Johnny's handsome features. "Even I would feel you had only got what you deserved. However, unlike the duke, I should be constrained from affection to help you."

"Johnny, you know me better than that. All I want is a means of meeting the duke. You know he's the most eligible catch of the ten thousand. Has been for years. You said yourself that's what drives him away from the season's buds." Her fingers twisted the material of her dress. Johnny had to help her. It was her only chance of pulling off an introduction to Camber, if you could call something like this an introduction. Certainly not a proper one.

"That's right. He's eligible, but you don't see him

getting caught, do you? He's avoided it for ten years and more. What makes you think you'll be able to bring him up to scratch?" He towered over her where she sat on the settee. She had that stubborn look in her eyes and her mouth was clenched tight. Exactly what she had done whenever Father had tried to get her to do something she was dead set against.

"Because he's bored by all of the women chasing him. He's bored with his mistresses. Didn't you hear he's just gotten rid of Mrs. Jones? She was his fourth one in less than three months. Surely, a man doesn't change his mistresses like he would change his horses unless something's wrong."

Johnny threw his hands into the air. "My God, Dami, you aren't supposed to know Camber has mistresses, let alone how many!" He was almost at his wit's end with this unreasonably obstinate sister. He'd never seen her in such a taking before over a man. He continued, "Just because the charmers are boring him quickly doesn't mean you won't do the same." Better to hurt her now than for the duke to do it. "What have you got that a professional lady of the night hasn't? Besides polish and willingness. Look at you."

He grabbed her by the shoulders and hauled her up, then pushed her ruthlessly toward the large beveled mirror that hung above the fireplace mantel. He turned her hard in the direction of the large looking glass, and stated, "Why, your gown is much too demure, you would have to dampen it, after you lowered the neckline by a good six inches or more. Do you think you would enjoy having the duke leer at your uncovered bosom? Next, your hair is old-fashioned, being as long as it is. You have no rouge or lip gloss to enhance your features. Your nails aren't painted, either. Add to that a lack of knowledge about dalliance and what have you got? Nothing that a man of Camber's sated appetites would want."

Dami stared into the revealing mirror and realized that everything Johnny said was true. Her image, reflected back at her with the lovely room for a backdrop, was definitely attractive, but most decidedly not exotic. She was like an English rose, while Mrs. Jones was like a tropical orchid. Dami's dress was all the crack, but it was still conservative. The high-necked bodice and loose sleeves of plum kerseymere trimmed in Brussels lace were fetching, but not beguiling. Her clear complexion and faintly tinted cheeks and lips were soft and inviting, but they'd never drive a man of Camber's stamp wild with desire.

"I will contrive somehow," she reiterated in a determined voice. "I . . . realize that there are many things I haven't any idea about, but I can learn. I know it's taking a chance, Johnny, but you must understand. To me he's worth the risk."

"More to the point, Damaris, you don't even know the man. You've never been introduced. You've never even talked to him. He's not the paragon you evidently think him to be. He's a rake and a libertine, Dami. He'd break your heart and take your innocence in the bargain."

"No, he wouldn't," she almost sobbed in her frustration. This interview wasn't going the way she'd expected. Johnny was remarkably quick-witted and stubborn about the whole thing. She had to show him Camber's good points. "At least, I don't think so. You remember how Papa always used to talk about

50

how advanced the duke of Camber's ideas on farming were. Why, Papa would tell his bailiff to get with the duke's man and find out about his new experimental ideas. Surely you haven't forgotten that?" The words were tumbling out of her mouth. She had to convince Johnny to help her or all was lost.

"Then, too, you must remember Father discussing the duke's enlightened ideas about mining. Why, just recently I read that he is sponsoring Sir Humphrey Davy's invention to prevent the inflammable fire-damp gas which issues from coal, often under pressure, from being set alight by the miners' lamps. That shows concern for the people who work for him," she declared. "You even said yourself that the gossip column in the *Gazette* should stop maligning the duke because he chooses not to use women and children in his mines." Her voice dropped to a whisper. "I know he's got a reputation with opera dancers, but he's also very generous when he ends the liaison."

"Dami!" The name exploded from Johnny's lips. "That does not recommend him in the least. Not to untried chits like you."

"Oh, I know I shouldn't know about those things, and that the duke shouldn't pursue them to the extent that he does, but after all," she looked at her irate brother slyly, "why should he be any different from any other gentleman in the beau monde?"

This last statement being a decided leveler, Johnny began to think he must concede the fight. She was right about Camber's being no different from any other man of his acquaintance, except in his honesty about his dealings. Most gentlemen managed to have their bit-o-muslins along with a respectable relation-

51

ship with a woman of their own class. Camber just chose to ignore women equal to him in birth and breeding.

Dami's pensive gaze worried him. She had the look she always got just before she did something outrageous. Like as not, she'd do it without his help. In that case there would be no one to help her if things got touchy. Reaching this conclusion, he told her grudgingly, "Okay, I'll help if I can. However, I can't promise that Harriette will. If she won't, you must promise me to forget this nonsense."

Elation rushed through Dami. For a while it had been touch and go as to whether Johnny would lend his support. She managed to keep her voice calm as she answered him. "Should Miss Wilson decide she can't help, then I will forget *this* plan. However, I won't forget my determination to marry the duke. Her refusal would only be a setback, not a defeat."

"I shall have to be content with that." Not taking his blue eyes from hers, Johnny reached for his fashionable beaver hat and clapped it on his head. "I'm on my way to see Miss Wilson. This is your last chance to change your mind."

With a slight shake of her head, Dami smiled. "I won't change my mind, Johnny, and I'm sure Miss Wilson will help me. They say she's lost her heart to Lord Ponsonby, who no longer cares for her, so I'm sure she knows the pain of loving someone who doesn't reciprocate the feeling." She added ingenuously, "And all I ask is one little introduction. It doesn't have to be elaborate."

"Even if she does agree to this, you must be careful not to be caught. If word of this ever got out, you'd be ostracized by the ton." He looked perplexed, "Don't know how I always let you talk me into these ramshackle schemes."

She decided to ignore his last comment. In this case, the better part of valor seemed to be retreat. She changed the subject. "Don't forget your walking cane, Johnny. Wouldn't want you to shame Mr. Brummell." Dami blew him a kiss and winked. "If you should be late getting back, I shall be at Almack's tonight. It's Wednesday, after all, and who knows, the duke might shock the polite world and attend."

She watched him stroll casually out the drawing room door. His hair was so black it shone with blue highlights, quite the opposite of her almost white curls. Their features were enough alike that upon close inspection they would be known for brother and sister, but never for twins. Usually they were well matched for mischief. It hadn't occurred to her that Johnny would oppose her plan as vehemently as he had. Up until their trip to London, she had always been the leader of the two. Perhaps Johnny was gaining that elusive quality the bucks called "town bronze." He was certainly becoming more independent.

Also, Johnny was frequenting the company of Harriette Wilson with a determination that spoke of involvement to the extent of trying to set her up. That much she knew. The servants talked, and her maid told her everything. Well, she intended to use that friendship to achieve her meeting with Julian. Who knew, she might even enjoy the role of courtesan. It definitely would not be bound by the rules that had governed her life to this point, strictures that she had trouble following no matter how hard her mother tried to impress them upon her. Now she would flaunt them to gain her duke.

She had been at the end of her tether when she fell into her current plan. It was the only way for a woman to go to the places Camber favored. If he wouldn't come to her world, where he could move with impunity, she would go to his. She would have to be much more circumspect, but she would manage. The trick would be to avoid persons she knew and places where they might be. Surely, the demimonde had haunts not frequented by all the masculine ton. And the duke must have private places where he took his lady friends to get better acquainted.

Having grown up in the country she had a pretty good idea of what "getting acquainted" must entail for the duke. But she had no idea of how to go about it. She brushed this thought from her mind as not concerning her for the moment. She was bent on marriage, and she didn't foresee that she would have any problem keeping the duke in rein. She'd never had trouble with a beau yet.

And she did so want to be married. Her goal in life was to marry and have children. She liked children. They were open and loving. Just what Julian needed to bring out the gentleness she knew he hid by his cool indifference. He'd be a good father. She could picture him now, down on the floor of a large, comfortable room with their children playing around him. A little boy with Julian's auburn hair and her brown eyes, his blond sister watching him adoringly.

The butler's discreet cough brought her back to the present and reminded her that it was getting late, and she still needed to get dressed for Almack's. A lady of fashion didn't materialize from thin air.

Almack's assembly rooms were stiflingly hot. The refreshments were insipid, and the conversation dull. Nothing new.

Damaris was bored, but not for lack of partners. Her gown of pansy purple with a low, rounded neckline and gored and ruched skirt became her ethereal beauty. The braided coronet of her hair enhanced the thick necklace of amethysts circling her slim neck and the matching earrings dangling from her delicate ears.

She and Kit were sitting out a country dance while they watched the ton at play. Tongue in cheek, Kit had been pointing out different personages to Dami. Being in her fourth season, Kit knew everyone and had deputized herself to introduce Dami to all of them in short order. So far, Kit had managed to get through most of them, with the exception of one, and he wasn't the duke of Camber.

"It's too bad so many have gone to Paris now that Napoleon is on Elba," Kit said. "Oh Dami, there is someone you haven't met yet. The earl of Perth." Here Kit lowered her voice to a dramatic whisper. "He's quite wickedly handsome. With a scar running from his eyebrow to the corner of his mouth. It's said he got it in a duel over a woman."

"How romantic. Was the woman worth the sacrifice? And who was his opponent?" Dami gave her friend a speaking look, before continuing. "Do you intend for me to make his acquaintance or is this all just to titillate me?"

"Of course I mean for you to meet him." Kit's response was indignant. "Look over near the windows. That's him, the tall, sinewy one leaning against the wall and eyeing all the women with that predatory gleam. He has the blackest eyes." Her eyes rolled to the ceiling. "Divine."

Dami turned to look at the gentleman under discussion. He was positively wicked. Dressed in the severe black evening clothes deemed *de rigueur* for Almack's, he oozed an animal magnetism. Powerful shoulders, slim hips, and muscular legs added to the deadliness of his looks. His face was narrow and aristocratic, with prominent cheekbones and deep-set midnight-blue eyes. A deep cleft in his chin and a long scar running from his right eye to his full lips finished the portrait of the complete rake. But to Dami his romantic appeal ended when she noticed the deep lines of dissipation etched at the corners of his eyes and mouth. He was a handsome man, but *noblesse oblige* allowed to run rampant held no appeal for her.

Noticing them watching him, he gracefully unwound himself from the wall and sauntered their way.

"Dami," Kit's voice went up an octave, "he's headed over here. I'm going to introduce you to him. Next to Camber he's the absolutely most sought-after man in town."

The earl reached them and bent into a smooth bow. His eyes never left Dami's face, and she returned his unblinking stare with her own. His dark eyes were warm with approval; she kept her brown ones cool. Something about the man upset her. Even in Almack's, the safest setting possible, the earl of Perth

56

made her uneasy. It was an unsettling feeling.

"Dami," Kit said, "may I present the earl of Perth, Jason Beaumair. He and my cousin Camber are friendly rivals. Just last week they had a race to see who could get to Bath the quickest in a racing curricle. Of course, Julian won."

Perth gave Kit a look usually reserved for young ladies who were found to be trying to their elders. Having tried to put Kit in her place, he addressed Dami. "May I have the honor of the next dance with you, Lady Damaris?"

Not knowing how to refuse gracefully, Dami assented. She felt unusually awkward as she got to her feet. The man unnerved her with his penetrating eyes, and the whipcord strength of his guiding hand on her elbow made her jumpy. They took their places in the set.

Perth continued to watch Dami with an intensity that brought high color to her face and neck. She tried to ignore his breach of manners and concentrate on the steps. To her relief, they were soon separated by the dance.

When they came back together, Perth remarked, "I don't usually find myself in a situation where the lady I'm partnering finds the floor more interesting than she finds me."

Her eyes flew to his, and she assumed a wide-eyed, innocent look. "Oh, but you see, I'm new to town and haven't had occasion to dance enough to be sure of my movements. Otherwise, I should fascinate you with my witticisms." She saw the wicked smile that came into his eyes and cursed herself for a fool to let his sally goad her into such a pert response. It was obvious from his regard that he now found her a challenge. She hoped he would not pick up the gauntlet her unwise words and look had thrown in his face.

He laughed at her obvious chagrin, but forbore to comment as they were separated again. Coming back together, neither one made any comments. Dami's brain was working fast. She remembered what Kit had told her their first day together. Putting it together with Kit's recent comment on the rivalry between Perth and Camber, she realized they were rivals in sports *and* love. Perhaps if it became known that Perth was attracted to her, which she thought she might be able to achieve, the duke would make a push to meet her. This idea was quickly discarded as she glanced up to find the earl's unsettling black eyes fastened on her. He looked so very wicked, and he made her feel so uncomfortable, that she knew she couldn't use him to meet Camber. She would never be able to carry out the role such a part would demand of her. A shiver of displeasure ran up her spine as his gaze continued to rake her body.

Dami glanced anxiously at the doors. Where was Johnny? It was getting late and she wanted him to be waiting for her when the dance ended. She didn't trust Perth, for no discernible reason, and she wanted to make sure he knew she had a male relative to take care of her. She craned her neck trying to see the door.

It was difficult to see anyone in particular, since the rooms were unmercifully crowded. Everyone and his wife, with their marriageable daughters in tow, was at Almack's for the Season's yearly market of flesh and fortune.

A sigh of relief escaped Dami as she saw her brother. It didn't go unnoticed by the earl.

Coming through the hallowed portals, Johnny made his leg to the Countess Lieven, one of the patronesses, and continued on his way to Kit without stopping. He reached Kit's side and waited for the dance to end. When it did, Perth returned Dami to his side. Both men nodded briefly before the earl took his leave. After the earl left, Johnny excused the two of them to Kit and yanked Dami unceremoniously toward the open balcony.

Once outside, he broke into a broad grin and declared in theatrical accents, "It's done, Dami. You can't back down now, even if you wanted. Tomorrow at midnight you make your debut at the Cyprians' Ball."

"The witching hour." Relief at being rescued from Perth made her flippant. "I've got a lot to do between now and then. This must go off without a hitch." After a thoughtful moment, she asked, "But what is the Cyprians' Ball?"

"It is an annual get together held in the Argyll Rooms and put on by the High Fliers. To get in is harder than getting into this place. So count yourself lucky that Harriette has agreed to sponsor you for the evening. Otherwise, you wouldn't stand a chance of admission." Johnny ran a critical glance over her toilet. "You certainly can't wear what you have on tonight, that's for sure." Johnny's inspection was followed by the wisdom of his experience. "Much as it goes against the grain, that purple confection you're wearing just isn't daring enough. No doubt it's pretty and just the thing, but it's not what a lady of loose morals would sport."

"Too modest, you say? I daresay, you're right." Dami sighed dramatically. "Probably ought to dampen my underdress too." She was forgetting the fear engendered by Perth as she exchanged light banter with Johnny. Anticipation of the next night lent vivaciousness to her voice.

"Just be sure that if you do, you wear a heavy cloak. Wouldn't want to catch a cold. Nothing puts a man off his lovemaking like a sneezing woman." Johnny's laugh was infectious.

"For a brother, dearest one, you certainly aren't doing much to help me maintain my maidenly innocence."

"I know you, my dear. You probably know as much as I do." A stern look from his sparkling blue eyes and a shake from an admonishing finger emphasized his words. "You are a baggage. Poor man doesn't know what he's in for."

With a toss of her delicate head, Damaris linked her arm with Johnny's and headed him back into the room. "Between now and tomorrow night, I must change my style of dress, even my mannerisms. You must coach me tomorrow while Mama is taking her afternoon constitutional. I wouldn't want to be found remiss at such an elite gathering."

Her husky laughter rang in the earl of Perth's ears as he stood hidden behind a palm on the balcony. Now, I wonder who Lady Damaris is plotting after, he thought. And with the help of her twin brother, no less. The curve of his full, sensual lips was sinister where the scar drew them downward. It appeared that his stay in town wouldn't be as dull as he'd originally thought.

Meanwhile, Dami and Johnny made their farewells to Kit and left for home. They both had a long day and night ahead of them.

Chapter Four

Dami grimaced as she surveyed herself in the full-length mirror. Her necklace and tiara were made up of huge diamonds circled by rubies. In itself that wasn't bad, but Papa had wanted to impress Mama with this particular gift, given after Simon's birth. Consequently, the choker was made of small connecting hearts that led to a large center one made from one of the largest diamonds in the country. This immense token of his love completely covered the dip formed by Dami's collarbone. Not to be outdone, the tiara was one mass of diamonds and rubies formed in a heart that stood inches above her coiffure. When combined with her thick curls, already piled atop her head, she was a vulgar-looking piece. It made her shudder and long to tear the things from her head.

Suzy's ohhs and ahs stopped her. As her lady's maid, Suzy had gone to great lengths altering the deep red dress Dami had on. Suzy had changed the once demurely rounded neckline to a low, plunging vee. It revealed Damaris's full breasts, cupping and lifting them upward. Next, Suzy had narrowed the skirt so that it clung provocatively to Dami's slim, shapely hips and legs. When combined with the jewelry, Dami looked, in Suzy's words, "just like a fallen woman." After that encomium, Dami felt obligated to stay as she was.

Her decision was further bolstered by Johnny's look of surprise as she met him outside her door. His light blue eyes seemed to pop from their sockets as he looked her over.

"You are looking very vulgar tonight, sis," was his only comment as he helped her on with her black satin cloak.

Dami's lips twitched as she watched Johnny's attempt to be a debonair buck. But his words had reassured her. "My feelings exactly," she answered.

While this was the effect she wanted, she still felt overexposed. She pulled the cloak tightly around her shoulders; the vast expanse of bare skin made her nervous. Then she pulled the hood full over her head to cover the flash of her headpiece.

Last, she glanced down the hallway to make sure Mama wasn't about. Lady Cleve was supposed to be away playing cards with some friends. It certainly wouldn't do to let her get even the slightest inkling of Dami's plans. She and Johnny had even contrived to give the butler and footmen the evening off — after the dowager left the house.

Without looking back, they swept down the stairs, out the door, and entered a hired coach headed for the Argyll Rooms.

Damaris peeked cautiously around the heavy velvet curtain that secluded the tiny alcove she had been nervously pacing. A view of sparkling abandonment met her eyes. Champagne was everywhere, and men and women circled the room to the strains of a waltz. The men were all in evening black and white, with a few exceptions; those being the die-hard dandies who insisted on their bright plumage regardless of the occasion.

But it was the women who really caught and held Dami's attention. She couldn't bring herself to call them ladies, although she wasn't any different than they this night. Their gowns of vivid colors fell around their bodies revealing all. They wore nothing under them. If Dami tried hard enough, she could discern the brightly rouged nipples of their bosoms blossoming over their low-cut bodices. That was, when she wasn't blinded by the flash of their opulent jewels, which they seemed to wear like badges of their calling.

She reined in her thoughts. This wasn't getting her anywhere, and it was getting late, even for the Cyprians' Ball. Camber still hadn't arrived. Thinking it might be better to leave, she sought out the Wilson sisters with her eyes. It didn't surprise her to see Johnny bowing over Harriette's hand. A low chuckle escaped her when she saw Harriette tap Johnny on the wrist with her fan.

The action diverted her. It seemed all courtesans did that. That made it seem more unjust than ever that Johnny had twitted her for doing the very same thing during their practice session.

His tutelage that afternoon had been a trial to her self-esteem. Irritation at being coerced into the ploy had made her brother's normally easygoing personality acerbic at best. At her third slap of his wrist with her fan, he'd exploded, saying, "I've had enough of this damned business. You've no reason to be doing this in the first place, and you'd best not hit the duke with that stupid fan as many times as you've hit me. I can tell you that." In sullen tones, he'd added, "And you'd better learn how to flirt, too. All you do is stare at a man until you put him out of countenance. That's no way to make a chap fall in love with you. Not to mention your penchant for heavy talk. Don't want to talk about Wellington's campaign. Don't want to talk at all."

His disgruntled words had put her in a momentary quake. She'd thought her progress in the deceptive art of dalliance had gone remarkably well. But if Johnny were any judge, there was a lot she lacked. However, after Harriette's display, she felt better.

Her eye was caught by a ripple in the teaming crowd as it milled around the ballroom, bringing her back to the present. It was Camber. He couldn't be ignored, with his auburn hair glowing hotly and his cool grey eyes surveying the room disdainfully. The fit of his black satin coat emphasized his broad shoulders and excellent carriage, while his skin-tight breeches showed the strong muscles of his thighs. They were the perfect foil for his sparkling white silk shirt, heavily embroidered waistcoat, and matchless cravat.

Chills ran down Dami's spine. He was such a striking man. No wonder every woman in England was eager for his attentions . . . regardless of what they were.

With a casual grace, he bowed to Harriette Wilson. Damaris saw him smile at something Harriette said.

65

When he smiled, the man was devastating. Strong white teeth flashed briefly in his unfashionably tanned face. His heavy eyebrows drew together as Harriette waved a languid hand, urging him to Dami's alcove. He looked as if he would refuse her command, but he offered his arm to the courtesan.

Disappointment soured Julian. It seemed that even Harriette could scheme against him. The news of his break with Alicia had spread fast. Now Harriette was trying to interest him in some innocent, or so she said, who was supposed to be quite out of the ordinary. He'd heard that story before. Still, he and Harriette were good friends and it wouldn't do to rebuff her. He'd just make sure after she left that this little climber understood he wasn't interested. Virgins, whether they were ladies of quality or ladies of easy virtue, didn't interest him. He liked his women to be experienced. It was much more interesting and less complicated that way.

To Damaris's highly charged imagination, Camber and Harriette looked like the Devil and his mistress bearing down on her. She took a deep breath to steady her nerves and still shaking hands. It had seemed so easy when she'd planned it. Everything had gone so smoothly, too. She couldn't mess it up now. But what could she say that would fascinate this sophisticated man? Her mind was a blank. Heaven help her, she wouldn't get a second chance.

The heavy curtain was twitched aside and Harriette and the duke entered.

Julian saw the delightful armful from The Swan. This time there was a marked improvement, if he ignored the gaudy, but obviously expensive diamonds she had draped herself with. A seductive red gown with a decolletage that plunged to reveal milk-white breasts shining like satin was only the start. This time, he noted with approval, she'd dressed her hair high on her head, with thick curls cascading down her neck. He saw her coral lips curve into a welcoming smile, with tiny white teeth glowing like pearls. It was an effort not to caress her creamy shoulder as he bowed deeply.

"Julian St. John, the duke of Camber, may I present Amalie?" Harriette used Damaris's middle name as they'd planned, and with a grin slipped out of the tiny alcove.

As the duke entered her domain, like a flash of inspiration, Damaris knew that the way to enslave him was to be open and fresh, yet never to tell him everything. She would be an innocent mystery lady. That was the type all the heroes in the Minerva Press romances fell in love with. Why not Camber?

"What a delightful surprise. I was hoping to find you again." His eyes remembered their first meeting as they rested on her lips. "How exotic and beautiful you are. Even moreso than I'd first thought, now that you are dressed to please." His left hand reached out of its own volition to stroke her sparkling white hair. "Your hair is truly a crown. I think it is what stayed in my mind the most distinctly."

"Thank you, Your Grace," she replied softly, her deep voice more raspy than its norm. Her tongue ran over dry lips, but she kept her eyes steadily on his grey ones.

A blush ran from her exposed bosom to her hairline as he made a comprehensive inspection of her. She bore the perusal, thinking she'd succeeded. He thought her exotic. She could hardly believe it. A daring dress, flashy diamonds, and makeup seemed to make all the difference.

"Should I bare my teeth also, Your Grace?" she asked in response to the look he was still devouring her with. "I've been told they're above average in whiteness and evenness. However, that was from a prejudiced party." She didn't wait for his reply as her brain raced ahead. She still hadn't risen from her seat, but the social gaff was made negligible by the humor evident in her voice and the situation she found herself in—she hoped. She decided to use it. "Does one stand and curtsy to a duke one hopes to snag in illegal bliss? As a question of etiquette, I fear it is beyond my abilities, Your Grace." It was very forward, but "nothing ventured, nothing gained" was her motto for this campaign.

Her quips caught him off guard. It had been his experience that, with the exception of Harriette Wilson, demimondaines had a depressing lack of humor and originality. Neither were they aboveboard about their intentions. He expected to be the hound, not the fox. This little innocent seemed about to prove his generality wrong.

His full, rich baritone rang out in a hearty laugh. "A feisty filly, but I'll wager you can be broken to the bridle. And I think I've already discovered the method." His voice dropped to a deep lull.

"Really, duke? Do you propose to try?" She tipped her head back and slightly to the side as she tapped one elegant index finger lightly against her chin. The attitude was definitely a challenge. How easy this art of flirting was. She felt exhilarated, drunk on the power to make Camber notice her with a gleam of interest in his usually cool eyes, and a genuine smile of amusement on his normally saturnine countenance.

"Of course," he answered the challenge with a grin of anticipation curving his firm lips. "A woman with your entrancing beauty and wit is rare. I'd decided the combination didn't exist."

"You don't think much of my sex, do you, Your Grace?" Her brown eyes were alight with interest. She'd known he would be a stimulating partner. Now she had to convince him she was worth the effort on his part.

"I wouldn't say I denigrate women. I just, shall we say, fail to find them infinitely fascinating. But I begin to think I might have been hasty in my judgment." He sat next to her on the small couch.

When she turned her head to look him in the eyes, Damaris found his lips inches from her own. She could smell the clean lime of his soap mixed with fragrant tobacco. It brought memories of their other encounters rushing in on her, and she knew she'd do anything to make him hers.

With her full lips slightly pursed, she leaned toward the duke until they were a hair's breadth apart. She gave a small prayer that her new position was seductive, and not an obvious ploy used by someone who was blatantly inexperienced. "Surely a man of your maturity doesn't make hasty decisions? Although, I must admit that you seem to take and discard ladybirds with a speed that does lead one to suppose you jump before you consider." That had been calculated to see if he'd already procured another divertissement. It wouldn't further her scheme if she had to compete against a legitimate lightskirt. She had no intentions of filling all the duke's needs. At least, not yet.

Julian's warm breath fanned her parted lips as his hot lips brushed against hers with his answer. "Are you trying to ascertain, without being blunt, whether or not I currently have a mistress?" His voice deepened and his eyes held hers captive. "Otherwise, from your mention of maturity, I must think that you consider me old. Which, I assure you, I'm not. I still have the use of all my faculties. As I'm more than willing to demonstrate to you." His eyes strayed to the fullness of her bosom exposed so conveniently by her position.

Dami couldn't keep a flush from mounting her high cheeks. It was his words and not his closeness. "To match your directness, Your Grace, have you a new kept woman?" She chose to gloss over his last words. She wasn't ready to get that involved yet.

Keeping his lips barely touching hers, Julian brought a hand up to cup her exposed shoulder carefully. A tremor shot down her back, starting where his warm fingers softly kneaded her skin.

"As I prepared to come here tonight, Amalie, I had no intention of setting up a new mistress. Now, I'm not so sure." The smoky tint of his eyes suggested more was to come. "To be honest, I have thought about you since The Swan, and was of half a mind to hunt for you. As I said earlier."

Triumph exulted her. It was followed by the urge to press her lips against the ones already teasing her with their proximity. She wanted to be kissed by him again. Taking a deep breath, she let it go in a long, soft sigh. She couldn't afford to lose control. The kiss would have to wait. Right now she had to play to win.

Her fingers, the well-shaped nails buffed to a shine, ran lightly along the row of pearl buttons on his shirt front. "Is there more, Your Grace?" She lowered her lush lashes so that she peeked up at him provocatively.

"Yes. Call me Julian. 'Your Grace' sounds too formal for what I have in mind." He slowly removed his hand from her shoulder, but his breath was still moist against her face from his closeness.

The words flowed over her nerve endings, leaving her tingling. "What is it you have in mind . . . Julian?" She knew what he meant, but she'd make him say it. It flashed through her mind that a gently reared lady would be offended at the carte blanche she knew he meant to offer, but it was the first step in her plan to win him. When she'd devised her strategy, she'd also prepared herself for this eventuality. That she was excited by his nearness, and was responding to him wholeheartedly, she pushed to the back of her consciousness. Time tomorrow to analyze that.

"Ah, Amalie, relax. You move too fast," he drawled, "even for a rake of my stamp." His mouth twitched. "The night is still young."

He's playing me like a sportsman would a trout on his line. Indignation made her eyes spark. She caught herself before any injudicious words passed her mouth.

In one quick movement, he was standing in front of her, bowing over her hand with a flourish. "May I have the honor of this waltz? I'm sure you are as graceful on the dance floor as you are sitting in this hidden alcove."

To help herself recover from the shock of his abrupt move, Damaris opened her fan and waved it slowly in front of her heated brow. It also gave her time to consider her next words. "Of course, I will dance with you, Julian. However, I must insist on first donning a mask." She'd thought this part out carefully and decided that, as unusual as it might look, it was the only way she could ensure she wouldn't be recognized.

"A mask, sweetings? You can't mean to hide such beauty behind something so mundane as a piece of cloth?" His words were laced with curiosity.

"Alas, but that's just what I intend to do." She brought the delicate fan to a stop just below her eyes, which were dark and mysterious from the judicious use of blacking. "There might be gentlemen whom it would be better did not recognize me. You understand, Julian." The throaty timber of her voice gave the words the exact meaning she'd intended.

His jaw clenched before he extended his hand to help her rise. "Of course," he replied in measured tones. "But if you are trying to remain incognito, might I suggest that a mask will only make you the more conspicuous?"

Standing, she turned slightly and extracted a black lace confection from her reticule. She used the act of bowing her head to fasten the strings to hide her knowing smile. It was going better than she'd dreamed possible. He was already showing signs of jealousy . . . she hoped. "That is a risk I shall just have to take, for it would be worse if I were recognized." The words were meant to tantalize him.

She didn't see the tightening of his hands into hard balls.

With her back turned, she also didn't see him reach for the ribbons that would tie the concealing fabric to her eyes. As he grasped the strings, fire licked up her fingers where they touched. He was so close she could feel the heat emanating from his large body as his hands moved in the silkiness of her hair.

His voice was as raspy as hers when he told her she could turn around. "The lace doesn't hide your beauty. I would recognize you anywhere. Let us hope your *former* admirers aren't as perspicacious."

"Certainly," she replied grandly as she took his arm and swept past the velvet hangings he was holding aside. A jigger of doubt tugged at her. If he could recognize her even with the mask on, then might not someone else also figure out who she really was? It was enough to make her start shaking, but she couldn't turn back now. What excuse could she make to suddenly deny him the waltz? None, unless she was willing to add more fuel to his already piqued inquisitiveness, which she wasn't. There would be too many times in the future, at least she hoped there would be a future, that his sense of something unusual would be aroused. She didn't intend to overload their first encounter. Just add some spice to the play.

The light of the ballroom momentarily blinded her after the shadows of the alcove. Without waiting for her eyes to adjust, Camber drew Dami into an intimate clasp and twirled her rapidly to the music. They spun around the large dance floor, her dress billowing out behind her, her hair streaming down her back like rays of moonlight. She felt giddy, as though she'd consumed far too much champagne.

Her face glowing with pleasure, she smiled into his intent face, inches above hers. The fire in his eyes discomfited her at the same time that it excited her. Warmth spread from his muscular arm encircling her supple waist, making her feel as if he held her in a red-hot vise.

"You're holding me much too close for propriety," she said breathlessly. Simultaneously, she pushed halfheartedly against his broad chest where it rubbed the delicate material of her bodice. She could have bitten her tongue as she realized that the type of person she was portraying wouldn't mind the closeness. Would, in fact, have relished it.

"Do you want me to loosen my hold?" His bold gaze raked her face as he bent his head to place a butterfly kiss on a wisp of molten silver that had escaped from the confines of her diamond tiara.

She shivered deliciously as his lips brushed her hair. "No," she sighed, "I think I must be crazy to let you hold me this way." Her dreamy, liquid-brown eyes held his, "I've never been this close to a man before. I didn't know it was so potent."

"You mean, you've never felt this close to a man before," he drawled.

"Actually, I . . ."

Before she could continue, Julian brushed her trembling lips with his firm ones. "Don't bother to explain, Amalie. I don't want to know. It doesn't matter how many men have gone before me."

She parted her lips to tell him he was wrong to judge her so, when a flash of sanity reminded her of the role she was playing. Even though she'd asked Harriette to explain that she was new to this endeavor, she really couldn't expect him to believe it. Especially after the hints she'd thrown his way in the alcove. Pressing her mouth firmly shut, she closed her eyes and immersed herself in the feelings his nearness aroused.

They flew around the crowded area. Couples moved to let them by. The arrogant duke and the beauty in his arms had the attention of all.

"This must be how it feels to fly. Free from all earthly restraints," Dami mused. Her head was flung back, resting on Julian's satin-covered shoulder. "No wonder a wild bird will die before staying in captivity for long."

His eyes held hers in a long look. Faster and faster they spun, their bodies moving as one. Dami felt the torrid strength of Julian's rock-hard thighs through the thin silk of her skirt, they seemed to twine and mesh with a will of their own. Emotions she'd never known existed coursed through her. Her heart beat with a rapidity that alarmed her.

Lost in sensations, it was full seconds before Dami realized that the music had stopped. Julian had been equally lost. Abruptly, he stopped them before a large Grecian pillar, where Dami clung to him, slightly dazed and out of breath.

"How enervating," she exclaimed.

A slow smile softened the harsh planes of Julian's face as he watched the slender woman in his arms. Her left arm was still around his neck and her right hand was caught in his large left one. He gently kissed the back of her hand as it lay in his, then turned it over and pressed a passionate kiss into her soft palm.

"You must be thirsty. Sit here on this chair, behind this column. This way, you will be out of the way of everyone. I'll fetch you some champagne." He ran a long finger down the edge of her gown, ending where her breast swelled above the tight fabric.

Fiery bolts licked up her chest, inflaming her face and chest. "You are much too bold in your attentions, Your Grace," she chided. "This is much too public a place for you to touch me as you do."

"Have you forgotten where you are, Amalie?" Inquiry once again in his voice and look. "You are at The Cyprians' Ball, not a debutantes' ball. What we are doing, and what I would like to follow it with, are quite acceptable here. Look around you and you will see that I speak only the truth."

She quickly lowered her eyes before he could see the shock of surprise in them. Yes, she'd forgotten where she was and what she was posing as in the heady delight of the dance. She didn't need to look around as he'd suggested. It was patently obvious what was going on. She'd forgotten in the intensity of her reactions.

"Please, Your Grace . . ."

"So formal when not in my arms. I can tell that I shall have to endeavor to keep you there always. Otherwise you will constantly be 'Your Gracing' me. Not exactly what a man expects to hear on his lover's lips." With a chuckle at her obvious discomfort, he turned and left her to go for their drinks.

Caught up in the feeling he'd invoked, Dami didn't notice the tall, elegant figure of Jason Beaumair, the earl of Perth, approaching her.

"Ah, milady," his suave voice interrupted her reverie. "I see Camber has deserted you. Mayhap I will be able to entertain you in his stead?"

Dami looked up into the insolent stare of Jason Beaumair and wondered how to handle the situation. She'd been in his arms just the night before at Almack's. A twinge of uneasiness assailed her and she felt her hands go cold and clammy as they clenched in the folds of her dress. What to do? She didn't know if the character she was attempting to play would be familiar enough with the earl to call him by name, or if she should pretend not to know him? Beaumair solved the problem for her.

"Come, you don't have to play the game with me, Lady Damaris," he said.

Her eyes widened in shock. "You are mistaken, my lord," she replied haughtily. She couldn't admit his hit; she would brazen it out. He couldn't know who she was. She had a mask on and it was the Cyprians' Ball; no lady of quality would be there. He was roasting her, hoping to get her away from Julian by piquing her interest. That was all. They were, she reminded herself, rivals for the favors of fashionable impures. It was the way things were done. That was the only thing he was interested in. Her identity was safe. There was no way he could know. Her thoughts ran chaotically through her fevered mind.

"Tut, tut, milady. If you intend to play dangerously, you should always remember to hide your hair. No one else in London can boast such an unusual color. Not even your twin." The insolent posture of his body dared her to deny his statement.

She continued to stare at him disdainfully. "Really,

my lord, you are becoming a bore." In her agitation over his recognition, she forgot her role. No woman looking for a wealthy protector would spurn the earl, but Dami was unaware of that. "Your joke is in poor taste." The husky quality of her voice was tinged with coldness.

"If your hair didn't give away the game, your voice certainly would. What sport do you play with Camber, my pet? I trust, for your sake at least, that you know he plays deep."

Becoming thoroughly alarmed, but determined to bluff her way, Dami snapped open her fan and started to flick it vigorously. "I daresay you consider yourself to be a wit, my lord," her straight nose tilted upward ever so slightly, "but I consider you to be *de trop*." She waved the fan under his chin. "The duke is returning, and I doubt if he will appreciate your having subjected me to unwanted attentions."

"Is that the stand you intend to take? Rather dangerous for a green chit. As your whole disguise is." With a casual glance over his shoulder, he continued, "Remember, I know your real identity. You would be ruined if it leaked out that you are playing the part of cyprian to Camber's rake."

Like a bird of prey, he grabbed her chicken-skin fan in his strong white hand. His hard black eyes never left her face as he deliberately broke one of the slats and then dropped the delicate toy on the floor.

Dami stared at the fan. Lying on the tiles, it looked like an exotic bird that had been mutilated by a rapacious hawk. Ravaged and left to die, forgotten about as soon as the deed was done. She picked it up.

Her eyes were heavy-lidded and filled with desperation when she lifted them. Camber was standing in front of her with their glasses. "It is time I left, Julian." She forced the words through thin lips and clenched jaw.

One look told Julian that something had happened while he had been gone. "Of course, Amalie. Let me get your cloak and I shall order my carriage brought around." He was full of concern for the obviously distraught girl. In her exposed vulnerability she reminded him more of a young girl than the experienced woman he knew her to be.

"No!" She forced her voice lower. "I have my own carriage. If you will just escort me back to Harriette, I will be on my way." She stood as she said the words, her hands gripping the dainty fan until the sharp cracks of the remaining slats brought her to an awareness of her actions.

"If I take you to Harriette and leave you now, how will I know where to find you? For I do mean to see you again, Amalie."

His determination would have thrilled her minutes ago, now she was numbed by the possibility of impending disaster. Surely, Beaumair meant to ruin her. But why? She didn't even know him.

"In fact, I want to take you driving tomorrow at eight. Where may I pick you up?" Julian's voice was determined as his strong hands reached out and took her shoulders.

Trying to regain control, she replied without thinking. "I shall be outside the marquis of Cleve's town house." The words were out before she knew it. Even then she was too upset to ascertain the effect they were having on the duke.

A look of surprise permeated his face, while his whole stance became stiff. "As you wish."

He took her to where Johnny was talking with Harriette Wilson. A curt bow and frozen smile were all he would vouchsafe her on leaving. Dami was too upset to notice his frosty demeanor as she turned to Johnny and begged him to take her home. Even under the cover of the mask, it was obvious her face was ashen.

Chapter Five

Frost nipped her nose as Damaris sneaked out the back door of Rose Arbor. The flowers the house took its name from bloomed in profusion, their scent wafting through the morning sunshine to twine around her. Even the wrought iron seat, situated back from the well-tended gravel path, was warming. It was here she stopped to worry over her dilemma.

A deep sigh shook her as she rolled her neck to lessen some of the tension. She hadn't slept well last night. Naturally exuberant, her anxiety over possible exposure had left her tossing and turning. She had dark smudges under her large eyes and a pallor in her cheeks that was even more pronounced than usual.

Perth scared her. His demeanor had held a subtle threat, and she didn't know how he had figured out who she was. But if he could, others might also.

Even so, the die was already cast. Should her last night's activities become known, any aspirations for social standing she might have would be blighted. Ergo: She ought to continue as she'd started. If Perth wanted to ruin her, he had enough ammunition already. Being fainthearted wouldn't mitgate the scandal one iota.

Unclenching her balled fists, she nodded her head with determination, shrugged in resignation, and rose from the bench and headed for the gate leading to the front of the house.

She forced her legs to carry her forward in a semblance of carefree energy. It was time for Camber to pick her up, and tired and worried as she was, she didn't want to keep him waiting. A servant might chance to glance out any one of the numerous front windows and see him. Then there would be the devil to pay as she tried to explain how he came to be there at eight in the morning, and her getting into his carriage with no abigail *and* then not returning until late in the day.

For now, Suzy would tell Mama she had a headache and was keeping to her room. When it was time to leave for Lord and Lady Snow's rout, she would make a miraculous recovery.

With this devious thought, she rounded the back corner of the building and saw Camber just drawing up in a black high-perch phaeton drawn by a magnificent pair of spirited bays. A twinge of apprehension sped through her at the sight of the restless beasts. She had never gotten over her fear of horses.

The fear was quickly forgotten as her eyes moved to Camber. He was dressed in a coat of light blue superfine over buff breeches and glossy Hessians. Around his neck he'd forgone the intricate cravat in favor of a more casual belcher neckcloth tied in a simple knot. A jaunty curly-brimmed beaver hat was tipped over his high brow, and tan driving gloves covered his hands.

Dami was glad she'd taken care over her toilet. Dressed in a pale yellow round dress, a golden-brown spencer with matching trim, dark brown gloves and walking boots, and a chip straw bonnet, she felt confident of holding her own with the sartorial duke.

It was too late now, but she wished she'd remembered to pinch some color into her wan cheeks. Instead, she took the three recommended deep breaths, squared her shoulders, and moved forward to meet Camber.

With an ease born of physical conditioning, he jumped down from the seat, threw the reins to his tiger, and advanced to take her hand. "You're looking lovely at this ungodly hour," he complimented her with practiced ease.

For a moment, Dami longed to see him lose some of his polished sangfroid. Anything to make him seem more human and more affected by her as a person. When he was so smooth, she harbored doubts of her scheme. She began to feel like another object that he was collecting.

"Why, thank you, Your Grace," she responded, careful to keep all irritation out of her voice.

"You're even prompt. A rare quality in a woman," he continued in the same vein as he handed her up into the high carriage. "I was afraid that you would keep me waiting at least a half hour, which would have been difficult on my cattle."

Before letting go of her hand, he turned it over and rolled the kid glove back to expose the underportion of her wrist. Never letting his eyes wander from hers, he bent and kissed the tender piece of skin where her pulse beat close to the surface.

Dami felt a flush mount her face at the unexpected sensual act. She longed to let her lashes drop to hide her eyes, but knew that wasn't the response he expected of her. So, she kept her wide brown eyes on his grey ones. Thus, it was impossible to ignore the flash of heat that emanated from his.

Camber was obviously satisfied with her response. A look of confidence turned the corners of his full lips up while he perused her charms. After what seemed an eternity to Dami, he relinquished her hand and walked around to his side of the phaeton.

Upon settling in, Camber took the reins from his tiger and flipped the man a gold coin, saying, "Take yourself off for the day, Tom."

The man bowed his head and turned away. For Dami, it wasn't too soon. When tipping his head to his master, the tiger had sent a look of leering appreciation her way. It offended her, not being used to that kind of regard from anyone, let alone a servant, but she bit her tongue. In the role she was playing, she must get used to insults of that type. Or at least be able to tolerate them.

Out of the corner of her eyes, Dami saw Camber send a knowing look at his tiger as he flicked his whip, setting the bays into a canter. Her attention was jerked back to her companion by his next words.

"If I didn't know better, Amalie, I would have said you must be the young lady of the house. So perfectly do you ape the styles of a demure lady of quality." A thin grin barely curved the corners of his sensual lips. The look he'd seen his tiger give her had brought his irritation from the night before slamming back.

The cutting words brought a spark to her eyes. Why

84

did she love this cad? It was obvious he was interested in her person, but he never let a chance go by to put her in her place: the place he believed her to belong in. But she kept looking straight ahead with her chin up. His comment didn't deserve an answer. Instead, she let the cool morning breeze defuse her irritation with the man.

She forced herself to examine the street they were on. At this hour, most of the beau monde were still in bed. But the less wealthy denizens were already out and about on their errands and merchandising. Consequently, Camber had to pay attention to his driving until they got out of fashionable St. James Court.

"Where are we going, Your Grace?" The remnants of anger made her sound breathless.

While waiting for an answer, Dami grudgingly admired his skill with the reins as he tooled them through the crowded streets. His hands were steady, his face showed his concentration.

He finally spoke. "Didn't I tell you last night, sweetings?" Camber sliced her a look before returning his attention to the sprightly animals.

"No, you didn't, Your Grace," she answered calmly. It was obvious that he was baiting her. Well, she would play his game . . . for now.

"I thought for sure that I had," he mused softly. "Perhaps the haste with which you gave me my congé in favor of young FitzHubert left me no time to say what I was thinking."

Although his voice was smooth and uninflected, Dami knew he was put out over her turning to Johnny. Well, there was nothing she could do about it. She certainly didn't intend to tell him that Johnny was her brother. Instead, she would play on his jealousy a little. If his reputation were true, until he bedded her he would tolerate a small amount of needling. It was, after all, the chase that excited him, not the surrender.

"Why, Your Grace," she tittered and tapped him lightly on the forearm with her gloved fingers, "you certainly can't be jealous of that child, Johnny FitzHubert?"

She saw dark clouds forming in his grey eyes and was hard-pressed to contain the genuine laugh that threatened to spill out. What a temper he had. No wonder he was such a deadly opponent in battle. He was that rare man who could contain his anger and use it to win.

"I'm never jealous, Amalie. Remember that," he answered. For all its softness, his voice was dangerous sounding. "And I refuse to share what is mine. You are mine."

A thrill of excitement ran down her spine at his words. He already felt possessive of her. Her plan was going better than she'd hoped.

At the same time, she felt a twinge of irritation that he considered her an object for his amusement, and not a human being with feelings and emotions and intelligence. Well, she would soon show him there was more to this chit than clothes, hair, and body. She would dazzle him with her mind.

She opened her mouth to introduce the topic of the Peninsular War. She screamed.

Without a break in movement, Camber pulled his team to a halt. Cursing under his breath about the lack of a tiger to hold his cattle, he jumped lightly to the ground. A frown pulled his brows together as he turned to Dami.

"Here, Amalie, hold these reins. All you have to do is keep a tight grip on them." He was gone on the words.

Dami watched from her precarious position on the phaeton as Camber strode up to the farm wagon positioned dangerously in the middle of the road. It overflowed with a boutiful harvest on its way to market, while the fat farmer berated the still donkey hitched to it. Arms flaying wildly, cheeks rosy from anger, the man's shouts could be heard over the hustle and bustle of the crowd enjoying the spectacle.

Camber waded into this arena and immediately took charge. Like a general commanding his troops, he ordered the mob to move back, then motioned for the farmer to release the donkey's bridle and fall back. Grasping the reins, Camber gave the recalcitrant animal an authoritative pull to which the donkey immediately responded. Within minutes the wagon was on its side of the road.

After the farmer drove away, Camber shrugged his broad shoulders to return his slightly awry coat to its previous fastidious fit. Then he picked up his beaver hat, which had fallen as he'd helped the farmer pull his donkey to the left side of the road, and sauntered back to the phaeton.

One auburn eyebrown raised. "I see that you've managed to keep my cattle from running away with you, Amalie." He eyed her gloved hands holding the reins firmly. "It would appear that you are a very unusual woman for your, shall we say . . . calling.

Not many women would be able to handle my bloods. Even those born to the task." He gave her a shallow bow. "I extend my compliments."

She eyed him balefully. He'd all but said she was a tramp. That he'd also praised her, she ignored, as it had been backhanded. Three deep breaths, and she had herself under control. He had only called her what she was attempting to portray. She should be glad that he was so easily taken in. Honest to a fault, she admitted to herself that her fear of horses had made it hard for her to keep the pair of Thoroughbreds under control.

"La, Your Grace, 'tis nothing," she cooed.

He flicked a suspicious glance at her as he vaulted into the seat. The swift move put him right next to her, so close she could see the tiny red-brown hairs on his wrists as he took the reins from her now slack hands. His riding gloves couldn't disguise the sinewy strength of his fingers. His grip on the ribbons seemed light, but the horses responded immediately.

A fleeting thought flashed through her mind. It would be so easy for him to control her the way he did his team. She shivered and broke into gooseflesh before she got control of herself.

"Are you cold?" he asked solicitiously.

"No."

"If you are, don't be afraid to tell me. Your outfit is very fetching, and your spencer looks warm, but I know that looks are often deceiving where a lady's clothing is concerned." He gave her a wicked grin, and continued, "I can very easily stop and get you a blanket."

"That won't be necessary. I'm quite warm." She had

to turn the topic of conversation. It certainly wouldn't do to let him know why she'd shivered, he was already too complacent about her.

From the corner of her eye, she cast him a surreptitious glance before returning her attention to the busy streets. She would introduce Wellington's Peninsular Campaign. Camber had fought in it, been a hero in it, and she wanted to impress him with her ability to follow a subject generally eschewed by members of the delicate sex.

"Hhhrm," she began, "you fought with Wellington in the Peninsula when he was still Wellesley, didn't you, Your Grace?" It wasn't the best of starts, but it was better than nothing.

He raised one thick eyebrow and gave her an oblique look. "Yes."

She was nonplussed by his unresponsive answer. He was supposed to start a monologue about his adventures, albeit expurgated for her ears. Instead, he said nothing, driving his only concern.

Taking a deep breath, she continued, "What did you think of it?" It was hard to keep the irritation out of her voice when he still looked uninterested. She decided any response was better than none. "I've heard that it was fought for nothing. I mean, what good did it do us to fight that war? It's not like it was on our land, or that Napoleon even threatened us. Why, it was obvious at the time that the War Ministry wasn't at all interested, either." That ought to goad him.

Not taking his eyes from his task, he asked blightingly, "Is that what you believe or are you just repeating what some man has told you?"

Frustrated, she blurted, "I'm trying to start a conversation about something that has always interested me. After all, we lost a lot of men in that war and the price of our commodities has skyrocketed as a result of the hostilities with the Emperor. That alone makes the subject worth dissecting. It's the English people who have suffered for keeping Napoleon's dreams of world domination from becoming true." She paused for breath and to watch his reaction.

At these heated words, he pulled the coach to the side of the road and stopped it. Then he turned to gaze at her long and hard. "You're absolutely right. Our commodities have gotten too high for the ordinary Englishman to purchase them easily. Corn is the perfect example. But the real crime is to the men who fought. With Boney defeated, they've been thrown on an economy no longer able to support them." His voice was bitter and his eyes were like chips of flint. "But I'm sure these things aren't what you're really interested in. Why should you be different from anyone else? So, I will satisfy your vulgar curiosity about a bloody war fought to prevent a distasteful future."

She returned his stare unflinchingly. "No," she started before he broke in on her.

"Very well. You're correct about the Prime Minister's not being particularly interested in the war. However, all of that changed when Perceval was assassinated in 'twelve and Liverpool took over. Then Wellington got the support he needed." A shadow crossed his eyes. "I wish it could have happened sooner." He scowled and fell silent.

"Why?" she prompted. "Was it because of the

90

hardships you and your men had to suffer?"

He was gazing into the distance now. "Some. You know, there were times when the men didn't get paid for six months or longer. Many times their boots had no soles and their uniforms were tatters that barely covered them."

His voice was strained now, and she put her hand hesitantly on his arm holding the reins. She was beginning to regret bringing up the subject. She wanted to talk about the politics and economics involved, not the suffering. Suffering was something very private, and she hadn't realized how concerned Camber was about it. She knew that most people were also unaware of this side of him.

"Do you know," he said, "while our men were going without we were sending millions of pounds to the continent to bribe the other powers to fight their own wars with Napoleon so we could go home to our insulated little island and not have to worry about the possibility that Boney might conquer the rest of the world and come for us."

Dami watched him and began to realize that there was more to the man sitting next to her than an idle Corinthian who had everything money could buy; more than she'd envisioned in her wildest flights of fantasy. More than ever, she wanted him to be hers. Only now she was beginning to have doubts of her ability to be his equal. The feeling was strange to her, and she wasn't sure how to cope with it.

Deep in revery, he kept on. "Even our own officers were uncaring about the enlisted men who served under them. I remember one time in particular. Word reached the duke that there were wounded men lying outside in the road of a small town because there wasn't room to billet them. Straight away he mounted his horse and rode hell bent to find out what could be done for them. When he reached the town, he found that there were quarters, but they were occupied by the officers. Wellington immediately ordered the officers to give up their rooms to the wounded men." A harsh laugh escaped him. "They did so grudgingly. The next day, knowing his men all too well, Wellington went back to the town to make sure his orders were still being followed. The injured men were back out in the streets." He paused.

Dami's deficiencies weighed heavily on her as she sensed his agony. Very aware of her inability to carry on light conversation for any length of time, she had fallen back on her knowledge of the wars against Napoleon. But she had not intended for this to happen.

He added, "The duke put the offending officers under arrest and cashiered them for disobedience to orders." He sighed deeply and pulled himself back to the present with an effort. This was quickly followed by a sarcastic cast to his features and a cutting edge to his voice as he said, "Is your voyeuristic urge for excitement sufficiently satisfied by what I've told you? There is nothing glamorous about war. It is something done to preserve one's country and way of life. It is not a pleasure to be enjoyed. Definitely not something a man discusses with a lady of breeding. But then," he added cruelly, "you aren't a lady, are you?"

He had lashed out at her so quickly she was caught off guard. All she could see were her castles in the air falling down around her. Instead of impressing him with her intelligence, she'd disgusted him with her interest in a subject he remembered with pain and distaste. She'd always considered him to be a glory-seeking egotist, whom she loved in spite of his faults. If she were perfectly honest with herself, she even had to admit that she'd entertained visions of turning him from his callous ways and making him a humanitarian. The shoe seemed on the other foot now.

She was silent for several seconds before saying, "I wasn't seeking vicarious thrills, as you so baldly stated. I am honestly interested in what went on. I had a bro . . . I mean cousin who fought in the war." She crossed her fingers in the folds of her gown. "He was in the infantry. Enlisted. And I was curious as to what it was like during that time. He would never tell me all the details."

"Now you know why," he said harshly.

He turned his head forward and gave an abrupt flick of his wrist for the horses to start moving again. Dami was pitched back into the soft squabs as the carriage bolted into movement. With one hand she grabbed her bonnet, using the other to grasp the edge of the seat.

She turned cautiously toward Camber. His forbidding face made her turn away and close her mouth without uttering the comment she'd started to make. Better to give him time to cool off and come back to the present.

They traveled some distance in the resulting chilly atmosphere.

The awkward silence was broken by Camber's quiet voice. "There are a lot of people out there who wait with bated breath to hear all the gory details. Then they rush posthaste to the first social gathering and repeat the gruesome stories they've just wheedled out of some poor fool. Those people thrive on the suffering of others. That has always nauseated me."

It wasn't much, but Dami realized that it was as close to an apology as he was going to come. She was satisfied.

The distance was eaten up by the smooth team as they pulled the light racing vehicle along the road. She noticed it was getting more rural, and Camber still hadn't said where he was taking her.

She knew she should be apprehensive at the lack of information, but she trusted him implicitly. He didn't have a reputation as a ravisher of women. Besides, now that she knew a little more about him, she felt sure he would protect her with his life if need be. Not that he loved her, or felt anything but lust for her, it was just his nature to care for the weaker member.

Still, she found her palms becoming wet in their butter-soft gloves and her neck muscles tensing up again.

"Will you tell me where we are going, Your Grace?" she asked politely.

He smiled down at her, his good mood returned. "I told you last night that my name is Julian, and I intend for you to use it, or suffer the consequences."

She ignored his comment, willing her treacherous heart to stop its pounding as she remembered his words. To give herself time, she asked her question again.

"We are going to a little house I own in Kensington," he replied. "I thought you might like getting away from the stench and heat of London for the day."

She felt his eyes on her as he said this. Without a doubt, she knew he kept it for his mistresses. Fresh from the country she might be, but she wasn't so uninformed that she didn't know that gentlemen of rank and fortune kept their current ladybirds in comfortable lodgings of their providing. It also reminded her that he was a flesh-and-blood man: a womanizer. She'd almost forgotten while he talked about the miseries of the war.

"Mmmm," was all she said to his statement.

Minutes later, Camber pulled up in front of a cosy little house, obviously built in the last twenty or thirty years. The front door was crowned by a small fan inlaid with colored glass, and the two front windows were spaced an equal distance from it. The second level had four smaller windows, and the final story had six even smaller ones.

Camber pulled his bays up as a young boy came to take them. The duke jumped down and flipped the lad a coin, saying, "Take them around to the stable, Jem, and see they get a good rubdown." Then he circled the phaeton to hand Dami down.

It seemed there was even a stable of sorts with this house. He must own it, she thought with a sardonic grin. Of course, it would be infinitely cheaper and more convenient to own the place. That way he wouldn't be paying for it if it chanced to be unoccupied, which she doubted ever happened. Also, owning it, he was assured it would always be ready for its newest tenant.

He took her arm and steered her toward the house. The front door was opened immediately by a middle-aged woman dressed in black bombazine. Her greying hair was pulled severely back from her face into a tight bun. Her blue eyes were cool, but her manner was everything expected of a superior servant. It seemed Camber employed only the best help, regardless of where their work put them.

He guided Dami into the sunny foyer, where he took off his hat and gloves and laid them on a small inlaid table reposing against one wall under a massive gilt mirror. When she had her bonnet off and her gloves removed, Dami followed his example.

Then he took her into a bright drawing room, calling over his shoulder for the woman to bring them tea and sherry. The walls were painted cream, which showed the pewter-blue curtains and furniture to perfection. On the floor was a thick Axminster carpet done in matching tones. An elegant fireplace took up one whole wall. Everything was done in impeccable taste.

Turning, Camber pulled her into a close embrace. One hand found its way to the nape of her neck where it held her captive in his arms. His lips hovered over hers. She could feel the warmth of his breath on her cheeks.

"How do you like my little home-away-from-home?" he whispered.

Breathless, the blood rushed through her, making a loud noise in her ears. He always did this to her. All sense of proportion seemed to fall away when he held her against him. If she weren't careful, she'd be in his bed before she accomplished her goal.

She took a deep gulp of air, her words coming out in a rush. "I haven't seen enough of it to tell yet. Why don't you take me on a tour?" That way she would get out of his arms. He was far too dangerous to her peace of mind to let him stay this close.

"Are you trying to get away from me, sweetings?" he teased lightly. "I assure you that you are perfectly safe in my embrace."

"From everyone but you, Julian."

A carefree laugh was his answer, but he let her go. She moved quickly out of the circle of warmth he'd enclosed her in. For a moment she felt cold and bereft, and she ran her hands up and down her arms several times as she moved to the relative safety of the fireplace.

"Why are you moving over there, Amalie, when the door is over here, and we are about to take a tour of the house?" A gleam of amusement lit his grey eyes.

Steadying her clamoring nerves, Dami moved gracefully toward the door. He met her there and put her cold hand on his arm. Together they left the room.

The first floor was comprised of the drawing room, a cosy library done in wood and brown tones, and a small, elegant dining room. Leading to the second floor was a staircase of mahogany with a beautifully carved banister. It was wide enough to allow the ladies of several years prior to pass down it without crushing their crinolined skirts. Upstairs were two bedrooms, which he rushed her past. There was even a modern water closet. The last floor consisted of four small rooms set aside for the servants.

After viewing the servants' quarters, Camber took Dami back to the master bedroom. Entering the large bedroom, she stopped. The carpet and drapes were deep crimson, and the large, well-cushioned chairs were covered in red chintz. The bed caught her attention.

At home her bed was done in bright yellows with golden curtains ringing it to keep out the cold while providing some privacy. Not so here. Ruby-red chiffon flowed to the floor from a circular ring on the ceiling. She could see every detail of the bed through the gossamer fabric. It would have held four people easily, and it was covered in opulent satin pillows. Their plush decadence screamed voluptuous abandon to her frayed nerves.

"What do you think of this room?" the duke questioned lazily.

All she could do was look, her eyes glazed. Then, for no reason, her eyes lifted again to the ring securing the poor excuse for a bed curtain. It wasn't a ring. It was a large mirror.

When she didn't answer, he added, "If there is anything you don't like, feel free to tell me. It will be changed immediately."

Was he laughing at her? She floundered emotionally as she pulled herself up straight and headed for the door. "No, everything is perfect," she tossed over her shoulder in a tight voice. So this was where he made love to his mistresses. No wonder he had such a reputation as a lady killer. Everything was set up to precipitate the fall of the woman. It was overpowering. She had to get out.

Her back stiff, she descended the steps to the drawing room where the tea tray waited. With a poise she didn't feel, she sat at the small chair in front of the silver set and started pouring out the dark brew.

She set one for Camber on the opposite side of the table so he wouldn't be able to touch her easily. Then she filled another cup for herself and liberally laced the liquid with cream and sugar.

It was this scene that Camber saw as he entered the room.

He moved casually to the chair across from her and sat down. Equally nonchalant, he picked up his cup and took a long drink. The cup made a light click when he set it back into the saucer.

At first, Dami almost laughed out loud watching the large, muscular man pick up the dainty china teacup. One sip almost emptied the small thing. But she remembered the bedroom and why she was here. She sobered instantly.

His eyes never wavered from her face. "I have a proposition to present to you, Amalie," he stated bluntly, "and now seems as good a time as any to discuss it."

She blanched under his cool appraisal.

Chapter Six

"You understand, this is a business deal." He leaned back in his chair, his bulk overpowering its delicate lines, his fingers templing in front of his chin. "I will pay you four hundred pounds per annum, with a thousand to be deposited into funds in your name upon occupation of this house." His eyes never left her face. "I feel this is a very generous settlement. Do you have anything to add?"

His arrogant assumption that she would accept very nearly sent her into a paroxysm of anger. Knowing this was why he had brought her here didn't help mitigate her fury at his high-handed statement of terms. Her backbone stiffened.

"Your offer is everything that is considerate, Your Grace," she said, in as diplomatic a tone as she could muster under the circumstances. "But, I'm afraid I shall have to turn it down." Ordinarily, she was sure she would have blushed at their lack of delicacy in talking about such a private act, but her anger carried her through.

"Ah," he said ruminatively, "you mean the money isn't good enough." He paused and raked her with an analytical eye. "Pardon me, but I hadn't realized you rated your person so highly. Shall we say then, five hundred a year? I'm a generous man with those who please me . . . and I'm sure you will do that."

Dami ignored the sarcasm in his voice as she purred, "I'm certainly worth every penny of five hundred, *Your Grace*, but that isn't the reason I must refuse your flattering proposal." She saw his brows starting to pull together in a frown. "I have every intention of accepting you, but I need time." She dipped her eyes bashfully. "You see, that is, this is very hard to say," she muttered, not acting now, "this is the first liaison of this nature I've ever considered," she finished in a rush. Now she was blushing in earnest, her anger forgotten in her embarrassment.

"What!" he ejaculated in surprise. "I don't believe it. Now look here, Amalie, you're a very fetching chit, but you can't gammon me into raising my price. I'm already preparing to pay you more than I've paid any other woman. I won't increase it, though goodness knows I want you."

Her discomfort dissipated as quickly as it had come. The gall of the man to say she wasn't worth more. She was worth much, much more. She was worth every groat he owned. She was going to be his duchess. Dammit if she wasn't.

"Not worth it, am I," she fairly shouted, rising up in her chair. She settled a baleful eye on him. "How dare you talk about me as though I were a piece of cattle you are considering purchasing for your amusement?"

"But, my dear," he drawled, "isn't that exactly what you are?"

"No," she hissed.

"I doubt it." His voice was void of inflection as he continued. "Don't mistake me for a flat, Amalie. I understand perfectly why you ran to Johnny Fitz-Hubert last night."

She listened to him in astonishment. She had thought that was over and done with, now he was dredging it back up.

"*When* you accept my very generous offer, Amalie, you will no longer be connected to FitzHubert — in any way. I have yet to be cuckolded by a woman. I don't intend to start with you." Even though he said it quietly, the statement held all the searing quality of an ultimatum.

On her dignity, she replied frostily, "There is nothing illicit between Johnny and myself."

"Your use of his Christian name belies you."

"We are friends, nothing more. Besides, I use your given name," she replied heatedly.

"Precisely."

"There is no correlation." But she'd blundered badly. Furthermore, there was no way she could right his wrong assumption without spilling the applecart.

"Of course," he said casually while he examined his already perfectly manicured nails, "there may be another connection between you that you refuse to admit to."

Dami's eyes started wide. Lucky he wasn't looking at her. "Why, of course there isn't. There isn't any 'connection,' except that of friendship."

"In that case, this discussion is closed," Camber said. "However, I hope I've made my conditions for you to occupy this abode perfectly clear. I don't share what's mine, even if it's only my mistress."

Not only didn't he believe her, but he talked about her as though she were an inanimate object designed for his pleasure, with no feelings of her own.

"You cad!" She threw caution to the winds. "You act as though you've only to beckon and I'll come running. Well, let me tell you, my lord duke, I won't. When I choose, and not a minute sooner, I will become your light lady." She pounded her fist on her chair arm for emphasis.

Camber smiled at her smugly. "I will arrange to have your things brought here tomorrow."

"You will not." Her hard-won calm was in tatters. All she wanted was to wipe the complacent satisfaction off his face.

The hand still holding her teacup came forward in an arch. Before either of them realized what she intended to do, she flung the tepid tea in his face. She dropped the empty cup onto the table. One hand covered her mouth as she gasped, "I'm s-sorry. I-I didn't mean to do that."

Camber took a handkerchief out of his coat pocket and carefully wiped the liquid from his face. His face was hard planes of fury.

"I take that as your final refusal." His words fell like chips of ice.

Now that her hurt at his callous handling of the situation was alleviated through action, Dami felt contrition. She could see all her plans crumbling down, because of her impetuous temper.

"Oh, dear," she wailed softly. "Please excuse me, Your Grace," she added and lunged from her seat to the doorway. Without closing the door, she sped up the stairs to the retiring room on the next floor.

She reached its safety and immediately began to pace the floor. Everything had been going so well until she lost control. It stood to reason that it wasn't a love match for Camber. She should have prepared herself for his lack of romance about the situation. But she hadn't. Her hopes that he would feel something more for her than lust had clouded her honest appraisal of their relationship. Now she had to pay the consequences of her actions.

Tears welled in her eyes as she pondered the mess she had wrought in just a few minutes. All her years of planning were for naught unless she could repair the damage she'd just caused. She had to think up something good—immediately. In the next few minutes, she had to go back down those steps and tell him why she had lost her temper . . . and why she still couldn't accept his proposal. Not only that, but she must convince him to continue seeing her.

She paused in midstep, the glimmer of an idea coming to her. It just might work, and it was her only chance.

Her brain worked frantically as she took a handkerchief from her reticule and dabbed at her eyes. The blacking she'd put on this morning had run a little with her tears, but it was soon set to rights. She straightened her hair and opened the door.

Minutes later, she was again seated across from him. To his jaundiced eye, she looked perfectly at ease. Conversely, his once casual sprawl was now compressed into a pose of arms crossed over his chest and one gleaming Hessian tapping belligerently against the floor.

She gave him what she hoped was a reassuring smile. One hand was stretched entreatingly across the small table toward him. He ignored it.

Her dry tongue ran over her lips on reflex. "I'm sorry about the contretemps, Julian." Perhaps using his given name would soften him. "But, you must believe me when I tell you this is the first time I've ever been in this position." She paused to gauge his reaction. It was definitely unrelenting. "It's a long story, but if you will bear with me, I promise to make it as short as possible without losing the details," she entreated him.

His face and posture lost none of their reserve as he gave her a minuscule nod.

Dami took the still wet handkerchief from her reticule and dabbed at her eyes before lowering it to her lap. "This isn't easy." She could hear her mother berating her already for her impetuosity. "I'm the only child of the marquis of Cleve's deceased bailiff. Father was the younger son of a country squire, so while he got a good education, he didn't have much of an inheritance. In order to support himself and Mama, he went to work for the old marquis over twenty years ago. Upon Father's death, several months ago, the current marquis asked his brother, Johnny, to bring me to London and see that I got a job as a governess."

Dami paused, spread her hands helplessly in front of her, and grinned ruefully at him. At least he was listening to her. "I'm sure you can tell already, even with our short acquaintance, that I don't have the disposition to be a successful governess. I'm much too headstrong and opinionated. And I don't have any

105

accomplishments. I can't sew, or sing, or watercolor. But I came to town anyway because I didn't know what else to do."

She shrugged resignedly and pleaded with her eyes. "Please, put yourself in my place. The only job a genteelly raised female can fill is one I'm not temperamentally or educationally suited for. I was fast becoming destitute when I saw you that evening at the play. The one you attended with Mrs. Jones," she added naively. "You looked so debonair, and Mrs. Jones seemed so happy with her lot, that I decided then and there that the life of a courtesan had to be better than trying to insinuate myself into the role of a downtrodden governess." She ended with a small shrug, her eyes downcast.

It was hard to keep from smiling. The story was so simple and so believable. Ladies of breeding found themselves in this same position on a daily basis.

"Hmmm." Camber pondered her tale. "It could be true. It would certainly explain how you act the part of a lady. The hardest to swallow is how a young woman of your upbringing could bring herself to crush her scruples and allow a man to keep her in the capacity that a mistress fills." He gazed at her speculatively.

"As to that," she started glibly, then stopped short. This was the critical part. She had to be convincing. "Why, I'm used to some small luxuries that only money can buy, and everyone knows that in addition to being the recipient of her mistress's ill temper and her master's misplaced lusts, a governess is very poorly paid. I decided that if I must suffer another person's mistreatment and a man's unasked-for passions, then I will be paid for it."

"There is much to be said for your reason. I would probably make the same choice if I found myself in a similar situation," Camber concurred. "All of which brings us back to the start of this whole fracas. You've admitted that you intend to become some man's inamorata, so you might as well start with me." An engaging grin warmed his face. "I'm wealthy, titled, and considered reasonably attractive. You could do worse, you know."

His abrupt change of tactics caught her momentarily off guard, and she just looked at him in astonishment. It was near impossible to keep up with the man. He changed his moods as quickly as a chameleon changed its colors.

"Yes, well, as I was saying. I intend to become a kept woman, but I haven't reached the point yet where I can do it." At his darkening eyes, she hastened on, "You said yourself that you didn't know how a woman reared as I have been could become some man's plaything overnight. I'm telling you now . . . I can't."

"Are you trying to tell me, in your estimable way, Amalie, that you don't intend to gratify me with your presence in my little abode?" Camber's voice was silky soft.

Dami knew she had to tread warily now. "No. I'm saying that I need time to make the adjustment. It isn't every day that a gently reared young girl goes from innocent to wanton." She was pleased with her phrasing. It had just the right ring of righteous priggery, but not without abandonment.

Camber was relaxed again. His eyes were sparkling

in enjoyment of their little banter. He was even leaning back in the chair once more.

"How much time do you anticipate that you will need to make this . . . um, transition, sweetings?" He wondered how long she intended to try and carry out this charade. "Just because I choose to believe your touching little story, and that only because it gives a plausible reason for all your little accomplishments that most women trying for the post you profess to aspire to don't possess, doesn't mean I plan to play your dupe for long."

She gave him a flirtatious look from under her heavy lashes. "This is no game, Julian. A leap of this sort must be taken carefully and after due consideration."

"How long?"

"Only until I feel comfortable with you," she rushed.

"How long?"

"I don't know . . . exactly." He was losing the complacent look he'd worn just moments before. "Please don't rush me. It will be much better for both of us if you let me come to you naturally."

"I would have thought you'd already come to me 'naturally,'" he commented sarcastically. "You know, if you'll only admit it to yourself, you melt every time I touch you." He was looking smug again.

"Melting and succumbing are two different things, Your Grace," she answered primly.

"I see," he said on a sigh. But it was obvious by the drumming of his long fingers on the chair arm that he didn't "see" at all. "Well, I've had enough of this play and the day is getting late. Since you refuse to provide us both with a very pleasurably spent evening, we might as well head back for St. James. No doubt, the estimable Johnny will be awaiting his protegée."

At his words, Dami stood up and headed gracefully for the door. Camber was beside her as she reached it. He put a hand under her elbow and turned her to face him. They were scant inches apart and she could smell the scent he used and see the individual pores of his skin. Little auburn hairs had come loose from his Brutus and lighted like rays of sunset on his forehead. She could feel herself weakening as tremors started in her stomach and radiated outward.

"Be sure you don't take long, sweetings. I'm not a patient man when I want something." His voice was low and throaty.

Without a word, she turned and walked into the hallway. The woman with the tight bun was waiting with their things. Dami donned her spencer, hat, and gloves quickly. It didn't strike her as smart to linger longer in this seductive house. The very thought of its purpose lent her strength to consider going against everything she'd ever been taught. No. It was too soon for that.

The ride back to town was uneventful and cold. What had been a beautiful spring day had turned into a lovely evening, but it was still too early in the season for much warmth after the sun started to go down. Fortunately, they would have light until early in the evening. They would need it, having left Kensington after five.

No one was about, being too busy preparing for their activities later in the evening. Aware that her mother would be safely in her room getting ready for a ball, but that the butler would undoubtedly be manning the front door, Dami asked Camber to put her down some distance from home. After giving her a quizzical glance, he acquiesced. She agreed to meet him early the next morning for a ride in Green Park.

Her mind was in a whirl as she ascended the front step. The door was opened by Smithfield, the butler.

"Good evening, Lady Damaris," he said in censorial tones.

She knew them well. He'd been with the family since she'd been in leading strings, and he knew she'd been up to something.

"Good evening to you, too, Smithfield. Is my mother about?" She kept her voice light.

"She's in her room, my lady, getting ready for Lady Snow's rout."

Dami was well into the hallway when she turned back to Smithfield and gave him a conspiratorial wink. "Well, in that case, we really shouldn't bother her about my coming in late. Don't you agree, Smithfield?"

Unable to resist her—he'd dangled her on his knee when she was a babe and he was only a footman—he bowed his agreement.

Relief flooded her as she bounded up the stairs to her suites. If Smithfield was with her, the whole household would keep mum. She burst into her room to see Suzy laying out a silver crepe gown for the night's round of entertainment.

"Suzy, I've decided not to attend tonight. I will tell Mama that I still have the headache," she said in a rush, then collapsed onto the big yellow bed.

Somehow, her room looked insipid and drab to her.

Only this morning the bright yellow had cheered her. Now it seemed the perfect color for a child still in the nursery.

With a start, she realized she was comparing it with that disgusting red room. She refused to admit to herself that the red room had excited her, even as it had repelled her. She flounced up in irritation.

"My lady," Suzy broke in, "your mother expects you to go with her. Even Lord Jonathan is going."

"All the more reason for me not to. I don't think I could stand Johnny harping at me all night for the gory details of today." She sank wearily into a large wing chair by the fire. "And I really do have a headache, Suzy. Much too much has happened today. It is all crowding my brain." Dami passed a limp hand over her forehead.

"As you wish, my lady." Suzy moved to put up the ball gown and turned down the covers of the maligned yellow bed.

"I think I will do my room in grey with a touch of red," Dami mused.

"Pardon?"

"Oh nothing, Suzy. I was just thinking out loud."

Dami didn't notice when Suzy left the room. It had taken all of Suzy's self-control not to ask her mistress for the "gory details," but she knew that if Lord Jonathan wasn't going to be told yet, she certainly wasn't.

Shortly thereafter, there came an imperious knock on Dami's door. Recognizing it as her mother's, Dami scrambled under the bed covers. She was still fully dressed, but she pulled off her gloves and hat and stuffed them under the bed, then she hunched down until the comforter came up around her ears. Only then did she call admittance.

"Damaris, what is this I hear?" bellowed the dowager as she marched into the room.

"I don't know, Mama," Dami answered sweetly.

"Don't try to gammon me, my girl. You know very well that I am referring to your having the headache. You never have the headache," the marchioness said awfully.

Prepared for this, Dami said, "But I've never been to London before either, Mama. It's such a dirty, smelly, noisy place that it's a wonder I haven't gotten sick sooner." For good measure, she added, "I'm a country girl at heart."

"Very well, miss." She gave Dami a close scrutiny before turning to leave. "But mark my words, young lady, if I find you've been up to some lark, to use your brother's cant, I shall take some bark off your hide." Pleased with herself, the dowager hurried to meet the rest of her party.

"I pray you won't, Mama," Dami whispered to her retreating back.

Much later that night, Dami lay tossing in her bed. The events of the day kept repeating themselves. It was going smoothly, too smoothly.

For the first time since plotting her scheme, she allowed her doubts to surface. It was past time she looked at what she was doing and owned up to what the consequences could be. For her and for her family.

As Perth had so willingly pointed out, if it became

known that she had gone to the Cyprians' Ball all of polite society would shun her. Then she had capped it off by going to Camber's love nest. No one, absolutely no one, but a lady of the evening would do that.

A lady of the aristocracy who was having an affair with Camber might take his money or his jewels, but she would never let him openly support her. Even then, the lady would have to be wondrously discreet, and she wouldn't be a young miss. She would either be married presently or a widow.

There was no doubt but that she was breaking all the taboos.

Then there was her family. She knew that should scandal break, they would stand by her. It would be hard on them, but they wouldn't let her down. That was what hurt the most. She hadn't even considered them when she'd started the whole mess.

Now it was too late to turn back. She knew Camber wasn't in love with her. He'd made that abundantly clear today when he'd told her his "business" proposition. Having no tender feelings for her, he would only laugh at her dreams of making him fall in love with her.

That was, he would laugh if he didn't kill her for making a fool of him first. He wasn't a man to take lightly being played for a flat. Hadn't he said today he had no intentions of being cuckolded by a woman? She knew that usually referred to intimate relations, which they hadn't had yet, but wasn't she doing the same to him in a different sense? Her thinking was convoluted, and not making much sense in her exhausted state, but she knew the essence was right.

Suppose she did tell Camber, and begged him to

understand. He'd shown how empathic he could be toward others. No, it still wouldn't help her. She would still lose him.

Kit had said that the woman Camber finally made his duchess must be above reproof. After what she'd done, Dami most positively wasn't above reproof. In Camber's mind, she would be a fallen woman, whether she'd made love to him or not. She'd done everything but.

That she loved him enough to do something this drastic wouldn't sway him in the least. He didn't love her.

There was no other choice left her, but to continue as she'd started. She would lead him on as long as she could and hope he fell in love with her. He had to.

Chapter Seven

The past weeks had taxed Dami's ingenuity to the utmost. It was becoming more difficult to persuade her mother that she was adequately chaperoned by Johnny during the day and that she truly did suffer from headaches in the evenings, thus allowing her to leave parties early. Deception was becoming almost second nature to her, and it ate at her inherent integrity to have it so. Most times she only allowed herself to meet briefly with Julian. She didn't trust herself to resist him otherwise.

However, today she convinced Mama that she and Johnny should go to the British Museum. And so they had, but now she was in a shaded corner in the gardens awaiting Julian, while Johnny kept a discreet distance preparatory to leaving upon the duke's arrival. Julian had promised her a picnic in Twickenham, returning early enough for Johnny to pick her back up before the dowager could start to worry.

Dami's head really began to ache. She rubbed fiercely at her temples, wondering why Julian wasn't there yet. Glancing up at the sound of boots on gravel, she saw him. He drew her as a bee to honey.

The thought made her smile.

"I see you find me amusing," he said, but smiled in return, his hair sparkling in the sunshine and his grey eyes like silver. A charcoal-colored morning coat hugged his broad shoulders, and dove-grey knit pantaloons showed every muscle in his strong thighs.

"It was nothing." She couldn't tell him he was honey to her bee. "Shall we go?"

"If you wish." He offered his hand. "I thought you might want to tour the museum first. At least that way, you will be able to sound like you actually viewed it, in case the dowager asks."

"No need, my lord duke." Her face was bland and her voice toneless as she rattled, "Opened in 1759 and located in Montague House."

"A scholar!" He chuckled. "I believe I'm wooing a bluestocking."

Dami watched him, her arms crossed tightly on her chest, her left foot tapping a martial beat. But his humor was infectious, and she felt a smile tug at the corners of her mouth. "Really, Camber, what is so funny?" she said.

"My dear, Amalie, you must realize no man wants an intellectual for a mistress."

"And why not?" His words were the same litany she'd heard her life through.

"Well," he paused to think, marshaling his defenses. "A man has his male associates to talk politics, war, and other sundry topics with. That is why one patronizes clubs."

She shook her head in resignation, unwilling to fight with him. "You mouth today's platitudes with practiced ease, Your Grace."

He looked at her quizzically and cocked his head to one side. She looked pensive standing in the shadows, and he felt the strangest urge to reach out and take her into his arms and comfort her. Instead, he tugged gently on the hand he held, and said, "We had better go or it will be too late." He winked broadly at her. "We wouldn't want the dowager marchioness to get suspicious before you make your decision."

He had decided to woo her slowly, but he couldn't keep the hot gleam of desire from darkening his eyes as he watched her move to him. He tucked her hand into the crook of his elbow and bent his head to softly nuzzle a wisp of hair that had come loose from the knot of silver on her crown.

The pungent, but pleasing smell of tobacco wafted to Dami, mixed with the spicy scent of his aftershave. She moved impulsively closer, unconsciously begging for the intimacy of his body with hers.

Sparks shot from the contact of their hips. Both stopped to stare stunned into each other's eyes. She watched him, held spellbound by her response to him. She had always thought she loved him, but it seemed that her feelings when she first started this masquerade were weak imitations of the response he aroused in her now.

Pulling in the rein of his emotions, Julian turned and guided her to his waiting phaeton. He was glad he'd let his tiger go. He wanted Amalie all to himself.

He helped her into the high-perch carriage, and they set off at a sedate pace. Dami was acutely conscious of his nearness in the narrow vehicle as one of his spread thighs rode lightly near her own, sending a tingling awareness of his masculinity racing through her.

To break the tension, she asked, "Milord, er, what do you think of this lovely spring weather?"

He smiled before replying seriously, "I believe it is perfect for our picnic. Not a cloud in sight, so we don't have to worry about being drenched while we enjoy ourselves."

There was a wicked gleam in his eye, and Dami found herself torn between anticipation and dread. Since their trip to Kensington, he had been the perfect gentleman and hadn't pushed her. There had been moments when impatience tightened his lip or caused anger to reveal itself in his drawn brows, but not often.

Twickenham, on the outskirts of London, was still rural. Its grassy banks ran in unbroken green splendor to the muddy waters of the Thames . . . and very few people frequented it. This was its major attraction for Dami. She had stressed her need to keep their friendship secret by telling Julian the dowager would kick her out if she knew, and until she was sure she truly wanted to make her living as a man's mistress, she didn't want to burn any bridges. He had acquiesced, but she could see him chaffing when she refused to attend one of Harriette Wilson's renowned sorties with him. He had gone without her that time. He never brought it up again, but she could sense his tether running short.

Julian pulled the phaeton up near a nest of poplars and handed her the reins before jumping to the ground. Every muscle tensed in her as she held on to the leather controlling the high-spirited horses. Luckily, Julian promptly took the reins from her and tied them to a tree.

He took her by surprise when he turned and clasped her around the waist, lifting her into an exuberant twirl. Her skirts swirled around them in billowing mauve wings. Both were laughing and breathless and dizzy when he finally let her feet touch ground. She leaned against him for support.

Starch from his shirt mingled with the smell of freshly scythed grass. Somehow the mixture conveyed security and comfort to her. She could hear his heart beating strongly and feel the rising and falling of his chest. Nothing would have pleased her more than to stay in the warmth of his embrace, her senses reeling from his closeness.

Julian felt her relax against him, but being an old campaigner he knew better than to follow where his thoughts led. Instead, he put her carefully from him. "Why don't you spread the blankets," he released her to get them from the floorboard, "and I'll bring the basket."

His pragmatism broke the bubble, and Dami jumped for the blankets. She grabbed them hastily and sped to the copse of trees. Dappled sunlight played through the leafy roof and frolicked on the warmly scented grass below. Birds chirped merrily, concealed in branches, as they began their spring courtship. She flapped the spread up, letting it ride the air currents down to the emerald carpet.

Entering the glade, Julian smiled at her nervously smoothing the cover. He crossed to her with the picnic basket and set it in the middle of their makeshift table. He motioned her to sit, following when she complied.

Julian pulled a cool bottle from the hamper and said with a flourish, "The best French champagne to be had since Napoleon turned Europe topsy-turvy. In fact, my father put this down. And," he rummaged in the basket, "two crystal glasses."

He set them down and removed a large loaf of fresh bread and a hunk of creamy yellow cheese. The aromas blending together made Dami's stomach rumble.

"I hear you approve of my choices." He put one forefinger against her stomach, barely indenting the fabric of her gown.

Dami's muscles contracted sharply. "I'm famished," she said, moving away from his disturbing finger. "What are we going to cut the food with?"

"Our fingers. But first," he removed a corkscrew from the basket and drove it into the champagne stopper, "I want to propose a toast to a most beautiful woman and a perfect day."

Dami felt herself blush hotly, more at his raspy voice than his words. "I've never had champagne before." At his look of disbelief, she rushed on, "Well, maybe a small sip, but it's been so hard to get in recent years, and I don't seem to appreciate it properly. It just seemed I ought to let others who enjoy it drink it."

He listened to her with a tolerant grin, but filled her glass anyway. "You will like this. I promise."

His eyes promised more than champagne, but Dami let him persuade her despite her better judgment, and her hesitation was barely noticeable. She raised the glass to her lips and took a tiny sip. Surprise widened her eyes. "Why, it's delicious!"

He smiled complacently. She was too inexperienced to realize the high quality of the bubbling wine she consumed as though it was lemonade.

On an empty stomach, the alcohol hit her like a sledgehammer. Before she finished the first glass a warm lassitude began spreading insidiously through her limbs. She extended her now empty glass.

"If you please, Julian, I should like more."

He refilled her glass and offered her a hunk of bread. She took the wine but shook her head at the food, grinning impishly.

"I don't want to waste this nectar of the gods." She swirled the golden liquid until the bubbles rose into tiny effervescent puffs. "Surely, when the Olympian gods talked of ambrosia they meant this delectable liquid and not some earthy, solid substance such as food." In a twinkling her second glass was gone, the empty goblet waving under Julian's nose to be refilled.

Julian munched bread and cheese, watching her carefully through lazy eyes. Three glasses were certainly her limit, and he recorked the bottle.

Dami leaned back onto her elbows, head lolling down between her shoulder blades. She could feel the pleasant warmth of the late morning sun bathing her in its relaxing rays. A whispering breeze tickled her exposed neck, fluttering lightly as a lover's touch through her wayward curls. She stretched luxuriously.

"More nectar, please," she said through barely moving lips. She didn't open her eyes, but leaned heavily onto one arm so she could extend the other with her empty glass.

Julian laughed softly. "I don't think so, sweetings."

He took the glass from her hand. "You've had enough."

Her eyes snapped open; her head pulled up. "Of course I haven't had enough. Now stop funning, Julian." She smiled her dimple into being. "Just a little more. It won't hurt."

He shook his head and put the bottle back in the basket.

"Julian," she purred, leaning back again, "be a dear and get me another wrap. It's getting chilly." When he didn't move, she asked, "You do have another cover, don't you?"

"Amalie, you are as transparent as a whore's nightrail." He stood up, taking the basket with him.

Her gaze shifted from his face to the basket. Springing forward, she grabbed the handle before he had time to tighten his hold. In a flash, she sped past him, her trilling laughter floating through the scented air.

Hot on her trail, Julian tackled her before she broke through the sheltering trees. In a long swoop, his arms grappled her hips, locking around her so that she fell to the ground cushioned by his body. The basket flew from her hands as she brought them up to his chest. Surprise knocked the air out of her as they landed with a thump.

One of his hands broke its grip on her side to tangle in her wild curls, pulling her face to his. Trapped, Dami felt the hard length of him under every inch of her. Her mouth was crushed against his, its tender petals expanding under his pampering care, his tongue teasing her response. Tip to tip, they met and retreated. Gratifying heat washed her body, taking her inhibitions with it.

They strained together on the fragrant ground, his hand at her waist holding her tight to his rising desire, his other hand pulling her head gently back to give him access to her exposed neck.

Fire whipped through her as he laved the sensitive skin below her earlobe. Her arms snaked up around his neck, forcing him lower, until his ravaging mouth moved against the barrier of her dress.

"Amalie," he groaned into her cloth-covered bosom, "come with me. Say yes and stop torturing us."

Her senses craved something she had no name for or experience of. With a will of their own, her curves molded into the denseness of his masculinity and her mouth responded to his nips with playful antics of its own. Her blood flowed through every pore, hot and pliable as melted wax.

Sensing her surrender, Julian rolled her to her back and pressed his advantage. His hands moved to cup her face, pressing her cheeks so her mouth became a receptacle for his fluid, suggestive tongue. Darting deeply into her hot moistness, he urged her to respond before pulling back, luring her tongue to follow into him. They were lost to their surroundings, and he was prepared to take as much as she would give.

Dami moaned into his tutoring mouth, her breasts arching into his covering chest with a need of their own. Her sensitive skin felt abraded by the roughness of his starched shirt, the gold buttons of his coat scoring into her.

Her stomach tightened into a hard knot, and her

legs parted automatically to allow him closer proximity. Her abdomen churned in a seething mass until she thought it would burst.

Then her feelings began subtly to change. Dami wasn't sure when the tremors first changed from pleasure to something different. It was a gradual transition that left her feeling breathless, her ears ringing. Lifelessly, her hands fell back from caressing Julian's shoulders and neck, her legs curled up under his heated body, and her shoulders began to hunch into her chest.

"Julian," she groaned. "I don't feel too good." Her stomach heaved and she doubled over, knocking into his groin with her knees.

With a suppressed gasp, Julian rolled free of her, his own pain washing over him.

Meanwhile, Dami turned on her side, curled into a tight ball, and screwed her eyes shut. "Oh, I think I'm going to be sick."

She moaned, covering her green-tinged face and white lips with her hands.

Recovering, Julian squatted by her side. He braced himself, put one arm under her shoulders, the other under her bent knees, and lifted. Careful not to jog her more than needed, he returned to the blanket, where he wet his handkerchief in the bottle of champagne. Since the wine was still cool, and the nearest water was the slime of the Thames, he felt it better that she reek of alcohol than continue in her hot misery.

Dami tried to swat his hand away. "What are you putting on me?" Brief memories of the first time she'd met him wandered through her misty mind. "I don't intend to smell like I've spent the afternoon in a gin parlor when I was supposed to be viewing the British Museum. How would I ever explain it to M . . ." she stopped to catch herself, "the marchioness?" She wrinkled her nose. "Please, let's go now."

Julian's brows drew together. "Are you sure you'll be all right? Perhaps you ought to rest a little longer."

"No," she protested. "I'll be all right once we're moving in the fresh air again. At least, that's what all the gentlemen say when they are foxed and still want to go hunting or riding." She struggled to a sitting position, grateful for the duke's supporting arm around her shoulders. "If you Corinthians can continue on, then so can I."

"You're a game one, sweetings." Julian bent to kiss her puckered mouth. It was a fleeting touch of respect and liking.

Her eyes flew to his, to be captured by the kindled silver spark that she was beginning to see more of. He helped her to the phaeton and started out slowly. After several miles, Dami felt better.

"At this rate," she rallied, "I should be fit as a fiddle by the time you get me back to Johnny." She wasn't going to tell him that her head felt as if someone had taken a pair of hot tongs to it.

As they neared the outskirts of London, she asked him to pull over. "I need to put my bonnet back on," she explained.

Pulling to the side, Julian leaned over and took the hat from her shaking hands. "Let me put it on." At her look of protest, he added, "Trust me. I will make sure it is on straight and the bow properly tied." Good as his word, it was soon done. "Now, pull down your veil." At her sheepish grin, he said, "Did you think I didn't realize why it had to go back on? If so, you must think me very dense. You've had on a hat with a veil at every outing, or a cloak with the hood hiding your glorious hair." He raised a roguish eyebrow. "I'm convinced that you've bought out all the milliners' supply of concealing headgear." With that, he started the team forward again.

They were soon in front of the museum. Johnny was waiting impatiently, pacing in front of his racing curricle and snapping his riding crop against his boot.

Julian watched him prowling before saying sternly, "Be careful with her, young jackanapes. She's feeling under the weather. Don't go trying to race that contraption of yours in these crowded streets." On the words, Julian got down and went around to help Dami. He lifted her lightly to the ground, his arms tight around her as she slid down his torso so her chin was even with his cravat.

Dami felt a kiss, soft as summer rain, on her shoulder just before Julian handed her into Johnny's vehicle. She looked up to see him smiling warmly at her before he jumped into his phaeton and drove away in the manner he'd warned Johnny against.

Clicking his horse forward, Johnny shot her a knowing look. "The 'disreputable duke' looked like the cat that ate the bird, and you look horrible." He grimaced and pinched his nose. "Smell terrible, too. What have you two been doing?"

"Not now, Johnny, please. My head is throbbing, and my stomach feels like I've eaten tainted food."

"I'm your brother, and like it or not, as long as Simon is gone I've got to look out for you.'" He stopped to consider his words. "Not that I'm doing it the accepted way, mind you, but I don't intend to let His Grace take advantage of you, no matter how clandestine your meetings with him are." He pulled his horses up in alarm. "He hasn't, has he?"

"Don't be ridiculous," she snapped.

When they reached home, Dami slithered down and walked with dignified grace into the house and up the stairs. At the landing, she broke into a jagged run down the hall to her room. Once there, she pulled her bonnet, pelisse, and shoes off, leaving a trail from the door to the bed. Her moans filled the quiet room. She would have to send a message to Mama asking to be excused from tonight's festivities.

She was recuperating in bed with a cup of hot chocolate when the dowager burst in. Although it was several hours after Dami's return, the liquor still hadn't worked its way through her system. Her eyes were red-rimmed and dull.

"Well, missy," her mama addressed her by wagging a long finger under Dami's nose. "Don't tell me you have another headache, for I don't believe it. You are up to something, and I told you before, I won't countenance any of your shenanigans here. It would be the worst sort of folly." The words rushed out before she got a clear look at her daughter in the dim room. "Hmmm, you really don't look very good." The dowager felt Dami's forehead. "You don't have a fever, but you certainly can't go anywhere as out of looks as you are tonight. But tomorrow you will go regardless." Then she bent and gave Dami a kiss on the nose.

Dami watched her mama leaving and smiled.

Mama was prone to gruffness, but underneath there beat a heart filled with love for her children, the children of her sorely grieved lost love. Dami sighed and fell asleep.

Two days later Dami sat frowning over one of the daily newspapers. The morning sunshine flowed into the large breakfast room window.

"Why the glum look?" Johnny asked as he helped himself to poached eggs, kidneys, and toast and marmalade from the laden sideboard.

She watched him sit down and proceed to fill his mouth with a mixture of all three before saying, "Have you read His Grace's latest speech to the House of Lords?" At Johnny's negative shake, she continued, "It's very good. Once again, he's arguing the plight of returning soldiers. You know," she stopped, a worried look on her face, "the more I learn of him, the more I worry that this foolhardy plan of mine will come to naught." She set the paper down and slumped forward, both elbows on the table, her chin in her hands. "I mean, if anyone leads him to the altar it won't be a worthless chit with no accomplishments. A man of his stamp isn't going to marry unless his bride is a nonpareil."

"Don't belittle yourself, Dami," Johnny said around a mouthful of egg. "It ain't like you're ordinary." He swallowed and then used his fork for emphasis. "True, you ain't skilled in what most ladies do, but Camber can afford to pay a housekeeper to run his establishments. You are a bluestocking," he paused, groping for the right words, his face comical, "but, while it won't do for me, it might for him." At her look of astonishment, he added hastily, "Stands to reason. He's active in politics. Takes intelligence. He'll need a wife who can talk on different subjects."

"Johnny, you've certainly changed your tune." She sighed heavily. "But there's more to it than that."

"You think I'm stupid that I don't realize that? You're worried about that noble thing. Yup, thought so. You worry about those things too much if you ask me." He waved his fork airily. "Listen to me. Camber may be concerned with his soldiers, but you're concerned with your children. The orphanages and schools you've established at Green Leaf are every bit as important as what he's doing. And don't you forget it." He drained his cup and rose to leave. "Got to go. Tattersalls has a fine little filly. Old Riley's rolled up and selling all his stock."

He was gone on the words, but he'd lifted her spirits. She might not measure up in her mind, but she loved Camber, and she was conscious of social injustices—at least a little.

Dami sat listening to the count de Bourville rave about the abilities of his tailor. She could well understand why. Although an emigré, the count was complete to a shade in his maroon double-breasted coat and grey knit pantaloons. His shirt points were moderate, and his cravat was done in a simple knot.

"Milord, how do you find our country?" she asked, genuinely interested.

"I find it *enchanté*." He twinkled at her, then sobered.

"I owe your country a great deal. It has housed me and given me a respectable means of supporting myself."

She meant to ask him more, but the butler announced in sepulchral tones, "Jason Beaumair, the earl of Perth."

Her head snapped toward the door. With his dark hair and eyes, his swarthy complexion and slashed cheek, he resembled her fantasy picture of a pirate. She shuddered with foreboding. He must have a purpose for coming; he'd never graced them with his presence before.

Dami watched her mama glide over to him and begin fussing about him. Despite his unsavory reputation, he was still one of the two most eligible men of the haute monde; the duke of Camber being first.

Then the earl was bowing over her and flicking a contemptuous glance at the count sitting next to her, who rapidly removed himself. "May I sit here, Lady Damaris?" He indicated the evacuated spot, sitting before she could reply.

She caught her breath in apprehension. Her intuition told her this wasn't a social call.

"Are you enjoying your time in London? I believe this is your first season, isn't it?" He turned sinister eyes on her.

Dami knew open defiance would do her no good, but she wasn't sure she could carry subservience successfully. "Yes, milord, it is. I do find it vastly entertaining. Much like the country, only on a much more grand and sophisticated level."

His lower lip curled. "Remarkable. Does Camber know what he is getting into?" He looked as if she were an unusual specimen of insect he had just discovered. "You aren't his usual sort. You have intelligence. Something I've never known His Grace to value in a woman before."

Her eyes flashed. Even though they were in her mama's drawing room, she didn't intend to stand by docilely while this man dissected her and made disparaging remarks.

"Pray, don't lose your temper." He raised one strong, tanned hand in protest, laughter momentarily relaxing his harsh features. "I only came to request your company next week." At her look of alarm, he continued insinuatingly, "It will only be for the evening, and it will be for the cyprian you portray so delightfully. I will return you unharmed."

"Really, milord Perth, you can't truly expect me to accept." She kept a tight rein on her willful tongue. Nothing would please her more than to give him a biting set down, but she was in no position to do so. He could ruin her.

"Oh, I think you will accompany me." His smile was sly. "After all, we share a secret. One you wouldn't care to have bandied about."

The fiend. He intended to hold his knowledge over her like a Damocles sword. She lifted her chin in defiance, but her voice, chilled and clipped, answered, "Put that way, I have no alternative. What time do you want me?"

"I will send you a note." He rose gracefully and made his farewells with panache.

When all the guests were gone, Dami tried futilely to escape to her room. "Dami," the dowager's commanding voice cut through the air, "the earl of Perth seems inordinately interested in you. First a dance at Almack's and now this. You could do worse."

Dami looked in disbelief at her mama. "That is only twice in two weeks, Mama. Really, you can't think he has formed a *tendre* for me." She forced a weak laugh.

"Hmmm." The marchioness was imposing in her purple afternoon dress. "I think we need to be more kind to the earl," she commanded before sweeping from the room.

Dami collapsed against the wall, uncertain whether to laugh or cry. Things were certainly getting out of control. Julian pushing her to meet him for dinner tonight, and now this. She was straining the boundaries of her mother's leniency already. How was she going to explain these further complications?

Luckily, the dowager planned a quiet evening at home, so Dami felt assured she could sneak out without her mother's being aware of it. Johnny had been dragooned into escorting her to the hotel and waiting with her until Julian showed.

Getting dressed, Dami was as nervous as she had been before the Cyprians' Ball. Again, Suzy had altered one of Dami's evening gowns. This time, it was a golden muslin trimmed lavishly with cream-colored Brussels lace. After Suzy's ministrations, the bodice was scooped low enough that Dami's bosom threatened to overflow the lacy cups, and the back dipped daringly low. The skirts were left alone, but Dami decided not to wear a petticoat, thus making the normally modest muslin seem clingingly transparent. She piled her hair in a loose topknot, allowing strands to fall like molten silver down her neck and nape. No jewelry this time.

Dami smiled, remembering the gaudy baubles she had worn at their first meeting. Tonight simplicity would be appropriate. Somehow she had to get Julian to love her, possibly even propose to her, before he learned her true identity.

Suzy wrapped a heavy wheat-colored satin cloak around Dami's shoulders, and Dami pulled the copious hood up until it left her face in mysterious shadow.

When she descended the stairs, Dami saw the butler was otherwise occupied, while Johnny perambulated the foyer in his impatience.

"Going somewhere after you drop me off?" She surveyed his casual attire. "Just don't forget that you have to pick me up later." As long as he didn't get trapped in some gaming hell, or even worse, Harriette Wilson's parlor, she knew he would come for her on time.

"Tom, that is Sir Bastian, and I are going to a gaming place he knows of in Pall Mall. Supposed to be all the crack." He ushered her outside to a waiting hackney, something she'd insisted on so that there wouldn't be any chance of someone's recognizing Johnny's distinctive beige and black phaeton.

They arrived quickly, and Dami descended to go into the imposing building and inquire of the clerk if the duke of Camber were there. Johnny would wait fifteen minutes before leaving.

Dami approached the clerk with all the poise she could muster, knowing full well from the disdainful look he bent on her that he was well aware of the type of woman she was trying to pass as. He peered down his long, skinny nose at her, but she knew he couldn't see her features, and while he might not approve of her reason for being here, he wasn't about to anger the duke by telling her to be off. Besides, she had a good suspicion that rendezvous of this nature were frequent here. Private dining rooms provided a lot of privacy.

Surmounting that obstacle, she climbed a ponderous stairway behind a maid, feeling her hands begin to slick over with perspiration. She hadn't wanted to be quite this isolated with Julian after the incident at Twickenham, but he had made it clear that he was losing patience and that if she continued to put him off he would look elsewhere.

She sneaked surreptitious looks at the heavy paneling and wall fabric as they turned down a badly lit corridor. At the end was a closed door made of heavy wood. Dami swallowed. They would certainly be cut off from the rest of the world.

The maid opened the door and beckoned her inside. A roaring fire sent light flickering through the small room. Deep ruby carpets muffled her footsteps as she approached the small table pulled cosily up to the flames. It was simply set, with fine china, crystal, and silverware. On a tea tray nearby sat several covered dishes, and a bottle of wine chilled in a bucket of ice.

She allowed her hood to fall back as she turned to more fully examine the room. A gasp died in her closed throat. A man stood in the shadows near the door. Relief sighed through her when she recognized Julian.

He was dressed in his favorite black with a frilly

134

white lawn shirt. Dami shivered, her pulse beginning to race as she surveyed him, unable to ignore the powerful attraction she felt for him.

She raised her eyes to his knowing ones, a fiery blush engulfing her from cheeks to chest. He neared her and laid warm hands on her shoulders to undo her cloak. Trickles of liquid heat spread from his touch down to her toes.

Trying to break his spell, Dami said breathlessly, "I didn't know the Clarendon Hotel provided this kind of service. However, I don't see any bed." She knew immediately it was the wrong thing to say. His eyes took on a hooded look of smoking sensuality. "I mean, not that I expected one, or even want one. Well, it's just that everything is so intimate. I just thought that a rake would have to do this in his own home—or that of his mistress." She moved from his imprisoning fingers, her cloak falling away in his hands.

She heard him catch his breath as his eyes devoured her rapidly rising and falling breasts. Her hands came up instinctively to ward him off. "After all, I'm new to this." She licked dry lips, not realizing the moisture imparted a sheen that made them eminently desirable.

Julian ran a forefinger along the outline of her bodice, his sword-sharp gaze never leaving the fluttering lace that showed, more than anything, her nervousness. He wondered if she knew how strong his attraction was to her. Watching her dilated eyes and puckered mouth, he doubted it. She was seductive, but not intentionally.

To calm himself, he said, "No diamonds? That's one thing to be thankful for. You won't blind me with your ill gotten gains."

Abruptly, he turned and draped her cloak over a chair, then indicated she be seated at one of the chairs around the table. She moved to comply, and heard his sharply indrawn breath again. Taken unawares, she turned to stone, waiting for him to do something. Soft as a feather, she felt his fingers tracing the ridge of muscle that defined her back. Warm and sweet as honey, his touch drizzled down her spine.

"You have a beautiful back. Well shaped and straight. Smooth as finest silk." His finger floated up and down. "This dress is very becoming."

He held the chair out for her, and Dami sank into its supporting frame. She kept her eyes lowered, unsure of Julian or herself. Things were going too fast. Again.

He sat across from her and poured them each a glass of wine. It was cool to the touch, and she took a grateful sip. Champagne. She looked at him and saw him smiling.

"Yes, it is the same vile stuff I gave you the last time." He chuckled. "Only I beg of you, don't drink it like lemonade tonight. I've no wish to have you sick again." At her pained look, he added, "Not that you aren't as lovely inebriated as you are sober, but nauseated isn't how I like my women when I make love to them." His voice was the raspy sound of a drawn sword.

He was dangerous. More so than ever before. She didn't know if it was the cozy intimacy of the room, or her growing love for him that gave him the increased power to make her succumb to the hunger in him.

Dami cleared her throat. "I read your speech to the House of Lords."

"Did you?" He leaned back in his chair and stretched his legs toward the fire. "I hope you were suitably impressed." He lifted the lid off one of the nearby containers, letting the savory smell of roast beef loose. "I told them not to bother us again. I will serve you."

He was changing the subject, bringing it back to the hotly disturbing reason for their presence here. "I thought you did a superb job of pointing out the hardships faced by returning soldiers," she persisted. "Had I been there, and a member, I'm sure I would have been with you."

"Roast beef, sweetings? It looks like we have potatoes and Brussels sprouts. I hope you don't mind, but I told them to make the meal simple. I don't want to linger over food when there are so many other more pleasing ways to spend the evening with a beautiful woman. Especially when that woman is one's mistress."

"I'm not hungry." She felt like a cornered rat. He had her right where he wanted her, and she'd helped him maneuver her into it. "And I haven't agreed to be your mistress."

He handed her a plate heaped with food. "You will." He turned his attention to eating.

She pushed her food around, her throat too tight to swallow. She watched belligerently as he leisurely finished his meal and poured himself another glass of wine. He brought it to his lips, taking a long, slow drink as he watched her over the rim.

"I had intended to woo you gently over candlelight

and good food, with the champagne thrown in to help you relax. As you said, there's no bed in here, but there is one in the other room." He indicated a door that Dami had hitherto not noticed.

Her blood ran cold and thick, paralyzing her. He sounded like a man talking about a horse, or a piece of furniture, nothing like the lover she'd grown accustomed to.

"I realize you are new to this, Amalie, and I've tried to be considerate, but I find that my patience is running thin." He surveyed her thoroughly while taking another sip. "You come here dressed more boldly than many a demi-rep, taunting me with your barely concealed charms, then play the prude."

He meant every word, the jumping muscle in his jaw told her that. He put his empty glass down and stuffed his fists into the pockets of his pantaloons.

"Amalie, you must decide now. Either you accompany me into the next room, and do so willingly, or you walk out the same door you entered and we never see each other again. I've never been known for my patience, yet I've found reservoirs of it with you that I never knew existed, but the river has run dry." His voice was harsh, cracking on the last word. "Decide."

Dami sat stiffly, her hands clenched in her lap. She felt moisture gathering everywhere but her mouth. There was no choice to make. From the start, she'd known it would come to this and what she would do when it did. Only, she had hoped she would be able to make him love her before she had to give herself to him.

Her head sank so that she wouldn't have to look into his rapacious eyes. "As you wish, milord." The words were a soft whoosh of sound in the silent room. The smell of burning logs was pungent in her nostrils, and every whorl on the silverware stood out in stark relief. Never before had all her senses been so strongly attuned to her surroundings.

She heard him rise, then felt his hand at her neck, intimately stroking her nape. The smell of his tangy aftershave blended with the starch of his shirt scratching against the sensitive tingling of her back. She knew the two scents would be irrevocably mingled with her memories of this night. Rising at his pressure along her spine, she turned blindly toward the closed door. His arm was snug around her, and she was unsure whether it was to support her jerky movements or to keep her from running away.

Somehow they were in the next room. Everything was a blur. She knew there was a large four-poster bed swathed in heavy cloth, and that to enter it would be like being cut off from the rest of the world, immured in a small cell. Dark and frightening, it would close around the two of them as he took what he wanted with no thought for her. Oh, she knew he would be kind and take his time initiating her into physical union, but there would be no love. None of the magic that she felt sure made the coupling of a man and woman greater than any delight the body alone could provide.

She turned blindly into the hard prison of his arms. His hand forced her face up to his, his fingers making her mouth open for him. His tongue entered, daring hers to pursue him in an erotic game of chase. She was molded to him by his free hand roaming the length of her exposed back, leaving trails of fire in its wake. Dami felt her breasts melt into the rock hardness of his chest, spreading to flow over him, turning turgid where they rubbed through the minuscule fabric of her bodice, pricking him with her response.

But her mind was numb. A barrier of haze had risen up to cloud her eyes even as her every fiber responded to the sexual intensity of his assault.

He felt her surrender and lifted her swiftly in his arms, striding to the enclosed bed. She heard him kick away the stairs for mounting the high bed. Then she was through the velvet curtains and Stygian darkness engulfed her. Unable to move, she heard him removing his boots, then shrugging out of his coat, pulling his pantaloons off, and finally yanking off his shirt. Dami began to swallow convulsively, pulling in great, heaving gulps of air. She wanted love, not this animal melding.

Fright and disbelief turned her cold and clammy. Her eyes screwed shut as he eased himself onto the feather mattress. The heat of his rangy body penetrated the whisper of material separating them. She could feel him responding to her. She lay still, hoping he would let her go. Knowing that even if he didn't she would still love him, still hope that she could make him love her before he tired of his new plaything.

She felt his warm champagne-scented breath waft against her neck as his erotically stimulating lips sucked and nipped her earlobe. One of his hands lay lightly at her collarbone, stroking up and down the sensitive portion of skin that ran to the top of her bodice.

"Amalie, respond to me." His voice was heavy with desire, his tongue persuasive as it traced down to the hollow of her neck.

She felt him shifting to cover the length of her with his naked body. Muscles she'd never known existed tensed, and her stomach knotted into a quivering mass, but she managed to turn her face from the sensual attack of his lips, tongue, and teeth. Her mind fought for control against her languid body that clamored for more of what only he could give her.

After an eternity to her strained nerves, he rolled off her. Her breathing was shallow and rapid, her fingers curled cruelly into the palms of her hands.

"Is this how you intend to fight me?" His voice was almost conversational, but the leg riding her thigh was hard as hewn oak. "You will let me enjoy your body, but you refuse to enjoy mine."

She felt him shift again and opened her eyes. He was lighting a candle, then hovering above her on one elbow, his eyes slits of ice. What could she say to him? Not the truth. She said nothing.

"What do you want from me?"

He sounded as if he truly meant it. His face showed curiosity and something else she couldn't name, having never seen it before. "I want time. I want . . . I want respect." The words tumbled without preamble, and tears began to well up. Her breathing, so light seconds before, was again deep heaves. Her chest felt squeezed dry. She wouldn't cry. "I want . . . oh, I don't know what I want. Except I don't want our first time to be here, in the impersonal coldness of a hotel. Where we have to sneak to meet and then sneak to get away."

He ran one finger in butterfly softness along her trembling lips. "How was I to know? You've always insisted on secrecy before. I thought this is what you would prefer, and then you continued cold, despite the message of your dress and body. I lost control."

"Oh, Julian." She reached her arms around his neck, her heart beating warm and fast where seconds before it had been encased in ice. "I want to be more than a mistress to you. I want to share your interests. I want to feel you next to me more than when you're making love to me." She pulled him down until her face was burrowed in the hardness of his corded neck.

He stroked her hair thoughtfully. "You don't want much, do you," he teased, but his voice was low and pained. "Amalie, I've never let a mistress get as close to me as you want. I don't know if I can, or even if I want to."

She stiffened. She'd pushed him too far. Now he was going to send her packing.

Julian rolled to his back, pulling Dami with him. One hand tangled in the curls falling from her bun, the other glided up the ridged smoothness of her back. "I like your back, Amalie. It's feminine, yet strong." He laughed. "I sound besotted with your back, and I never knew I had a back fetish." He stopped. He knew he was just talking. He didn't know what to do with this strange woman-child. She aroused feelings in him no other woman ever had, but she asked too much. "Amalie, I can't give you what you want."

She pushed away to lie at his side.

Julian turned to look at her. The tracks of her tears were barely visible in the scanty light. He leaned

142

forward and traced the salty ribbon with his tongue, stopping before he reached her mouth. He knew that if he kissed her again, his body would rule his mind, and he would take her regardless of her wants.

"Amalie, get up and go get your cloak. It's time you went home." At her anguished look, he added, "You're free again. But I don't know how long I can continue to hold myself in check." He watched her crawl out the opposite side of the bed. "Amalie," his voice made her pause, "I want to continue seeing you."

A small smile of relief curved her lips and hope flared again. "As you wish, milord."

Chapter Eight

Julian scanned his recent invitations.

"Your Grace, if you will please be still, these warm towels will make it easier to shave your beard. It will also be closer." The harassed man tried valiantly to fix one towel around Julian's chin and neck.

"Yes, Williams, but I can't very well read my mail if you've got my head tilted toward the ceiling, can I?" Julian continued doing the chore.

He didn't add that he'd decided to make a long overdue appearance in society again. For that purpose, he needed the perfect activity. He found it in the form of Lady Sefton's ball. While he never attended any of the functions, he was always included on any guest list, and he always had his secretary pen a polite refusal.

This time he would go. It was past time for him to see what his future betrothed looked like. Perhaps even talk to her and ask her to dance.

The letter to Simon asking permission to pay his respects should have reached Paris by now, and Julian felt it behooved him to move forward with his acquisition of a bride.

"All right, Williams, I'm through. Do your worst." Camber leaned back and allowed a gratified Williams to apply all the hot wraps he could wish.

The whisper-thin muslin of her primrose ball gown swayed provocatively with her graceful movements. The high bodice and low square neckline accentuated the slender ripeness of her figure. Her neck arched gracefully, emphasizing the regal shape of her head, which was crowned by her silver hair clasped in a diamond circlet. Curls cascaded delicately down to her nape.

Dami was doing a country dance with a young sprig of fashion. His black jacket and pantaloons were in direct contrast to his pea-green waistcoat. He was definitely no threat to her peace of mind. Certainly not like Camber.

The dance ended and her escort took her back to Johnny and Kit. Dami glanced at the entrance. The ball was a shocking squeeze, and someone else was arriving. The tall newcomer had his back to the room as he bowed gracefully over his hostess's proffered hand. There was something alarmingly familiar about that strong back, with broad shoulders narrowing to slim waist, all encompassed in a smoothly tailored black coat.

He turned and his grey eyes pierced her brown ones. What was he doing here? He didn't attend these functions. He was heading in her direction.

"Oh, no," she moaned. With strength born of desperation, she clutched Johnny's forearm.

"Dami," Johnny complained as his right hand tried

to pry her fingers from his arm, "you're wrinkling my coat. Surely, I don't have to remind you that a gentleman of fashion doesn't wear untidy clothes." The twinkle in his eyes belied his reprimanding words.

"Oh, do stop being goosish, Johnny," she expostulated. "Look who's headed our way." Frantic, she pulled him onto the crowded dance floor.

"You know I don't like to waltz, Dami," he told her, very much on his dignity.

"Johnny, Camber is here."

The succinct statement stunned Johnny, making him stumble. "You must be mistaken."

"I'm not. He's standing with Kit right now." Her eyes darted to the devilishly handsome duke. His eyes were blazing at her, and his hands were clenched stiffly at his side.

"Whew," A low whistle escaped Johnny before he remembered where they were. "What are we going to do now? This isn't the time or place to tell him who you really are. From the looks of him, he's furious and won't listen."

"He's the cynosure of every scheming female in this room," she grumped. Jealousy kept her momentarily blind to their perilous situation.

"We're about to be thrown to the lion, and you're worried about competition? You're a cool one. If we don't figure a way out of this, neither one of us will be in any condition to worry about other women."

Johnny had managed to maneuver them to the opposite side of the room. A brief sense of escape made Dami bold. "We must bluff our way out of this. We shall tell him that Lady Damaris has rushed unexpectedly to Green Leaf to care for her old nurse and that I've taken her place tonight," she finished.

"What a cawker," Johnny said. "It won't work. He's much more likely to think we're trying to bamboozle him, which, of course, we are, and to reach the conclusion that nothing you've told him is the truth. Then you'll be in the suds." A smug look accompanied this facer.

"Johnny, what an abominable thing to say. And you're my brother." She drew back stiffly, thus giving herself an unobstructed view over his shoulder. The duke was right behind them, leaning nonchalantly against an elegant Grecian pillar. The anger emanating from his slitted eyes, and his usually full, sensual lips compressed into a tight line belied his relaxed pose.

"He's here," she whispered through numb lips.

"I know he's here. But being on this side of the room will give us a small reprieve. Time to work out the kinks in your Canterbury Tale before we have to actually present it." He twirled her to a stop. "Even the duke of Camber can't cross a room this crowded in under thirty minutes," Johnny finished in thankful tones.

"Can't I?" came a silky-smooth voice.

Up close he was overpowering. The black, close-fitting jacket and breeches did nothing to hide his virility. The whiteness of his shirt pointed up the darkness of his scowling visage.

His right arm snaked out and caught Dami's left wrist in a crushing grip. "You, FitzHubert, stay put until I return," he growled. "As for you, madam, you're coming with me."

"No I'm not, Your Grace," Dami replied. She drew

herself up to her complete height and tilted her head back slightly. The better to look down her well-bred nose at the odious man.

The shadow of a smile crossed his darkened eyes as he took in her stratagem. "Unless you want to cause a scene, Amalie, you will come with me. And come docilely."

"You're hurting my wrist," she said petulantly.

"If you're not careful, my girl, I'll do a lot more than hurt your wrist." He forced her to his side, where the heat of his thigh burned into hers through the layers of material separating their flesh. "Trying to gain respectability, Amalie?" he taunted. "You didn't wear a slip before, yet tonight you do. Interesting."

"You, Your Grace," the title held a wealth of contempt, "are insulting. And despicable." But her knees felt weak and her breathing was labored.

"You didn't used to think so, my sweet," he drawled.

"I do now." She fairly flounced. "Release me and we shall talk like two sensible adults."

His gaze was devouring the creamy expanse of her bosom as it heaved under the flimsy bodice. "You're a beautiful woman, Amalie," he whispered tightly. "My loins are on fire for you."

She gasped in shock and her free hand raised of its own volition to strike, but Julian chose that moment to turn and head toward a nearby door. Her arm dropped to her side. It wouldn't improve the situation if she angered him further. He still had her in a viselike grip, forcing her to follow him from the room.

With an economy of motion, he strode down the

hall until he reached a closed door, which he threw open, and dragged Dami through. Momentarily releasing her, he turned and closed the door. Dami used the temporary freedom to put the room between them.

The room appeared to be a small sitting room, elegantly furnished in the popular Egyptian style. A long, low settee with crocodile feet, and several chairs, more decorative than comfortable, were grouped around a small table. The French windows, with their heavy emerald velvet drapes pulled back, gave onto a typical English garden.

The still smoldering embers of an old fire gave off just enough light for Dami to make out the expression on Camber's face as he watched her. It scared her and excited her at the same time. He wanted her, and she knew she was playing with fire to bait him. It didn't stop her.

"You certainly know your way around this house . . . duke," she said sweetly. Her limpid brown eyes watched him as her delicate hand lightly smoothed the gold brocade back of the chair she was using as a shield.

His jaw twitched. "Experience, my lady cyprian." His pupils dilated and his irises turned black as his heavy lids drooped. He took in every curve of her luscious figure.

"I told you before, I have all my teeth, and I'm not a horse you can inspect before you buy," she flared. His intense inspection had caused a flush of heat that penetrated to her very toes.

"You're incredibly beautiful with the glow of the dying fire setting your hair ablaze. Anger only makes you more desirable," he murmured. "Are your breasts and thighs as creamy and perfect as your neck and arms?" He watched her flinch.

"You're an animal," she snarled.

"You make me that way, Amalie. The fire causes tantalizing shadows to form in the hollow of your bosom." He was slowly advancing on her.

"Keep away from me. Keep away or I'll scream." Her threat fell on deaf ears. Quickly, she backed farther away, pulling her protective chair with her. The incongruous sound of the chair legs scraping on the wooden floors seemed to bring him to his senses.

A grin softened the hardened angles of his face. "My dear girl, you look ridiculous lugging that awkward chair around."

Her indignation flared at his uncomplimentary observation. "That's easy for you to say. You aren't being stalked by a female-devouring predator."

"I'd like to devour you, sweetings, but in more congenial surroundings." He grinned wickedly. "That is, if you can control your baser instincts long enough for me to get us there."

"You're a boor. I don't have to stay here and be subjected to your insults and vulgar insinuations." First last night at the Clarendon and now here. In her anger, she forgot her danger and made to sweep regally by him on her way to the door.

"Not so fast." He reached out and encircled her waist in the corded muscles of his arm. Like the tide moving to shore, he pulled her to him, chest to chest, so close she could see the moisture on his upper lip and smell the light fragrance of his cologne. "You're going to tell me what you're doing at a respectable ball. I can't believe that even young FitzHubert is so lost to propriety that he fails to realize a woman of your calling can't be here."

She could feel the pounding of his heart where her fingers rested lightly against the fine silk of his shirt, but she was incensed at his callous assumption of her lack of respectability. "I was enjoying myself, Your Grace," she said with venomous sweetness. His sharply indrawn breath coupled with a fierce anger scared her.

"I wouldn't think a tame thing like this ball could keep you entertained. It was my impression that you had more interesting pursuits in mind when we last talked."

"You might be surprised at what interests me, Your Grace," she hissed at him. The air from her lips stirred his auburn locks where they fell across his wide forehead. She felt him shudder, and she licked her dry lips in mute anticipation.

"Perhaps, but I doubt it. I've had plenty of experience with women of your stamp, my dear," he drawled. "A whore's a whore by any name."

She drew back her slipper clad foot and swung it full force against his shin. She grimaced at the shooting pain that lanced up her leg, but Camber released her as he doubled over in pain, his hand going to his silk-clad shin.

As soon as he let go, Dami rushed to the relative safety of the fireplace, close to the poker.

"Vixen! I ought to beat you." He was furious. More so than when he'd dragged her into the room.

"Better that than subjecting me to conversation fit only for a bawdy house." He had insulted her enough to last her a lifetime. She might be playing the part of a gentleman's convenient, but she still hadn't given him any cause to say the dreadfully hateful things to her that he had, and especially after last night's interlude. "I'm sick and tired of the way you fling my lack of social standing in my face every time we meet. You want me in your bed, the least you could do is show me a little respect. If not for myself, at least because I'm a human being. You do it for the men who used to fight under you. Does being a woman make me any different?"

His eyes were hooded as he watched her standing ramrod straight against the mantel. "My men were honorable. Engaged in the defense of their country. Can you say the same of yourself?"

The implied disgrace of his words tore at her heart. Surely she had chosen the wrong way to reach his heart. Or even if she did, he would never respect her or countenance her place at his side as his duchess. "No." The single word held all the futility of her position.

"Exactly."

Her head drooped on a neck too weak to hold it proudly. But a tiny bit of rebellion made her add, "You are a hypocrite. You know that."

"Yes, but that is my prerogative. I have the money and rank to allow me to do as I wish. You don't." He moved to the settee where he settled himself comfortably against the silk cushions.

She turned her back on him, her hands clenched in outrage. "Oh yes, I'd forgotten. Rank has its privileges. As long as one is a gentleman."

"Precisely."

"What if I were a lady of noble birth and I wanted to take you for a lover, my lord? What would you think of me then?" She was on dangerous ground, but that was nothing new.

"A lady of genteel upbringing wouldn't contemplate becoming my mistress. Unless she were a widow or married to another man, in which case she wouldn't be offered the chance." His tones were smug and righteous.

"You disgust me, Your Grace. It's all right for a man to carry on. To drink, gamble, and . . . yes, whore, but your woman must be above all that. She must reside on a pedestal of respectability."

"The woman I deign to marry must come to me untouched." His eyes were like flint.

"The perfect woman. Must she also enjoy the marriage bed? Or do you plan to cuckold her?" Her voice was barely audible, facing away from him as she was.

"A delicately nurtured female doesn't concern herself with the carnal side of marriage. She provides the heir and is a hostess."

She turned to face him, belligerence uppermost in the line of her lips, the curve of her body. "You mean she submits to your animal lusts so that you can have a son to carry on the illustrious title of the duke of Camber."

"Yes. But enough of this. It doesn't concern you, Amalie." He patted the cushion next to him. "Come and we will discuss us. There are many things still not ironed out."

She was beautiful in her anger, and she was cruel. "I'd forgotten about the little details of 'us.' Foolish of me. After all, when you tire of making dull love to your duchess you plan to come to me, where you intend to enjoy all the illicit pleasures of abandoned sex."

He was equally hurting. "Very crudely put, but essentially accurate."

How could she continue to love this man? Yet the thought of never seeing him again was more than she could bear. He'd been the center of her existence too long for her to tear him out of her being because he thought her good enough to be his whore, but beneath consideration for his love.

Her movements jerky, she moved to sit next to him. A possessive arm circled her proudly held shoulders. She wouldn't let him beat her into submission. She would continue to fight.

"This is much better, don't you think?" Without waiting for her answer he continued, "Have you decided when you will move into my house?"

"No." The bald answer caused him to frown. Seeing it, she hastened to follow up. "I need more time. I want to get to know you better. It's obvious from our 'discussion' here that there is much we don't understand about each other. I thought, after the Clarendon, that you understood."

"Amalie, I'm asking you to be my mistress, not my lifelong companion. All I require of you is that you be entertaining in and out of bed. That doesn't include deep philosophy."

His enclosing arm was pulling her closer to him, while his hand made little curlicues on her sensitized shoulder. She was slowly suffocating. His nearness, her inability to refuse him, and his condemnation of her all combined to awaken her awareness of him as never before.

"Never doubt I intend to grace your bed, but I want more time." She was adamant. Every particle of her screamed out against giving in to him. She would make him respect her.

"I don't have much left," he said enigmatically.

"Neither do I. Johnny has told me to be out within a fortnight." Silently she asked her brother's forgiveness. She had to force Camber into making the necessary arrangements to see her again, before she agreed to become his mistress.

"I see. What exactly do you want me to do?" He continued to hold her, but his fingers had stopped their erotic play.

"I want you to agree to see me every day—without trying to seduce me."

"You ask a great deal." Both hands were now resting lightly on his knees. His eyes contemplated the french windows dispassionately.

For a moment, Dami thought she'd lost her gamble. He was so detached from everything she'd just said.

"You win." He rose to tower over her. "Stay here. I'm going to talk some sense into that young fool who brought you here." He turned and strode to the door. He yanked it open hard and turned to her once more. "Don't leave this room. I'll be right back."

The door slammed shut behind his highstrung body.

A sigh of relief flowed from Dami. She'd won the skirmish. It had hurt, intolerably, to hear him talk of her as though she were a piece of merchandise he could pick up and discard at will. Particularly when she knew he didn't feel that way about the men who'd fought with him. But she was a woman, and women either went to bed with men before marriage or after. If they did it before, as he thought she did, then they were automatically bad. If they didn't, they were good.

But was being "good" any better than being "bad"? A shiver ran through her. She doubted it. To be required to live a life barren of feelings and love. That would truly be hell.

Lost in contemplation, she got up and wandered to the French windows. It was a warm night. The heady smell of roses permeated the dark air.

When Camber returned with an agitated Johnny, the room was empty. The French windows stood open, a breeze blowing the heavy curtains into the room.

Camber cursed heavily. "It would seem she had an urgent appointment elsewhere." Without a backward glance, he crossed to the open casement and walked out.

Johnny stared after him before muttering, "Oh Lord, the fat's in the fire now." He returned to the ball, but didn't see either Dami or Camber again that night.

Chapter Nine

At ten o'clock the following morning, Julian found himself knocking on the door of the marquis of Cleve's town house. Not that he was a stickler, at least not in his own affairs, but he felt responsible to warn the boy that it was bad ton to introduce women of dubious morals into the house of a lady of the ton, no matter how close the shady lady was to one.

He wouldn't be doing this if the boy weren't soon to become his brother-in-law. Too, he felt he owed it to Simon to help his younger brother through the shoals of functioning in the polite world.

His wandering thoughts were brought quickly to heel by the unblinking stare of a most proper butler.

"I'm here to see Lord Jonathan FitzHubert. You may tell him the duke of Camber wishes to speak to him on a matter of concern to both of us," Julian responded to that worthy's impartial face.

Julian quickly found himself in a very impressive drawing room. The walls were tall and the ceiling was done in plaster relief. The windows were framed by heavy pale blue velvet drapes. With a nonchalance born of breeding and fitness, he sauntered to the marble fireplace and leaned one shoulder against the cool material. It didn't surprise him to see Johnny soon come rushing into the room.

"I say, Your Grace, nice of you to call. Didn't expect it and all." Johnny had the unhappy knack of blushing when he was flustered. He blushed. "Not that it isn't an honor." The duke's cool gaze on him didn't help matters. "Butler says it's a matter of interest to us both?" He had a sinking feeling that he knew what this was about.

Julian carefully flicked a piece of imaginary lint from his coat sleeve. "You see, about last night." He felt damned awkward combing this pup's hair when he did things just as bad. But it was his duty. "Not to mince matters, it isn't the thing to bring women with, shall we say, tainted backgrounds to functions held by a lady of quality." He gave Johnny a piercing look. "Do I make myself plain?"

"Ah, you mean Amalie?" Johnny had known something was coming as soon as he'd seen that empty room last night.

"Exactly." Julian straightened up and walked toward Johnny and the door. "I don't want to make a big to-do about it, but I thought you ought to be warned. As a friend of Simon's, of course." He allowed a warm smile to show his even teeth and lighten his eyes. "All you need is a little time to acquire some town bronze. This was just a small mistake that no one else is aware of."

Julian was gone before Johnny could think of anything adequate to say. He certainly wasn't going to tell him the truth.

From her curtained window, Dami watched Julian

descend the front steps. She'd heard a carriage pulling up twenty minutes earlier and had been shocked to see it was Julian's. He'd spent that time with Johnny, with no summons for her, even though he knew that Amalie lived somewhere in this house. Had she pushed him too far during their last two meetings?

She was deep in thought, and Suzy had to address her several times. "Lady Damaris, this was given to me by a small beggar boy." Suzy held out a screw of paper.

Dami took it curiously. She untwisted it and read the contents. Her teeth snapped shut. Perth was certainly sure of her, writing to demand she be ready at ten the following Monday. She crushed the paper and threw it viciously into the fireplace.

Pop! Julian's head whipped back, sharp pain splintering his chin.

"Sorry, Your Grace, but you haven't been thinking about your form." The words were respectfully reproachful. "This is the first time in many months that I've been able to land one."

Julian rubbed his sore jaw and smiled ruefully at his opponent. Gentleman Jackson, ex-pugilist, with his own training rooms where he catered to the pink of the ton, watched him speculatively. It was true, he didn't have his mind on what he was doing. "You're right. I think I'll call it quits for the day." Julian picked up his shirt from a nearby chair and headed to wash down and dress.

Walking home from Gentleman Jackson's, Julian found his thoughts again distracting him. When

Jason Beaumair waved, asking to join him, Julian's mind was only half on what he was doing. The chit was becoming an obsession with him.

"Been to Jackson's?" Perth asked casually.

"Yes, and he landed me a facer," Julian responded ruefully. "What about yourself, Jason? Just out for a stroll or going somewhere?"

"I was going to Jackson's, but if he's in good enough form to get through your guard, I don't think I want to." Jason surveyed Julian nonchalantly. If he didn't know better, he'd say the man was preoccupied. He smiled. Perhaps now was the time to propose his plan. "I say, Julian, would you do me a favor?"

Julian watched him warily, all his attention brought to focus on the one man in society he felt the closest ties with. They were two of a kind, both from the old aristocracy, wealthy as Croesus, and rebels. "What is it you need?"

Picking his words carefully, Perth began. "There's this ladybird who is unwilling to let the thing end." He gave Julian a conspiratorial wink. "You know the kind. Anyway, not wanting to create a distasteful scene, I agreed to squire her one more time. Tomorrow we are supposed to go to Covent Gardens, but meantime, I've entered into a liaison with another lovely bit-o-muslin. So, I was wondering if you would accompany us and entertain my old flame."

Julian chuckled. "Don't tell me you've gotten yourself into something you can't get out of. That isn't like you, Jason, but . . ." It might be just what he needed. Amalie asked too much of him. Perth's old mistress might interest him, at least for one night, and then, who knows, it might dampen his obsessive

160

craving for Amalie. "I'll go. What time and where do I meet you?"

"I'll call for you in my carriage around ten next Monday." Perth doffed his curly-brimmed beaver and headed back in the direction Julian had come from.

Julian watched the earl stroll away, and his brows drew together. Why was he having twinges of guilt? He had made no vows of fidelity to the chit. He certainly hadn't asked her to marry him, and no one was ever faithful to his mistress (or his wife, for that matter). She asked too much.

He glanced around to see several ladies across the street watching him. He knew that if he gave them the slightest encouragement they would descend on him like vultures, so he frowned even more fiercely. He knew that his excursion into the polite bastions of the ton several nights ago had probably aroused all sorts of expectations in the hearts of marriageable chits and their mamas. Not to forget speculation in the minds of everyone. Well, let them worry about it. He had no intention of enlightening their vulgar curiosity.

Meanwhile, what to do about the infuriating woman who wouldn't stay out out of his mind? He marched home, angry at himself for letting her affect him this deeply, but determined to see her again.

Dami heard her mother's door close and knew she was leaving for a card party. The dowager had a passion for cards. Tonight Dami had again begged to be left behind. Every time she had ventured out since the fracas at Lady Sefton's, she had been beset by prying people. She managed to fend them off, but she was the cynosure of all eyes, and would continue to be until the beau monde found something else to gossip about. The dowager, equally curious, but in more control, had finally relented and let Dami stay home. But Dami knew that soon her mother would call a reckoning. Thank goodness it wasn't yet.

Suzy was brushing Dami's hair when there was a knock on the door. "Come in," Dami said, wondering who was looking for her at this late hour.

Johnny entered. He looked the worse for drink, but otherwise seemed in good spirits. Striding into the room, he waved Suzy away. "You may go, Suzy, I've got something to discuss with Lady Damaris."

After the maid was safely gone, Dami looked at her twin, one eyebrow raised. "You are certainly home early. Did you lose too much?"

He grinned hugely. "Don't really enjoy gambling, only go because it's all the crack. But that's not why I'm here." He dropped onto her bed and wiped his forehead, his Brutus even more wild than his valet had intended. "Am I tired. All the tongues are wagging about you and Camber. It's all I can do to keep them from tearing me apart, so eager are they for minute details of the latest on dit. Your little confrontation at Lady Sefton's ball has spread. Even those on the social fringes are aware."

"I'm so sorry you have been beset with a notorious sister." She said the words jokingly, but a small kernel of truth lurked in them. She was truly becoming notorious, and if she weren't careful she'd find herself ostracized even before Perth had a chance to expose her.

"Yes, but I was beginning to live with that and who should walk in as bold as brass? Camber." He waited for her reaction. Her mouth hanging open, eyes wide as two dark tunnels, was worth it. "Yes, he walked right up to me in front of them all. We had to leave to get some quiet where he could talk." He stopped to let her stew. "He wants to see you again. It seems you can't give him a disgust of you no matter what you do. He doesn't even suspect you aren't who you claim to be. It seems he's so aloof that no one has the gumption to tell him who it was he really yanked off the dance floor."

"Johnny, will you stop this infuriating rendition of minutia and get to the poit."

"The point is that he wants to take you to some masquerade tomorrow night. Don't really approve. It's not the place one takes a gently reared young lady, or a fella likes his sister to go to, but then I remembered, to him you're some demi-rep, so I couldn't say no." He peered at her curiously. "Does it bother you that he holds you in such low esteem that he'd suggest such a thing and intend to carry it out?"

"Of course it bothers me, you sapskull, but what can I do about it?" Hurt made her harsher than she intended. "I'm trapped in this disguise. If I reveal myself, he will throw me over for sure, and then I'll never get a chance to win his love. If I remain in this disguise, at least I have a small chance of winning his affection. Unless I completely alienate him with my unusual requests." Dami prowled the room, her face a conflicting mess of hopelessness and frustration. "Do you have any better suggestions? Because if you don't, I shall meet His Grace for this masquerade.

163

After all," her mouth twisted bitterly, "hasn't my whole association with him been a masquerade?"

Having to agree with her, Johnny gave her the pertinent details before departing for his own bed and what he felt to be a much deserved sleep.

The next night Dami donned her heavy wool cloak over a brown domino and sneaked out the servant's entrance. Again she'd pleaded indisposition with her mother, and again the dowager had allowed her to stay home. Something wasn't right, but she couldn't afford to find out what.

She rounded the corner of the house and slipped into the hackney coach Johnny had procured. She gave the man directions to Julian's apartments, her fingers tight on the opening of her cloak and her heart like a thundering storm.

The cab stopped in front of the imposing set of rooms. Dami jumped out and paid the driver. With a wry smile, she wondered if it ever occurred to Julian that a true dependant waiting for a governess's job wouldn't have the ability to continually pay for the transportation she took to reach him.

He was waiting for her in the shadows of his doorway, a black domino over his arm. He took her elbow and ushered her into his carriage.

Sitting so close her thigh stung him, Julian said, "I'm glad you could come tonight."

She smiled timidly. All of a sudden she felt shy with him. Too much had happened too soon. "I'm glad you asked, milord."

"You called me Julian before. Do you think it is too much to ask that you continue to do so?" One finger traced the rim of her half-mask.

He felt like a firebrand next to her, the heat of him scorching her senses. "I wasn't sure if you still wanted me to."

"If I didn't want you to use my Christian name, I wouldn't have gone to the trouble of seeking out that puppy and giving him my message."

There was no answer to that. She knew he had apologized, in his own way, for the confrontation at Lady Sefton's. His low opinion of her still rankled, for Johnny had been prompt to tell her of his visit, but she was forced to accept it while she played for time.

She felt him shift, pulling her close so her head rested on his shoulder, and his arms were snug around her waist. She felt safe and warm and cared for. If only it could always be like this. Neither said any more, both content to luxuriate in their rapport.

The building housing the masquerade was jammed with the lower portion of London's populace. Dami watched avidly as persons she was sure never graced a grand drawing room milled around them, jostling and joking boisterously and crudely. Occasionally she saw a woman dressed in the manner of a cyprian escorted by a man whose clothes proclaimed him to be wealthy, even if his location didn't. She knew these were gentlemen out with their lights-o-love, and her heart sickened realizing anew that Julian was treating her similarly by bringing her here. Yet, what else could he do? There were precious few public places he could take her. She'd trapped herself.

They entered the large ballroom, and the smell of unwashed humanity mingling with the cloying scent of heavy musk nearly made Dami swoon. She felt that

London Bridge had tumbled down on her unsuspecting head. Feeling Julian's hard strength solidly next to her, she shrank into his embrace.

Sensing her nervousness, Julian held her close, cursing himself for bringing her there in the first place. He had wanted to see her, but knew he couldn't trust himself alone with her. He'd promised. She ignited his senses too much, even as she demanded behavior from him that forced him to fight his baser urges.

He guided her to the dance floor, where couples were swaying to the strains of a waltz. Many of the people were beyond being capable of propriety, if they even cared. The women turned rouged cheeks to their bosky companions, while their partners fondled them in areas better left for private.

To Dami, it was a sea of exposed white bosoms and bare legs. She thanked her guardian angel that she'd left the Cyprians' Ball too early to see it degenerate to this level. She wished she weren't here to see this. Then she was in Julian's arms and all else was momentarily forgotten.

He pressed her to him, their bodies flowing together as they circled the room. Dami knew they were too close, but she didn't care. No one knew who they were, and—she felt a fiery blush—they had been closer than this several nights ago.

She could hear his heart beating in her ear, slow and strong. His domino was silky against her cheek, and his arm was warm and comforting around her waist. She wanted this moment to last forever. Too soon, the music stopped, and Julian led her off the floor, his hand possessively at the small of her back.

Before either realized it, the crowd pushed between them, dragging Dami away in its wake. Fear clutched her. Where was Julian? She heard him calling her, but the multitude kept forcing her further away. She called futilely to him.

The next thing she knew, her arm was clasped by Henry the Eighth. "Unhand me, sirrah," she demanded.

Henry only laughed. "Well, well, my pretty. Are you interested in becoming one of my wives?" The man almost rolled on the floor laughing at his own joke.

"Release me." She was glad her voice was almost free of squeaks.

"No, no, you can't be so cruel. Fair lady, I only want to do what every other male in this room does." He pulled her away from the gaudy throng.

Dami yanked backwards, hoping to make him lose his balance, or at least make her abduction more effort for him than he wanted to expend. "If you don't let me go, you will be sorry." Fear edged her voice. Despite the man's jocular words there was a hint of cruelty in his devouring eyes and the curve of his narrow jaw. "Please, I promise to make it worth your while if you return me to my escort." She tried the new tack, desperate in her growing dread of what the man planned.

"Tut, tut, my dear, you don't take me for a flat, do you?" He leered back at her, dragging her on the end of his arm. "There is only one way you can make any of this worth my while—and it isn't by taking you back to your lover."

"Oh, no," she moaned. She also realized for the

first time that his voice was cultured. She was in the suds now. She didn't recognize her captor, but it didn't much matter. Her name had been bandied about enough since Lady Sefton's that he would know her, provided he even bothered to unmask her.

They were in a small alcove before Dami could do anything more. In a corner, up against the wall, was a settee just large enough to hold them both. Her jailor forced her down onto it and followed her with relish. She could see him licking his chops in anticipation. Strong, frighteningly strong arms in green velvet closed like iron bars around her. His head bent to hers, his breath stinking of strong liquor. He ground his wet, soft lips against hers. Dami bit him.

Suddenly, she found herself prone on the small couch, her would-be-lover covering his bleeding mouth with a white hand. "You'll pay for that, bitch," he said through clenched teeth, his free hand back preparatory to slapping her across the face.

Dami closed her eyes and waited for the blow. She was trapped under his body and knew she couldn't get away, but maybe he would draw back after the slap and she could unbalance him and escape. She held her breath. The blow didn't come. She opened wary eyes.

Julian was behind her captor, the man's hands secured in his. As she watched, Julian pulled the man backwards so he fell onto the floor. Then Julian stepped on his neck, pinning her assaulter to the ground.

"You are lucky she is unharmed and that I don't wish to kick up a dust here." Julian growled the words as he pressed his foot harder into the man's neck until his prey whitened. Anger corroded what little control Julian had left as he turned to see Amalie crouching on the couch, her face drained of color and her eyes too large for her pinched face. It stabbed through him that he could very easily kill the knave under his foot. Instead, he released the man and grabbed Amalie, propelling her out of the alcove.

He dragged her through the crowd until they were in the fresh air. Then he huddled her into his waiting coach and yanked her into his arms. He buried his face in her hair, smelling the clean, fresh scent of her. "I'm sorry, sweetings." He took a deep, ragged breath. "I never thought about the danger you would be in from bounders like him when I brought you here. Please forgive me."

Dami reached a hand to stroke his cheek, free of the domino he'd flung onto the opposite seat. "It's all right, Julian. You were there when I needed you."

"No, it isn't," he reiterated. "I was insane when I realized I'd lost you. I knew you didn't know how to go on in a place like that. I'm ten kinds of a fool to have even suggested taking you there." He sighed into her hair, holding her snugly against his rigid body. "I don't know what to do with you, sweetings. I just don't know."

"Oh, Julian." Hope lurched through her.

They were silent until the carriage drew to a stop. Dami disengaged herself from his encompassing warmth and looked out the window. They were in front of Rose Arbor.

"Oh, Julian, you shouldn't have brought me here," she said softly.

"I couldn't stand the thought that something else

might happen to you tonight. I had to see you safely home." His voice was gravelly, and yet sweet from the words he was saying. "And I can't keep you with me because I'm a worse threat to you than any man."

Dami couldn't help herself. His self-reproach broke down her last barriers. She flung herself back into his arms and kissed him. She kissed him with all the pent-up love and horror the night had brought her. Her lips talked to his of her longing. Her tongue met his in a pagan dance of passion shared and given freely. Her mind numbed as her body exulted to the feel of him, the care he expressed for her.

He put her from him. "You must go, my dear, before anyone sees my carriage."

Her lips were swollen and red from the kiss she'd initiated. Julian wanted badly to take her back into his embrace and kiss her into mindless submission. He wanted to take her home with him and care for her. The thought jarred him into gently pushing her from the carriage. He remained outside the house long enough to see her let herself into the back gate.

Chapter Ten

Dami dragged herself, bleary-eyed, from bed the next day, her heart singing. She was sure Julian was beginning to care for her. Then her emotions plummeted. Tonight was her assignation with Perth. Now, more than ever, she needed to keep him from exposing her. She was too near her goal to have it wrecked by Julian's learning her real identity before she could convince him they were meant for each other.

Several hours later, she surveyed herself with satisfaction. The full-length mirror showed a young governess. Her silver hair was braided and pinned tight to her scalp, and her slim, graceful figure was shown to disadvantage by an ill-fitting drab kerseymere dress buttoning high on her long neck. Serviceable shoes peeked out from the unfashionably full skirt.

If Perth intended to flaunt her, he was in for a disappointment. Dami knew she couldn't stand him up, but he would derive no pleasure from her company.

She intended to blend into the background, and the wig Suzy was procuring would be the final accoutrement. A dull, mouse-brown wig was the maid's goal. If the chit would only return before it was time for Perth to pick Dami up at the Drury Lane Theatre.

The door burst open. "Oh, milady, I done the best I could." Suzy rushed into the room, her hair awry and her apron skewered around. Hanging from her hands was a milliner's box.

Taking the box from the girl's unresisting fingers, Dami laid it on the bed and removed the top. "What is this?" she cried. She lifted hands covered by an orange-red fluff ball. "I asked for something ugly and inconspicuous—not ugly and garish!"

"There weren't nothin' else, milady." Suzy stood desolately wringing her hands.

"It's too late to get another one, too," Dami mumbled to herself. Heavens, but she was going to look a fright. She had no choice, though, since she didn't want to be seen with Perth as Lady Damaris, and he'd specifically stipulated no mask, and she knew that going to Covent Gardens with no concealing mask meant she had to hide her hair. It was too unusual a color, but not, she thought wryly, any more unusual than this wig.

Resigned, Dami went to the mirror and settled the wig on. "Oh, no," she wailed when the offending item was properly secured. A thick fringe of heavy bangs dragged her high forehead down, while the remaining hair was gathered into two bunches, one on each side of her head just above her ears. These tails, for they reminded her of an unkempt horse's mane, were crimped into cotton-candy fullness. It was all the crack—if the wearer wanted to be considered fast.

All her efforts to affect being a nonentity were for naught. The contrast of the "governess" gown and the "fast" wig threw her into sharp relief as an eccentric.

Dami twitched the offending bangs and stooped to get her smothering wrap. Maybe she could wear the cloak all night with the hood pulled up to hide her hair. If not, at least no one should recognize the strikingly fashionable Lady Damaris in the eccentric old maid she now resembled.

Thirty minutes later she was huddled into a dark corner outside the Drury Lane Theatre watching Perth's crested coach draw to a stop not more than twenty feet away. Dami scurried forward to meet Perth as he descended the steps to look for her. She careened into him and would have fallen if he hadn't grabbed her firmly at the shoulder, knocking down her hood in the process.

"My, God," he said, his face twisting in disgust. "You've certainly disguised yourself this time." He handed her into the carriage.

It was a comfortable chaise, well sprung, with deep wine velvet squabs. She dimly perceived two people seated across from her and the earl, but she was too embarrassed and scared of discovery to lift her head to see who they were. However, something kept nagging at her, pricking her much the same way Julian's presence always did. Finally, she raised her head just enough to see her fellow passengers.

"Oooooh," oozed from her frozen lips. Camber was sitting directly across from her, his arms crossed belligerently over his broad chest, his hair tumbling rakishly over one eye.

"Is something wrong, my dear?" Perth asked solicitously.

Dami said nothing, but she would have sworn there was satisfaction in Perth's dark eyes. The game was up for her. Even if the earl didn't reveal her true identity, Julian would never trust her once he realized she was the ladybird Perth had picked up. And how could she convince him different without giving the game away? Then he would despise her for pulling the trick in the first place. She moaned again, and thought seriously of pleading with Perth to drop her off because she was too sick to go on.

Cogitating on what to do, Dami still hadn't bothered to look at the fourth occupant of the coach. A pearl-white hand wielding an ivory fan that swatted playfully on Camber's wrist soon enlightened her. It was Mrs. Jones, and she was clinging languidly to the duke's shoulder, her eyes gazing soulfully up at him.

Infuriated beyond caution, Dami failed to comprehend the duke coolly shaking Mrs. Jones off. All Dami saw in her red haze was him acting as "that woman's" escort.

Well, she'd show that . . . that libertine . . . that rake, that he couldn't drop her without so much as a by-your-leave. She'd make him pay all night.

Sitting abruptly up, Dami swept the replaced hood from her head and shook her curls out before turning her own hooded eyes on Perth. Distaste stiffened her back, but she was determined to show the cad across from her that she didn't need him.

"Oh, la, Jason," she sounded like a simpering ninnyhammer, but she didn't care. "I do declare, this is so exciting. Going to Covent Gardens and all. I've never been there before." She leaned into him, turning her face up to his, pouting her lips, hoping she looked seductive.

The earl smiled sardonically down at her and whispered, for her ears only, "Very good, my dear. It's too bad your dress somewhat mars your performance." He flicked a glance at Camber. "But I do believe your fish has taken the bait." Perth brought his

174

forefinger up and lightly caressed Dami's mouth.

She barely kept herself from drawing back. Somehow, she sighed with contentment and allowed her head to fall to Perth's shoulder. She'd give him his money's worth tonight, since it was obvious that he'd engineered the whole thing.

Camber stared at her, a hard glint in his eye. She couldn't tell whether he recognized her or not, but just for good measure, she lifted her face and gave him a dazzling smile, her dimple out for all to see. A storm broke over his demeanor, and she saw him jolt up. Satisfaction made her smile smug. He'd seen through her red wig. Good.

She turned back to Perth and tried to look limpidly into his eyes. The smile in his as he surveyed her efforts didn't help her any. She wished she had a fan so she could use it as Mrs. Jones was, tapping Julian imperiously on the shoulder to gain his attention. Dami fumed.

"It would be better," Perth murmured in her ear, "if you would stop tapping your foot."

Dami's mouth thinned, but she stopped the errant foot, only to catch her fingers drumming against the seat. If only they would reach their destination. She needed to get out and walk before she exploded, saying things she'd regret. She wasn't about to give *him* the gratification of knowing he'd hurt her. She'd convince him that she had planned to meet Perth all along.

The carriage stopped, and with an expertise born of practice, Perth soon had them all ensconced at an isolated table for four. They were far from the crowds, but close enough to hear the orchestra and get to the dance floor if they wished.

Dami watched Julian surreptitiously. He certainly didn't seem inclined to favor the lovely bit-of-fluff at his side with his undivided attention. In fact, he seemed to be ignoring Mrs. Jones as his jaw twitched and his eyes bored into Dami's. Just what she wanted. Now she'd play lightskirt to Perth's rake—and she'd play it to the hilt.

When Perth put an insinuating arm around her waist, Dami checked her first implulse to draw away, and instead covered his hand with hers. She reached up and kissed him teasingly on the cheek, wagging her head so that her hair bobbed up and down.

"Oh, you are such a flirt, Jason," she trilled. Her raucous laughter echoed around them. A small shudder worked through her. If looks could kill, Julian's would have put her six feet under.

Not content, she got to her feet and pulled Perth to his, dragging him bodily to the dance floor. When he put his arms around her, she moved closely into his embrace.

"Don't you think you are overplaying your role, Lady Damaris?"

"No."

"Tsk, tsk. Remind me never to play a woman false. You females are as poisonous as a viper when crossed." He swung her around so that her skirts and hair billowed out.

To an onlooker, they were a couple involved with each other to the exclusion of all else. Dami made sure her appreciation of Perth's company was visible to the couple still seated at their table. Even so, she was beginning to feel apprehensive. Julian hadn't stirred or said a word since she'd entered the carriage, and he was now patently ignoring the widow, who was brazenly trying to gain his attention.

Danger was just beginning to trickle down Dami's spine when a well-manicured hand came to rest heavily on Perth's shoulder.

"My turn, old man," the duke of Camber said, dangerously low.

The breath caught in Dami's throat as Perth relinquished her with a mock show of regret. Her feet and hands felt cold, while her face felt like stone. She gulped rapidly.

Camber pulled her straining body to his. He was as hot as an iron to her, exacerbating her already flushed condition and making her squirm to put distance between them.

"Are you trying to draw more attention to us than your ill-considered garb already is?"

The taunting words fueled her temper. "What I choose to do is no concern of yours." She tried to twist her right hand free of his viselike grip. "I'm tired of dancing. Let me go."

"My pleasure. When I'm finished with you." He came to a sharp halt, throwing her off balance so that when he headed toward a darkened pathway she was forced to follow his momentum or fall.

Her protestations fell on deaf ears as he dragged her into a pavilion. Vines grew profusely around the structure, increasing the privacy already afforded by its dark location and surrounding shrubs.

"Leave it to you to know exactly where these are." She turned her back on him.

"My reputation precedes me, as usual." His dry

tones were tinged with bitterness. "But so does Perth's. Turn around and look me in the eye, Amalie. I want to see your face when you explain your presence with him tonight."

She whirled around, sputtering, "Me! Explain? How about you? What are you doing with the enticing and already once discarded Mrs. Jones?" She glared at him, jealousy swamping any precautions or worries she might otherwise have had.

"You forget yourself, Amalie. I don't owe you any explanations. You are, if you will remember, my mistress. Not my wife. As such, you are at the disadvantage by being caught with Perth." His autocratic bearing was blurred by his hand rubbing wearily at his temples. "I can only suppose that he has paid you well to cuckold me."

Dami squashed the pang of concern his tired action roused in her. "The earl hasn't paid me anything! Furthermore, I'm under no delusions where you're concerned. How could I ever forget you consider me your mistress? An object for your physical gratification. To be put aside like a used toy when something more interesting presents itself. How can I ever forget the shallowness of our connection?"

"If you are just for my pleasure, sweetings, then you aren't performing your duties." He leaned against the wall of their enclosure, his eyes heavy-lidded. "You have been the confoundest woman it has ever been my misfortune to tangle with. So far you have led me a merry chase, beckoning on the one hand, holding me at bay with the other. And just when you present your biggest demand—asking for more than my body—you flaunt yourself under the protection of

Jason Beaumair: second to none in the art of seduction." He looked her over speculatively. "Ordinarily, I wouldn't put up with this behavior from any woman."

"You wouldn't! Well, you certainly are the pot calling the kettle black. First you try to buy me into your bed and when that doesn't work you use kindness, and when that fails you take up with your old *chère amie*." Tears glistened on her lashes, picked out in diamond brilliance by the filtered moonlight. She didn't want to cry, but she couldn't continue the way they'd been. More than anything she wanted him to refute Mrs. Jones. She didn't even care how he did it. He could say it wasn't what it looked like, or even that it was, but that it was only for one evening.

Julian took a step toward her, holding out his arms, and she flew into them. The pressure of his embrace was oddly reassuring to her shattered nerves.

"You're the only woman, except my mother, who has ever been able to move me with tears." He laid his cheek on her frizzed wig. "I'm only here because Jason told me he had been unable to rid himself of one ladybird so he could woo another. I was to be the decoy to draw the unwanted one off. It appears, however, that I've been used for something deeper." He tipped her face up. "Look at me, Amalie. Alicia means nothing to me. She never has, and I would never be unfaithful to you with her."

Radiant joy filled her. She forgot everything else as she lifted on tiptoe to kiss him. His lips felt like down as they moved across her eyelids and down to her arched neck.

With a contented sigh, she relaxed into the cradle of

his arms. Sliding against his coat made her wig go askew, so Dami moved infinitesimally away to resettle it.

"Why did you wear that ridiculous thing?" Julian asked. "You certainly do look an antidote, in that so modish wig with your brown wren dress." The words were softly jibing, but his eyes held something warmer.

Not taking offense, Dami said, "It's rather complicated, but the gist is that I didn't want anyone to recognize me." She bit her lip and lowered her eyes, praying he would let the subject drop.

"I'm glad you treat us equally on that stead." His eyes were turning frosty. "However, I'm still interested in why you're here with him." At her look of alarm, he gathered her up again. "I'm not accusing you of being his mistress, I think I've finally worried that bone thin, but there's something going on here that both you and Perth are privy to and from which I'm excluded. I feel you owe me an explanation."

Dami knew she looked mulish. She couldn't help it. That was the way she felt. "I can't tell you, Julian, not yet." She watched helplessly as thunder brewed across his face. "I'm asking you to trust me. This shouldn't affect us." Even while she said the words, she knew they weren't true. There was a big chance that once he learned the truth he would never trust her again.

"Amalie, I've revealed a lot of myself to you tonight. I'm asking you to reciprocate." He held her at arm's length.

"Please, Julian, trust me. Don't force me to tell you yet. I will as soon as I can." As soon as you love me, she thought. Anguish racked her as she felt him

180

drawing away.

"You want me to trust you when it involves a man of Perth's stamp?" His harsh laugh grated along her spine. "When you wouldn't trust me about Alicia until *after* I'd told you everything?"

"It's not the same."

"How so?"

"Because I don't have your reputation, that's how!" She knew immediately that she'd gone too far. This time she'd pushed too long and welshed on her unspoken part of the bargain.

"So, we're back to my past. It seems mighty convenient for you. Then let me act up to it." He yanked her against him, slashing his mouth across hers, brutally sapping her strength and her spirit. Panting, he raised his head to say, "You are my mistress, though you've yet to live up to your obligation. As such, I expect you to have no secrets from me that involve the earl of Perth. Or any man. I know your play of affection for him tonight was only to pique me because you thought I'd betrayed you with Alicia. I understand that, but I will not allow you to put me off about why you were with him in the first place."

Dami could feel his barely restrained violence in the trembling of his thighs against hers, in the tensile strength of his fingers digging into her shoulders. Despair penetrated bone-deep in her. She was truly caught in her own trap. She'd forced him full circle, until she was back in her original place as his mistress.

"Nothing you say or do can make me tell you before I'm ready." She stood up to him with rivulets of sweat running between her shoulderblades.

Furious at her willful refusal to trust him with her secret, Julian tossed her from him and turned his back to her, trying to master the inferno she'd ignited.

Dami watched his back, saw the bunched muscles in his neck and shoulders, and knew she couldn't continue to hold out against the buffeting of his anger. If she stayed, she would relent and tell him everything. Then he would denounce her and throw her aside. Nothing in his past handling of females indicated differently. She fled.

Calming down, Julian turned to face Amalie. Even if it meant he must continue to play her dupe, he wasn't going to let her go. The words telling her it would be all right were on the tip of his tongue. She was gone.

"Damn," burst from him. She didn't realize the danger she faced unescorted in Covent Gardens at night. "Amalie," he yelled into the dark pathways. He wasn't surprised when she didn't answer. The ninny-hammer.

The next sixty minutes of Julian's life were spent in fruitless searching. Finally, he retraced his steps to their table, only to see that Perth was also gone. Alicia sat in majestic solitude, obviously put out.

Approaching her, Julian was succinctly informed that Perth and his light-o-love had left a good thirty minutes earlier. Bowing to pressure, Julian hailed a hackney for Alicia where he quickly deposited her after prying each of her ten fingers loose from his jacket.

Later that night Julian sat ensconced in his library,

a half-empty tumbler of brandy clenched in his fist, scowling at the cheerful fire. Drat the woman. He was spending an inordinate amount of time pondering the havoc she continued to wreak on his sangfroid.

Why, he had even told her that he wouldn't be unfaithful to her. To her! A cyprian! What was he doing? He knew she wanted marriage; what woman didn't? But that was not an option for them. He owed it to his name, if not to himself, to marry someone from his own world. Hadn't he set in motion plans that would eventually leg-shackle him to Lady Damaris FitzHubert, sister of his best friend? Yes. He needed an heir, and it was a responsibility he couldn't shirk.

He didn't know what he was doing anymore. If any of his old cronies from the Peninsula could see him now, they wouldn't recognize the cool colonel who had led charges with no thought of personal danger in the befuddled man combing his wild hair with shaking fingers.

Julian swallowed the last of the liquor and set his glass on the nearby table with a resounding whack. The chit was like a drug on him. The more he got, the more he needed. He buried his face in his hands, disgust warring with the determination to have her at any cost.

A soft scratch on the door, followed by a loud knock when he didn't respond, finally elicited "What!" from him.

"Your Grace," his factotem said hesitantly, entering the darkened room apprehensively, "I've a message that was just delivered. The man was in the livery of the earl of Perth, and he said it was imperative that you read the note immediately."

Grumbling, Julian took the paper and quickly scanned its contents.

"The fiend!" Crushing the paper, he surged to his feet. His eyes were shut till lines creased around them and his mouth was a slit. "Is this some Cheltenham Tragedy they both hope to perpetrate on me?" The words ground out of him, even as he opened his eyes and smoothed out the badly battered note to reread it.

"No." She and Perth might have a secret between them but he knew her integrity to be too great to allow her to pull this sort of shabby trick on him.

"Stevens," he said, moving rapidly to the door, "have my phaeton brought around immediately. I will be leaving as soon as it is ready. Tell Williams to pack a fresh shirt and cravat." The words were bullets of command. "I'm on my way to Felixstowe, and I don't know when I will return."

If Perth meant what he threatened, he would ravish Amalie if Julian didn't get there by tomorrow evening. Even as he jumped into his carriage, he found it hard to believe that Perth, his old friend, was capable of the actions he hinted at. Unless it was . . . no, he put the thought aside. That had happened four years ago. Surely they were past that now.

With a flick of his wrist, he sent his matched greys sprinting.

Chapter Eleven

Dami examined herself in the mirror hanging above the jug and bowl she was washing her face in. Her eyes were gritty from lack of sleep, and her mouth was dry from apprehension. She made a moue of disgust as she tried to twist her silver hair into a knot at her neck. Wisps insisted on coming loose to wave around her cheeks. She'd discarded the red wig at Cheltenham, finding it not worth the discomfort. Disgusted, she whirled around and made for the door. The earl of Perth required her presence immediately in his private parlor.

She made her way down the hall and entered the room without knocking. Sweeping her skirts in, she pushed the door shut and advanced to the fireplace. A cheery blaze belied the sinister intent of the room's male occupant. She took a deep breath and faced Perth.

"Why did you abduct me?" She kept her voice firm, but she stiffened at the sight of him. His coat hung over the back of the chair he lounged in, his cravat dangled untied, and his eyes shone. Her lips curled. "You have certainly made yourself comfortable." Determined to do likewise, she sank into the chair facing him. Between them was a serviceable oak table holding a half-empty bottle of wine.

Perth's answering smile was saturnine. "Please, make yourself comfortable, Lady Damaris." He grabbed the neck of the bottle and extended it in her direction. "May I offer you some wine? It's not the finest, but it is decidedly superior to what I expected." She jerked her head in refusal. "No? Too bad." He put the bottle down, then took a sip from his full glass.

"Well? Do you intend to explain yourself, Perth?" If his manner hadn't infuriated her so, she knew she would be shaking in apprehension. Her eyes darted around the room. It was small, but clean, with heavy chintz curtains on the single window and serviceable knot rugs scattered on the wooden floor. There were two large chairs near the fire, which they occupied, and a sofa against the far wall that was almost lost in the shadows. She guessed it to be brown like the rest of the furnishings.

"Finished with your examination, Lady Damaris?"

She nodded, searching his face for the sarcasm that was absent in his voice. "You must have a very good reason for risking both our reputations this way."

"To me," he said, putting his empty glass on the table. He leaned back and steepled his fingers in front of his chest. "And you have been priceless as the tool to effect my revenge, not to mention the pleasure I've derived watching you lead Camber about with a leash." He ran his forefinger along the scar on his cheek. "Fascinate you? It's taken me a long time to reach this level of complacency about it. Camber gave it to me."

"Oh!" She stifled the sound as best she could behind her hand.

"I thought that would shock you. If he had stopped at this, I would still call him friend, but he didn't." He smiled, then turned his gaze to the mantel clock as it struck the hour. "He should be here soon. When we stopped at Cheltenham, I sent a lackey to Camber with instructions to meet us here."

"Now I know you're insane," she said. "Surely you don't expect Julian to follow us." She hoped she sounded incredulous. As much as she hoped Julian would come to her rescue, she didn't want Perth to be prepared. "Especially after our exhibition tonight," she emphasized.

"My dear, I expect him for exactly that reason. It confirmed my suspicion that Camber has finally met a woman who interests him for more than her body." He watched her blush. "You should be the first to know you haven't made things easy or . . . uhm, rewarding, for him. So, there must be more to his pursuit of you than his normal selfish urges."

Dami squeezed the arms of her chair until her knuckles turned white. When would he stop playing with her?

"You are controlling yourself admirably, but I doubt if the landlord will appreciate having nail rents in the upholstery of his chair." He smiled as she jumped and jammed her hands down at her sides. "Not that the material is expensive."

"I've changed my mind. I'd like a glass of wine now." She glared at him when he raised one eyebrow in disbelief before pouring the liquid. "Thank you," she muttered, much tempted to say nothing.

"As I was saying. We had a small misunderstanding four years ago concerning Lady Christine Julie St. John." He refilled his glass and took a drink. "It seems I was looking above myself when I asked Camber for her hand."

"I beg your—" The words jumped from her before she could shut her moth. She blinked several times. "You wanted to marry Kit? She never said a word." Cynicism and something else Dami couldn't name twisted his face, making his scar stand out in white relief against his swarthy complexion.

Perth eyed her over his glass rim. "She never knew." At her look of disbelief, he said, "Strange, but true. I was the soul of propriety: never asked her to dance more than twice in one evening, took her sedately driving in Hyde Park, once escorted her and Lady Sebastian to the theater." His eyes dimmed with memories. "I loved her and wanted everything done properly so she would have no hesitation in accepting. I spoke to Camber without telling Kit my intentions, but I flatter myself that she would have accepted." He put his empty glass on the table, got up, and strode to the fireplace. Leaning one arm along the mantel, he continued. "This is the very inn, even the same room, I asked Camber's permission." He mocked himself with his smile. "Ironic, isn't it. Four years ago tonight Julian and I fought a duel over Lady Kit and my honorable intentions. Tonight we will fight a duel over Lady Damaris-cum-Amalie and my not so honorable intentions."

His harsh laugh jolted Dami out of her shock.

"Why did Julian refuse you?"

"He said I was a loose screw and a rake. Not what he intended for his precious cousin." Bitterness dripped from each word. "It didn't matter that I loved her and intended to do everything in my power to make her happy. My reputation preceded me — and with him, of all people!"

"My reputation preceded me" echoed through her mind. Julian had said those very words to her just hours ago. She looked at Perth, her eyes dazed by her thoughts. "I'm sorry," she managed at last.

"Don't be." His voice was harsh as he turned his back on her. His next words were muffled. "Tonight I intend to even the score."

"Oh no . . ." The words were a soft moan as the realization hit her fully. Perth intended to fight Julian, and he was deadly serious about it. "You carry a grudge a long time."

He swung to face her. "Isn't losing four years of your life something to begrudge?" His legs were long, his stride purposeful as he neared her. Taking her shoulder, he pulled her up. "But don't worry, Lady Damaris, I don't intend to kill Camber, only scare and humiliate him." At her puzzled look, he elaborated. "To scare him about your safety. Yes," he said when she blushed, "he will worry about your maidenly modesty, but don't be scared." He released her shoulders and moved back. "I have no intentions of hurting you. You are, unfortunately for you, only the tool of my revenge. I'm sorry if you must suffer, but console yourself with the thought that he cares for you or all of this would be . . ." The sound of carriage wheels outside was loud in the stillness of early morning. A satisfied smile curled Perth's lips. ". . . impossible."

Dami sprang from her chair and rushed to the window. Yanking the curtain aside, she peered through the haze to see an elegant black phaeton, drawn by a pair of matched bays, being taken into the livery by the ostler. Noises came from downstairs: an imperious voice demanding the whereabouts of the earl of Perth and the obsequious answer of the innkeeper.

Whack! The door slammed against the wall. Framed in the doorway was the duke of Camber. His eyes flashed dangerously. His curly-brimmed beaver tilted arrogantly to one side. His feet, in their immaculate Hessians, stood shoulder distance apart. The hem of his five-caped buff-colored garrick whipped around his calves.

Dami sank back into her chair, her eyes rounded by the fury he emanated. Not so Perth.

"My dear Julian," he said, advancing on the duke, looking as though he were welcoming a guest in his own parlor, "how considerate of you to answer my summons so quickly. Let me help you." Perth reached for Camber's coat.

"No, thank you," Camber said, undoing the fashionable brass buttons and shrugging out of the heavy folds.

Dami averted her eyes from him. The intensity of his anger filled her with dread. She'd never seen him so hard-faced or heard him so ice-voiced. Was this the guise he presented his enemies in combat? If so, it was no wonder he was a many-times-decorated war hero. Her knees began to tremble under the hiding skirts, and she was grateful she didn't have to stand. She'd probably swoon.

Camber tossed his coat onto the couch and carefully peeled his black riding gloves off to lay on top of the coat. His voice was controlled. "Because of something that happened so long ago, Jason? Those were our salad days and yours was calf love." He saw the agony in the blue eyes of the man he had called friend. "More, then. You've certainly hid it well." Glancing at Amalie, he added, "However, you shouldn't have dragged her into this. It isn't her fault you and I fought, with the understanding that the loser must abide by the winner's terms. This is taking the situation too far." He strode to Dami and reached for her hand. "Come, Amalie, you go up to your room while Jason and I settle this once and for all."

At his imperious tone, she stood up automatically. For a second she flirted with the idea of saluting him, but decided not to when she saw how compressed his lips were. Instead, she said, "Julian, please, leave it be. Perth has offered me no insult—had no intentions of doing so. Let us leave now and forget this whole thing has happened."

He stared at her as though she were insane. "Forget this? Forget that you have been alone with him for the past five hours, that your reputation is ruined?"

She couldn't hide her smile. "What did *you* wish to do with my reputation, milord?"

"That is different." He drew himself up. "I fully intend to care for you. *I* would never use you as a tool for revenge on another." He took her elbow and began propelling her toward the door. "And if that isn't enough, consider this. If I don't stop him now, he will only think of another way to force this fight on me. Possibly in an even less honorable way." He flashed a black look at his enemy. "If that is possible."

"Tut, tut," Perth said, enjoying himself immensely. "Sour grapes doesn't become you, Camber."

Camber's nostrils flared, causing Dami to shiver with apprehension. She knew it was up to her to stop the coming confrontation—both men were too caught up in their emotions.

"Oh . . ." she moaned, putting her hand to her forehead and slumping back into Camber's arms. She prayed he'd be quick enough to catch her before she hit the floor. Stopping their fight was one thing, injuring herself in the process, quite another.

Camber grabbed her around the waist, checking her fall with his thighs. She fluttered her eyes open. His look mixed concern and chagrin. She let her eyelids droop to hide her thoughts.

"Amalie," Camber said to her, "are you ill?" His tone implied doubt. "You aren't trying to gammon me?"

Her answer was another low moan and complete shutting of her eyes. Doubt her! She'd show him. She went limp, her head lolling and her fingers dragging the ground.

"Very interesting," Perth murmured. "I would never have thought it of her."

"Right." The clipped word held a treasure of meaning. Camber looked down at the prostrate woman. If this was another ploy of hers, one designed to stop the duel, he would give her a tongue-lashing she'd never forget. He scooped her up into his arms and carried her to the shadowed couch where he deposited her as carefully as his frustration would allow. Under his breath, he hissed, "You'd better be in a swoon, Amalie, or you will rue this little exhibition." Though he watched her carefully, she didn't move. "Send for a maid, Perth," he said over his shoulder, "while I loosen this bag of a dress." He knew that if anything made her betray herself it would be his hands on her.

It took every ounce of control she possessed, but Dami didn't stiffen, not even flinch, when his warm fingers touched her neck. Without a pause he unbuttoned the gown and pulled it apart near the neck and upper chest. The palm of his hand rested against her left side, making her heart beat in double-time. She hoped he would attribute it to shock. She didn't think unconscious people could blush. She hoped she hadn't done so.

Camber felt the thumping of her heart and observed the flush that suffused her face and torso. Perhaps she had caught a cold. He would leave it at that for the present.

The door opened and Perth reentered with the landlord and a maid. He raised his eyebrow at Camber. When Camber shook his head, Perth turned to the maid. "Put the smelling salts under her nose."

Dami tried to prepare herself. She started coughing, her eyes watering, as the first whiffs assailed her. Trying to look as natural as possible, she opened her eyes to see a dark-haired girl, buxom and with brown eyes, watching her with a worried frown.

"Oh. Oh, my," Dami groaned. She felt truly sick now. "I . . . did I pass out?" She looked past the girl, who had moved to one side, to see Julian's reaction.

He was grim-faced. "Yes, you did."

"Oh, dear." Her voice was almost inaudible to the other occupants of the room. She allowed her eyes to shut before she started rubbing her temples. She collapsed back against the arms of the couch. "I must be starting a megrim." She opened her eyes tentatively, shut them at Julian's scowl. "I . . . you see, I always swoon when a megrim is coming on. It's my warning to get plenty of laudanum—quickly." She didn't dare look again. Someone was chuckling softly. It sounded like Perth.

"Just what are you trying to say?" Julian enunciated carefully, staying his distance from her.

Dami pushed up on her elbows and opened her eyes. "Oh!" she squeezed her eyes shut and fell back. "I feel like someone is driving a lance into my head. 'Tis always thus." She opened her eyes and furrowed her eyebrows trying to look racked with pain. She stretched one arm out to Julian. "Please, Julian, before you do anything else, please, please, procure me some laudanum." At his skeptical look, she allowed her arm to drop. "If you don't, I fear . . . truly fear . . . that I shall be tortured with pain for the rest of the day." He watched her stonily. "Perhaps even two days." She looked up through her lashes. "Sometimes as long as a week."

That ought to move him, she thought. But no, the man was heartless. Her ire built at his look of patent disbelief.

"Careful, Amalie," Perth intervened. "Or you will worsen your condition. You are starting to turn the color of a radish." He turned to Camber. "I've waited four years to maneuver you here, Julian. I can wait long enough to get your lady some laudanum."

Dami turned to him gratefully. His eyes gleamed with amusement. He could ruin everything. "Thank you," she murmured. She transferred her attention to Julian. "Surely, if he can postpone your slaughter of each other, then so can you." That was daring, but she was getting desperate.

"All right," Julian capitulated.

"Thank you, milord," she said.

The maid was sent to the nearest apothecary. While she was gone the three of them kept an uneasy truce. The minute hand of the mantel clock ticked loudly. Dami glanced surreptitiously at it. It was time she started recovering a little.

With a small sigh, she struggled to pull herself up and propped her head against the back of the sofa. Then she dragged her legs until her feet fell off the edge and hit the floor.

Camber roused himself to move to her side. "Feeling better?" He took the hand she offered him before squatting down in front of her. Softly, he said, "Forgive me for doubting you, but it seemed too convenient." He watched her. Her face was pale and her hand shook in his. "I'm a cad to have doubted you."

She smiled tentatively. The warmth of his palm made her shake. He was so masculine, even in his concern for her. "Please, Julian, help me to sit up. I'm feeling a little better, but," she put her freed hand to her eyes, "I hope that maid returns soon."

He helped her to sit before positioning himself next to her to prop her up.

Julian's chest against her cheek made Dami's breathing quicken. His thigh rubbing hers made her feel dangerously lethargic. If that dratted girl didn't return fast, she would become overheated again. She needed to conclude this farce before she gave herself away.

The door opened and the maid bustled in, her cap askew and her hair flighty from her rush outside in the cold. " 'Tis all they had," she said breathlessly.

Not waiting for more, Dami struggled to her feet, putting a hand on Julian's shoulder to steady herself. "Thank you," she said to the maid.

"Here, sit down," Julian said, taking Dami's hand from his shoulder and rising. "I will get the laudanum for you." He put his hands to her shoulders and pressed her back to the couch.

"No, no," she began in a shrill voice. In more modulated tones, she said, "That is, you don't know how much I need." A deprecating smile at his arched brows and she plunged on. "I take a very large dose, having taken it for some years now, and I have to have it in wine. That is the only way it will sit in my stomach without making me sick." She stood again and shrugged her shoulders in resignation. "So you see, Julian, I must be the one to prepare it."

She tried to keep her agitation from showing in her eyes as she waited for his answer. Her hands were shaking again, and she hurriedly buried them in her skirts. This day was becoming a marathon filled with hurdles.

Finally, after she thought she would collapse from nerves, he answered her. "All right, Amalie. If you feel it is best, then I won't stop you."

She bowed her head, then turned to the maid. The bottle of laudanum was large and heavy. "There is enough here to floor a horse," she muttered, going to the table where the wine and glasses still stood. Secretly, she was glad of it, as she had a mule to floor. "Julian, Perth," she kept her back to them, "would you care for a glass with me? It always seems so lonely to me to drink by oneself. Don't you agree?" She didn't wait for their answers, but began to pour.

One glass she filled a quarter full of laudanum, then topped it with the strong-tasting wine. The other two she filled strictly with the liquor. With a brilliant smile, she turned and carried a glass to Julian and one to Perth, then retrieved hers. "To a satisfactory ending of this duel," she toasted. All three took a sip. A sigh of relief escaped her as the two men gulped theirs. "Would you care for more?" She waited, stiff with expectation.

"I believe I would," Perth answered.

"Has a taint," Camber said. He looked at her suspiciously.

"Yes, it does taste a little off," she agreed, "but Perth commented earlier, before you arrived, that it isn't the finest." She kept her eyes wide and innocent.

"Probably so," he answered. "Yes, I will take more."

She fetched their glasses and once again turned her back to them. One glass she filled a third full of laudanum, topping it with wine, the second had all wine. She faced them again and passed out the glasses. This time both men drank more leisurely.

Had she given Julian enough to knock him out?

She didn't know. Sipping her own wine delicately, she tried to watch him without seeming obvious. Did his eyes droop just a little? Was his mouth the teensiest bit relaxed? Turning her gaze, she caught Perth watching her with a question in his eyes. She let her look skim past him.

"Would you care for more?" she asked again, jumping to her feet to grab their glasses before they could refuse. She repeated her prior actions, pressing the refilled goblets on the gentlemen. "I think I need some more, too," she muttered, thankful that the laudanum bottle was too dark to see inside. She returned to her seat near Julian with a nervous laugh.

"What's wrong, sweetings?" He leaned close to her, slurring his words ever so slightly.

"Uh, nothing," she managed. He was beginning to look a little foxed.

"I'm glad," he said, "because now I am sure this is a poor-quality wine. You would think that being this close to the coast, and with the embargoes on French imports finally lifted, that the landlord would carry a better quality."

Dami watched him openly now. His eyes were glazing over and his movements were slowing down. She was sure that he would soon succumb to the drug.

He set his empty glass on the floor and flung one arm around her shoulders. He was heavy, leaning against her. She looked into his eyes where the black of his pupils dwarfed the color of his irises. As she watched, understanding dawned on him, and with it an anger that finished the job the drug had begun, until his eyes seemed obsidian chips in a face of white marble.

"You've drugged me with the laudanum," he thundered, but his voice was weak and floated out.

She cringed back from his arm, unsure how strong he still was. In the background, she heard Perth chuckle. She flicked him an irritated glance. The man was forever laughing at what she did.

"You'd better have a good reason, my girl," Julian interrupted her concentration on the earl, "or you will rue it when I . . . finally . . . wake . . . up. . . ." His lids drifted down and his body sagged onto her, pinning her under his weight.

She pushed at him, but was unable to budge him an inch. "Help me," she commanded Perth.

He rose to tower above them, a smirk turning his face into a mask of sinister purpose. "It would serve you right if I left you to suffer under him until he regains consciousness, but since I'm not that malevolent, I will extricate you from his unloverlike embrace."

Later, Dami found herself free of Julian and standing in the room Perth had ordered for her upon their arrival. Next door to her, Julian was sleeping off the effect of the laudanum she'd bludgeoned him with. On the other side of her, Perth was resting, planning to wait out Julian's recovery. She hadn't planned on that. Somehow, she didn't quite know how, she had intended to convince Perth to flee Julian's wrath before it was too late. To that purpose, she'd screeched at him for thirty minutes, saying that he would only be killed or gain himself another scar on the opposite side of his face. Instead of scaring him, she had first amused him, so that his guffaws

...ght the landlord inquiring if everything was ...actory; then she had finally irritated him, so ...at he had sent her packing to her room while he had Camber removed from the parlor.

At a momentary standstill, she sought another plan. There had to be something. She couldn't achieve this much only to see it fade like smoke with no fire to stoke it. "Aha," she mused. "I have it now." She rang her bell, summoning the landlord.

Chapter Twelve

An hour later Dami knocked on Perth's door. At his "come in," she entered, unable to keep the smile off her face. He glanced up at her, simultaneously finishing his last bit of eggs.

"You seem pleased with yourself." His eyes narrowed, but immediately relaxed.

"I am, milord," she answered. She glanced toward the bed, but felt no fear on that account, so she went to a small chair closer to him and sat down.

"I suppose," he said, taking a long drink of his warm ale, "that you are up to something else. Somehow, though, it doesn't worry me." He finished the drink and wiped his mouth with the large white napkin.

"I imagine you will be secretly relieved when you find out." She leaned back, still smiling. "It appears to me that you aren't all that eager to fight Camber."

His look was enigmatic. "Perhaps."

"Well, anyway, I've solved your problem of how to back graciously out of the situation you've gotten yourself into without looking like a coward. I know how you gentlemen put honor before all else . . . or something like that." She sat up straighter, preparing to lower her surprise on him. He yawned. "You must be getting tired, Perth. It wouldn't surprise me."

"It wouldn't? Now, I wonder why?"

He didn't look too concerned. In fact, Dami thought he looked almost amused.

"To be honest, it would surprise me if you weren't tired." She couldn't help it. Her voice was smug and her satisfied smile wouldn't go away, no matter how she tried to wipe it off her face.

"I imagine it would. You must have laced my ale with enough laudanum to down a horse."

Dami's mouth dropped. "You knew?"

He got up from his chair and moved to the bed. He loosened his shirt some more, pulled off his boots, and reclined on the well-worn brown comforter.

"A guess, but one based on carefully watching you the last month. I must admit to being a little surprised at how Camber fell for your performance earlier." He shook his head, a grin tugging at his lips. "I knew he was besotted, but until then I didn't realize just how much. Still, it was a performance that the great Siddons would envy." His eyelids drooped, and he seemed to force them open.

"I was rather proud of it myself. Although I must admit to some serious qualms when you insisted on chuckling at everything I did." She would be magnanimous. After all, she had won.

"How did you get the landlord to agree to drug me?" There was only mild curiosity in his slurred words.

"That part was easy. I threatened him with the magistrate if a duel were fought here, then I emphasized to him how notoriety of that sort would only hurt his business." She was very satisfied with her skill.

"Silly chit," he chided, tumbling down her complacency. "That kind of notoriety would have improved his business. But if he was bacon-brained enough to believe you, then he deserves what he gets." He yawned heartily. "More important, how do you intend to keep Camber from skinning you alive?"

"I . . . I don't know yet. But," she brightened, "I don't anticipate any unsurmountable problems. I trust he cares enough for me to understand that I couldn't let him risk his life in a duel with you."

"Hmm . . . you might be able to do that, but, Lady Damaris, you'd best be careful how you go about it. You haven't told him that you aren't the lightskirt he believes you to be," at her nod of agreement, he went on, "and he won't take kindly to being made a butt of your game. Camber has always been able to laugh at himself—within reason, but being bamboozled by a woman he is half in love with will be quite a different story."

His eyelids sank down, and his hands, which had been on his chest, slid to his sides. Dami realized that he had fallen asleep. Her brow furrowed with worry. Perth had warned her of something she was only too aware of. She pushed the fear aside. Right now she had to get Perth out of here before Julian woke up.

With a sigh of relief, Dami sank into the cushioned chair drawn up to Julian's bed. He should be awakening soon, and she wanted to get the next ordeal over with as soon as possible. Even though it was early summer, and stayed light till late in the evening, the sky was beginning to turn hazy. Carrying out her plan had taken longer than she'd anticipated. Luckily, Julian had slept through the day. She must have overdosed him.

A movement on the bed caught her attention. Julian's eyelids were fluttering open. His pupils were still large, but some of the glassiness was gone.

"How long have I been sleeping?" His voice was raspy and low.

"It's going on nine," she answered, getting up to fetch him a glass of water. "Here," she handed him the glass, "this will help with the cotton mouth." She tried to smile, but her apprehension made it stiff.

"Thank you," he said, taking the glass. He downed the contents in one long gulp. Sinking back into the pillows, he gave her the glass. "That did help, but don't think playing the Good Samaritan is going to save your hide when you're the reason I'm in this condition."

To play for time, she took the glass back to the washstand and carefully placed it near the pitcher. When she felt sufficiently composed, she turned to face him. "Would you rather be bleeding to death from a sword wound?"

She let that sink in while she returned to her chair. Sitting in it, she noticed it didn't feel as warm or as safe as before.

His brows drew together. "You are a meddlesome wench. Neither Perth nor I intended to kill." He raised on one elbow and glowered at her. "Until you learn to tell the difference, I suggest that you keep your nose out of men's business."

"Humph! You are ungrateful. As it is, I arranged it so that neither one of you had to fight and take a risk, and," she leaned forward to emphasize each word, "I did it in such a way that neither one of you lost face. I drugged him, too."

"That's rich! Neither one of us 'lost face.' Hah! If it became known that a slip of a chit drugged us both we would be the laughingstock of London." He leaned forward until their noses were inches apart. "Neither one of us would *ever* live it down."

"Ingrate." She flounced to the door. "See if I ever try to help you again."

"If you didn't get into every scrape that came your way, I wouldn't have been in a position to need your help." He sat up, gingerly holding his head every inch of the way. "And while I'm thinking of it, what did you do with Perth after you drugged him insensate?"

"That was the easy part," she answered with a small smile. "I got a message to the captain of his yacht, which he had in the harbor and had threatened me with. The captain came for him and I suggested that the earl leave the country for a couple months." She put her hand on the doorknob.

"No you don't, minx," he ordered. "Come over here and let me sample the wares I was willing to put my life on the line for. And if you're lucky, I'll forget this last contretemps. Besides," he laughed fully, "it is worth it to think of Perth passed out like a baby and being carried to his yacht and told not to return — and all done by a slip of a girl."

She caught herself laughing with him before she pulled herself up sharply and glared at him. One minute he berated her, the next he expected her to put herself within his grasp for amorous pleasures!

He caught her hand and pulled her toward him. She

came to a standstill so close that his face was level with her bosom. If he chose he could reach out and touch it with his lips.

"You've redone your buttons," he said regretfully. "I was hoping to find them still open." He sighed theatrically. "Now I shall have to go to all the trouble of undoing them again."

"Oh," she gasped, "you certainly won't go to all that trouble." She pulled away, but he held her immobile.

"Come here, Amalie," he said softly, pulling her onto the bed.

Thigh to thigh, they sat with his arm circling her waist like a band of iron. She thought her breathing would stop on her, so hard was it to get a breath. Heat licked her body everywhere she made contact with his.

She brought a hand up to smooth back her hair, licked dry lips. "I need to get back to my room."

"You don't mean that, sweetings," he murmured into her ear.

His warm breath wafted against the side of her neck, making her skin break out in goose bumps. If she didn't get away soon, she would be lost. Or found?

"No," she paused, "I mean, yes, I do mean that. It's time I went to my room and sent a message to Johnny, that is John FitzHubert, telling him where I am."

His lips nuzzled her earlobe. "Surely after this long, a message can wait a little longer. I haven't properly thanked you for, uhm . . . saving me from Perth's diabolical plan."

She whipped her face around, trying to catch the sarcasm in his eyes that she heard in his voice. "You're laughing at me." She reared back. "I only did it for your own good."

He pulled her back and laughed softly, causing his teeth to nip gently at her ear. "I know you did, sweetings. And I only want to show you that I am properly appreciative of all the trouble you went to. Conniving of that order must be exhausting."

"It was." She stiffened her spine. She wasn't going to let him woo her after he'd ranted at her and then mocked her. It wasn't safe to be in a room alone with the man, particularly when there was a bed present.

Shadows crept into the corners of the room as the sun sank lower over the green countryside. Dami glanced nervously around the room, searching for a candle.

"Looking for something?" he asked from the fragrant nest of her hair.

His words flowed over her like warm wine. "Isn't there a candle we can light?" she said in a rush, desperate to draw his attention away from her sensitive skin.

"I don't know. I haven't seen this room in daylight." He continued to cuddle her, his lips moving moistly over the heated flesh of her neck.

"Well, there must be." She pushed against his chest to no avail. "Julian, please. I don't want this. Not like this."

"Amalie, what do you want?" When her lips parted, he said before she could, "I know. You want love. You have that. I love you. I love you more than I ever thought it possible to love a woman. I want to give you everything it is possible for a man to give a woman."

She stared at him. His words were terse, but they winged to her heart and eased it so that she melted toward him. He loved her. He wanted to marry her.

"Oh, Julian, I thought I'd never hear you say those words." She raised her hand to cup his jaw, momentarily sidetracked by the roughness of the beard he was growing.

"I never thought to say them."

Without thought, she was back in his arms. Her hands twisted into his hair, pulling his lips to hers. Not allowing him to move, she held him close, felt his fingers kneading the tight muscles of her back as they stair-stepped to her hips.

Warmth and something else she had so little experience of that she was afraid to name it made their way through her body, starting at the pit of her stomach and working outward in waves of pleasure. She sank into the warm caress of the mattress. Julian's hands played over her, leaving buttons undone where they went. Her own stumbled over him, until they both lay naked on the bed.

His lips locked to hers, evoking sensations she wanted to continue for ever. His strokes soothed and excited her at once. His body, with its dry, hot skin riding hers set her afire.

His mouth left hers and he began to rain stinging kisses down her face to her neck, down her chest to her hips . . . lower.

"Don't," she managed, as her fingers grabbed his shoulders to pull him back.

Immediately he was back, his lips resting against her flushed cheek, his arms cradling her to his chest. Her breathing began to return to normal. She was thankful for the dark that kept her from seeing his face in this most intimate of acts, that kept him from seeing her.

"Julian," she whispered, "I don't think I can go through with this. I truly don't." She burrowed her face into the hollow of his shoulder, felt herself shiver when his hand ran down her back.

"Trust me."

He began to kiss her, butterfly touches that tickled. His fingers traced swirls on her back and shoulders, working down to her waist, twisting lower, tickling so lightly that it was exquisite pleasure. Flicks that barely touched her skin sent shivers through her. His lips glided to hers. He played with the nerve-rich skin of her mouth before asking admittance with his tongue.

Too bemused to stop, Dami opened up to him. His tongue and teeth stroked and nipped her, while his fingers continued their journey of delight. Caught in the seductive appeal of her senses, she flowered under him. Tension built with each caress he gave her, until she felt she could take no more.

"Julian . . ." Her lips were moist and swollen from his.

"Hush, Amalie. I won't stop. Don't worry."

Distantly, she knew his voice sounded strained and harsh, but it floated by her as rapture pulsated through her.

Later, she lay in the nest of his arms, rubbing the hairs that rimmed his nipples. She felt warm and satisfied, tired but exhilarated.

"Julian?"

"Hmm?"

"Was that all? I mean, not that I didn't enjoy it, but

I thought there was something else. At least," she stopped, unable to express what she'd seen farm animals do when coupling.

He laughed softly. "No, that wasn't all, Amalie. You are still virginal."

"But, I thought you wanted . . . that is."

"Yes, I wanted, still want, but I first wanted you to experience the joy I can give you without the pain."

A sliver of moonlight twisted through the heavy curtains to fall on his face. His eyes were silver in the cold light. Looking at him, the angles of his face pronounced, his lips full and sensual, she felt doubt assail her again. She had given him almost everything possible. He said he loved her. She hoped he hadn't lied to her.

"Planning to welsh on me now?" He said the words easily, but she felt the arm around her shoulders tense. "Because if you are, at least tell me before I get my hopes up."

There was a wicked gleam in his eyes, and she sensed he'd just made a joke, though she didn't know how. "You find me amusing," she said and found her voice sounded petulant.

"Infinitely." He pulled her into the curve of his body and stroked her hair back from her face so that it fanned out behind her on the pillow.

She raised her face to say more, but his finger on her lips stopped her. She stared at him, caught by the look in his eyes. His lips lowered to hers.

Chapter Thirteen

Dami stretched long and hard, pushing outward with her hands. Something firm, but yielding, stopped her. Memory flooded back. Her eyes flew open.

"Good morning." Julian's eyes smiled into hers.

She grabbed at the sheets to cover her bosom, which had become exposed during her stretch. Averting her eyes, she mumbled, "Morning."

Squirming to put distance between their naked bodies, she worried about what one said to a man who had made love to one the night before. She supposed it was academic, but she couldn't ignore him. Neither could she bring herself to look at him. A hot rush colored her as pictures of their lovemaking flashed through her mind. Unable to stand it, she turned her back to him.

Julian smiled at her missish behavior, so at odds with the wanton of last night. After getting over her first shock, she had responded more fully than his most vivid fantasies had ever portrayed her doing.

Still smiling, he ran a finger down the ridge of her backbone.

"Amalie, it is only I. You can look me in the eye." His finger lingered at the swell of her hip.

His words soothed her, while his finger made her throb. She rolled to face him, the sheet pulling tight across her full bosom, eager to experience again with him the fullness of their love. But now she had to tell him who she was. Now that they were to be married, he needed to know her real identity.

Looking at the tenderness in his grey eyes, usually so cold, she hesitated. She didn't want the warmth to turn to disgust, and heaven only knew she'd been warned often enough about his views on women to know he wouldn't take kindly to the charade she'd pulled on him.

She took a deep breath and willed her eyes to stay on him. "Julian," she plucked at the sheet, pulling it higher, hoping that by covering her bareness she would also give herself more strength, "Julian . . . I'm," her courage deserted her, "I'm not a good housekeeper. I wasn't raised to keep a home, I was raised to manage an estate." Her eyes pleaded. He was intelligent, surely he would realize she was trying to tell him she wasn't what he thought. Only a lord's daughter would be taught estate management. "I feel it only fair that you know I won't be able to run your households the way you expect."

His laugh was soft. "That's what housekeepers are for. As for the estate, why, since you are the daughter of an estate manager it's not surprising that you learned the rudiments." He kissed her on the nose. "Don't worry, that's not what I want you for anyway." He grinned lasciviously and ran his eyes, now hot with need, over her.

She blushed. Somehow she had to make him understand.

"What I'm trying to tell you is that you will have to be patient with me after we are married." She cringed back from his look of thunderstruck amazement. She had bungled it. "I'm a quick learner. I will be able to do things competently after several months. But I will need time. I only tell you this because I realize that as a duke you will be doing a lot of entertaining. I know that as your wife I will be expected to arrange these things and be a proper hostess." She stopped. Her heart was beating so fast her throat was closing painfully.

Without a word, he drew away from her, his face an unemotional mask. She moaned softly and closed her eyes. She knew her inability to keep house and be a proper hostess would be hard to accept by her husband, but this bad? When was he going to say something? The mattress moved, and she peeped at him. He was getting out of bed and pulling on his breeches.

Buttoning the waistband, Julian pulled a chair near the bed. Dami sat up, pulling the covers with her. She knew the next minutes were crucial to her future. Her fingers trembled and sweat broke out on her palms. She wished she could get dressed too, then perhaps she wouldn't feel so vulnerable.

"Amalie." He had started sprawled out in the seat, but saying her name brought him erect. "Amalie, I am a duke, and my name goes back to Henry the Eighth. Consequently, my wife must be of impecca-

213

ble lineage and unblemished reputation. I owe these things to my name, my dependants, and my heirs. This is something I can't alter to suit my own needs as a man."

Her face blanched. She knew what was coming next, and she wanted to stop him. Her hand raised to ward off the verbal blow she knew was coming. She didn't feel the sheet slither down to her waist.

"Amalie, this has nothing to do with how I feel about you, but you must understand that though I love you, I can't offer you marriage. Sweetings, I want to live my life with you, but because of who I am I must do it discreetly. Meanwhile, also because of who I am, I must marry a woman who is conversant with my world and acceptable in it."

Her face was white. "So, I'm nothing but another fancy piece to you. Another Mrs. Jones to be shrugged aside when the next trollop comes your way. All your pretty talk of love was just a ruse, is still just a ruse, to trick me into surrendering to you."

"Amalie, nothing is changed. I still want to take care of you. Only, I can't marry you. This arrangement isn't unusual. It is done all the time."

She stared at him in horror. "You are a hypocrite. I believed that you would put love before the material expectations of your world. I see that I was wrong."

"You're overwrought," he said curtly. He donned his shirt and boots. "I'll be in the parlor. When you are dressed, join me."

Dami heard the door close behind him. To think she had worried that he would be unable to accept the trick she'd pulled on him! To think she was gullible enough to believe he offered her marriage even though he thought her below him socially!

She pulled herself out of bed, unaware of her nakedness, and went to the small oak desk where she pulled out a sheet of paper, pen, and ink to write Johnny a long overdue letter. After sanding it and folding it, she rose, put her drab brown dress on, and rang for a maid. She gave the letter to the girl and told her to send it by messenger.

That done, she collapsed into the chair. Suppose she told Julian her true identity and forced him into marriage. The fiery glow of revenge tempted her to this course, but she knew it wouldn't work. She wanted love, had wanted him because she thought him capable of love strong enough to overcome all boundaries. She had given herself to him with that belief.

A scratch on the door brought her back to reality. The maid peeked in. "Pardon me, ma'am, but His Grace sends his compliments and requests your presence."

She went below. Without knocking, she pushed open the door to the parlor and strode in. He was sitting near the fire, a decanter of brandy on a table near his arm, a half-empty snifter in his fingers.

"Milord," she said frostily, "you wished to see me?"

His face was ravaged. "Yes, I did, Amalie. Please be seated." He waved to a chair several feet from his. "I know how I've hurt you. I didn't mean to mislead you, I thought you understood my position." He put his empty glass down. "Look at me." She turned to face him, her lips set in mutinous lines. "Is there any

215

possibility of rapproachment?" At her stony gaze, he said, "I thought not. I want you to know I will do anything in my power to help you. If there is a child from our union, I expect you to tell me so that I may support you."

The sounds of a large coach pulling into the yard distracted her. Ignoring his last words, she went to the window where she pulled back the curtains to see Johnny jumping out of a traveling chaise.

"Johnny is here. He will take care of me." Without looking at him she walked out of the room and descended the stairs.

Johnny met her in the tap room. She went up to him and put a hand on his shoulder. "Let's go now."

"Blister it, Dami, I can't let that bounder get away with what he's done to you." He shrugged off her hand and made for the stairs.

Her voice stayed him. "Johnny, your calling him out would only cause exactly the kind of scandal we want to avoid."

The dead quiet of her words stopped him. He turned and guided her into the closed coach.

Dami kept her eyes cast down, seemingly fascinated with the pleats she was making in the gold muslin of her morning gown. She hadn't expected this interview with her mother to be easy, but somehow she hadn't expected it to be this horrifyingly hard, either. She found herself shrinking from the picture she painted of her portrayal of a cyprian and Camber's reaction to her.

"So," the dowager rounded on her, "you even went

so far as to share Camber's bed and now you tell me you refuse to tell him who you are and force his hand." For a second, her eyes held pity. "He would have to marry you then."

"No, Mama, please. If he can't love me for myself, I would as lief not have to spend the rest of my life in the enforced intimacy of marriage." She bit her lip. "And if I don't become in the, uhm . . . family way, then there is really no reason to do so."

"No reason?" roared Lady FitzHubert. "No reason?" She raised her fist to her forehead and struck a theatrical pose. "What kind of henwit have I raised?" Dropping her hand, she glared at Dami. "Listen well, my gel, you have been dishonored. Should that become known, no amount of dowry or social pull will get you a husband. Do you understand what I am saying?" Dami nodded. "You will remain a spinster the rest of your life. Is that what you want?"

Dami wrung her hands. Of course that wasn't what she wanted, but what choice did she have. She had fallen in love with an idealized version of Camber, had given everything she possessed to that vision, only to lose it all.

"Better not to marry than to marry for convenience only." She wouldn't let this defeat her. "You, of all people, Mama, ought to know that a love match is the only kind. You and Papa were in love. You can't deny it. Everyone who saw you together commented on it. Would you force something less on me?"

The dowager sank down beside Dami on the settee. "No, child, I wouldn't, but the enormity of what you've done is beyond belief. Why didn't you come to me instead of going off in that half-baked fashion of yours?"

"Because you wouldn't have allowed it." That was unanswerable, and Dami held it to her parent's credit that she didn't try to refute it.

Lady Cleve took a deep breath and made her decision. "That's settled, then. Right now we must decide what to do with you in the meantime." She furrowed her brows in thought.

"Kit is going to Paris and has asked me to go." That had been last week, but Dami supposed the offer still stood. It would be the perfect excuse for her to drop out of London society. "Kit's mother, Lady Sebastian, is taking her, and Simon is still there on Wellington's staff."

The dowager stood up and paced to the fireplace. "That might work. Yes, that's it. We will nose it about that you have been suffering from chicken pox for the last couple of days—to explain your absence—and that you have decided to follow the rest of the ten thousand to Paris to celebrate Napoleon's defeat and incarceration in Elba." She swung around. "I will follow in several weeks. After I have scotched any on dits still linking you with Camber because of your shameful behavior at Lady Sefton's ball. But remember, if you find yourself with an embarrassing reminder of your folly, you are to contact me immediately!"

"Yes, Mama," Dami said demurely. It wasn't the solution she had dreamed of when she had first set out on this crooked path, but it was much better than she had any right to expect after what had happened. A wiser girl would have known better than to fall in love with a womanizer—no matter how charming he might be.

Julian leaned back, put his feet up on the grate, and reread the note from Lord Liverpool. What the devil was going on that the Prime Minister had to contact him now? He couldn't expect him to drop everything and rush off to Paris. He finished the letter for the second time. It appeared that Liverpool expected just that. Some damn fool had intimated that Napoleon planned to escape from Elba. Well, that was old mutton. He tossed the letter in the fire.

Whom did he owe his first loyalty to: himself or his country? It was a week since the debacle at Felixstowe. Watching Amalie leave and not rushing after her had taken all the self-discipline he had. It had been like watching a part of his soul walk out of his life. The fright that thought conjured had held him immobile while she drove off with Johnny FitzHubert. At the same time, the sight of FitzHubert had ground in the fact that he had already offered for Lady Damaris FitzHubert's hand and been accepted by Simon FitzHubert. As a man of honor, he could no more welsh on an offer of marriage than he could cut off his right hand. He smiled ruefully. Cutting off his right hand would probably be easier.

But the urge to go after Amalie and offer her the marriage she prized so highly had cost him emotionally.

"Damn," he said, jumping to his feet. Jerking open the door, he yelled, "Bring me my hat and gloves. I'm going out."

It was a balmy night and early enough to still be light as he made his way to Whites. The club was deserted, except for one other gentleman reading the daily paper. As he approached, Julian realized it was Lord Liverpool. It was too late to turn around, so he decided to brazen it out.

"Ah, Camber," Liverpool said pleasantly, laying his paper aside. "I was wondering when you would grace Whites again. Been waiting for the last two days. Have a seat." He pulled up a red leather wing chair.

Not wanting to seem more churlish than he already had, Julian sank into the chair. He felt doom moving in on him. "I was out of town for a couple of days, and when I got back I had a mound of correspondence to wade through." Even as he made the excuse, he denigrated himself for falling into the trap. It wasn't that Liverpool was an imposing personality, for he wasn't. It was what the man stood for: God, and country, and the Union Jack.

"Right. Well, not to use roundaboutation, are you going to accept the assignment? You know how hard it will be if Boney does escape. We've no way to stop him. All our best troops are still in the Americas, and the other allies will follow our lead or lack of one."

Julian rumpled his hair. "I know, I know."

"Wouldn't have asked it if there were another way. Wellington sent a special courier to ask for you in person. Seems the duke holds you in high esteem." He toyed with his quizzing glass. "And it's not as if you have a wife or children to consider."

Julian winced. No, it wasn't as if he had that to contend with. A mistress who had jilted him didn't count. "Just how serious does Wellington think this is?"

"Very. You see, we've had a leak in the War Ministry for some time now. In fact, some of our troop strength and locations have been leaking out for the last four years. Nothing major enough to cause us to lose a battle we would have otherwise won, but enough to lose more lives than needed."

Julian winced at that. "It appears that you have an irrefutable argument. Under the circumstances I must bow gracefully to your need. Just what exactly is going on?"

Lord Liverpool beckoned to a nearby waiter. "See that we are undisturbed." Then he turned back to Julian. "Our information indicates that the leak is someone on Wellington's staff in Paris, someone who is also high in the War Ministry. Wellington will have that for you. This same leak also seems to be involved in Bonapartist plots to free Napoleon. At the present, this is the most serious problem."

"Just what do you expect of me?"

"As you know, with Boney's incarceration in Elba, everyone and his wife is in Paris right now. If you were to show, it wouldn't cause comment. Particularly as you are known to frequent the, uhhrumph, uh . . ."

"Less genteel places?"

"As I was saying. You could keep your ears open for any hints or someone looking for people sympathetic to Bonaparte's cause. Then pass the information on to Wellington and never become dangerously involved." At the fierce look in Camber's eyes, Liverpool explained, "Not that you aren't known for your courage, but no sense in risking yourself when you no longer have an heir. Might even meet a suitable miss while you're there. Well, it doesn't hurt to be on the lookout."

"You are perfectly clear, and as I'm sure you already knew, I am forced to accept this assignment." He rose and made a shallow bow. "If you will excuse me, I have a lot of packing to do."

Late that night, lying in his bed for the last time, Julian pondered the situation he found himself in. He was in love with a woman he couldn't marry and so was forced to give her up since she would settle for nothing less; engaged to the sister of his closest friend whom he'd never seen, let alone met; and about to embark on what could be a dangerous assignment, regardless of how Lord Liverpool chose to gloss over the danger.

He grunted and turned to his side. His life was becoming more complicated with each passing day. Still, he might be able to turn this trip to his advantage. He could see Simon and feel him out personally about his sister. Maybe get out of his untimely betrothal?

He flipped to his back again and grimaced. That would solve nothing. Even if he managed to get out of this engagement, he still had to marry and father an heir. Might already have fathered an heir.

Chapter Fourteen

"Simon," Dami said, entering the large drawing room of their Paris residence, "the footman said you wanted to talk to me."

The tall, slim man standing by the windows turned as she spoke his name. Simon and Johnny should have been twins, she thought, looking at the dark curls and laughing blue eyes that looked so much like Johnny's. The only major differences were Simon's stronger jaw, square and determined, and the lines carved into his cheeks that hadn't been there a year ago. He'd lost weight too, though you couldn't tell it by the snug fit of his dark blue morning coat.

"Dami, come here and let me give you a proper hug." His grin was infectious as she flung herself into his arms. "I couldn't do it last night with all the bustle and hustle of your arrival." He squeezed until she yelped. "Yup, you're still the unladylike baggage who would squeal at anything, regardless of the situation and the people present." She made a face at him as he put her down. "Better sit down."

"Why?" Surely tales of her kidnapping and subsequent interlude with Camber hadn't reached Simon.

She wrinkled her brows suspiciously. Johnny, moonling that he was, would know better than to tell Simon something like that. Or he'd better.

"To start," he interrupted her thoughts, "what are your first impressions of Paris? It's very hectic, and I expect that you and Kit will have every minute packed with outings." He sauntered to the sideboard where he poured some ratafia for her and some port for himself.

"Well, since it was after midnight when we arrived last night, and I have been lolling about in self-pity the last two weeks due to seasickness and then carriage-sickness, I can't say I've formed any impressions." She took her ratafia and sipped delicately at it. She knew Simon well enough to know her opinion of Paris wasn't what he was leading up to.

"Hmm. In that case, you won't mind if a friend of mine escorts you around. You know, shows you the sights." He studied his wine as though something of immense importance lurked in its depths.

"Simon, I don't see how one leads to the other, but I suppose that Kit won't mind if a friend of yours accompanies us." She gave him the ghost of a smile. "It isn't a woman, is it?"

"No, my dear, it isn't." His blue eyes, turning serious, watched her. "It's an old friend who fought with me in the Peninsula, even saved my life at one point when my horse was shot out from under me"

"In that case, I must be on my best behavior with him." She rose and walked to her brother, putting her arms around him and resting her head on his shoulder. "I owe him a great deal."

He rubbed her head with his chin. "Yes, well, that

aside, he's also a great gun and a man I'd be honored to call brother."

She pulled back. "Just what are you trying to say, Simon?"

"I've bungled this badly. I've been asked for your hand in marriage. Of course, I gave my consent, but stipulated that you must be agreeable." The smile he gave her was lopsided. "I can't force you into a union that is distasteful to you, no matter how I might want it."

"Simon, you are placing quite a burden on me, and you haven't even told me the gentleman's name." It was impossible to tell Simon that no respectable man would want her now, and that having been so thoroughly disillusioned by Camber, she wanted no man.

"Don't look so aggrieved, my dear. He is everything that is agreeable and quite a catch."

"Please, Simon, stop the quizzing and tell me his name." She felt dread gyrating in her stomach.

"All right. It is my war buddy, Julian St. John, duke of Camber."

Dami's eyes went wide with shock. "Oh, no," she wailed and collapsed in a heap.

When she awoke, Dami found herself on the purple sofa in the drawing room. The matching velvet drapes, trimmed in gold thread, were pulled against the strong afternoon sun. There was no fire in the grate because of the heat. And she was surrounded by people.

Bending over her, concern creasing his face, was

Simon, on her left she perceived Kit, and at her feet stood Johnny.

"Heard all the racket," Johnny offered, "and couldn't leave the house without finding out why you was screaming like a banshee."

She grimaced at him. Leave it to Johnny to put it as ungraciously as possible. "I'm sure," she said, trying to sit up.

"Here let me help you, Dami," Kit said, putting an arm around Dami's shoulders.

"No, no, let me," said Simon. "You're barely big enough to take care of yourself, Kit, let alone trying to lift Dami. Besides, it was my fault she fainted." He helped her up while Kit plumped the sofa cushions. "I tried to lead into it, but I guess it isn't every day a young lady barely on the marriage mart receives an offer of mariage from the most eligible bachelor in the ton."

Dami's eyes met the startled ones of her twin. She decided it would be best to try and stand. She needed to be near Johnny to keep him from blurting out anything.

"Please, Johnny, come help me stand up. I'm convinced that if I don't start moving immediately, I will become a permanent invalid."

Simon frowned, and Kit looked puzzled, but Dami's imperious tone set Johnny jumping. He moved forward, elbowing Simon out of the way, and grabbed her by the waist.

"The fat's in the pan now," he muttered for her ears only.

She gave him a quelling look.

"Who wants to marry her?" Kit asked.

"Your cousin," Simon answered.

"Camber?" Johnny expostulated. "I say, not the . . . ouch!" He glared at Dami who gave him an angelic look.

"Yes, Camber," Simon said with a satisfied smile. "He wrote me two months ago asking for Dami's hand, and of course I gave him permission to court her. Unfortunately, it seems he was unable to locate her in all the bustle of the season. Anyway, so he said yesterday."

"Yesterday?" Dami felt herself getting dizzy. This had to be a bad dream that would go away as soon as she could wake herself up. She pinched her arm hard. Nothing happened. "What do you mean, 'yesterday'?"

"He was here yesterday. Seems he wanted to come see what all the fuss is about here, what with all the cream of London society flocking here for the summer. Thought while he was here, he'd pay a visit and confirm that I still feel of the mind to allow him to approach you. Of course, I told him the same thing as before." Simon smiled at Dami. "It is your decision, but I strongly urge you to accept."

"I say," Johnny began again, "she can't very well do that. Not after . . . ouch!" He turned his head to Dami and muttered under his breath.

"What is wrong with you, Johnny?" Simon said, "You sound let in the attic." His eyes narrowed suspiciously. "Is there something I ought to know about?"

"No, of course not, Simon," Dami inserted. "I'm sure all Johnny is worried about is Camber's reputation." She tried to keep her voice light. "You know he is known for consorting with unacceptable persons."

"Be that as it may," Simon said, "it doesn't make him any less a desirable *parti*."

"Of course not," Dami said bitterly, "he's a man. If a woman carried on as he does, she would be ostracized by one and all."

I know it's not fair," Simon said in a soothing voice, "but it is the way of our world."

Dami saw the worry on Simon's face after her small outburst. Perhaps she could use it to advantage. She certainly couldn't accept Camber's proposal. Moreover, she didn't want to. He was only marrying Lady Damaris FitzHubert to use her as a brood mare. Somehow she would get around this difficulty and punish Camber in the process. She would make him rue the day he made Amalie fall in love with him, all the while planning to marry her alter ego, Lady Damaris. And all that aside, she couldn't very well let him see her and realize that the Amalie he had seduced was really the sister of his best friend. He would revile her for deceiving him at the same time he would feel forced to marry her anyway.

"I think I am beginning to feel faint again," Dami said in a weak voice. "I think I need to go to my room. If you will excuse me." She turned to go, pulling hard on Johnny's sleeve.

"You're the one who's sick, Dami, not me," Johnny said ungraciously.

"But you are the one who must help me up the stairs, brother." She emphasized the last word. Outside, with the doors closed, she released Johnny's arm.

"What's all this about, Dami?" he asked in an injured voice. "And look at my Hessians. There is a smudge on each one, thanks to your foot. It took my valet all morning to polish these to a mirror shine, now he will have to do it over."

"Is that all you can think of? After you almost told Simon everything?" She could feel her anger at Camber boiling up into her berating of Johnny. "If you had stopped to think, I wouldn't have had to step on your precious boots. Honestly, Johnny! You know I can't marry Camber—don't want to now—but I can't tell Simon why, either. If I did, we would both be in the fat, since you have aided and abetted me from the start."

He looked at her, for once bereft of words.

"What we must do," she mused, "is come up with another plan to put him off of marrying Lady Damaris. And I think I have an idea."

"Oh no, you don't," Johnny said. "That's the last thing you need."

"No, no. This one will be perfect. Come along," she said, pulling him up the stairs to her room. "This one will be fail proof. Trust me."

Kit stood in the drawing room talking with her cousin Camber, chills of excitement creeping along her spine. She knew Dami was up to something. When she'd gone up to her room earlier, Dami had refused to let her in. Putting her ear to the door, Kit had heard noises indicating a large amount of activity. That, coupled with Suzy, Dami's maid, leaving the house twice in one afternoon and returning with a very large hat box, led Kit to assume the worse. Dami was up to her old tricks. Finally realizing that Dami was adamant about not seeing her, she had sent in a message that Camber would dine with them.

"Cat got your tongue, Kit?" Camber asked. "You have barely spoken a word since I arrived — which is unusual at best, dangerous at worst."

"Oh," she strived for nonchalance, "nothing so dramatic. I am still in shock at the speed with which we traveled here, only to find you ahead of us. It must have been a precipitate decision on your part."

"Hmmm. You might call it that." He surveyed the other occupants of the room. "I gather we are dining *en famille*."

"Yes, Simon felt it would be best if only Mother, Johnny, Dami, you, he, and I were present on our first night. None of us has been feeling well. Mother and Dami were sick the whole trip across the Channel, and then even more when we hit the rutted roads. France's roads are deplorable."

"Ah, but they haven't benefited from the brilliance of Mr. Macadam, as we have. Consequently, even their large roads are only comparable to our shabby country lanes, all dirt and potholes." He looked around the room again, raised his auburn brows at Simon. Simon shook his head. "I wonder what is keeping Lady Damaris. She isn't still sick, is she?"

Kit darted a glance at the door. "No. But she did keep to her room all afternoon, so it's possible she has a touch of something." The sound of the door caught her attention.

"Oh, my goodness," she whispered.

Camber gulped audibly. "A vision," he murmured.

Simon took a drink just as he looked up. "Ah, ahem —" He choked on his wine, spilling some down the pristine whiteness of his shirt.

"Dami?" said Lady Sebastian in amazement.

"Strap me, we're in for it now," Johnny muttered, to no one in particular.

The object of their attention threw a quelling look at all concerned and sailed into the room. Her hair was hidden by a hideous black velvet turban, a large silver ostrich feather sticking up in the back. It accentuated her high forehead and the flesh-colored cloth that masked her from hairline to chin. The eye-slits effectively hid her eye color in the faulty light of the candles. She made for Kit and Camber.

Pulling up short, Dami extended her hand and dropped into a deep curtsy. Rising, her eyes flew to his face. No matter what he had done to her, or what she intended to do to him, she knew in that instant that she loved him irrevocably. Putting aside the urge to stroke his cheek, she said in a gutteral voice, "Your Grace, I'm pleased to make your acquaintance."

"The pleasure is mine," he answered, raising her. He gave her a once-over. Her gown, while the latest crack, fit her figure loosely. Either she had no figure and wished to disguise the fact, or, he thought cynically, she has lost weight since its fitting. However, the brandy color was very becoming to her complexion, or what he could see of it on her shoulders and bosom. He supposed her to have a bosom, howsoever small it might be.

"Thank you, milord," she said, breaking his train of thought. "Are you here long?"

He tried to see the color of her eyes, thinking he saw them twinkling. "Only as long as necessary. I have a few business matters to clear up, since trade has

231

once more commenced with France."

"Oh," she sounded shocked, "you can't mean you are engaged in . . . *trade*."

He shuddered inwardly. She was a snob, and there was nothing he detested more. "Not exactly. I am a part owner in stock on the Exchange that has dealings with France. Consequently, I thought it might behoove me to check matters out, in case I should sell out."

His tones were bland, but Dami was sure she detected undertones of loathing. Good! She turned to Kit, who continued to stare rudely at her. "Cat got your tongue?" Kit muttered something that was drowned in Camber's laugh. Dami could feel her temper rising. She worked her tongue around the cotton handkerchief stuffed in her mouth before rounding on him. "You find me amusing, milord? I suppose that is a good sign, considering your intentions." That shut him up, she thought with satisfaction. "Excuse me," she said, and made her way to Johnny.

Johnny saw her approaching and looked desperately around the room. She reached him before he could decide.

"Don't be so anxious to leave, brother dear." She gripped his sleeve.

"Dash it, Dami, this is the outside of enough. You never said you intended this." He gaped at her. "Ugh! but you look ugly. And what did you do to your voice? You sound like a bullfrog."

"Don't be crude," she said, pinching his arm.

He yanked his arm away. "First you ruin my boots and now you're trying to rip my coat. How am I ever going to cut a dash in fashion if you are forever undoing what it takes my valet hours to do?" His tirade wound down and he found himself beginning to enjoy the situation. "Did you see the way Camber looked when you entered? Why, I heard him gulp way over here, and it must be at least twenty feet away."

"Yes, he was rather rude." She giggled, stopping immediately when Simon approached them.

"What is the meaning of this, Dami?"

When he used that tone, she knew she was in trouble, but she had her tale ready. "Please," her whole body implored him, "don't give me away until I am able to explain *all* to you."

"It's a queer business, Dami." He gave her a rueful once-over. "I hope you have a good reason for this."

"I'm sure she does," interrupted Lady Sebastian. "But even if she doesn't, it's worth it to see Julian discommoded for once. The boy has become entirely too complacent about his place in life as it is." She winked broadly at Dami. "I'm behind you, my girl."

Dami found the older woman's bravado reassuring. She conveniently pushed from her mind the widow's reputation. Lady Sebastian, Miss Rosalie Smith-Jones before her marriage to the younger brother of Julian's father, was the spitting image of her daughter, with titian hair and green eyes. Their similiarity ended there. While Kit was everything agreeable, her mother was considered ramshackle. Even the death of her husband, three years earlier in a hunting accident had only temporarily blighted her spirits. Kit was prone to say her mama was the most fatiguing person she knew. But Dami found Lady Sebastian to be a kindred spirit.

Somehow, when they paired off for dinner, Dami found herself with Camber. She knew that to convince him he didn't want to marry her, she had to spend time in his company. On the other hand, he didn't need to look so handsome in his severe black evening clothes. And they didn't need to fit his figure so faithfully that they brought back images of their last time together. Hot flashes seemed to course through her body, making her burn and freeze by turns. She snorted.

"Did you say something, Lady Damaris?" Camber asked with a wicked grin.

"No, milord. I merely sneezed."

"Ah. I like to see a girl with a healthy sneeze, it is a good sign of lusty appetites."

She shot him a look of loathing, which she knew he couldn't see through her mask. Drat the man, he was baiting her. Well, two could play at that game.

"Oh, yes, we FitzHuberts are known for our appetites. Why, Mama," she silently apologized to her slim parent, "quite loves to eat. She can consume seconds at every course, and naturally she has a most flattering figure. Round and soft, the kind Prinny so admires." A picture of the overly endowed matrons the Prince of Wales favored gave her a sense of minor revenge.

"And do you enjoy your food also?" He kept his voice conversational as he helped her to her chair. "One wouldn't think it to look at you." His eyes raked her, not missing a single bagging seam.

"Certainly. Mama was my size when she was my age, you know." She bowed her head to concentrate on her plate.

"I see. Then let me help you to some of these lovely pickled herrings and some of that side dish of creamed asparagus." Camber began to load her plate with heaping proportions.

What had she gotten herself into, Dami thought as she watched the mound grow. She shot him a fulminating glance.

"Do you take your mask off to eat?" he inquired politely.

"No." She didn't want to talk to the man. Inspiration hit. "I don't usually eat at the table." She turned to him in a confiding manner. "You see, I just had the chicken pox, which was why I didn't go about much in London, and have still got some nasty scars that haven't healed yet. That is why I wear this inconvenient mask in company."

"Please, don't consider me company," he returned suavely. "But I have it on the best authority that you left for the country to nurse your old nanny."

"Oh, but I did." She laughed nervously. "But that wasn't until later." She had to change the subject. "Your Grace, even though you are interested in courting me and becoming part of the family, you are still company until we set a date. Besides," she added ingenuously, "I don't want you to take a disgust of me."

"Dear lady, nothing you do could disgust me."

"I'm so glad," she murmured, swallowing gulps of air.

Her belch made Simon drop his water glass.

Kit choked on her fish.

Lady Sebastian's fork missed the potato she was aiming for, clattering against her plate.

235

Johnny muttered under his breath.

Only Camber took it in stride. "Gracious, that was loud, Lady Damaris. I imagine we shall get on famously."

Dami felt her vexation with the man growing. He was so bent on marrying birth and position that he was willing to overlook any character flaw. Well, they would see just how much he was willing to endure for the perfect wife.

Dinner was interminable. Dami felt her stomach churning and several times was brought to the blush by its loud rumbling.

"It appears your stomach does not appreciate your decision not to eat in public. Perhaps you could take pity on it and take a bite of something."

The look he gave her was so sympathetic Dami wanted to land him a facer. Instead she ignored him. She couldn't very well eat with this great wad of cotton in her mouth.

After dinner the gentlemen accompanied the ladies to the parlor without taking their solitary port. Dami made for the pianoforte where she began to pick out a country ballad, knowing two out of three keys she hit were wrong. It was just proof of another accomplishment lacking in her repertoire. Worrying at the cotton that had kept her from eating, she adjusted it so she felt confident she could sing.

Entering the room, Camber went straight to the pianoforte, where he assiduously turned the music pages for her, keeping his eyes decorously centered on the top of her head.

Sitting next to Simon, as far from the music as possible, Johnny grumbled loudly. "Do we have to listen to this caterwauling? A cat being hung by its tail sounds better."

"Hush," Simon ordered.

Still grumbling, Johnny excused himself for bed. He'd had enough of his sister and her schemes for one day.

Lady Sebastian and Kit positioned themselves to get the best view of the couple making the noises that passed for music, for Camber had added his voice to Dami's and it wasn't much better.

After two songs, Camber excused himself, pleading an early day tomorrow. He bowed deeply over Dami's hand.

"I have enjoyed this evening more than I imagined possible," he said in a voice rich with innuendo. His lips lingered on the back of her hand, which he held too long, even managing to squeeze it before relinquishing it.

"Likewise," she muttered ungraciously. He was setting out to seduce her just as he'd seduced Amalie. She despised him. If only her body wouldn't shiver when he touched her, or grow warm and languid with memories when his thigh brushed hers.

As soon as the front door closed, Lady Sebastian and Kit also made their excuses. Dami rose to go with them.

"Not you," Simon barked. Dami froze in place. "All right, young lady. What was the meaning of tonight's performance?"

To gain time, she carefully undid the strings holding her mask on, then pulled her turban off, setting it aside, and last turned her head to extract the bedraggled piece of cotton from her mouth.

"Yuck!" She threw the damp material in the fire where it sputtered before catching flame. Taking a deep breath and squaring her shoulders, she turned to face her brother.

"And it had better be good, after making a laughingstock of yourself tonight."

"I'm testing Camber," she said. Simon's mouth dropped. "He has such a wild reputation, I don't think I can be happy married to him, unless he is also kind."

"Go on," Simon prodded when she hesitated.

"Can't you see," she choked on the words, "he only wants a wife to have an heir by. He doesn't care who he marries, because he will always have his ladies of the night."

"So you are trying to give him a disgust of you. Why don't you take the easy way out and tell him no?"

"Because he hasn't asked yet. I hope that by presenting such an unsavory image to him he will never ask." She began to pace the room. "If he loved me it would be different."

"He won't fall in love with you if you continue to act this way."

"Then I don't want him. I'm only giving him a chance to rise above his baser self."

"You aren't making sense, Dami," Simon said. "How can he rise above his baser self and fall in love with you when the woman you present him with isn't even yourself?"

"Maybe I did overdo it a little tonight." She collapsed into a chair, hugging herself against the sudden chill. "It's just . . . I don't really understand."

I can't explain, she yelled silently. I only want to punish him for what he's done to me. This is the only way I know how. And I can't let him recognize me or I will be ruined. She tried again. "I want to see if he can care for me even though I am disfigured. If he can, then I will feel better about marrying him. It will show that at least he has compassion, even if he doesn't have honor."

Watching the agony in her eyes, Simon got up and went to her. "My dear, if you don't want to marry him, you have only to tell me and I will convey the message."

She gulped before flinging herself into his open arms. "Oh, Simon, I don't think I know what I want. Only, please, don't expose me. Not yet. Let me see how he will react to a woman who isn't pretty or witty. If he won't love me, at least let me make sure that he won't abuse me either."

Looking into the earnestness of her face, Simon promised. "Much against my better judgment. But only because I am sure that Julian will prove to you in the end that he will be a good and considerate husband."

"Even though he will never love me or be faithful to me?"

"Dami, that is the way of the world. Camber will never knowingly embarrass you with his other interests and he will take care of you and your children."

"I think I've heard that line before," she mumbled, disengaging herself from his arms. "But somehow I have always expected more."

Chapter Fifteen

"Dami," Kit cornered Dami in bed the next morning drinking coffee, "what was the meaning of last night's performance? For I can assure you that Mother hasn't stopped rolling. She found the whole thing too amusing for words and plans to back you to the hilt even if she never learns why. I, on the other hand, already know that you have a *tendre* for Camber and that you should have been at your scintillating best."

Dami took a sip and set her cup down. She had known she would have to tell Kit an edited version of what had happened so far. "Sit down, or else you will probably fall down when I explain." She grinned impishly as Kit flopped on the bed. "It's a long story, but the gist is that I have been impersonating a bit-o-muslin with Johnny's help and in that guise have already made Camber's acquaintance."

Kit's mouth fell open. "You what?"

"That's right. Moreover, I have been alone with him numerous times and have even seen his Kensington house where he lodges his current lady loves."

"Never say." Kit's voice held grudging admiration.

"Yes, I have, but I am not his mistress. I refused that dubious honor, holding out for marriage. Something Camber was unwilling to offer one of such lowly birth as he thought me to be. Consequently, I called the whole thing off and came here to start anew with someone else." Dami crossed her fingers at the white lie. She was here to nurse her wounds, not find another.

"If that's so, then why the elaborate disguise?"

"Because Camber knows me as Amalie, the daughter of our estate manager. He never knew, and I don't intend him to ever find out, that the woman he was trying to seduce was Lady Damaris *Amalie* Fitz-Hubert. When Simon told me Camber wanted to marry me, I saw red. He will marry a woman of good birth and breeding without love, because he is a duke, but he won't marry a woman he professes to love because she hasn't got the breeding lines he considers necessary. I intend to punish him—after I lead him a merry chase."

"Dami, I sympathize with your anger, but I think you are headed for trouble. Camber isn't one to mess with, not if you hope to come out unscathed." Kit sat up and looked carefully at her friend's flushed face and thin body. "And it already looks as though you've been burned. Since we left London you've lost weight, and the sparkle you used to approach everything with has dimmed."

Dami bent to drink more coffee. "You refine too much on changes wrought by travel sickness. In a couple of weeks I will be fit as a fiddle. As rosy and firm as a fresh apple."

"If you don't tangle with Camber. You forget, Dami, I've seen women come and go with him, and he's always the one who ends it, regardless of the woman's wiles."

Dami raised diamond-hard eyes. "This time it will be different. He will learn that love is important, too,

241

not just bloodlines. I intend to prostrate him."

Julian glanced around the library in the duke of Wellington's rented Parisian hotel. It was dark and austere, like the man who frequented it. Walnut paneling covered the walls where there weren't bookshelves, and chocolate-colored leather covered the furnishings.

"Yes, sir," he said in response to Wellington's inquiry as to whether he had been apprised of the situation.

"Good," the great man said. "Then you are prepared to start immediately, for I can tell you, we haven't much time. Yesterday a rabble-rouser was arrested in one of the seedier parts of town. He was passing out pamphlets emblazoned with violets, Napoleon's symbol. There are serious plans to free Bonaparte, and all our efforts to prevent them have leaked to his supporters before we can even put them into action."

Julian whistled low. "This is more serious than Liverpool led me to expect, but it only increases my determination to plug the leak. I gather there are three suspects?"

"Yes." The duke handed him a sheet of paper with three names written on it. "Burn this before you leave this room." There were two English names and the count de Bourville, a French emigrè.

"I understand," Julian said, memorizing the names. That finished, he got up and threw the crumpled paper into the fireplace where it ignited in a burst of flames. He turned back to the duke. "If you will excuse me now, I'd best start laying my groundwork." He bowed and left.

Coming out of the library he ran into Simon going in.

"Going to Talleyrand's dinner tonight, Julian?"

"Got to," Julian answered, taking in his friend's dapper appearance. "You certainly don't bear any resemblance to that young sprig you call brother — not in the wardrobe department, at least." He grinned as he remembered Johnny's chartreuse waistcoat the night before.

"Thank God," Simon said with heartfelt relief. "Johnny is young and still thinks the best way to cut a dash is by dressing the perfect macaroni." His eyes flitted away, coming back to rest on Julian's. "About Dami. She isn't usually such an original. Ahem, that is, recovering from the chicken pox, and then an arduous trip and all."

Julian clapped him on the back. "Relax. I'm sure her sickness has only momentarily addled her brain. Nothing to fret about. Good breeding always tells out." He gave his friend another reassuring slap on the back, then donned his jaunty beaver, and sauntered out the door.

Simon watched Julian until he was out of sight. Perhaps Dami had something when she said Camber was too concerned with antecedents to see the individual behind them. He shook his head to clear it of these unloyal thoughts, and entered for his interview with the duke.

Meanwhile, Camber strolled along the rue de Clichy, taking in the warm air and English visitors. He passed Lady Oxford's rented hotel with a grimace.

Tomorrow he would be at her latest rout. The woman entertained as lavishly here as she did in London.

Within hearing distance was a group of English, loudly extolling all the virtues of the Louvre, filled with Boney's plundered artwork, versus the beauty of the Tuileries, the old Bourbon palace. He frowned at their rude ethnocentric attitude as they talked about the wonders of Paris, simultaneously denigrating its narrow streets and lack of gaslights. To get away, he turned at the next corner. A walk would do him good. He had many things to think about.

Genuine amusement turned his sensual mouth up and lent a spark to his grey eyes as he remembered Lady Damaris's outrageous behavior the night before. Was her own hair that bad, or was she simply a slave to the fashion that said ladies should wear turbans every hour of the day? Then her mask. She was the second woman he had met who hid her face at their first meeting. Would she be as beautiful as Amalie when she discarded it? He doubted it.

The thought brought all his hurt and bewilderment surging to the surface. It had pained him to tell Amalie he wasn't offering marriage. But he had his name to consider. No St. John had ever married away from duty. His father had been lucky in loving the woman responsibility had dictated he take to wife.

Unfortunately for him, he doubted if he would ever love Lady Damaris. How could he, when he was already in love with Amalie? If he had an heir, he could forgo marriage and live with his Amalie. Alas, he had no heir. He had to beget one, and there was no way around it.

Coming out of his reverie, Julian found his feet had

led to Simon's residence. He knew it wasn't good ton, but he intended to call on young Johnny and see if he knew Amalie's whereabouts. He couldn't stand the thought that she might be alone and destitute . . . or even worse, another man's plaything.

He rapped at the door and handed the austere butler his card. The servant led him to the same drawing room as the one of last night's musical entertainment. Just the sight of the pianoforte made Julian wince. Lady Damaris had a voice that would cause the dead to run, and his wasn't much better. Not to mention her inability to play. He was tone deaf, but even he had been unable to ignore her less than mediocre playing.

"Milord," Johnny's voice caused Julian to turn around.

"Ah," Julian began, momentarily made speechless by Johnny's morning attire, "Lord Jonathan." He paused to take in the full elegance of his host. The whelp was dressed in skin-tight canary-yellow breeches, a cherry waistcoat that stopped short of his waist, another waistcoat on top of that made of white satin and embroidered with pink roses, and a cutaway morning coat of bath superfine the color of stone. The only decent things were his top boots, which were polished to a nice shine. Really, Simon should take the stripling in hand. Julian swallowed his remark on the cloths. "I trust your trip here was uneventful."

Johnny was suspicious at Camber's bland question. There was something smoky here, or his name wasn't Jonathan Lewis FitzHubert. "Tolerable, Your Grace. My sister suffered from travel sickness, but aside from that and the deplorable roads in this country, there was nothing out of the ordinary." He'd bet a monkey Camber wanted information about Amalie. Well, he'd keep mum, and see how a man of Camber's repute handled a situation like this.

Seeing the belligerent set of Johnny's shoulders, Julian very nearly lost his temper. He could see the chucklehead wasn't going to make this easy, but there was no help for it. He had to make sure Amalie was safe, and this was the quickest way.

"Do you go to Talleyrand's tonight?" Camber asked. "You don't mind?" He sat down in a chair near the tall wainscoted window, not waiting for Johnny's invitation, since it didn't seem to be forthcoming.

"Not at all," Johnny managed, blushing at the necessity for his guest to seat himself. "Yes, we go tonight. And you?"

"Tedious, but necessary. I saw Simon earlier and have contracted to go with your party." He hadn't, but he could easily rectify that. Feigning nonchalance, he crossed his buckskin-clad legs. "I'm looking forward to getting to know Lady Damaris better. She is quite an unusual chit."

"Dami is a diamond of the first water, sir." Even though Camber's words were noncommittal, Johnny found himself taking offense at what he felt was implied. However, he couldn't very well tell the duke that Dami was hiding behind her ridiculous costume so that Camber wouldn't know he had already seduced her and then refused to do the honorable thing.

"I'm sure she is," Camber said in a soothing voice. The bantam cock was touchy. "By the by, my apologies for our last meeting, although I suppose strictly

246

speaking we didn't meet in Felixstowe." He kept his eyes wandering the room, alighting on Johnny only long enough to gauge his reaction.

"No, we didn't. If we had, I would have been constrained to take, er, certain measures. However, the lady being wronged felt that it would only make a bad situation worse." It felt good to put Camber in his place, even though his tightened jaw made one the teensiest bit apprehensive. Camber was said to be deadly with pistol or sword.

"Quite" Julian answered, at his most repressing. "How is the lady doing?" When he saw the shuttered look come over Johnny's eyes, he added, "I mean her no disrespect. I want to do anything in my power to see that she doesn't suffer."

Johnny studied the duke. Camber did seem sincere, and Dami had played an outrageous trick on him. And the duke had reacted just as he had predicted he would so long ago when Dami had first broached the subject with him. And Johnny knew that if Camber knew Amalie's true identity he would marry her, that being the honorable thing to do, and Camber being honorable above all else. He relented.

"She does well, milord." More he couldn't say without giving away Dami's new game. Drat the girl, she was going to get them into another hobble.

Just then, the door opened and Lady Damaris, her mask in place and a fashionable purple turban with another exotic ostrich feather tickling her ear, burst into the room.

"Oh, Johnny, Smithfield didn't say you had company." She made a pretty display of embarrassment. "I don't want to interrupt you gentlemen." She backed

247

to the door, chewing hard on the cotton to keep it from choking her.

"No, you aren't interrupting anything," Camber hastened to assure her. "I was just leaving." He rose gracefully and made a bow to her before turning to Johnny. "I will see you all at eight."

Dami watched the duke take his leave before turning on Johnny. "Well?"

"Well, what?" He decided to make her work for her information. He might as well get some fun out of this mess she'd gotten them into.

"You know," she said, untying her mask and yanking the handerchief out of her mouth. "Yuck! this stuff tastes awful, but my voice is so distinctive I have to disguise it somehow." She threw it into the fire and turned back to her twin. "He was here for a reason, and he asked to see you."

"Perhaps he wished to discuss fashion with me?"

"If anything he probably wished for some of those green visors you gentlemen wear when you gamble. The better to dim the glow of your attire." She sprawled into the same chair Camber had just vacated.

"Insulting me won't get you the information sooner." Johnny rose and went to the sideboard to pour himself a portion of brandy. "Care for some?"

"Stop stalling."

He returned to his seat, and took a leisurely sip of his liquor. "Why did you barge in on us? Afraid I might be indiscreet?"

"Yes. You are too loose with your words, twin, and I don't want Camber to pry something out of you that would make him suspicious. Under the circumstances, I felt it behooved me to join you as soon as I saw him walk up. Unfortunately, I had to don my outfit first."

"He asked about Amalie." She turned to stone, giving Johnny a modicum of satisfaction for having to have gone through the uncomfortable interview with Camber. "He's a downy one, Dami, and make no doubt. If you're not careful, he will find you out. But, anyway, he's concerned that Amalie may need help."

"Hmmm. I may be able to use this to advantage." She stared off into space.

"Oh, no," Johnny groaned. "I wish I'd never said a word to you. I wish I'd told the duke I was out." He admonished her with a wagging finger. "Don't you go trying anything more than you've already started. Things are complicated enough without your adding to them. As it is, I don't see how we can continue to fool him when he has decided to start attending acceptable functions. Don't see how you can continue to delude him when his express purpose for being here is to court you. Stands to reason he intends to get to know you. In order to do that, he's got to spend a lot of time with you. More time he spends with you, the more similarities in character and figure you have with his lost Amalie. In short—he will find you out."

"Brilliant deduction, but I intend to throw a red herring over the trail. And I think I know just what it will be, but first I must give things some time to settle out." She rose and headed for the door with an air of distraction. She tossed over her shoulder, "Thanks, Johnny. What you've told me is invaluable."

Johnny watched her leave with a harassed look on his face. He recognized that lost-in-the-clouds look she wore: Always came just before she brewed her next caldron of worms.

Dami looked around the table. They were twenty to dinner at Prince Talleyrand's house, mostly British and Russian. The food was sumptuous and the wines continuous.

So far she had managed to sip some wine and move food on her plate at such a rate that no one noticed she wasn't eating. She only hoped her stomach wouldn't growl and embarrass her, since there was no way she could eat with the cloth in her mouth.

When she had first entered the parlor on Camber's arm, everyone had stared quite rudely before remembering their manners. A little judicious mingling and she had set everything to rights by explaining her chicken pox and thus the temporariness of her condition.

Now she leaned to her dinner partner on the right, the count de Bourville, and whispered, "Is it true that Talleyrand conspired with Czar Alexander to overthrow Napoleon in 1808? And with the permission of Joseph Fouche, Boney's minister of police?"

"Shh," he cautioned. "Yes, it is true, but we don't talk openly about it. It is too tender." He grinned, abashed. "Is that how you say it?"

Taken by his little-boy charm, Dami laughed. "Tender is perhaps not the best word, but it is appropriate." She liked the count.

He had easy, unassuming manners that heightened the aura of slim elegance he exuded. Sandy brown hair, in a Stanhope Crop, and light brown eyes with lush lashes provided the perfect touch to his restrained dress. He affected neither the extreme of the dandy or of the Corinthian, managing to straddle both with panache.

"Does the czar stay here with Prince Talleyrand? I heard that he has upon occasion." She couldn't keep the awe from her voice. "He is such a magnificent man, and so charismatic."

"Are you falling for his fabled charm also?" de Bourville lamented. "I had hoped that you, at least, would be impervious. It seemed, but forgive me if I am out of line, that in London you were much more concerned with the man behind the outer face."

Dami brought her fan up to swat lightly at him, then thought better of it. "I am impressed by the czar's bearing and easy manners, not by the man himself. It seems to me he can't be very discerning, since he was taken in by Napoleon for some time. If I remember correctly, it took the brutal slaying of the duke d'Enghien to take the scales from his eyes. Even Napoleon couldn't convince people that a man visiting his mistress was really plotting the emperor's downfall."

"My dear lady," de Bourville said, "you are much too harsh. If anything, the czar's perspicacity is at fault, because he failed to see the rationale for Napoleon's action. And besides, your talk of d'Enghien is *de trop*, since your host has also been accused of being party to d'Enghien's execution."

Unable to stay out of the conversation longer Camber leaned toward Dami and said, "Really, Lady Damaris, d'Enghien's activities shouldn't be bandied about." His eyes gleamed with amusement as she

251

turned away from his gaze, but his voice was serious when he said, "What was done to d'Enghien, a royal Bourbon prince, was unprincipled and showed a lack of coherent thought on the part of Napoleon and his ministers, but that was only the beginning of Alexander's disillusionment with Boney. It was further compounded by neither one's living up to his promises to the other."

Dami listened to Camber proudly. He was so informed that he never failed to hold her attention. His knowledge and intelligence were a strong magnet to her own intelligence and ideals. His shoulder rubbed hers, bringing back unwanted memories of their night together. She could feel herself blushing under her mask.

She felt eyes on them and looked up to see Talleyrand carefully studying them. For a moment, she allowed her eyes to meet his. She wondered if he could fathom her thoughts behind the concealing mask, and decided he couldn't.

Turning, she caught the czar devouring Kit with his eyes. It would be interesting if Alexander intended to set Kit up as his latest flirt. He had more of a reputation as a lady's man than Camber, but then Kit knew how to handle womanizers.

Camber moved back into his chair again and Dami suddenly realized how cold the dining room had become. Her arm felt like ice where his arm had warmed it. Thank goodness the dessert plates were being removed and she could soon escape from such close proximity to the man.

At the signal to rise, Dami and the other ladies left for the music room, to be followed almost immediately by the gentlemen. Unwilling to play an active part in the repartee going on, Dami found a corner and sat down. From her location, she watched de Bourville join the ranks of Kit's admirers, only to see him outmaneuvered by Alexander.

Julian entered the room and sought out the lady of his choosing. Lady Damaris was seated in the shadows of a corner. He shook his head slightly before approaching her. Her evening gown was a very becoming rose silk, with bell sleeves and a bell skirt that was heavily embroidered with burgundy roses. Unfortunately, she failed to fill out its flattering lines. At her throat she wore a circlet of pearls. If any jewels hung from her ears, he couldn't tell for the mask. A shudder rippled through him. He was beginning to wonder if the mask was just an affectation and her chicken pox nothing but the excuse of a young woman bent on making herself noticed. If so, it was too bad.

He stopped in front of her. "Do you mind if I sit next to you, Lady Damaris?" Without giving her an opportunity to reply, he lowered himself onto the straw silk cushion of the settee. Nonchalantly, he draped one arm on the back of the seat and allowed the other to rest negligently on his knee. "Are you enjoying yourself? You and de Bourville appeared to be on the best of terms."

Dami fanned herself, wishing the mask didn't block the cool air. "The count and I have always found we have a marked similarity in thought." Could Julian be jealous? All the better. "He knows just how to make a woman feel appreciated. It must be his French finesse."

"I'm sure he has had much practice."

"Yes, I suppose you are right." The urge to strike at him was overpowering. "But then he does it with such polish that I am sure his practice has always been with ladies of genteel sensibility." She kept her voice smooth and innocent.

Julian eyed her sharply. So Lady Damaris had claws. Well, he would blunt them. "You speak as though from experience. Am I to assume that you know the difference?" He raised his quizzing glass to study her.

She shot him a fulminating glance, realizing too late that he wouldn't see it. Instead he was looking at her through an odious black enamel quizzing glass. "You may *assume* whatever you like, Your Grace."

"Careful, Lady Damaris," he replied, "you are beginning to spit. Come," he said imperiously, standing and reaching for her hand, "walk with me to the balcony. I am convinced you are hot behind that mask."

She scowled at him. Either she went with him or caused a scene. She allowed him to raise her and guide her out the doors. It was a warm night, with the stars brilliant pinpricks and the moon a full circle of silver light. She took a deep breath, inhaling the fragrance of honeysuckle that climbed the brick walls.

"Lovely night," she said, hoping to keep things on an impersonal level. He was much too close for her comfort.

"Yes, it is," he agreed, not looking at her. The chit was irritating in the extreme and he meant to teach her a lesson.

Without warning, he turned her into the circle of his arms, pinned her hands behind her, and with his

254

free hand lifted her mask enough to bare her lips. He didn't really want to see the scars she said she carried.

"Unhand me, si . . ."

His mouth slashed across hers, bruising in its intensity. He forced her teeth open with his tongue. For long minutes he attacked her with his kiss, unaccountably aroused by her breasts pressing into his chest and her hips flush with his. Surprise at his response made him release her, and the mask fluttered down to cover her swollen lips.

She gasped for breath. "You are not a gentleman."

Recovering himself, he answered, "I have never claimed to be . . . unlike some I might name." He leaned against the railing and watched her breast heaving, wondering idly if she would strip as well as his Amalie. The thought of his love brought a scowl to his face. With a curt bow, he left her on the balcony.

Dami watched his retreating back. The beast hadn't even excused himself. Fury lashed at her, and her agile brain whirled with plans to make him regret his recent actions . . . and not so recent actions. She turned into the soft breeze, lifting her mask to let it cool her heated countenance.

"Lady Damaris," de Bourville's voice brought her whipping around, "I saw you and the duke come out here, but only he returned. May I be of assistance?"

She turned to contemplate the night sky. "I couldn't ask it of you. It is too much."

"No, milady, you may ask anything of me. I am yours to command."

A slow smile curved her lips. "Well, perhaps just a little." She moved the cloth in her mouth around as it

255

was threatening to choke her. "It's the duke."

"Of course. A man with his reputation and a young woman of your sensibilities, it is no wonder." He moved closer to her.

"I know, but Simon does so wish for me to accept Camber's advances." She sighed, "He has asked for my hand, but I am loath to accept, knowing of his proclivities."

"Everyone knows of His Grace's proclivities. I am so sorry for you. Do you require that I call him out for you and put an end to his life?"

The suggestion shocked her. She certainly didn't want Camber to be put an end to. "Oh, no, I couldn't ask that of you. But . . . well," she turned to him, her hand beseeching him, "you might help me in another way."

He bowed to her. "Anything."

"I have thought that if I could prove to Simon that Camber is nothing but a hard-hearted rake who will never treat me with decency then I might be allowed to cry off of the marriage they are both forcing on me. Don't misunderstand me, Simon loves me, but he is inordinately fond of Camber and thinks he will make me a good husband." She lowered her voice. "But you and I know different."

"Most assuredly."

"I have thought that . . . this is a convoluted plan, but I think it will do the trick. To start, I have recovered from the chicken pox and may take this mask off without any scars showing, only I have hesitated because I was hoping it would dampen Camber's determination. It hasn't. But he has never seen me without it, in fact, he would not recognize me without it. So, I have thought and thought and have decided that I must play the part of another woman and get him to fall in love with me in that guise. Then when he still insists on marrying me as Lady Damaris I will be able to convince my brother that Camber is a cad through and through." She untied the strings of the mask and allowed it to drop, then lifted her pleading eyes to de Bourville's stunned ones.

"This is a dangerous scheme you concoct, Lady Damaris. Should it become known, your reputation would be finished."

She laughed ruefully. Little did he know that it was no more dangerous than what had gone before. "I am aware of that, but any risk is worth taking if it removes me from *his* clutches." She watched him carefully, noting when his eyes turned from worried to skeptical to speculative.

"You must allow me time to consider, but" he grinned, erasing the calculating look that had come over his face, "I believe I will help you. I have no wish to see you go to another."

She had the grace to blush. But no qualms would prevent her from her revenge. She would appear as Amalie, the woman Camber claimed to love, and then she would taunt him from the arms of another man. It would be sweet justice.

Chapter Sixteen

Dami gave her horse the signal to canter despite her rapidly beating heart. She would never be comfortable on a horse, but it was part of her plan to be seen riding in the Bois de Boulogne with de Bourville.

She flashed her companion a smile, which was returned by a very warm one. "It is the perfect day for this adventure," she said, looking at the bright sky.

"As you say, Lady Damaris," de Bourville answered with a small bow from his saddle. He brought his stallion up close to hers. "You are lovely without that hideous mask. I am glad you decided on this plot so that I may bask in the beauty of your smile. Even your voice is as I remembered it." He gave her a quizzical look. "How did you change it so?"

She laughed. "I stuffed a handkerchief in my mouth, and let me tell you, it was most uncomfortable."

The look of admiration in de Bourville's eyes made Dami blush. She must be careful and not encourage him to put more emphasis on their partnership than she intended.

"Look," she said, excitement making her jump, "there are Kit and Camber, coming our way. I knew Kit would not fail me."

"She is in on this too?"

Dami shot him a look. Did he sound disappointed or disapproving? "Yes, she is my best friend, and as Camber's cousin the person most able to get him to go riding in the park at this unfashionable hour. Why, if gossip is to be believed, I am surprised and disappointed that we have not met any soldiers bent on dueling."

"Lady Damaris, you shouldn't know about those things," de Bourville reproached her.

"Ah, but I do. Indeed, all of Paris knows."

As Kit drew closer to Dami and the count, she became more interested in seeing what Julian would do. According to Dami, he considered her to be a lightskirt and might very well not want to stop. She would take the matter into her own hands.

"Julian," Kit said, "there is the count de Bourville, and he is with a lady. Do you know her?" It was with a supreme effort that she managed to keep the excitement out of her voice.

"Yes."

The word was clipped and Kit shot him a glance. Camber's jaw was clenched to the point of twitching, and his hands were holding the horse's reins in a death grip. This might not have been such a good idea, she thought belatedly. There was no telling what her cousin would do in a situation like this.

"Let's stop and talk with them." Kit spurred her horse on, convinced that she must reach de Bourville and Dami before Camber, or he would very likely ride past them.

"Kit," Camber said. "That is hardly the kind of woman you would wish to be introduced to."

Kit could see by the expression on Dami's face that she had heard Camber's words. She groaned. They were in for it now. How she wished she had ignored Dami's plea for help. But she stopped her horse next to Dami's.

"Lady Christine," de Bourville took up his part, "how delightful to see you."

Of necessity, Camber reined in his bay stallion, a look of such anger on his face that even Dami cringed before she regained her own fury at his cavalier treatment of her. The smile she gave him was so wide, she knew her dimple was in evidence. His scowl only became deeper.

"Count," Dami touched de Bourville's arm lightly, "do you intend to introduce me to your friends?" She watched Camber's eyes narrow.

"Of course," de Bourville said. The introductions were short and to the point.

Dami was introduced as Amalie Dupree, a surname she had thought of at the last minute. It was to pique Camber, since he already knew she wasn't French and very likely didn't have a French name. It achieved its end. The look Camber gave her was black.

Dami's eyes flamed her challenge. "I am delighted to meet you, Lady Christine, Your Grace. Would you care to join us? We are exploring the area. In fact, just as you were riding up the count and I were discussing the duels that are constantly fought here."

"Did you know that the Bois de Boulogne was once the hunting ground of the Valois kings?" de Bourville inserted.

"No, really?" Dami gushed.

"How edifying," Camber said in blighting accents. The other three ignored him.

A mischievous glint lit Dami's eyes as she gave the duke a surreptitious look. "I wonder who hunts in it now? You don't suppose it could be the French hunting for Englishmen to duel with?"

"Miss Dupree," Camber said, "that is a subject no well-bred lady would discuss." He ran a derogatory eye over her, taking in the dashing moss-green riding habit trimmed in black military braid, the jaunty hat with its rakish feather teasing her cheek, and the impeccable boots.

The urge to bring her riding crop across his arrogant face was extreme. Instead Dami turned to de Bourville. "Jacques," she deliberately used his first name, "you promised to take me to Tortoni's for ices after our ride." She pursed her lips into a provocative pout and noted with satisfaction that Camber's jaw tightened.

"So I did, Amalie, my love," de Bourville replied. "If you will excuse us." He made his bows.

"Ta, ta." Dami waved her hand vaguely at Kit and Camber as she and de Bourville moved away.

Camber swore under his breath. His mind raced. What was she doing here, and with de Bourville of all people? And claiming a French name.

"Julian," Kit said sweetly, "won't you take me to Tortoni's, too?"

He gave her a speculative look. "Kit, you are not to

become acquainted with Miss Dupree."

"But why ever not? She seemed perfectly present-able to me."

"She may appear respectable, my dear cousin, but I know different."

"Surely you don't mean—she can't be de Bour-ville's mistress!" Kit said, round-eyed. For a fleeting instant, she thought she saw pain in Camber's eyes.

"I refuse to discuss it with you!" He kicked his horse lightly into a walk. "Yes, I will take you to Tortoni's. I wouldn't want you to say you've been deprived."

Kit chuckled. "Never."

From her vantage point at an outside table, Dami watched Kit and Camber approaching. The almost imperceptible shake of Kit's head should have been a warning to Dami to go easy. Instead she put on her most brilliant smile.

"Won't you join us, Lady Christine, Your Grace," she said loudly.

"Oh yes, how kind of you," Kit said quickly.

Camber's expression was thunderous, but he for-bore to comment. Instead he pulled a chair out for Kit who sank into it and rolled her eyes. He placed himself next to Dami.

The waiter brought a second set of ices. Dami took the opportunity to feast her eyes on Camber. He was dressed in a bottle-green coat by Weston and buff breeches that tucked into Hoby-made top boots. His hair was windblown from his ride, but that only added to his appeal. She felt herself thawing toward him until she encountered the icy look in his grey eyes as they rested on her.

Camber said, "Kind of you to allow us to join you, de Bourville. Not every man with so lovely a companion will let competition near." He gave Dami a very telling look.

What is he up to now, Dami thought as she took a sip of her ice.

"Ah," de Bourville said, "but I am very sure of myself. My Amalie and I are the best of friends." His tone implied more, but his face was smooth.

Dami rested her hand on the count's arm and gave him a melting smile.

"So I see," Camber said dryly.

"Oh," Kit said in an excited voice, "isn't that Jason Beaumair walking over there?"

"Where?" Camber said, his eyebrows snapping together.

"There. Oh," disappointment dragged Kit's voice down, "he has disappeared around a corner. I must have been mistaken."

Dami gave Kit a measuring look. Did Kit care for Perth? She forgot the thought at Camber's next words.

"I see you are finished, Miss Dupree. So have I, but the count and my cousin are still enjoying theirs." He stood up and extended his hand. "Walk with me."

His command set Dami's hackles up, but it was what she wanted so she agreed. He extended his arm and she put her hand on it. Together they strolled off, to all the world a picture of English propriety.

They walked some distance, neither speaking, then Dami felt herself being pushed into the alley they were passing. She sputtered indignantly, "Just what do you think you are doing, *Your Grace*?"

"Exactly what you are afraid I am doing." He backed her against the wall, his hands on either side of her. "Just what is your game, my sweet? Surely de Bourville isn't as fat a pigeon as I, and you threw me aside."

She eyed him angrily, refusing to feel the heat of him so close to her. She could smell the citrus of his aftershave.

Not pretending to misunderstand him, she played her trump card. "He offers marriage, Your Grace." She crossed her fingers in the folds of her dress and silently vowed to explain to de Bourville why she had had to implicate him to such a degree, but right now she must concentrate on the infuriating man who made her breath come faster, no matter how she denied him.

Camber looked stunned, but he didn't release her. "He does? Then he is a bigger fool than I thought him."

The words cut her to the quick. She could feel tears threatening, but she would not give him the satisfaction of seeing them.

"He is an honorable man," she said, as calmly as she could.

"And are you an honorable woman to give him Haymarket wares? Is it also honorable to marry one man when you love another?"

She gasped. "You go too far!"

"Do I? We shall see."

Looking at the heat in his grey eyes, she knew his intentions. She twisted her head to the side, but his hand gripped her chin and brought her face to his. It was like dying to feel his mouth on hers again. Sweet, bursting pleasure filled her with a longing for more.

She forced open her heavy eyelids, wanting to see the same slumbrous look on his face. But sharp, calculating eyes met hers. She plummeted back to reality. Determined not to let him overcome her again, she pounded on his chest with her fists.

"Stop it. You are reprehensible." The words were an incoherent sound against his demanding lips. When she thought that she would faint from lack of oxygen, he released her. She sagged against the wall.

Camber pulled back from her, forcing her to steady herself. "So coy? Or has your conscience begun to prick you?"

She ran past him into the busy street. So incensed was she that she tramped into a mud puddle, splattering her hem and boots. "Oh!" she cried in vexation. "Now look!"

"If you'd taken my arm, like a lady, I would have led you around it." He gave her a superior look. "But all this bickering hasn't accomplished what I set out to do."

Now come the questions, Dami thought, biting her tongue to keep it silent. She would let him hang himself.

"Aren't you the least bit curious about why I am in Paris?" he asked. "For I am dying to know how *you* got here and why. And you can't tell me de Bourville brought you, because I checked up on him for my own reasons and know he came over the week before you and I went to Felixstowe."

She searched in vain for some reaction from him about Felixstowe, but he was as unreadable as stone.

265

What had happened between them was an everyday, or almost everyday, occurrence to him. It had shattered her world; it was a mere bagatelle to him.

She sniffed and raised her chin. "I am not in the least interested in your reasons for being here, and I do not intend to tell you mine."

He took her unproffered arm and began to guide her back to Tortoni's. "Then I will tell you anyway. I am here to woo my future bride, and I believe *you* are here to get me back."

His presumption was insufferable! "You, Your Grace, are an overbearing, conceited coxcomb. I doubt your future wife will take to you if you treat her as you have treated me."

"I treat her like the lady she is, but then you already know that, since you know her." He watched her for some reaction, but it was her turn to be cool.

"Do I?" She relished the opportunity to give him a much deserved setdown. "You must mean Lady Damaris FitzHubert. She told me, just yesterday, that you were hanging out for her and that she intends to lead you on and then refuse you." She turned to face him.

He stared at her. "I beg leave to doubt that, madam."

"As you wish."

Without more ado, he returned her to de Bourville and took Kit away. Dami couldn't keep the complacency out of her voice when she turned to toast the count with the second ice he ordered for her.

"To our future leveling of the duke of Camber, and to my engagement that will never take place." De Bourville met her ice with his in a flourish. She couldn't help the twinge of pain at the thought that she was throwing away the only man she could ever love because he wasn't in love with her.

Julian cursed as he ruined his fourth cravat. "Williams," he bellowed, "come here and tie this damned thing."

Williams approached warily. His Grace was unusually moody tonight.

"Now help me with this jacket. Thank goodness, Brummell brought black into fashion for evening wear. I don't think I could stand to wear the odious colors Johnny FitzHubert thinks are all the crack." He squeezed into the tight coat, then twitched his silk-embroidered white satin vest into order. Picking up his malaca cane, white gloves, and chapeaux bras, he said, "Don't wait up for me. This affair at Lady Oxford's promises to be long and boring."

He left his lodging uncertain whether to walk through the unlit, filth-strewn streets, or to take his coach. Calling a French linkboy, he decided to walk. The air, although filled with malodorous smells, would be better than the stuffy interior of a coach. He had purposely put Amalie out of his mind since meeting her earlier, but now, before seeing Lady Damaris tonight, was the time for him to decide what to do about Amalie.

He followed the bobbing, flickering light of the linkboy with half his mind. Seeing the chit had been a shock. A pleasant one, until he had recognized de Bourville. He would stake his reputation that Amalie hadn't known the count in England. And de Bourville had some shady dealings here in Paris. He had heard rumors that the man frequented Silves's, a well-known Bonapartist cafe. Not exactly the behavior one expected of a man who was part of the Home Office's staff. The count would bear closer watching.

Meanwhile, what did he intend to do about Amalie? He still wanted her. Their kiss had only intensified his yearning.

"Monsieur?"

With a start, Camber realized he was at Lady Oxford's and the linkboy was holding out his hand for pay. He flipped him a franc before mounting the impressive stone steps and rapping smartly on the door.

A stout butler, his accent obviously English, said, "Come in, Your Grace." He bowed Camber in and led him to double doors that opened into a large room sparsely furnished and sparsely peopled.

"His Grace, the duke of Camber," the servant intoned.

Camber entered the room taking a quick lay of the land. De Bourville had Lady Damaris buttonholed in a far corner, Simon and Kit were exchanging lively conversation with Lord and Lady Oxford, and his aunt and Johnny were talking with the duke of Wellington and Stephen Moresby, another Home Office staffer who was here with Wellington. It seemed tonight was to be a select party.

Dami looked toward Camber in time to see Lady Oxford rush to his side. "Just look at her," Dami muttered to de Bourville. "She is toadying him to no end. And now Simon," she said in disgust as her brother went to Camber and slapped him on the back.

"Console yourself, Lady Damaris," de Bourville said, "in the fact that you will have the last laugh over the duke." He patted her hand tenderly as it lay in her lap.

Dami drew herself back, intending to give the count a reprimand for being too intimate, but thought better of it. His eyes held a sly message that said louder than words that they were conspirators and must stick together. "You are right, of course," she managed to choke out around her cloth. Rising she said, "It is time I put the next stage of my play into action. Excuse me."

She approached Camber, her head high. "Good evening, Your Grace. I was beginning to think you weren't coming."

Julian purposely moved his eyes down her. She was filling out, and not unattractively. Her gown of rose muslin scooped low over her breasts to be caught up by maroon ribbons. It accentuated their high firmness. He noticed it also showed her to have slim hips. The sleek lines of a race horse. It could be worse.

"How could I miss it when I knew you were to be here?" he said, deciding to flirt outrageously with her.

Her laugh was guttural. She swallowed and readjusted the handkerchief, thankful he couldn't see behind her mask. "You are such a tease, Your Grace."

He bowed slightly in acknowledgment, wondering all the time if what Amalie had said was true. "No, you mistake me, Lady Damaris. I only pay homage to the beauty I imagine is yours. But tell me, are we to have the pleasure of meeting you face to face sometime in the near future?"

"La, I suppose you must, but my scars aren't quite healed yet." Her voice simpered as she fluttered her hands.

He captured one of her hands and pressed a kiss to it. She yanked it back. "I don't intend to bite you. Human flesh isn't my idea of a delicacy," he said.

"Mmmm." She wasn't going to pick that up. Instead she sidled closer until their thighs and shoulders were touching. "Do come and sit with me."

Camber gave her a measuring look. Was she about to start fawning on him as Amalie had said she intended? He resigned himself to the inevitable after glancing around to see everyone else forming up at tables set for whist. Now was as good a time as any to get to know her. He should ask her to go riding with him, but he preferred to wait until she took off that grotesque mask.

They sat down at the couch she and de Bourville had occupied, the count having moved on to play cards. Their conversation was desultory, dealing with the weather, Paris's deficiencies, and the wanton behavior of the French aristocracy.

Camber couldn't stifle a yawn. "Please excuse me, Lady Damaris, but I was up late last night and up early this morning." She was also one of the most boring talkers he knew. She had nothing substantial in her repertoire of polite conversation, but then, most society chits were the same.

"That's a whisker," Dami said before she caught herself. She'd done her best to bore him, she didn't want to ruin it now. To cover her slip, she laughed and put her hand on his arm. Little ripples of delight traveled from the touch to her stomach, making it knot. To cover her shiver, she asked, "Have you been riding in the Bois de Boulogne? Kit said she went there this morning, but it was much too early for me."

He gave her a sharp look, but not being able to ascertain anything through her mask, he decided it was an innocent question. "Yes. I accompanied Kit. It is too bad you didn't get up, for the park was beautiful and virtually deserted."

"Ah, but the effort is much too great. After all, nature palls on one so early in the morning. Don't you agree?"

Camber's answer was noncommittal. What was he getting himself into? She was a dead bore, and he didn't even know if she was presentable.

"However," Dami leaned into him, saying, "I might be persuaded to try if you were to ask me."

That was the last thing he wanted to do. He pulled back slightly. "That's very generous of you, but I wouldn't dream of inconveniencing you like that."

"How sweet of you," she tittered. "But it would be no inconvenience if it were for you."

He stretched his neck.

"Is something the matter, Your Grace?" she asked.

"Oh, it's just my cravat. It is a bit tight. My man sometimes forgets about comfort when he is bent on fashion."

"Oh."

It was said demurely, but Julian suspected she was laughing at him. She was making a play for him that would shame a courtesan. In fact, since he had come into the room she had stuck to him like a merchant sticks to a creditor he is afraid will skip town before paying the shot. Perhaps he should be equally bold and scare her off.

"Since you are so determined, Lady Damaris, why don't you ride with me tomorrow afternoon. I shall take my curricle so that we may be alone." He allowed his voice to lower to a seductive purr. "It's past time that we became better acquainted, don't you think?"

"Yes, that would be ideal," she answered in dulcet tones.

"Good." He plucked her hand from his jacket and turned it over to kiss the underside of the wrist. "Until tomorrow."

Her heart twisted at his familiar action. She watched him as he made his way to Lady Oxford. No matter how she baited him or how she blackened him in her own mind, he still had the power to make her throw caution to the winds for him. If only he loved Amalie enough to marry her.

"Why aren't you playing cards?" Johnny said, taking the vacated seat next to Dami.

"I would lose, my mind is so preoccupied." She sighed and leaned back. "I shall be so glad when this is over and I can go back to the way I was before."

"Never be the way you were again," he answered unthinkingly, only to see her body tense. "That is, having been to London and Paris and all."

"Just so," she said dryly.

"By-the-by, de Bourville is a good chap. He's promised to take me to the Salon des Etrangers next week. Hear it's all the go." Johnny looked immensely pleased with himself as he straightened the sprout-green waistcoat with gold embroidery, which hadn't been disorderly to begin with.

"The Salon des Etrangers? I don't believe I've heard of it."

" 'Course not. It's not . . ." He stopped, realizing his mistake.

"It's not a place a lady knows about," she finished for him. At Johnny's pugnacious look, she added, "You've already started, so you might as well finish and tell me all about it. Or I will tell Simon that you intend to go." It was blackmail, but someone needed to keep tabs on Johnny. For all his assertions that he was bang up to the mark, she knew he wasn't.

"That's underhanded," he grumbled. He gave her one last chance to retract her threat before saying, "It's a gaming place, run by the marquis de Livry. All the crack. Only the richest and most aristocratic patrons. Nothing to worry about."

Dami saw the flush on Johnny's cheeks and decided differently. But she said, "Oh, in that case then, I shan't feel anxious over you. Particularly, when you plan to go with de Bourville."

Chapter Seventeen

"He will be here," Dami said with conviction. To emphasize her words, she flicked her whip in the air. The sudden action made her mare prance, and Dami's face turned white. She would never be comfortable on the beasts.

Johnny looked at her in consternation. "I hope not. You are running close to ruin by flaunting yourself about without your mask. What if an acquaintance happens by and sees you and then the next time sees you with the mask back? What do you intend to do then?" In his nervousness, he jerked at the reins, causing his stallion to sidle around.

"If you can't manage your horse better, then perhaps you should take to walking." Dami knew it wasn't a nice thing to say, because ordinarily Johnny was a very good equestrian, but he was irritating. They were both nervous. "Have you no spirit?"

"Not when your reputation, which I might add is already tarnished, is at stake." Her hurt look caused him a pang of conscience, but she needed to be tethered before she did irreparable harm, not only to herself, but also to her family.

"I've told you before, Johnny, sometimes you have to take risks. I'm betting that no one we know will be here this early." She craned her neck, looking for the horse whose hooves she could hear. "I intend to teach Camber a lesson he won't forget!"

"Humph! I doubt you'll succeed—but speak of the devil."

Dami, in her guise of Amalie, was ahead of Johnny. She prodded her sedate mount into a walk, stopping next to the duke. She took a deep breath to relax her nerves, made taut by riding and by anticipation of this meeting.

Her stylish riding habit added to her bravado. She knew the pale blue material trimmed with silver showed her at her best. And the little boat hat, lavishly trimmed in silver, that perched on top of her curls had been an inspired choice.

"I hoped you would be here, Your Grace." It was audacious of her, but she would attack while her courage lasted.

He doffed his hat to her. "I see you aren't with de Bourville this morning. Has he let you off the leash long enough to stretch your legs?"

The smile went out of her eyes. Trust Camber to start off on the attack, too. "The count is a very understanding fiance," she sniffed.

Camber grinned at her. "If you were still mine you can be certain I wouldn't let you out of my sight."

"Except for those times when you must be with your bride, you mean." She gazed wide-eyed at him.

The flush under his tanned skin let her know she'd scored. She was glad, for his possessive words had made her overly warm.

"Touché," he murmured ironically.

Listening to them, Johnny shook his head. "If you two will excuse me, I will go for a short canter before Da . . . Amalie and I must leave." He tipped his hat. "Your servant, Camber."

After Johnny had gone, Dami once again took the offensive. "Have you told Lady Damaris about me?"

"A gentleman doesn't discuss his diversions with a lady," he said in a cutting tone, "particularly when that lady is to be his wife."

"A gentleman," she said icily, "does not discuss his intended wife with his, er *diversions*."

"Touché, again. Consider it a sign of my love for you that I fall so low as to break that unwritten law." He was still cajoling her.

"I see Johnny coming, Your Grace." She turned her horse.

He noted how her hands shook as she guided the reins, and how pale her face was. "Amalie," he said. "I would like to see you again. A place less public than this, where we might talk at length with each other."

She turned her head away. He reached a hand across to hold her reins. "Come now, my dear. Surely de Bourville won't miss you for one evening. Tonight, perhaps. For dinner."

Dami's heart was pounding. "Yes, all right," she said after a pause. "Dinner at the Palais-Royal." It was the only place she could think of that was well lit at night, where she could feel safe—whether from his passions or her own, she did not analyze.

She kicked her horse into a canter toward Johnny, leaving Julian staring after her with an odd expression on his face.

"Lady Damaris," Camber addressed her as he guided his spirited cattle down the Avenue Des Champs-Elysées toward the Place de L'Etoile where Napoleon had started erecting his Arc De Triomphe, "I am flattered that you have come."

He was dumping the butter boat on her, but she could match him. "So kind of you to offer. I'm sure I must be the most envied girl in all of Paris."

"You flatter me," he murmured.

The Champs-Elysées was a broad avenue lined with large, healthy trees and thronged with carriages and pedestrians. It would also take them to the Rout de Longchamps which runs through the Bois de Boulogne.

As they passed the area where construction on the Arc de Triomphe was stopped, Camber said, "Thank God that monster was defeated. Just looking at his plans for this triumphal arch shows his grandiose scheme for himself as conqueror of all Europe."

"Oh, you're talking about Napoleon again. How interesting." Dami yawned into her lemon kid glove. She kept her head down as though contemplating the weave of her skirt. "Don't you think this buttercup-yellow dress is vastly becoming to me? I particularly like the turban. So *comme il faut*."

"Vastly," he answered, his expression bland. The chit was a nitwit. Nothing in her swaddled head and masked face but fashion and the weather.

Reaching a quick decision, Camber swung them around the circle of the Place de L'Etoile and headed back to Simon's house.

"What? Quitting so soon, Your Grace? But it is still early. And see, it is quite crowded. I am convinced that this is the time to be out and about."

"I abhor traffic jams. They aren't good for my high-strung cattle." He jerked lightly on the reins. "As you can see, they are nervous. I really must beg your indulgence and take you home before their highbred sensibilities lead them into bolting."

"But of course," she said sweetly. He must think me especially gullible to be taken in by that when he is the most talked-about whip in all of England, she thought.

"Isn't the weather lovely?" she said. She saw his hands tighten on the reins, but the horses didn't shy this time. He had perfect control. "It is so warm and sunny."

"Quite." He pulled to a stop in front of her house. "Please forgive me for not helping you, but with no groom to hold these spirited animals it would be sheer folly for me to let go of the reins."

"I understand, Your Grace," she said lightly as she descended on her own. "I enjoyed the ride."

"It was my pleasure," he answered at the same time he signaled his bays to start.

Later that afternoon, Dami pulled the ice-blue satin coverlet up to her chin and fell back onto the matching lace-trimmed pillows with her eyes closed.

"Oh, Kit," she said faintly. "I have an excruciating headache. I really don't think I will be able to go to the opera with you tonight."

"Gammon!" Kit exclaimed. "But it might fool my mother," she added thoughtfully.

"I say, Dami," Johnny chimed in, "you ain't seriously going to go with Camber to dinner, are you? I remember the way you looked after the last time, even if you choose to forget it."

She gave him a dampening look. "It is part of my plan," she said with a superior air.

Just then, there was a knock on the door followed by Lady Sebastian St. John, Kit's mother. With her eyes half shut, hoping the face powder added pallor to her already pale cheeks, Dami awaited the widows's first words.

"What's this?" Lady Sebastian said. "You can't be sick, Dami. Why, we have such an entertaining evening planned. De Bourville is part of our party, and I'm sure Julian will be around somewhere for you to quiz with your disguise."

"No, no, ma'am," Dami answered weakly. "I have a most severe headache. I seem to be more prone to them as I get older. You don't suppose," she said in a voice filled with horror at the possibility, "that it is an affliction of advancing age?"

"Tut, tut, child," Lady Sebastian responded, "I am much older than you and I certainly have never been prey to them." She went to the window and opened the drapes, letting in the bright evening sun. "There, that should make you feel better in a trice."

Kit and Johnny rushed to shade Dami from the light. "Oh, Mama," Kit remonstrated, "How can you be so unfeeling. Dami was complaining that the harsh glare was compounding her pain."

"Ooooh," Dami moaned and slid deeper into the covers.

"Well, if you insist." Kit's mama closed the drapes again. "What a poor time for you to have a start like this, my dear," she addressed Dami. "You were never a sickly sort, and I have known you since you were in leading strings."

"Oh, no, ma'am," Johnny interposed, "you should have seen her in London. Never seen a horse as sick as she was. Something in city air must not agree with her. Isn't that right, Kit?"

"Oh, yes, quite right."

Dami peeped through her lashes. Lady Sebastian had a speculative look on her face, which turned to amusement as she said, "I suppose we shall just have to leave you here then, and you'll miss all the fun. Ta, ta." She blew Dami a kiss and left.

Flinging the covers back, Dami sat up and said, "Now, you two run along, I haven't any time to lose. When I'm ready, Johnny, I'll send Suzy to get you."

"What do you mean? I'm not going with you tonight. Devonshire may enjoy a *menage à trois*, but I don't think Camber does," Johnny grinned.

"Don't be a goose. You know I need your escort to the Palais-Royal."

He winked at her before leaving.

Dami pulled the hood of her cloak closer around her face, and leaned to whisper to Johnny, "Who is that man over there?"

280

"Which one?"

"The one who looks like he hasn't eaten in a month and has eyes like a wild boar's. That one. He's in a pink coat and black pantaloons."

Johnny looked where she pointed. "Oh, him. He's probably a 'hawk.' "

"What is a 'hawk'?"

He looked at her, exasperation writ plainly on his face. "A 'hawk' is someone who has gambled his fortune away, but can't stay away from the tables like a sensible man would. He drinks to excess and don't eat. Gambling and drinking, with gambling much the stronger, are his passions. Does that satisfy you? It's not something you should know about."

"It seems that there is nothing of interest that I should know about."

"Pardon me," Camber's voice interrupted them, "but I hope this is Amalie with you, Johnny." He couldn't stop the wince caused by Johnny's outfit.

"Anything the matter, Camber?" Johnny asked, seeing his look of pain.

"Nothing that won't soon be alleviated." He held out his arm to Amalie. "It is you, isn't it?"

"Yes," she giggled. "Good-bye, Johnny," she threw back as they walked away. "It was Johnny's waistcoat, wasn't it? He thinks he apes the dandies, but personally, I find his taste abysmal."

"I couldn't agree with you more. I really must talk to Simon about doing something with the cub before he offends one of these Frenchmen and finds himself challenged to a duel."

"Surely, they wouldn't call him out over his dress!"

"Look around you, sweetings. There are French

soldiers everywhere, they are as thick as fleas on a dog, and every one of them is itching to pick a fight with an Englishman. The reason is merely a formality."

She took a more comprehensive look. The Palais-Royal was packed with soldiers looking the worse for drink as they propositioned the prostitutes plying their trade, while the upper crust of England and France ate at the numerous sidewalk cafes, or drank along with the soldiers. It definitely didn't look like the place for a woman to be. Or Johnny, for that matter. She hoped he would come to no harm.

They spent the next half hour strolling the busy thoroughfare, watching the people and lingering in the cool of the park situated inside the rectangle of buildings that formed the Palais-Royal. It was so colorful, and so many people of importance were there, that Dami was sorry when Camber said it was time to go.

"Where are we going?" she asked him as he led her to his carriage.

"It is a surprise. I doubt you have been there yet."

"Do you go frequently?"

"Not in the last eleven years or so," he answered with a grin.

"I forgot. That was stupid of me. With Napoleon loose, no Englishman has been here."

"Not stupid, sweetings, impulsive. But I gather you are always impulsive, and I wouldn't have you any other way." He flicked her nose after settling her into the coach. "With you I never know what to expect, but I know it won't be the weather or the latest gossip and fashions."

Shortly, the carriage stopped and they entered the Cafe des Milles Colonnes. Dami's eyes were round as saucers as she looked around at the opulent setting. Seated on a royal throne, the very center of attention, was a woman swathed in velvet. The gown was daring and her lips and cheeks were rouged to a glaring red.

"What manner of place is this?" she whispered to Camber.

"The perfect place for us. The woman on the throne is the hostess. She is also a noted French demimondaine." He broke off to tell the maître d' he wanted a corner table, well hidden from prying eyes. To Dami, he said, "I know your penchant for avoiding public stares, sweetings. This is the perfect place to do so, for all the men here are without their wives or on the go for a mistress, while any respectable women who come here definitely don't want to be recognized."

She maintained a stony silence. He wasn't going to get a response from her, because she was afraid she would say too much. She forced herself to relax and look at it objectively. It was no worse than going to the Cyprians' Ball, and it was positively better than meeting him at the Clarendon Hotel for a private supper. And it would be something to remember in her no doubt lonely old age.

The waiter seated them, taking her cape and giving Camber the menu. "Shall I order for you?"

"Please." She didn't feel up to reading French tonight.

Their table was barely big enough for two, with a candle taking up a large part of the center. Dami could feel Camber's legs on the outside of hers. It was such an intimate touch that shivers ran hot and cold from their contact.

"I'm glad you wore that dress," he murmured. "I like the gold color and the creamy lace. Not to mention the daring dip in the back. You have a very lovely back."

She dropped her eyes from the heat in his.

The waiter arrived then with champagne. "A toast," Julian said, raising his glass. "To us." He held her gaze as he downed the contents of his glass. His eyes wandered to the low bodice of the gown, lingering there. "Your gown brings back memories of our first dinner together. Just as before, you aren't wearing any jewelry with it." He reached into his coat pocket and brought out a slim box.

Dami watched him in dismay. So he would try to buy her again. He opened the lid to show her a bracelet of diamonds set in white gold. From their sparkle in the candlelight, she knew they were diamonds of the first water.

"Oh I couldn't accept that," she said quickly, "It is too expensive."

She was temporarily saved by the arrival of their food. When the waiter had left, Camber said softly, "I am not accustomed to having my gifts refused. Are you going to take the diamonds, or must I keep them for another woman?" His voice was as hard as the gems he pushed on her.

"Keep them for your next doxy, milord." She rose abruptly from her seat. "I find I've quite lost my appetite. It is time I left."

The waiter rushed over to them, bringing her cape, which he helped her put on. She pulled the hood up and stalked out of the cafe. Camber, having taken care of matters with the waiter, caught up with her at the door.

"Where are you staying?" he demanded curtly.

She sighed. "The marquis of Cleve's hotel." She knew it was still too early for them to have returned from the opera.

He flagged his coach and helped her in. "Don't you feel the least bit awkward being in the same house with my future bride?"

"I wish you would stop throwing that in my face! I can't help the circumstances that put me in that household, and I certainly can't help that you choose her over me." She bit her lip and turned her face away from his.

"Amalie," he said, cupping her chin in his palm and turning her back to him. "Why do you fight me like this?"

Her eyes were luminous with unshed tears as she searched his face for something she could not at that moment have put a name to.

He brought his mouth to hers. When she parted her lips for him, he crushed her to him. He devoured her. The intoxication of his kiss bubbled through her veins, seeming to join with the champagne to make her senses float. She reveled in the feel of him pressed to her, chest to chest, thigh to thigh.

He drew back, undoing the ties of her cape so that he could place his lips at the base of her throat. With butterfly kisses, he traveled down to the edge of her bodice. His tongue darted along the line where skin met material, leaving a moist trail of sensation in its wake. His hands kneaded the muscles of her back, arching her into him.

She longed to slide into the completeness of his embrace, to merge with him for their mutual pleasure and love. Where he touched her, her skin felt on fire, urging her to press closer.

She slipped her hands inside his coat and around his waist, feeling the heat of his body as it penetrated the thin silk of his shirt. The rapid beating of his heart excited her as she roamed his back with her fingers.

"Amalie," he moaned, raising his lips from her peaked breasts, "say you will come with me. There's no need for you ever to return to the FitzHuberts. I will keep you and love you all the rest of my life."

His mouth brushed her chin on its way to her earlobe, but his mention of the FitzHuberts knocked awareness into her, even as she shuddered at the exquisite pleasure his lips and hands gave her. She pushed weakly against his chest. It did no good. His lips captured hers again in a slow languorous kiss that roused her most primitive emotions. Now, instead of pushing him away, her fingers curved into the muscle of his chest, pulling him toward her.

The carriage jolted to a halt.

"I . . . must . . . go," she managed between soft, clinging kisses. "Julian," she turned away, "we will see each other again, but tonight let me go."

His hands fell away, taking the heat of their passion with them. Without a word, he helped her tie her cloak and then assisted her down and up the steps to the door. Before allowing him to knock, she kissed her fingers and placed them on his lips. The stiff line of his mouth softened under her touch. Not

286

waiting for his reply, she turned the handle. Entering, she heard his shoes on the marble steps as he returned to his coach.

It was all she could do to keep from turning and watching until he was out of sight. Instead she glanced up at the butler to see what Smithfield thought of the irregular proceedings. His raised eyebrows asked a question she would not answer.

She mounted the steps to her room. Suzy was long ago in bed, so she undressed herself then sat at her dressing table brushing her hair. Tonight had opened old wounds and old pleasure that should have been left to fade with time. Revenge was no longer so inviting.

Julian caught himself whistling "All the World's in Paris," a popular British tune of the summer, as he pushed open the door to Wellington's office. The great man was sitting behind his desk, looking over some documents.

"I got your message, sir." Julian stopped in front of the full desk.

Wellington looked up and waved him to a seat. "Have a seat, Camber. I wanted to give you some new information. It seems the Silves's is becoming known as a Bonapartist cafe. Since you're new in town, I wasn't sure if you were aware of this."

"Yes, I was and now that you mention it, I think it would behoove me to go drink some coffee and exchange the time of day with some of its patrons."

"My thoughts exactly." Wellington shuffled some papers. "Well, don't let me detain you, I know you'e busy."

Taking the hint, Julian rose to his feet. "If I learn anything substantial, I'll be back."

Closing the door behind him, Julian heard Simon calling him. He turned to see his friend walking in his direction.

"Been in to see the duke?" Simon asked.

"Yes, he had a tidbit of information to pass along to me about Silves's."

Simon gave a knowing nod. "That's a regular hotbed of activity. Not that all of Paris isn't. The French may be defeated, but they definitely aren't downtrodden."

"That reminds me. I saw your brother in the Palais-Royal last night. Mind, he wasn't doing anything to precipitate trouble, but I wonder if he's totally aware of how close the situation here is to igniting."

"That's a good point. I do need to speak to him about that. Since their arrival, I've been just getting them settled, what with the negotiations on the peace treaty and the threat of Napoleon's escape from Elba." Simon rubbed wearily at his temples. "It seems there's never enough time in the day. At least Dami doesn't cause me trouble."

"Oh, does she usually?" This was interesting. Perhaps he could find out something to Lady Damaris's credit besides her birth and fortune.

"Don't suppose I should be telling you, of all people, this, but she's been prone in the past to get into more scrapes than is deemed acceptable for a girl." Simon smiled, smoothing out the worry lines in his forehead. "But she's been exemplary here. That's

. . . well, that's nothing." He thought better of telling his friend about Dami's ruse. If Camber developed a *tendre* for his sister, then it would be better if he didn't know how she was testing him. Nothing worse to cool a suitor's ardor than knowing he isn't trusted.

Camber raised an eyebrow but let the subject of Dami drop. "Perhaps you might contrive to teach that brother of yours some taste. The colors and dandy fashions Johnny follows are enough to put a fellow off his equilibrium."

Simon laughed. "Yes, I fear I must take the scamp aside and depress his pretensions to Brummell's throne."

On that note, they parted ways.

Since it was late morning, Julian made his way to Silves's to try his luck at flushing game. Sauntering up to the busy cafe, he gave it a once-over before making his way to the table de Bourville was seated at. The Frenchman was deep in conversation with another man, and oblivious of Julian's approach.

"Good morning, de Bourville." Julian broke into the first conversational lull. "May I join you?"

The count jerked around, his normally mild countenance registering surprise and then suspicion, quickly changing to acceptance. "Of course. My friend here was just leaving." He stared pointedly at the other man, who got up reluctantly and left without another word. "What brings you here, Camber? I don't believe I've seen you here before."

Julian signaled the waiter before answering. "Then you must haunt the place, for this is indeed my first time here. Simon FitzHubert recommended it to me just this morning as the ideal place for a good cup of coffee and stimulating conversation." He placed his order for coffee and croissants, seemingly engrossed in perfecting his French, but in reality making a more in-depth survey of the other denisons of the cafe.

"I wouldn't say I haunt the place," de Bourville said. "I believe, if my English is correct, that only a ghost or spirit of a dead person may haunt a place."

"Forgive me," Julian said, "I used a colloquialism. What I meant was that you must come here almost every day."

The coffee and pastry arrived, breaking the tension. Julian added the cream he preferred and buttered his croissant, allowing the count time to stew. He took a bite of the flaky croissant. "Exquisite. I must remember to thank Simon. There is nothing better than good coffee, pastry, and interesting companions. Don't you agree?" He looked for all the world like a man who has found his paradise.

"Like yourself, duke, I appreciate the better things in life. Unfortunately, my time is otherwise committed, so I must leave you to solitary enjoyment." Smooth as a snake, de Bourville rose and took his leave.

Julian watched him with a knowing smile curving his lips. This was an interesting development, but not totally unsuspected. The count would bear closer watching, and what better way than to hang about when de Bourville courted Lady Damaris and Amalie?

His smile disappeared. If de Bourville were doing what he suspected, then where did that leave Amalie? She had said the man had offered her marriage. And there was the French name she'd adopted. Could she be working for de Bourville—if the count was his man, that is. His mind rebelled at the idea, but for the sake of his country he didn't dare ignore it.

His pleasure in the morning's findings evaporated like water in the desert.

Chapter Eighteen

"What a bore," Julian muttered as he knocked on Simon's door. Smithfield, the butler, ushered him in, indicating that he wait in the parlor.

Entering the room, Julian stifled his surprise at seeing de Bourville. "So we meet again, count," he said smoothly. "Do you join us for dinner tonight?"

Rising from his seat, de Bourville executed a brief bow. "What a coincidence, duke. Yes, Lady Damaris asked me this afternoon. She stressed good English beefsteak and potatoes at the Cafe des Anglais on the Boulevard des Italiens. But," he murmured sinking back into his chair, "she didn't mention it was to be a party."

Julian gave him a sharp look. Did he hear a disgruntled suitor in the words? He quelled his exasperation. If so, then his problems were trebled. Not only must he determine if de Bourville were the spy he suspected, but he must untangle Lady Damaris from the man's wiles at the same time he endeavored to do the same for Amalie. At least Lady Damaris's problems were made easier by there being no shadow of duplicity on her part.

"Your Grace, Jacques," Dami said, entering the room. Even though her face was swathed in its familiar mask, her body managed to convey artful confusion. "Smithfield didn't tell me there was any-one in here. I thought I would be the first. I'm so excited about eating English food for a change."

Julian groaned inwardly. She had no appreciation of the culinary arts, either, if she was excited about beefsteak and potatoes. "I'm sure I speak for the count as well as myself when I tell you we are delighted that you are early."

She simpered as he led her to a seat by the fire. "So nice of you."

Julian gave her a once-over. As usual, she was in a becoming shade, lilac this time, and a modish gown that hugged her curves. And as usual, her hair was covered by a turban.

"Lady Damaris," he said sitting down next to her before de Bourville could take the seat, "not to be impertinent, but when do you expect to be able to remove your mask? I'm eager to see the beauty I imagine behind the mundaneness of the cloth."

"Oh, oh, my," she tittered. "Why, I expect some-time next week. The scars are almost healed." She dipped her head.

"We must have a party to celebrate the occasion," de Bourville inserted.

"A splendid idea," Julian agreed. He was getting tired of this game the chit persisted in playing.

"Hello, Julian, de Bourville," Simon said, entering the room with Lady Sebastian on his arm and Johnny on his heels.

Kit entered next, her titian curls burnished and her petite figure shown to advantage in a bronze muslin evening gown. "I'm here at last," she said breathlessly, her cheeks flushed.

"So you are," Julian said, rising to take her hand.

"Yes, and not a minute to lose," Johnny said. "This

place is supposed to be dashed popular, and if we don't hurry there won't be room for us."

Julian drawled, "I took the initiative of reserving us a table."

Within minutes, they were in two carriages. Camber found himself with the pleasure of Lady Damaris's company in his curricle, which only had room for two.

"How are you enjoying your stay, now that you've had several days to get your bearings?" He asked politely.

"It's delightful. So many shops. Why, even Napoleon's private apartments at St. Cloud are on view, and," she lowered her voice in awe, "they are magnificent."

"So I hear," Julian said dryly. "Have you been to the Louvre? It is full of priceless art treasures the Emperor managed to confiscate during his victories."

"The Louvre? Oh you mean the museum? No, no, I fear I'm not much on museums. . . . Oh, look, there is Prince Talleyrand." She waved vigorously at the man, who returned it with a languid movement of his hand.

What a bore, Julian thought to himself. The chit has no conversation because she has no brain. He turned his attention with resignation to his driving. He was marrying her for her breeding, not her scintillating wit. But to spend the rest of his life the way he envisioned the rest of this evening?

Behind her mask, Dami smiled. He was tired of her, which suited her purpose. Now she must fawn on him and convince him that she would accept him, thus tying him for life to a woman who worked like a sleeping draught on him. Perhaps then he would turn to Amalie—and she would have him just where she wanted him.

The next morning, Dami paused long enough to hear Johnny's muffled "come in" before entering his bedroom. She gave the large, airy room, done in cool blues, a cursory glance. "Did you enjoy wherever it was you gentlemen went last night after supper?" She sat on a pale blue brocade chair near the large window that opened to the back of the hotel.

Johnny forced open one eye to peer at her. "My head feels like it is ready to come off, and all you can think about is where we went. Oh," he groaned and collapsed back onto the pillows.

"If you hadn't indulged, you wouldn't be in this condition," she shot back, a twinkle in her eye. "It must have been a wild place if you shot-the-cat—or merely boring. Did Camber stay with you two?"

"Never thought you'd ask." Johnny tried again to pull himself up. "What time is it, anyway?"

"Time you were up, but that isn't the answer to my question."

"Know it isn't. Ohhh . . . I'll bet neither de Bourville nor Camber has a hangover like this," he muttered. "Where's Johnson?" He looked bleary-eyed around the room. "Not like him to leave me suffering like this."

"I told him to give us some privacy. Surely you can manage without your valet for ten minutes. Or at least, that is what it should have taken to get the information from you, but you have managed to skirt the issue nicely."

"All right. I've had enough of your torture. Yes, Camber stayed with us the whole time." He rubbed his eyes. "The man was a leech. And a killjoy too. Wouldn't have thought it of a man with his reputation." He shook his head and winced at the pain. "Wouldn't let me play roulette. Said it was too deep for my pockets. Never heard the like."

"Camber was protecting you. He has a chivalrous streak in him." Dami said it to needle Johnny, but she knew it was true.

"Yeah, well, he didn't do a very good job of it," Johnny muttered.

"What did you say, Johnny? You are talking under your breath a lot this morning. Is this another symptom of your condition?" She wasn't sure whether to be irritated with him or amused by his attempts to gain sophistication. "I knew Simon should have gone with you, but he had some correspondence to complete for Wellington."

"Nothing," he said, his eyes skirting hers.

Her eyes narrowed as she focused on her twin for the first time. He looked terrible and he refused to meet her eyes. Had something happened last night he wasn't telling her?

"Johnny, what happened besides your drinking more than you could hold?"

"Told you—nothing." He was beginning to sulk as he slid back under the covers.

"I know something did, and either you tell me or I'll ask someone else."

"Go ahead and ask. Nothing happened." As a matter of honor, he knew the other principal would tell her nothing.

"As you wish," she said, rising and heading for the door.

She descended the stairs in time to see the butler admitting de Bourville. Eager to find out Johnny's secret, she entered the drawing room before Smithfield could announce her. She closed the door in the scandalized butler's face and pounced on the count.

"Jacques," she started, "what happened last night? Johnny is evading my questions, but I know something occurred to make him upset."

"Lady Damaris, you are in looks today." He gave her a roguish smile. "It is so nice to see you without that mask and turban. Your hair is too lovely and unusual to hide." He rose to kiss her outstretched hand.

Taking her hand back as soon as it was seemly, Dami sat next to him. "You are being as obstinate as Johnny."

"I am merely admiring your beauty." He bent close to her. "You are everything a man could wish."

Dami leaned away from the count, but still his breath fanned her face. She put her hand out to ward him off, but she kept her voice neutral. He was too enmeshed in her schemes for her to alienate him now. "You are too bold. Please, I need your help, not your lovemaking."

His laugh was delighted. "You are an innocent if you think this is lovemaking. This is merely banter. When I make love to you, it will penetrate to the core of your being." He leaned back, forcing his intense voice to relax. "But about your brother. Things got rather out of hand last night and he was . . . ahem, well, this isn't what one discusses with a lady, but I suppose you have a right to know."

"What are you beating around the bush about?" At his look of compassion, she moved closer to him. "It's not something dangerous is it? It's not . . . not a duel?" Horror widened her eyes.

"*Cherie*, I don't like being the one to bring bad news." He caught her fluttering hand in his, brought it to his lips. "I did everything in my power to prevent it. I still hope to stop it. I know how it would hurt you if anything were to happen to Johnny."

"How did it happen?"

"It was nothing he could have avoided." He took the opportunity to take her hand. "The Frenchmen are using every excuse available to challenge Englishmen to duels. Many of them, particularly the soldiers, were happy with Napoleon."

Pulling her hands free, Dami said, "Please, why?"

He grimaced. "The reason given was his clothes."

"What?"

"Preposterous, I know. But then, that was only an excuse. It was enough that Johnny is English, and wealthy."

"Oh, no." She collapsed against the cushions, closing her eyes against the vision of her twin lying prone in the Bois de Boulogne, the cold dawn breaking over his still body. "I must do something," she moaned.

"No, no, *chérie*, there is nothing you can do, but trust me to prevent it." He still held her hand, which he began to kiss in earnest. "I vow to you I will protect your brother as though he were mine."

Dami opened her eyes, forced them to focus on the count. His face was creased with concern, and she felt herself warm at his caring. "Thank you," she murmured.

"Don't thank me. It is the very least I can do for the woman I love."

Hours later, Dami decided she must take Kit into her confidence. Her plan would work better if the two of them joined forces. Knocking on Kit's door, Dami waited only long enough to give her friend warning.

"Kit, we have to act quickly—tonight—or Johnny's life may be forfeited." Dami paused dramatically in the doorway.

"Whatever are you talking about," Kit said from her dressing room where she was debating the merits of two muslin evening gowns.

Dami enlightened her.

Entering the Salon des Etrangers, Julian nodded to the marquis de Livry, the host, as he glanced around the room. It was busy tonight, but he had no doubt his quarry would be here to put a good face on the situation.

"Damnation!" There was Amalie, bold as brass, a thin black mask over her eyes and her hand on the shoulder of the soldier who had challenged Johnny to a duel. And next to her . . . he couldn't believe his eyes. The hair was black instead of red, but the face and figure were his cousin's.

Anger sharpened his perceptions as Julian bore

down on the lively group. With an effort he kept his hand from pinching painfully into Amalie's shoulder as he leaned over her and whispered into her ear. "Madam, this time you have gone too far. Come with me now, or I will drag you screaming from this room."

She turned a startled face to him, but the fury in his face warned her against refusing. "Excuse me gentlemen," she said, laughing as she made her escape, "but the duke *won't* be denied."

A ripple of laughter eased their leave. Julian gripped her wrist and pulled her through the nearest door and into a small antechamber. He saw her glance furtively around the dark room. Satisfaction at her wary action loosened his grip. She yanked her arm away.

"Just what is the meaning of this?" she confronted him.

"I'm asking you the same question. Just what do you hope to prove by making a spectacle of yourself in the most disreputable gaming hall Paris has to offer? And," he pointed a finger at her, "dragging my cousin into this!"

Even as he berated her, Julian felt the pull she exerted on him. She was in the red velvet dress of the Cyprians' Ball, its plunging neckline clinging to her bosom. Now he knew intimately the feel of her white flesh as it molded to his fingers and caressed his chest. Taking a deep breath, he forced down his raging desire for her.

"I suppose," he said, "that this revolves around the duel young FitzHubert is to fight."

"Yes, and I'm afraid that you can't stop me."

"I think you will find out different, sweetings," he

drawled, taking one finger and running the rim of her plunging gown. He felt her shiver as he cursed himself for a fool. Much more of this and he would have her on the floor and none of their problems solved.

"It's not your concern, Julian." She faced him defiantly.

"That's where you're wrong." He pulled back from her and forced his face into composure. "Johnny FitzHubert is the brother of my best friend and the twin of the woman I intend to marry."

She paled. One hand reached out to the wall for support. "Of course. I had forgotten your involvement."

"Just what did you intend to do?" he asked conversationally. "Perhaps I can help you," he added.

"Jacques is helping me." She turned her back to him, not seeing him wince at her use of the count's first name. "I hope to get the French soldier too drunk to shoot accurately. Johnny plans on deloping."

"How did you concoct this abominable plot?"

Smiling ruefully, she turned back to him. "It was really quite easy. Much easier to think of than it's been to execute. In fact, I had to practically blackmail Johnny into letting me come with him. As for Kit, she did it willingly."

"Ah. And how came you to know Kit well enough to enlist her aid?"

"Well, I didn't, but when Jacques told me what happened, I felt that two women would be better than one in enticing the soldier into overindulging. And . . . and I didn't ask Lady Damaris because I felt it would scare her too much." She felt inordinately proud of coming up with so plausible an excuse for her alter ego's absence.

"Very convenient," Julian said dryly.

"Yes, wasn't it," she smiled brightly at him. "But now I need to get back out and help Kit."

"Tell me, why do you call her Kit instead of Lady Christine?"

"She asked me to call her Kit," Dami said defensively.

"I see. And why did de Bourville succumb to your wiles?"

She saw his eyes darken and his lips thin and knew instinctively what he was thinking. "Oh, la, Julian, you know how it is," she played to his thoughts, batting her eyelashes. He deserved to suffer a little.

"I'm afraid I do, sweetings. But come, as you said, there is much that still needs to be done." He took her elbow. "Watch what I do, and play along with me, Amalie. I have already decided how to deflect the Frenchman from Johnny. Trust me, my way will be easier to accomplish than yours." He steered her back into the crowded room.

Dami took a deep breath as she took her vacated seat again and flashed a smile around. She paused momentarily on the count's face. He was looking angry.

"Gentlemen," Camber bowed around, "and ladies," he forced Kit to meet his eyes, "please allow me to join you." He sat next to Amalie without waiting for an answer. "Monsieur," he turned to the French soldier, "I believe we've met before, at the Cafe Silves's, but have not been properly introduced. I'm Camber."

Insufferable, Dami thought. The man speaks as though only to say his name is enough to explain who he is. "The duke of Camber," she inserted smugly.

"Your Grace," the soldier said, nodding. "My name is François Cancalle, lately a captain in Napoleon's army." He smiled defiantly around the table.

Dami stifled her gasp at the man's effrontery.

"Captain," Julian said, his eyes hard as tacks. "But that explains why you are to be found gambling with all the other 'hawks.'" His lips sneered at the man. "Of course, you don't have a family fortune to lose, as some others here do."

Had the man taken leave of his senses? "Julian," Dami said sweetly. "You promised to show me how to play roulette."

If Camber's plan was to goad the Frenchman into fighting a duel with him, she would rather go back to her original plan!

"Women," he murmured for the table at large, "they only understand what pertains to them. My dear," he turned back to her, "I intend to teach you all the games of chance, but only when I am finished here." Under cover of the table, he stepped lightly on her toes.

"Insufferable," Dami grumbled to herself, swiftly moving her feet out of his reach.

"As I was saying, before being so agreeably interrupted," his bland smile encompassed the table, "I image the life of a soldier of fortune at the gaming table is as exciting as that of a soldier of fortune under Napoleon."

"Monsieur, duke, your insinuations are beyond bearing." The captain reached out his hand and slapped Camber across the cheek with his glove. "I demand satisfaction."

"How dare you strike me, you French popinjay!" Camber surged to his feet. "Meet me in thirty minutes at the Bois de Boulogne, with your pistol primed."

"So be it," the Frenchman huffed.

"No, no," cried de Bourville, jumping to his feet. "Cancalle is already committed to meet FitzHubert there in a few hours. And where are seconds to be found at such short notice?" he added desperately.

Camber's eyes narrowed at the count's odd behavior. "Johnny will be my second," he said, looking at Johnny to get his confirming nod, "and you shall second Cancalle. That shouldn't be too hard, since it was you I saw him talking to the other day in Silves's."

This was unanswerable.

Dami looked from Camber to de Bourville and felt an unpleasant sensation go down her spine.

The sun was just beginning to rise and it cast a small glow on the two men as they paced away from each other in the Bois de Boulogne. In slow motion they turned, their guns leveling.

Bang! The deafening sound of pistols firing broke the silence. In pantomime, Cancalle slid to the grass, winged in the shoulder. Camber stood his ground.

From within the curricle, tears of relief slid down Dami's cheeks. Johnny was safe. And so was Camber.

Chapter Nineteen

Early the next morning, de Bourville called upon Dami. She greeted him in some surprise.

"Milord," Dami extended her hand formally, "how charming of you to call."

De Bourville took her proffered hand and kissed it. "I found I couldn't bear to remain away longer, *chérie*." His brown eyes burned into hers as he led her to a settee where he pulled her down next to him. "I have come to beg your compassion for a man whose heart is sorely tried."

Dami suppressed the smile his melodrama engendered. Even his thigh pressing tightly to hers did nothing for her. And his eyes, their soulful expression causing them to droop in what she felt sure was a very sensual manner, left her detached. She didn't think she could say anything without laughing, so she kept quiet.

"I am bursting with love for you." He dropped to one knee in front of her, grabbing her hand and

305

pressing it to his heart. "Feel how my heart beats for you? Say you will make me the happiest man in the world. Say you will marry me."

"Count, Jacques, please get up."

"Your wish is my desire," he said, sitting next to her again.

"You have taken me by storm. That is, I didn't expect this." He looked like an expectant puppy with his brown eyes imploring her to say yes. She would try to let him down gently. "I care for you, Jacques, but I don't love you."

"It doesn't matter, *ma chérie*. I will love you enough for two." He pressed closer to her.

Unable to endure his closeness longer, she leaned back onto the arm of the settee.

"I'm sorry, Jacques, but I can't marry you."

"Is it because I'm only a poor emigré who must make my way working for your government? If so, you must not let it stop you, for I promise you that soon I will have all my lands back and more. I shall be rich beyond your imagination." His eyes sparkled with his fervor.

For a second, he looked like a fanatic, and Dami found herself shrinking further from him. Her voice when she spoke was soothing. "No, it isn't that. Never something as paltry as that. And I know you will have your title and lands fully restored. Why, Louis has already started giving back what was lost in the Revolution."

His eyes sharpened like a ferrets. "The Bourbon king? Yes, he has made promises." He caught himself up. "Yes, that is it exactly."

She could see him getting himself under control as

he moved back from her and assumed a relaxed position. Her tension flowed from her.

"I haven't thanked you for your help last night," she said, hoping to take his mind from its errand.

"Bah! Last night was a bagatelle." He waved his hand dismissively. "I would give my life for you." He paused. "It is Camber, isn't it? I see by your blush that I am correct; don't bother to deny it." He rose. "I won't importune you further."

Watching the door close behind de Bourville, Dami reflected ruefully that she had never intended to hurt anyone but Camber. Perhaps it was time for the charade to end.

"You wished to see me?" Camber said, entering the duke of Wellington's office.

"Yes. Be seated, won't you." Wellington indicated a chair, and Camber sat. "We just apprehended a Frenchman passing out more pamphlets emblazoned with Napoleon's symbol—violets." He handed one to Camber.

Julian scanned its contents. "This is more inflammatory than the last. If the populace gets hold of this, we are headed for trouble."

"Exactly. It will incite them to riot under the belief that Napoleon's escape from Elba is imminent. We already have more trouble than we can adequately handle without this. You have to get to the bottom of this—and quickly."

"You're right," Camber agreed. "It seems our leak refuses to give us time. However, I have my suspect in hand." He leaned forward to give Wellington an update.

Thirty minutes later, Julian left Wellington's office for Silves's. He waved to Simon in passing, the sight of his friend bringing back last night's fiasco. He pushed the memory from his mind.

Nearing the cafe, Julian saw what he had expected. De Bourville was deep in conversation with another French soldier. Julian approached them, careful to keep his manner nonchalant.

"May I join you?" he asked them. His blood picked up at the startled look they gave him.

"But of course," de Bourville said, regaining his aplomb.

Without a word, the soldier rose and melted into the teeming crowd.

"A lovely morning for having coffee outside," Julian said, mentally smiling at how like Lady Damaris he sounded with his talk of weather.

"I enjoy most mornings here, Your Grace," de Bourville said.

Julian looked sharply at him. The count was slipping to admit to such a thing, and now that he took the time to notice, he could see that de Bourville looked distracted, too. He could see resolution forming on the Frenchman's face.

"Camber," the word was like a shot, "you are to be congratulated."

"I am?" Julian said. De Bourville was cagy, but what card was he playing now?

"Of a certainty. Haven't you just won the hand of the most lovely and talented woman in England — or France?"

Julian studied the man. He didn't look bosky, but

he definitely sounded it. "Not that I am aware of."

"Then it is only because you haven't asked for it, but I am assured that it is your intention to do so."

"Ahhh," Julian said, "I take it you are referring to my pursuit of Lady Damaris."

"But of course, doesn't everyone know that you are courting her? And isn't it obvious that she will accept?"

De Bourville's voice took on a bitter tinge as Julian leaned back in his chair to allow the waiter to place his coffee. Taking his time, Julian stirred in a liberal helping of cream.

Turning his attention back to his companion, Julian said, "I assume she will accept. Her brother has already agreed to my suit."

"Never doubt, she will have you."

"Tried your luck, old chap, and lost?" Julian found himself almost feeling sorry for the man. "But you know women and titles and money. They are forever looking out for the biggest catch. But you will be able to console yourself with the lovely Amalie."

De Bourville smiled bitterly. What a fool the duke was. "Tell me, Your Grace, do you love Lady Damaris?"

"What a question, and coming from a man of the world like yourself." It was Julian's turn to smile bitterly. "What has love to do with marriages between people of our station? We reserve that particular emotion for our opera dancers."

"Then if you lost the lady tomorrow you would not grieve?" The count leaned forward in his chair, his eyes lighting.

Julian scowled at him. "I would be sorry to lose a

lady of her standing — but 'grieve' is too strong a word."

"Ah!" Rising, de Bourville picked up his hat and cane. "If you will excuse me, I have matters of the utmost importance to attend to."

Julian watched the count's back disappear. The man was up to something havey-cavey, but he didn't think it had to do with spying. Not this time.

He lounged back against the twisted wire frame of the cafe chair and took a cheroot from his pocket. Lighting it, he took a deep drag, then blew one large, perfect smoke ring. The count had disappointed him. He had hoped that by bringing Amalie into the discussion, the Frenchman might be goaded to let something drop. Instead the man had acted as if the woman and what they were doing were the last things on his mind.

And the talk of Lady Damaris. Ugh! Marry the woman he might, but love her? She was a dead bore and would probably be as cold in bed as a whore discussing money.

He flicked the ashes of his cigar. He knew it would be a mistake to marry the woman. He would never be happy with her and never be faithful to her. Both their lives would be miserable. All his good intentions were nothing when he remembered the fire Amalie built in him. If only Amalie would take him on his terms, then he could marry for convenience and still be content with his lot. Guilt pricked at him. Lady Damaris wouldn't be happy to have a husband who openly betrayed her with his mistress. And he owed it to Simon to do better by his sister.

He pushed the thought away, surging to his feet.

Enough of that. He must force de Bourville to tip his hand, and at the same time see that Amalie's dabbling in espionage was covered up. Bile rose at the thought of his love's betraying the country he loved, but he knew that no matter what she did, he would try to protect her.

Chapter Twenty

Dami pushed into the parlor, flung off her black cape, and twirled till her black muslin skirt floated around her like smoke. "Do you like it?" she said, still spinning.

"Egad! So this is why you had me meet you down here early," Johnny said, a look of horror dawning on his face as he took in the plunging decolletage and lack of a slip.

"Tonight's the night," Dami hummed. She pirouetted and dropped into a deep curtsy at Johnny's pumps. Her skirts puffed around her like clouds, curling and clinging to her hips and bosom, floating around her slender waist. Looking mischievously up at him, she said, "Tonight I bring the proud duke of Camber to his shocked, nay, prostrated knees. Tonight, I tell him all."

"I knew I should have stayed in bed," Johnny moaned. "What you really mean to say is that tonight you plan on ruining any reputation you manage to have left and pull the family down with you." He groaned and made for a tray of port and glasses. Pouring himself one, he gulped it down before turning back to his sister. "I don't suppose Simon or Kit or Lady Sebastian know anything about this?" At her nod, he screwed his eyes shut. "And you expect me to escort you to Lady Oxford's masquerade early so you can be in place before they have a chance to tumble to your ruse and prevent it?" At her "yes," he continued, "And just what makes you think that I will aid you in still another ramshackle adventure?"

"Johnny, dear," she got up and went to him, laying her hand on his arm, "because I contrived to help you in your hour of need. Would you deny me? Why, this masquerade is the perfect opportunity to reveal myself to Camber and rub in his face the truth that not only will Amalie not be his mistress, but Lady Damaris will not be his wife."

"Cruel."

"Exactly."

"Come now."

"He snubbed me as a nobody because he couldn't let love overcome his cerebral workings, then wooed me as a lady with lukewarm motivation because he had no heart to overcome. He deserves to suffer!" She turned from her twin and picked up her discarded cape. "If you don't take me, then I will be obliged to go alone, and you know Paris has no lights at night, except at the Palais-Royal, and that isn't near Lady Oxford's."

"Once again, you win. But mark my words, Dami, you are going to get caught. I would have thought you'd learned your lesson at Felixstowe. It's not as if any other man will have you now. Give over. This goes too far."

She rounded on him. "You give over, Johnny.

313

Should I let Camber get off scot free after what he did to me?" She pulled her cape around her shoulders and fastened it tight at the throat. "Are you coming?" she flung at him as she opened the door.

With a sigh, ne joined her.

The trip to Lady Oxford's was short and stormy. Johnny continued to upbraid her, saying she would regret the night's work, and if she were smart, she would take the duke quietly aside and break the news to him gently.

"Johnny," Dami interrupted his monologue, "you are only increasing my determination to carry out my original plan."

They were still arguing when the carriage pulled up and the outrider opened the door for them. Giving the man her hand, Dami thanked him for his help and secretly preened herself on the shocked interest he had been unable to mask. If a man trained from the cradle not to show surprise at anything the aristocracy did couldn't contain his emotions, then she felt sure His Grace, the duke of Camber, would be equally nonplussed.

Since it was a masquerade, there was a receiving line, but no one mentioned names and no butler announced new arrivals. Pausing long enough to exchange pleasantries with their hostess, Dami quickly turned her attention to the room. She hoped Camber had come early, since she had hinted the other day as Lady Damaris that she had a surprise in store for him.

The massive ballroom was done in the Empire style made popular by Napoleon's Egyptian campaigns. The walls were a smooth grey, hung with massive paintings depicting his battles in Egypt. Red columns stood at each end of the room, flanking the large windows, which were hung with matching drapes and overlooked the inner courtyard. The floor was a herringbone pattern of parquet, perfectly suited for the gliding motions of the dancing couples scattered across it.

Finally, having almost decided that Camber had decided not to humor her, Dami spotted him near the orchestra.

"Your Grace." She approached him where he lounged against the wall watching the masked dancers exert themselves, "don't you recognize me?"

His eyes studied her from the folds of a black domino. "Should I?" His gaze ran over her figure. The filmy muslin drifted from the tight empire bodice to float around her ankles, showing black satin pumps. Her rosy nipples turned the material over them a darker shade. "Very lovely," he said, sounding as though he was discussing a horse and not a woman.

Dami felt herself begin to puff with anger. She pulled her chest up and her shoulders back. "Your memory must be faulty, duke. I believe I've told you before I am not horseflesh for your arrogant appraisal."

"Very nice, indeed," he said, taking in her jutting bosom. "Perhaps I do know you, or if I don't, will." He reached out to cup her waist. "The mask, however, must go."

His hot touch on her skin made her gasp, but she managed to maintain enough savvy to reach up and stay his hand. "Not yet. It lends piquancy to the situation and prevents nothing at this stage."

He bowed and let his hand drop. "Very well."

Without preamble, he swung her into the music. His severe black evening dress complimented her filmy black evening gown. Together they twirled in a world of smoky dreams and desire.

His arm around her waist and his hand holding hers firmly gave Dami a feeling of security even as his touch sent tremors of sensation racing through her body. She allowed her head to rest on his shoulder, uncaring of the looks they might garner.

His warm breath roved through her curls, sending them floating to his face. His lips moved enticingly on her forehead as he pulled her tighter.

Around and around they spiraled, their bodies pressing together like magnets with opposite charges. They broke apart with the movements of the dance, only to come inexorably back together.

Whatever else happened tonight, Dami vowed not to regret this last moment of closeness with him. Waves of remembered pleasure washed over her, leaving her weak in their wake. For a fleeting moment, she wished she were truly Amalie and could overcome her foolishly idealistic need for true love. She wanted to be with him no matter what the cost.

"You look like a wicked fairy, intent on making me lose my good resolve, for you feel all too real pressed against me. I am here to meet another woman, and I doubt if she would appreciate finding me with a woman of your exposed charms tight to my chest."

She pulled her head from his shoulder to watch his reaction to her words. "La, you are overbold. Simon would have severe doubts about your suitability were he to hear them."

He scowled down at her. "Simon? What has he to say to this?"

"Everything, and nothing." She felt him stiffen, and he loosened his grip on her. She stumbled at the lack of firm guidance as he chose that moment to put them in a twirl.

"Your hair is very beautiful and very striking. Am I mistaken in whom I think I hold in my arms?"

Her laugh was brittle. "That all depends on whom you imagine you are dallying with, Your Grace."

"The voice is melodious and well modulated. A bit deep and gruff for most men's tastes, but distinctive nonetheless — and strangely exotic."

"Has it ever been different?"

"And the body is full-bosomed and willowy, moving with a grace that is undeniable."

"I strive to please," she murmured.

"Yes you do. Even to the dress. A plunging concoction of midnight muslin that whispers around your charms, like mist on the moor, hiding one minute, revealing the next." His gaze plunged to her neckline. "Lovely skin and breathtaking attributes. One would think you came here pretending to be a courtesan."

Dami smirked behind her mask, even as pink crept up from her decolletage to stain the skin at the roots of her hair. "But isn't this a masquerade?" she said innocently.

With a dip and a twist, they were out on the balcony. The warm summer air moved against her heated skin in cooling strokes. She wished for a fan to feign unconcern with. Thankfully, she noticed no lamps or candles on the rails or walls and no moon, either. It was hiding behind a cloud. She moved to stand near the wall, her hands lightly touching the stone behind her.

"What game do you play tonight, Amalie?" Camber's voice was flat as he leaned negligently against the railing, his dark clothes a darker shadow in the night.

Dami turned her head to study the whirling couples moving past the door on her right. "Am I playing a game? And how can you mistake me for another woman, Julian? I thought you wished to marry me, or so Simon says. If such is the case, isn't your love strong enough to recognize me in disguise?" She said the words softly, not looking at him.

With a sigh, she moved away from the wall and turned her back to him. She didn't want to see enlightenment tighten his mouth and narrow his eyes when he realized her duplicity. She didn't want to see all her secret hopes against hope die as contempt entered his eyes.

His finger touched the small of her back where the thin gown met her flesh. "I would recognize this back anywhere, Amalie. I don't know how you got in here, I imagine Johnny FitzHubert helped you, but you have got to go. This is no place for you."

"Déjà vu," she murmured, turning to face him. With a smooth flick of her wrist, she untied her mask and let it drop to the stone floor. "I believe I've heard those words fall from your lips before, Julian." She made his name a caress. "Simon will be very disappointed in your perspicacity."

"Simon would never countenance your presence

here, any more than I can." He straightened up and extended a hand to her imperiously. "I know you are enjoying yourself, coming to an exclusive ball and taunting me with your knowledge of my plans to marry Lady Damaris, but it has got to end."

"Oh, it will, it will," she sighed. With a resolute squaring of her shoulders, she swept from him before he could stop her.

"Amalie," his voice rang in her ears as she made straight for Simon, Kit, Johnny, and Lady Sebastian where they were paying their respects to Lady Oxford.

Julian ripped off his domino and followed her. He was in time to hear Lady Oxford say, "Oh, Lady Damaris, you don't know how pleased I am to see you finally put off that disfiguring mask. And your hair. I never could understand why you saw fit to hide it as well."

Julian stopped. His body stone. Dami turned to look at him. His eyes, as grim and opaque as iron, looked through her. He spun on his heel and was lost in the throng.

"What is going on, Dami?" Simon's sharp voice jerked her around.

"I'm only proving to you that Camber isn't the paragon you perceive him to be," she answered, her eyes flashing and her mouth in a grim line.

"Ah," said Lady Sebastian with a knowing look, "the game of love is strewn with rocks."

Dami turned to her. "No, ma'am, the game of lust is finally dashed on the rocks."

"Even better," murmured the older woman with a wicked gleam in her green eyes.

"Dash it, Dami, I knew you'd make a muddle of it,"

Johnny injected. "Why, he gave you the cut direct."

Dami glanced at her twin, then back to Simon. "Not the proper thing for a gentleman to do after he finds out his fiancée isn't quite the demure nonentity he thought her. And in public, too."

"You must brazen it out," Kit said with authority as she took Dami's arm and guided her to where the count de Bourville talked with a mixed group of French and English gentlemen.

"Lady Damaris, may I have this waltz?" de Bourville asked. "It appears to be the only music Lady Oxford is allowing her musicians to play tonight."

Kit watched the couple enter the dance floor. She noticed her cousin who, surprisingly, was still there. At the moment, he was talking to several ladies who seemed to be vying for his favors.

On the dance floor, de Bourville said to Dami, "It was much harder than you expected."

"Yes, it was." She smiled, trying to look impudently at him, knowing she failed. "Not that I expected it to be easy, but I thought he would have better control of himself than to cut me in front of the entire English contingent in Paris." She couldn't keep the small edge of hurt out of her voice.

"No, that was not well done," he commiserated. "Should I call him out for you? Defend your honor? I would do it gladly."

Her smile turned wistful. "That is very gallant, but not necessary. It would only result in one of you being hurt and the gossips having their latest on dit confirmed."

Somehow she managed to follow his lead through the rest of the dance, but the glitter was gone from the evening. She couldn't help but notice the stares that were becoming more evident as time passed. Her imagination filled in the words her ears couldn't hear.

"*Ma chérie*," de Bourville said, halting their movements as the music stopped, "marry me and all of this will be only a nine days' wonder. I will take you away to my château, and you need see no one but me." At the anguish in her eyes, he said, "I love you so much it doesn't matter that you love him."

It was too much. She choked, "That is too, too kind, Jacques. I don't deserve it." She hung her head as he steered them to the privacy of a dark corner. "I could never make you happy or be happy myself." She raised her eyes to his, the tears beginning to fall. "It wouldn't be fair to you. You see, I would always compare you with him, and while he has many faults, he also has the redeeming quality of my love. No," she put an imploring hand on his sleeve, "I can't accept your offer. And besides," the words stuck in her throat, but she forced them out, "I belong to him . . . he has made me his, you see."

He quickly masked his shock, but not before it had pierced through her melancholy.

"That does not matter to me, *ma chérie*," he assured her. "I only burn that he dared to do such to you and then refused to marry you. Now, more than ever, I must insist you marry me."

From his position on the sidelines, Julian watched the affecting scene between Amalie, no, Lady Damaris, and de Bourville. He saw her hand on the count's arm, her brown eyes large with longing as she looked at the man, and the man's earnest face as he took her to a secluded corner.

Julian's emotions rioted. The heat of anger cooled, to be followed by relief that he could marry the woman he loved and not betray his responsibility to his title and name. But it was swiftly followed by disillusionment. She had played him for a dupe and even now was probably accepting de Bourville's renewed proposal.

He moved away from the group, only to freeze as a thought struck him. If Amalie was involved in Bonapartist activities, then so was Lady Damaris.

Chapter Twenty-One

Her chin high, Dami watched Camber leave the masquerade. She turned a sparkling smile on de Bourville, saying, "I believe I will have that glass of champagne you mentioned."

"At once." He bowed and left to procure it.

Her head was beginning to ache in earnest now. Her lips twisted in a smile. It served her right after all her posings in bed with a megrim.

"Here you are, Lady Damaris," de Bourville said, handing her a glass.

"Thank you." She sipped the sparkling wine. As it bubbled up her nose, memories of her afternoon at Twickenham with Camber bubbled through her thoughts. "I am not feeling at all well. I think I will seek out Johnny and ask him to take me home." She tried to smile graciously at the count, but knew she wasn't succeeding.

"Please, allow me," he said. At her protest, he pressed, "No, I want to take you home. You need someone who will be sympathetic." He led her to the door. "Do you have a cape?"

At her nod, he sent the footman to get it. With

tender hands he draped the cloak over her and tied it at her neck. The love and longing in his eyes were more than Dami could bear. She focused beyond his shoulder, wondering how she had ever made such a bumblebath of it all.

DeBourville helped her into his barouche, the hood up, and they were off. The filtered light of the lanterns cast eerie shadows on the brown velvet squabs and etched harsh lines on the count's face as he watched her. Feeling his eyes on her, Dami kept her attention concentrated on the streets they were traveling. As she watched, she noticed the buildings changing from the imposing brick fronts of large mansions with well-lit windows and ornate doors to smaller buildings, neat, but with ordinary doors and fewer lit windows. The streets appeared to be narrowing, as the walls they passed were getting closer to the sides of the carriage. Finally, the smell of open sewers became so strong that she was forced to hold her scented handkerchief to her nose. The buildings now had shutters over the windows instead of expensive glass, and some of the shutters hung drunkenly on their hinges.

She looked at the count with raised eyebrows. "Are we taking the scenic route?"

His face, grim minutes before, turned to her with gentle care easing the lines. "So to speak, *chérie*. We are going to my home."

She jerked up. "I can't go with you, Jacques, and you know it," she said.

"You can't go home, either, Damaris."

"Jacques," she began patiently, "I know you want to protect me, but this is something I must clear up

324

myself. It is, after all, of my own making."

"Not true. It is because of Camber and his high-handed ways that you find yourself in this compromising position. And what you told me." He grabbed at her hand, taking it to his cheek. "No gentleman would do what he did to you and then treat you so callously." The fierceness in his eyes died. "I want to care for you, and I will." He turned her hand over and pressed a hot kiss into her palm.

Dami controlled the urge to yank her hand from him. Where Camber's touch had left the fire of desire, de Bourville's left only icy dread.

"What do you intend to do with me?"

He reached out and stroked the silver curl that had worked its way loose from her chignon. His eyes followed his hand as though mesmerized. "You have such beautiful hair, *ma chérie*. It is like moonlight on the Seine."

"Jacques, please," she said curtly.

"I intend to marry you. It will be a civil ceremony only, but it will be legal. Later we will be wed in the church. After Napoleon is reinstated," he murmured.

Her eyes widened. She marshaled her thoughts. "I can't marry you. Simon would never countenance it. You are very kind to want to help me, but Simon has already told me that if I choose not to marry he will support me. Conversely, if I enter into a marriage without his consent, he will see that it is annulled."

"*Ma chérie*," he said, his voice like an adult speaking to a recalcitrant child, "*ma chérie*, you forget the world. Everyone saw you leave Lady Oxford's with me. When you don't appear tomorrow, or the next day, there will be talk. Next week, after our honeymoon, will be too late for Simon to have the marriage annulled." Sly cunning entered his brown eyes, turning them from their normal innocence to something sinister. "And even if I were to forgo the pleasure of bedding you, a doctor's examination would still show you to be no maiden."

"Oh," she gasped. How could a man she trusted so greatly, betray her like this! He was twisting everything she had told him in confidence to fit his nefarious plans.

Immediately contrite, he squeezed the hand he still held. "I'm sorry. That was cruel. It will not come to that, *chérie*. You will see. We shall be happy together. I love you. You will see." He settled back into the cushions, pulling her to him.

He wasn't rough, or even importuning. All he did was hold her to him, one arm around her shoulders, the other still holding her hand. Dami's skin crawled. Somehow, she had to make him see reason before he succeeded in his ploy to marry her. Perhaps she could convince him she would marry him willingly if he would return her home. Then, once safe, she could work something out.

"Jacques," she turned pleading eyes to him, "please, take me home. I will tell Simon I have decided to marry you. That will be enough. He will allow it."

"Oh, *ma chérie*," he bent to kiss the top of her head, "you are such an innocent. I can't let you go now. You know my secret, the one Camber has been sniffing around since he arrived in Paris. If I let you free now, you would go straight to your lover and tell him. Then where would I be? No, you must marry me. It is best for all. I will cherish you for the rest of your life. There will be no other woman but you." She stared, fascinated, into his eyes. "That is more than Camber would have ever given. He doesn't love you. I do."

"My God," she muttered. And what secret was he talking about? Something must have slipped her attention. Holding her body stiff as a poker, she turned to look out the window.

Returning to his lodgings, not bothering to change, Camber strode into the library. He sank into a large leather chair. There was something about the musty odor of companionable books that always worked to soothe his nerve-tightened body.

Loosening his cravat, he propped his feet up on a stool. Briefly, he wished for brandy, but rejected that, too. He needed a level head to decide what to do next.

There was no doubt that he would marry Amalie. All the problems that had hitherto held him back had been dramatically resolved tonight. Granted, she was a baggage, and would lead him a merry chase, already had, but he loved her, and as fate would have it, her birth and breeding were everything he could want. She would make him an exciting, sensual duchess.

A smug smile curved his lips and crinkled his eyes. Well-being permeated him. But first, he must manage to get her out of de Bourville's clutches and then insure that when the count was arrested she was in no way implicated. At the moment, it seemed an insurmountable task. He shrugged. He had no doubts of his ability to do it.

"Your Grace," his butler barged into his thoughts,

"there is a gentleman here to see you."

"At this time?" Julian didn't bother to turn around. "Tell him I am not home."

"Yes, sir," the butler made his silent retreat.

"I really think you must see me," said a familiar voice from the door.

Jumping up, Julian rounded on his uninvited guest. "Perth! Out of my house before I challenge you to a long delayed duel. Don't think I have forgotten Felixstowe."

"I didn't think you had," the earl said, entering and stripping off his gloves and beaver hat. "But this time I am not the villain in the play."

"I have nothing to say to you," Julian said wearily, taking his seat again. "Go away. I have problems to solve and don't have time for you, much as I would like it different."

"Yes, you do have problems, Camber. More serious than you think, or . . ." he paused to move in front of the duke, "are you already aware that Lady Damaris is right now on her way to a secluded house belonging to the count de Bourville?"

"What?" Julian thundered, jumping once more from his seat and taking a belligerent stance.

"You are beginning to resemble a jack-in-the-box," Perth drawled.

Julian's face darkened with anger. "What game are you playing now? When I left Lady Oxford's, Amalie, I mean Lady Damaris—damn the chit and her names—was dancing with the count. And even you must admit there is nothing in that."

"We can stand here and fence all night, or you can accompany me and I will tell you what I know on the

328

way." Perth eyed him coolly.

Julian reined in his anger and studied the earl. Perth was as cold as ice, and sounded about as emotional. Yet, once again, he didn't dare call the earl's bluff. Amalie—no, Damaris— was too precious to him.

With a shrug, Julian rose and went into the hallway, yelling, "My hat and coat. I am going out and don't know when I shall return." He turned back to Perth who was following him. "I trust you have your curricle ready?"

"Of course."

Ensconced in the two-wheeled racing vehicle, they bowled down the unlit streets, heading for the outskirts.

"Your explanation," Julian said. His eyes strained to see their direction in the light of the full moon. They had to reach Amalie in time.

"Such a dull story," Perth said, casting a glance at his companion, "but one I can see you will insist on having. After being put on my yacht in Felixstowe, and with such originality, I set sail for France. Word had reached me that Wellington was in need of subterfuge. That surprises you? It shouldn't. You must remember that I often worked behind the lines during the Peninsula campaign. With a French mother, I speak the language like a native. So, I came here to try and flush out the War Ministry's leak."

"Then why did they involve me?" Camber interrupted.

"You were to hit the more aristocratic environs, while I searched the sewers, so to speak. In fact, I was hot on de Bourville's tail the night of your duel with

Cancalles. The man was one of de Bourville's dupes. Anyway, from everything I can surmise, de Bourville has been in Bonaparte's pay from the start."

"I thought as much," Julian said.

"Yes, I knew you did. The count had all his hereditary properties returned years ago, but continued to stay in England until Napoleon's victories and his domination of Europe were assured. De Bourville must have been very surprised when Wellington defeated Boney. However, that hasn't stopped him. He is busy keeping the Bonapartist sympathizers alert to our every move, and he is deep into a plot to spring Napoleon from Elba."

"So far you have not told me anything Wellington hasn't already. What makes tonight so important?"

"Because tonight he has taken Lady Damaris to one of his restored properties to the southeast of Paris. And it wouldn't surprise me if he has revealed his double-dealings to her as well." He cast a measuring look at the duke. "It appears that they have been thick as spies, if you'll pardon the expression, the last couple of weeks. But whatever chase the lady has led you, I don't believe her to be a knowing conspirator with the count."

"How do you know where this place is?"

"De Bourville spends a lot of his time there, and I have trailed him to it before. However, I am not sure that is where he has taken her tonight. I only know this is the direction he headed in. I judged it more prudent to get you."

"Why me and not Simon?"

"Because you have already compromised the lady, and I thought you were prepared to wed her." He expertly guided his team around a corner. "If I was mistaken, you may wait here while I deal with the situation."

"You are a scoundrel, Jason," Julian said, shaking his head. "But you and I think alike."

"So I thought," the earl murmured.

Dami rounded on the count. "You can't keep me here indefinitely."

She shuddered at the thought. The room they were in was magnificent. Done in the rococo fashion, it was small by modern standards, but the inlaid mirrors and pale blue plaster walls made it seem large. Silver-gilded wood, carved into ragged C-scrolls, garlands of flowers decked with ribbons, and sprays of foliage were appliqued on the walls. The same gilded wood surrounded each mirror like a frame and was reproduced in the intricate carvings of the chairs and settees, which were covered in heavy silver satin.

"Do you like my hotel, *chérie*?" de Bourville asked from the distance of the fireplace with its lapis lazuli mantel.

"It's lovely. But," she frowned, groping for something he had said to explain the wealth, "how can you afford such luxury on the salary of a civil servant. Gone are the days when those positions were lucrative enough to make them desirable."

"Ah, you must have missed my remark on that." He turned to stir the fire with a silver poker.

Dami studied his back. It was so slim and elegant, not a fop, but not a Corinthian, either. She had thought him one of the most fashionable men she knew, next to Camber. His face was always so open and handsome, in a young-boy way. She was having trouble rearranging her perception of him. Like a nightmare floating away with the morning light, his words came back to her.

"You got this from Napoleon." She was stunned. Had a chair not been at her back she would have slumped to the floor. "You are a spy for Napoleon. But how have you kept it secret? What are you doing now, with Napoleon on Elba? What do you want with me?" The questions ran through her mind like a string of beads.

"*Chérie*." He turned to face her, his eyes shadowed in the faint light from the fire. "The only question you have asked that matters is about you. I intend to marry you and keep you with me always. I found you amusing in London, but knew you were above my touch," he spread his arms, "even with all this magnificence, since it will do me no good until Napolean defeats England. But, that time in Paris . . ." his voice lowered and his eyes became sparkling almonds in his pale face, ". . . when you took me into your confidence about your scheme to humble Camber, then I knew you would be mine. I admit to some doubts when you professed to love the duke, but when he told me in Silves's that he didn't love you, then—*then*—I knew without doubt that you were mine." As the last words left his mouth, he bore down on her.

She cringed into the skimpy seat, her heart pounding out a tattoo. Somehow she had to escape.

Belatedly, his words about Napoleon crystallized. She had to warn Wellington. This man was dangerous to her country.

He threw himself on the Beauvais carpet at her feet, his hands grabbing for her fingers where they were twisted together in the folds of her gown.

"You mustn't do this," she reasoned with him. "I'm not worthy of you. You know I don't love you, not as you wish, and that I love another man. Surely you can't want to saddle yourself with a woman who has given herself to someone else." She pulled, wiggling her fingers in his clasp.

"I don't care, *chérie*." He moved to clasp her around the waist. "I am bewitched by you."

Dami strove to remain calm. A plan—she must come up with a plan.

"Jacques," she smoothed his hair back from his forehead, "it will work out, but right now I need to refresh myself."

She forced herself to meet his eyes. As the cloud of passion cleared from his face, his eyes took on a suspicious look, then one of understanding.

"Of course. How inconsiderate of me," he said, rising and freeing her. "There are no servants here, not like there will be when Napoleon escapes, so I will take you to a chamber upstairs. I will give you thirty minutes, *chérie*, then I will return for you and we shall be married. By then, my valet will have fetched the man who is to marry us."

She acquiesced, following him up the most magnificent set of stairs she had seen in a private home. They were freestanding, spiraling up to the very top of the house, where a medallion carved in the de Bourville coat of arms looked down on all who used the steps. They passed several closed doorways before the count opened one and ushered her in.

"I will return shortly," he said, closing the door behind him.

Dami stood there in awe. This room was even more elaborate than the one downstairs. There were no mirrors this time, but the walls were a cream color lavishly embellished with gold-gilded wood carved into cherubs and hearts, love knots tied under them. The furniture was covered in a sumptuous gold brocade and scattered about the room on a cream Aubusson carpet that had threads of gold woven through it. On one wall a Gobelin tapestry depicted a scene from life at Louis XIV's court. The beauty of the room was overpowering. She began to understand why de Bourville would do anything to retain his inheritance.

But this wasn't getting her out of here. Against an outside wall hung heavily embroidered gold velvet, obviously curtains. She rushed to them and yanked the material aside. Yes, there was a large French window that led out to a balcony. She tried the handle. It was locked.

She stepped back. Did she dare break the glass? Would de Bourville hear and come back, catching her before she could escape? Did she have a choice?

She wrapped her right hand in the folds of her cloak. Swinging her arm back, she plunged it through the window. Shattered glass flew around her.

Were there footsteps in the hall? Her heart pounded in her ears.

She began to pick the glass out of the door. An eternity passed. No one came.

Several minutes later, she had a space cleared that

was large enough for her to squeeze through. Ducking her head and sucking in her breath, she went through the jagged shards. One caught at the skirt of her gown. The ripping sound of tearing material froze her.

She gulped, stepped onto the balcony. She became aware of her dress dragging the ground and tangling her feet. One side was torn nearly in half. She reached down and finished tearing it. Now her hem was knee high, showing her pink stockings.

She glanced at the sky. The full moon played on the balcony rail. She allowed precious time for her eyes to become fully adjusted to the dark. Her ears strained for any sounds. The night was as silent as a cemetery.

Moving to the rail, she looked over. Her luck was too good to be true. There was a trellis, covered with ivy, that led to the ground. It wasn't much, but she had grown up a tomboy.

She threw her leg over the rail, then positioned her hands as best she could, and brought the other leg over. Her feet were on a secure part of the trellis, but the width of the rail made it hard to hold on to. Her palms began to sweat. Her grip slipped. She let go with one hand and moved it to the wood of the trellis. She felt a splinter stab her finger.

The thick ivy touched her face, reminding her of the slithering movement of a snake. She shuddered, moved too quickly, and broke the trellis where she tried to plant her foot. She lunged to one side, moving her foot to another place.

Sweat dripped from her face. Her breathing punctuated every movement. The ivy tripped her feet and confused her hands as she sought purchase for her descent.

It seemed to last forever. Any second de Bourville would enter the room and find her gone. A sound in the garden below made her jerk. He already knew she was gone. He was waiting for her. She knew it. He was the one who had made the sound.

She bit her lips shut, trying to stifle the small sobs of frustration leaking from her. She touched solid earth. She started to shake. Turning, she anticipated the feel of his hands closing over her shoulders.

No one was there.

Her knees buckled, and she fell to the ground. De Bourville wasn't here. It had been her imagination. Exhaustion sapped her strength. All she wanted was to lie on the cold grass. She knew she couldn't.

Pulling herself up, she searched the enclosed area. There had to be a gate somewhere, or at least a place to hide. No, that wouldn't work. As soon as the count saw the door he would know what she had done. Hopefully, it would take him a while since the curtains should have fallen back to hide it. No, again. There were slivers of glass all around the carpet where she had thrown them in her haste.

She had no time. Tensed to trigger tightness, she loped toward a bare spot in the surrounding wall. She jerked to a halt and squinted through the night to see if there was a handle. There was. She wrenched it open and tumbled into an alleyway.

Where to go now? She twisted her head from side to side. There was nothing to tell her which way to go. Casting her fate to the winds, she set off to the right. Her satin evening slippers made no sounds on the cobbles, but they also afforded no protection against the jagged edges that protruded upward.

She sprinted into an unlit street. The tall buildings, once proud residences of the aristocracy, crouched like gargoyles in the dark. She looked apprehensively at the front of the hotel she had just broken out of. There didn't seem to be any movement. She didn't have time to wonder.

At a trot, she took the direction she thought most likely to lead back to the more populated parts of Paris.

Her foot landed in a puddle, The stench told her it was an open sewer. She gagged. Her nose wrinkled in disgust. She kept going. To her right, a dog sniffed in a reeking pile of garbage. If only she could make it home. She didn't want to see this squalor.

Her breathing was deep and labored. Several blocks away from her would-be prison, she paused to rest. Fatigue swamped her, making her muscles shake. She leaned against a brick wall. The odors seemed stronger here. She had to go on.

She looked around, her eyes dark pools of fear. Her bosom heaved, her hands splayed against the bricks at her back. She felt light-headed, and cursed herself for a weakling. Just as she felt she must faint, the sound of drunken singing met her ears.

"Oh, no," she gasped. She glanced frantically around for a place to hide. There wasn't even an alley close by. Perhaps if she shrank against the wall her black gown would hide her. In her urgency, she forgot her cloak was lying back in the garden, and her pale skin and silver hair stood out against the dark like beacons.

"What have we here," said a male voice in French. "Appears to be a woman," said a female voice.

Even in her anxiety, Dami found the time to wonder at her ability to translate the words. The voices were uncultured and the language idiomatic.

She looked from one to the other. The man was dressed in breeches that were torn at the knee, and his shirt hung out of the waistband. His hair was long and shaggy, and a bedraggled beard covered his chin. The woman was his counterpart. Her homespun skirt was a dirty brown and bagged around her rotund waist. The blouse she wore was dingy white and too tight at the bosom. Her hair was in a semblance of a bun, but hanks of it hung limply along her shoulders.

Dami cringed. Their breath beat her in waves of cheap gin. She knew nothing good would come of their finding her.

"Here," said the man, grabbing her arm and pulling her away from the wall, "Let's have a look at you in the light."

The woman came up and turned Dami's head from side to side, her thumb and forefinger pinching painfully into Dami's jaw.

"She isn't bad looking," said the woman. "A little thin for most of the aristocracy's taste, but she's unusual enough to make up for it."

The man ran his hands down Dami's bosom and waist, pausing at her hips, then said, "She's shapely enough. I think I'll sample the goods first."

"No, you won't," the woman said, slapping his hands away. "The gentlemen pay well for a virgin."

Shame made Dami feel sick. The man's hands on her had made her feel like a filthy piece of merchandise. The first coherent thought in ages entered her mind.

"I'm not a virgin," she whispered.

"We'll soon see about that," the woman said. "Bring her over here Pierre. I'll examine her in the doorway. And if she's telling the truth, then you can have your fun. It won't spoil anything for the lord I have in mind for her."

The man dragged Dami into the abscess in the wall. He pushed her up against the door while the woman began to fumble with her skirts.

"Let me go," Dami yelled. "Stop it!"

"Hold her tight," the woman said, "I don't want her kicking me in the face."

"My pleasure," the man said, pushing his chest up against Dami's, his legs splayed so the woman could work Dami's skirts up.

His gin breath beat at Dami. If she didn't faint first, she would throw up on the lout. She began to scream. Her arms heaved against the broad chest pressed to hers. She wiggled her legs. She tried to kick at the woman who bent at her feet.

Her foot landed with a soft thud against the woman's chest, sending her backward. In the ensuing space, Dami brought her knee up. With a satisfying whack, she felt her knee jam into the man's crotch.

"Awww!" he screamed, falling to the ground. "The bitch has hit my jewels."

He reached for her, but Dami nimbly sidestepped his flaying arms. She sped past, into the street. She knew it would be only a short time before the two were after her. The woman wasn't hurt that badly.

Dami sprinted down the cobbles. Her foot slipped in a puddle. She fell to her knees. The sounds of pursuit catapulted her to her feet. She rushed on in jagged spurts.

Her limbs ached. She tripped over a pile of garbage, caught herself, and went on. Her hair streamed down, obstructing her vision. She grabbed at it with one hand, yanking it back. Her mouth open, she panted.

She couldn't go much further.

Chapter Twenty-Two

As Perth's curricle rounded the corner, Julian's eye was caught by a flash of silver.

"Stop," he commanded.

Perth pulled the horses up and turned an inquiring eye to the duke. "See something?"

"Over there," Julian pointed.

A shadow flitted across the building just opposite them. A shimmer of silver floated at its top. Julian caught his breath. He jumped from the carriage and sped after the fleeing apparition.

He was gaining on her when he heard the sounds of other footsteps on the cobbles. Cursing, he turned to see who it was.

A beefy man, his breathing raspy, was lumbering toward him. As the man neared, Julian noticed he was holding himself. Julian gave a bark of laughter. The chit was handy with her knees.

Then he noticed the fat woman struggling to keep up with the man. He knew at a glance that she was a procuress. His blood turned cold, then boiled. With a snarl, he moved in on the man.

Julian planted a facer. The man careened backward, knocking down the woman. They fell with a crunch of bones and a yelp of pain.

Towering over them, Julian ordered, "Get out of here. And if you know what's good for you, don't let me see your ugly faces again." He waited long enough to make sure their skulking away was permanent.

He turned and continued his pursuit of Dami. She was nowhere in sight. Julian stopped and listened. The sound of someone hitting the ground and the resultant moans of pain started him moving again. He turned left at the next corner.

Dami stumbled, falling onto the uneven street. Her arms spread out in front of her to break the fall, her skirts foamed around her knees like black waves. She pushed herself up, twisting her head to see behind her. The silver curtain of her hair blinded her.

She struggled to a sitting position. Exhaustion hammered at her. Getting to her hands and knees, she pulled herself erect on will power alone. Her feet didn't want to obey her command to run. Her mouth was parched, and she could feel the pain of the bruises her multiple falls had given her.

Somehow she had to move. Tears of fear and frustration began to stream down her face. She started forward. Her arms swung out to balance herself as she began to run. Her movements were shaky, but she was making progress.

She screamed as strong hands circled her waist, lifting her into the air.

She was beyond reason now as she flailed at her

attacker. The filthy scoundrel wasn't going to have her. She would scratch his face to shreds before she let him handle her the way he had. As for the woman, she'd fight as dirty with her. Punch her in the breasts if necessary. Dami's hands curved into claws and her feet kicked wildly, preparing for her attack. Her teeth ground together, ready to bite if she had to.

"What a spitfire," said a deep, familiar voice.

She bared her teeth.

"No, you don't," he said. "If you bite me I will be compelled to put you over my knee and pop your bottom until you collapse. Something I should have done months ago."

She went limp as wilted lettuce. "Julian." The word soughed through her numb lips.

Other footsteps approached.

"So you found her," Perth said. "She must have escaped. It certainly looks it by the state of her clothing."

For the first time, Julian took a good look at her. Her hair hung in streamers down her back, and a large purple bruise was starting to show on her chin. She was covered with scratches and patches of dried blood. She could have passed for a street urchin if one overlooked the quality of the dress she wore. But the condition of it was deplorable. It clung to her like a negligee, and one side was rent to the knee showing her pink stockings and garter. He felt his desire for her mounting even as he fought it.

"What have you done to yourself? What did *they* do to you?" Julian asked, his voice harsh with strain.

"I should have killed them. Your hands and arms are bloody and your face is scratched and dirty. Not to mention your state of undress.

Animation came back to her, and Dami glared at him. "How dare you attack me? If it weren't for you, I wouldn't be in this position." She sniffed. "I climbed down a terrace of ivy. And they didn't do what they intended. No thanks to you!"

"Resourceful," Perth drawled.

"Don't blame me for your nefarious plots' going awry," Julian said. Seeing that she wasn't seriously hurt, his anger overcame his worry. "They must not have hurt you. Your tongue is as sharp as ever. If you had a little more self-control you would have never gotten yourself into this position. *I* didn't tell you to run away with de Bourville. And if you had to climb out a window, it only serves you right. You should have known better than to trust the man. You should have known better than to go about alone in an area like this, too. You were lucky the man didn't rape you, and the woman sell you to the highest bidder on an hourly basis in the brothel I'm sure she runs."

"How dare you, but how typical," she hissed into his face.

"Easy, easy, you two." Perth inserted the cool voice of reason. "We haven't time for this. We have a spy to catch, and Lady Damaris must get home before everyone and his mother realizes she never reached there."

She turned to stare at the earl. Then her sense of humor caught her. "How very droll of you, Perth. And so very practical. I would never have thought it of you after Felixstowe."

The earl put an arm around her waist and started leading her to his parked carriage.

"I will help her," growled Julian.

"If you wish," Perth said, "but it didn't seem you had the inclination."

"I'm not a sack of potatoes," she said. "And I don't need your help. I'm perfectly capable of walking under my own power." She pulled away from him.

"Suit yourself, minx."

They reached the carriage where Perth turned to Camber and said, "You take Lady Damaris home in the curricle, while I go on to the house."

"You can't do it alone," Julian protested.

"De Bourville is a Bonapartist spy," Dami protested, "You must both go to ensure he doesn't get away."

"So." Julian said, lifting her up into the carriage without her leave. "You admit to it. Well, it's a fine kettle of fish you've landed yourself in. My only regret is that I will have to tell Simon, and it will break his heart."

She rounded on him. "What nonsense are you muttering about now? If I didn't know better, I'd say you were let in the attic, duke."

Smiling, Perth said, "If *I* didn't know better, I'd say you were *both* let in the attic. Now, get her home, Camber, and don't worry about me. I know how to handle myself in a pinch." He swatted the rump of the nearest horse, setting it into a canter.

Dami turned away from Camber with a huff.

Reaction set in, and it was all she could do to hold her head up. Her back felt like it had the consistency of putty as it bent into the cushion. The tears she had been shedding when Camber caught her were dry, making her skin pull uncomfortably across her cheekbones. All she wanted was her bed.

Julian's voice brought her back to the present. "As much as I hate to leave Jason, he is right. We do need to get you home as soon as possible. And Jason is a street fighter. He'll survive and get his culprit." Julian gave a flick of his wrist, snapping the reins and speeding the horses through the narrow streets.

"Hmmph!" Dami snorted.

"What do you have to say for yourself now, Amalie, or should I say, Lady Damaris?" His voice was conversational, but the strain showed in the whiteness of his knuckles holding the reins.

"I don't wish to discuss it with you, duke."

"So we're back to the 'duke' business." He shrugged. "It's better than some things I've been called by you. But we have a serious problem here, and I think it would behoove us to figure out what we intend to do before we reach Simon."

"I have no problem, Your Grace. *I* didn't do anything wrong."

"Neither did I. You are the one who played me for a gull, although I haven't been able to figure out why yet. But that can wait. First, we have to decide just how much to tell your family, and then Wellington, about your complicity with de Bourville."

"What?" She turned on him, her eyes narrowed. "Just what are you implying?"

346

He ran his hand through his hair. "As much as I want to believe different, it is obvious that you were in cohoots with the count: the French surname, and the constant attendance on him. How you contrived in England, I don't know, but if your behavior with me is any indication, I imagine it was with ingenuity."

"What effrontery!" She glared at him. "I thought you graceless when you seduced me—a virgin—and then refused to marry me because I wasn't up to your weight socially, but you have finally torn the blinders from my eyes with a vengeance. Were I a man, I would end your despicable existence this instant." Her hands balled into fists, but she kept them pinned to her side.

Julian leaned back, surprise easing the harshness of his face. "Careful, or you *will* end my existence, and your own with it, by making me drive us off the road."

"Despicable," she muttered, turning away from his again. "Bounder, cad, scapegrace, jelly face . . . oooh!"

"No," he demurred, "not jelly face. The others perhaps upon occasion, but never jelly face. Come, let's be sensible about the whole thing. I don't think you did it for money, since Lady Damaris isn't exactly in need of blunt. It was just a foolish prank done out of boredom and pique. I can understand that, but it still doesn't wrap it in clean linen, and that we must do before we reach home."

"This is beyond everything. Never, not even after you ravished me, have I felt so humiliated. So belittled."

"That is carrying your outrage too far, madam. I did not ravish you. You cooperated admirably."

"A gentleman would never say that." The man was beyond all that was acceptable.

"Look at me."

"Never."

"All right, then, but don't go crying on my shoulder when Simon is forced to send you home in disgrace. And he will when he finds out that you have spent most of the night with a Bonapartist spy, not to mention having already encouraged him in your outrageous impersonation of a cyprian."

"You wouldn't!"

"Wouldn't what?"

"Don't play innocent with me, duke. You know exactly what I mean."

"I don't advise you to put me to the test. You have already run me through the gauntlet with your hoydenish ways, and I've a mind to effect some vengeance of my own. Now, if you have sufficiently vented your spleen, I suggest that we hash this out. We are within minutes of your home."

Looking around her, Dami saw that he was right. While she had no doubt Simon would never believe she had helped de Bourville spy, he would still be upset over her having been abducted by the man. Her reputation was probably in shreds by now. She sighed.

"All right," she capitulated, "what do you suggest?"

"That's more like it. I think you should tell them

the truth about being kidnapped by the count. They don't need to know the rest. I will take care that your name isn't implicated when de Bourville goes to trial. Meanwhile, Perth will catch de Bourville and keep the circumstances under wraps."

"I never intended to tell my family that I helped de Bourville, because I didn't."

"Spare me your denials," Camber said. "Aside from that, I will tell your family that you and I have decided to marry. That will take care of any embarrassment over your prolonged stay with the man."

Dami was enraged. "Frankly, Your Grace, I would rather have my reputation ruined!"

With that, she leaped from the slowing carriage to the street, uncaring of the risk she took. Landing at a run, she sped up the steps and burst into the hallway.

In the light of dozens of candles, she saw the entryway piled with boxes and trunks. It looked like an army had arrived. It looked like her mama was there.

"Famous! Just famous," she growled, trying to pick her way through the obstacle course.

"Amalie, dammit, Damaris, come back here," Julian bellowed, sprinting through the door. He ground to a halt inches short of a pile of trunks. "What the devil?"

"My question exactly," stated the dowager marchioness of Cleve, opening the drawing room door and emerging into the hall. She was dressed in her favorite lavender, this time in a traveling dress trimmed in grey that fit her elegant figure perfectly. She raised her lorgnette and slowly examined Dami and Julian where they stood in shock.

"Mama, I can explain. . . ."

"Lady Cleve, I can explain. . . ."

"I certainly hope so," the dowager said, turning her back on them and reentering the drawing room.

Feeling sheepish, Dami trailed her mother. She glanced at Camber, who was looking rather intrigued by her mama. She sniffed and positioned herself with her back to the fireplace.

"Dami, where have you been?" Simon asked, rising from his seat and going to her. He put an arm around her. "We have been so worried about you. And your face. My, God, you look like you've been in a brawl."

Johnny yawned. "Told you she was up to another one of her scrapes. Stands to reason, since that's all she's done is scheme since we left Green Leaf for London."

Dami suppressed the urge to stamp her foot. She should have known that of all times for her mother to arrive, that worthy lady would choose the worst. And to have the whole household up and about when she and Camber came trailing in. It was too much.

"You exaggerate, Johnny," Dami said.

"Do I?" he leered at her.

"Children, children," Lady Cleve said. "Save your bickering for later. Damaris come here and let me look at you."

Dami went to her mother. When the dowager took her chin in her hand, Dami winced.

"Humph!" Lady Cleve said. "You are a fright, child. But, I'm sure that after you are cleaned up and get a good night's sleep you will be good as new.

Right now you owe us an explanation." She released her daughter. "I understand that you have been missing since the masquerade?"

Dami made a frustrated sound. She looked around the room, taking in her younger brother's position, then Lady Sebastian and Kit on the sofa with Camber standing behind them. Simon hadn't budged from the fireplace.

"Well, I suppose you are all involved, since you will all be called on for information about my disappearance."

Camber cut her short, saying, "Would you prefer for me to tell them?"

"No, thank you, Your Grace," she managed as politely as her discontent at him would allow. "You see, de Bourville decided that since I don't wish to marry Camber, and Camber doesn't love me, and he, de Bourville does love me, that he would abduct me. All for my own good." She looked around at five startled faces. "So, he took me to his home with the intention of marrying me tonight, but when he let me go freshen myself, I broke through the windows in the room and climbed down the trellis into his garden and managed to escape. I was on my way home when Camber found me." She shrugged. "Nothing very much, really. It has all been resolved, with no harm to anyone." She decided to gloss over the later incident. It wouldn't do to get everyone so upset.

"Damaris, not again!" Lady Cleve expostulated.

"Again?" Lady Sebastian asked, her eyebrows raising.

"What's this?" Simon demanded.

351

Dami's eyes flew to Julian's. Was he going to keep mum? He stared at her, as though trying to read her thoughts.

"It was only another one of Dami's kick-ups, Simon," Lady Cleve said hastily.

"That's right," Johnny chimed in, only making it worse.

Dami saw Lady Sebastian look from her to Camber and then back again, and a speculative look came over the widow's face. Fortunately, she didn't say anything. Dami didn't think she could take an inquisition on the Felixstowe caper.

"One good thing has come out of tonight," Camber's voice cut the silence like a wire cutting cheese. All eyes turned to him. "Lady Damaris has consented to become my wife."

"I have not," Dami said. "You presume too much, duke."

"No, he doesn't," Lady Cleve said. "I shall brook no argument this time, Damaris. Things have gone too far. If Camber has asked for your hand, then you shall bestow it on him." She stared her daughter down. "Do I make myself understood?"

"Yes, Mama," Dami muttered, "but you don't understand."

"That's where you are wrong, my gel. You have been a hoyden from the moment you entered your teens, aided and abetted by your father. Your escapade before coming here was such that I had no choice but to help you make the best of it. Now, I am helping you to make the best of your most recent shenanigans."

"What is all this mumble-jumble about things happening in England?" Simon asked. "Seems that if it has a bearing we ought to discuss it, although," he glanced at the nonfamily members, "later might be better."

"I believe," Camber answered him, "that you and I ought to discuss this privately. I am fully capable of explaining all of this."

Simon studied his friend. "Let us go to the library, then. The rest of you had best get to bed. And Dami, that indecent gown deserves to be burned." He frowned. "If I had known what you were wearing to the masquerade, you would never had gotten out of the house. I suppose I owe that to Johnny." He scowled at his brother.

Johnny had the grace to blush. "She coerced me. Wouldn't have done it otherwise."

"Now I wonder just how much she 'coerced' you. No," he held his hand up to stop Johnny who looked like he was ready to open his budget, "don't tell me now. I'm not sure I'm up to handling any more this night. Come." He motioned to Camber.

The two of them left.

Dami glanced nervously around the room. Her mother looked like hell and brimstone, and she knew she was in for the worst scold of her life.

"If you will excuse me?" Dami murmured, "I believe I will go to bed." She began edging toward the door.

"Young lady," Lady Cleve said, "you will visit me first thing in the morning."

"Yes, ma'am," Dami said on her way through the

door.

Simultaneously, Julian and Simon crossed the foyer and entered the library. Like most rooms of its calling, it was paneled in wood, mahogany in this case, and lined with shelves full of books. Pulled up to the fire were two oversized chairs done in leather. The two men seated themselves.

"It was a close thing tonight," Julian said. "I don't know what she was doing with de Bourville in the first place, or all the details on how she escaped, but we're lucky to have her back."

The anguish in his friend's voice gave Simon something to think on. He was careful to keep his voice noncommittal. "That bad? Well, what counts is that she's safe. But what happened to de Bourville?"

Julian told him the pithy details as he knew them. When he was through, he said, "I want to marry her, Simon."

"I know that. You asked me for her hand months ago."

"Oh, that," Julian waved his hand. "That was purely convenience. She was your sister, had breeding, respectability, and a good dowry. She was merely an object that filled the position of duchess and bearer of much needed heirs." He turned to Simon. "It's different now. She doesn't believe it, and I haven't explained myself yet, haven't had the time, but I love her."

"I believe you, Julian. Your face when you entered the drawing room spoke more clearly than words of your feelings for her. But before I give my blessing to your real request for her hand, I must tell you that what happened tonight, while a bit much even for Dami, isn't out of character for her. If you wed her, you will be taking on a lifelong task of keeping her out of trouble. She is a madcap of the most accomplished sort."

Julian grinned ruefully. "I'm fully aware of your sister's proclivities. I can't reveal all of our dealings, because I promised her I wouldn't, but I can assure you that I have participated in several of her latest escapades."

"In that case," Simon said, extending his hand, "let's shake on it and have a bottle of champagne."

"Sounds good," Julian said. "I have fond memories of champagne."

Meanwhile, Dami lay sprawled on her bed. Tonight the relaxing blues of the room seemed cold. They also brought back memories of the blue-and-silver-gilt room in de Bourville's hotel. She shuddered and forced the memories from her mind.

What were Camber and Simon doing? If she knew the duke, he was making matters worse for her. Why couldn't he leave her alone? Hadn't she made enough of a fool of him? Or was he seeking revenge by telling Simon all? For if he did, it was a certainly that Simon would curtail all her activities for a long time to come.

But that might not be bad. She had been in many scrapes in her life, but never one to rival tonight's. There had been some bad moments in the alley when the man was mauling her and the woman was trying to examine her.

Shivers ran down her spine and tears welled up in

her eyes. The humiliation of it. The sheer, unadulterated terror of it. At the time she had been sure that she would be carted off to some unspeakable future and never see her family or Julian again.

Her control slipping, she curled into a tight ball and buried her face in her pillow. Sobs of release wracked her body until, near dawn, she fell into a restless sleep where dreams of a faceless man pursuing her down twisting lanes left her sweating and cold.

Chapter Twenty-Three

From her bedroom window, Dami watched Camber draw his phaeton to a halt before turning away. It was good to be home in England. The familiar green color of her bedroom soothed her taut nerves as nothing else could. She let the green and pink chintz drapes fall back into place and went to a pink and green striped chair near the fireplace. She sank into it.

Camber had left them at Dover to go to London. He had said he had some business to clear up. Probably the acquisition of his latest ladybird. The thought brought back the memory of his house in Kensington, and the red bedroom. With a shudder, she glanced around her room again. The only mirror she had was on her dressing table, and it certainly didn't show any portion of her bed.

She continued to sit as the sun went down and shadows crept into the corners of her room. Suzy's entrance to prepare her for dinner finally dragged her from her gloomy contemplation of the coming weeks.

"Milady," the maid said, "you've been sitting in here in the dark. Tsk, tsk."

Dami watched the girl light a taper in the smoldering fireplace and then light the branches of candles that were scattered around the large room. Within minutes a warm glow encompassed them.

"Is it time to dress for dinner?" Dami wasn't really interested, but she knew her mother would not countenance her not showing.

"Yes, and His Grace has requested your presence in the drawing room thirty minutes early." She watched her mistress. "He said he has something to give you."

Dami forced a yawn she was far from feeling. "I suppose he means to give me a ring, or some such nonsense."

"And your mother wants to see you before that," Suzy added.

"A regular circus," Dami grumbled. "I guess Johnny wants to see me, too."

"No, milady," the maid answered.

Dami rose and went to her dressing room. Thirty minutes later she surveyed herself in the mirror. She had to admit she was in looks. Her cheeks were flushed, giving color to her normally pale complexion, and her hair shone like polished silver. She knew it wasn't because of Camber's presence.

"Suzy, please fetch my mother's pearl choker. It will go perfectly with this grey silk gown. And don't forget the ear bobs, and bracelets. She smiled as the maid rushed to do her bidding."

Coming back into the room, Suzy approached her mistress with laden arms. "Cooh, but ain't they pretty," she praised as Dami lifted the lid on the jeweler's box.

"Yes, aren't they," Dami agreed.

With the girl's help, she finally managed to don the jewels. Lastly, she slipped a pearl ring on her engagement finger. Then draping a silver-spangled shawl through her arms, she posed in front of the mirror. She tried to suppress her giggle, but couldn't. The ear bobs dangled three inches from her lobe, dragging it down. The choker was six strands, banded with diamonds, and it rose up her neck making her look like a head sitting on a pearl basket. But the *coup de grace* was the ring. It was a mound of pearls and diamonds that resembled the type of rings often used to hold poison, so massive was it. With a flourish and a smirk, she left for her mother's room.

Knocking at her mother's door, Dami waited for permission to enter.

"You wished to see me," she said, moving into the shadows.

Lady Cleve turned to study her daughter. "Yes, I did. Camber is here." She looked again. "What on earth are you doing with my pearl set?"

"Wearing it, and I know the duke is here."

"Then you also know that he intends to present you with the traditional engagement ring, worn by the duchess of Camber, but where it will go decked out as you are, I don't know."

Dami remained mute.

"Damaris, I want you to marry the duke for your own good. If I thought he would make a bad husband, it wouldn't matter what has happened between you, I wouldn't force you to marry him. As it is, I honestly believe that the two of you can work out your differences."

Dami watched her mother. She knew her mother truly thought she was doing the right thing. "Mama, I know you want me to be happy, and you think that Camber will make me so." She felt the tears prick her lids. "And he would have, if he had wanted me as plain Amalie. And if he hadn't thought me a spy like de Bourville."

"What?" Lady Cleve rose and went to stand near her daughter. "You haven't told me this."

In a few pithy words, Dami enlightened her parent.

"So, this is the final thorn in your side," the dowager said. "I agree that it wouldn't sit well with me if my future husband thought me capable of betraying my country. Still, you must admit there were extenuating circumstances."

"Mama, how can you say so?" The tears came.

"Child, child," the dowager gathered Dami into her arms. "Hush, don't cry. It won't solve anything and it will make Camber think that he caused them, and I know from experience that there is nothing to make a man more infuriatingly superior than to think a woman has cried because of him. There, there, I know it hurts, but these are things one must work out before reaching the ultimate goal. In this case, your marriage to a man who I truly believe loves you, no matter how he has bungled the job."

Dami tried to pull herself together. Hiccupping, she asked, "Do you really think he loves me? I don't see how you can."

"I think the duke is still unsettled in his mind, but should come around nicely."

"Even after all he has done to me?"

360

"Well, you must admit that you asked for much of it. And he did come up to scratch without any coercing from Simon. That proves something."

Dami pulled away from her mother and wiped the last of her tears away with the back of her hand. "It shows that he has an inordinate amount of honor and pride. That speaks nothing of love."

Lady Cleve looked at her daughter compassionately. "You are still young, Damaris. When you reach my age, you will be able to see beyond the stupid trappings men wear to show their masculinity. Why, I remember. . . ."

Dami stifled her groan. She didn't want to hear again how Mama had finally forced Papa to admit his love for her. "If you will excuse me, Mama, Camber wants me to meet him before dinner."

Dami made her escape. Outside the drawing room doors, she paused to make sure her jewelry was in place, thankful that Mama had been too involved in their discussion to demand that she remove the pearls. She waved to the footman to announce her. That ought to reduce any pretensions Camber harbored about lording it over her.

He was standing by the fireplace, and it was as though he had only been away for an hour instead of four days. His auburn hair was curled in its customary Brutus, and his grey eyes sparkled as dangerously as they ever had. She noted the tight fit of his black velvet coat and black satin breeches. They were snug to his figure in a way that caused her blood to pound in her ears and her fingers to tremble in the folds of her skirt. His white shirt was modestly ruffled, and a diamond the size of a small button caught the folds of his cravat.

"You wished to see me, Your Grace?" She stopped with the settee between them.

"I did. I have something to give you, but I can see that it will be like one fish in a school of fish, and about as distinguishable."

"You speak in riddles." A grin curved her lips.

"And you understand me perfectly, Lady Damaris. As I've said before, we are suited to one another."

Her smile turned to a frown. Her hands clenched like talons on the carved back of the mahogany settee. "On the contrary." She attacked. "I believe in monogamy in marriage. You don't. I believe in the worth of the person overriding the worldly status of the person. You don't."

He approached her on long legs, striding like a conqueror approaching the conquered. "That is the past, this is the present. Give me your hand."

As he rounded the corner of the settee she fought down the urge to move around the opposite corner. She stood her ground, putting out her right hand.

"You are being purposely obstinate," he said, the tightening of his jaw the only indication that she was succeeding in her purpose. "Give me your left hand."

She extended it, a glint of satisfaction in her eyes at the knowledge that the next couple of minutes were not going to go smoothly for His Grace.

"So, your ostentatious and gaudy pearls even extend to your ring finger. After you are my wife, I will pick all your jewels. I won't have you going about decked out like a cyprian."

Her eyes kindled. "My father gave these to my mother."

"And they are in exceedingly poor taste, as you would admit if you weren't bent on irritating me." His eyes lightened with amusement. "So that is where you got those gaudy diamonds you wore at the Cyprians' Ball."

Remembrance tugged at her sense of humor. "They were gaudy, but you must admit, they fit in perfectly."

"Please remove that ring. The pearls and diamonds on it are enough to choke a horse."

She snorted and drew herself up to her full height, but one glance at his face and she pulled off the ring and transferred it to her right hand.

"Good," he said, taking her hand and slipping on a ruby the size of the nail on her smallest finger.

It winked like blood in the candlelight. "It's beautiful." The words slipped from her.

He raised her hand to his mouth and kissed it. His lips, warm and dry on her skin, drew her attention like a homing bird. She met his eyes, moved closer to him without conscious thought.

"I say, you two look cosy. All made up?" Johnny bounced into the room unannounced. "Mother will be glad to hear that. So will Simon. So am I, come to think of it. Never could abide the thought that you two would continue to fight like cats and dogs while the rest of us are forced to put as good a face on it as possible. Not the thing when all the gentry for miles around will be on us in the next couple days to help celebrate your engagement."

Dami jerked her hand free and scuttled around to

the front of the settee, started to sit in it, thought better of it, and sat in a chair.

"You have perfect timing, Johnny," Camber said dryly, taking the chair opposite Dami. "Have you thought of the theater? It seems all your family has some talent in that direction."

Johnny looked uncertainly from one to the other.

"Leave him alone," Dami said. "He isn't up to your metal, Camber."

Camber bowed his head. "Your wish is my desire, sweetings."

She ground her teeth, but said nothing. The talk was desultory until the dowager and Simon joined them.

To ease the tension, Dami said, "I just received a letter from Kit. She says they will be here next week."

"Good," said Simon, "I was afraid they would be unable to make it, and as Julian's closest relatives, it would be crass to have the wedding without them."

"True," Camber said, "but the Channel can't stay calm longer than a week at a time. It is like a woman that way."

All three men chuckled, Dami fumed, and the dowager smiled indulgently on the young people.

"Your wit overwhelms me," Dami said sarcastically.

Dinner was announced. Camber took Lady Cleve's arm, and Dami gave an arm to each of her brothers.

Dinner was strained, and over none too soon for Dami's comfort. She was grateful for the interlude of repose that the men's traditional drinking of port and smoking of cheroots by themselves after dinner would allow. Entering the room behind her mother, she went to get Adam Smith's *The Wealth of Nations* from the table where she had left it the other day. She was engrossed in his explanation of capital when the gentlemen rejoined them.

Following behind Simon, Julian located Amalie. No, he corrected himself, Lady Damaris; Dami. It surprised him to find her with her nose buried in a book . . . and those pearls. As it was, her grey gown was still becoming, the bodice higher than what she wore as Amalie, but better fitting than what she'd worn in Paris. For the first time, he noticed that she had put back on the weight she had lost. He made a beeline for her.

"Reading one of Mrs. Radcliffe's novels?" he said, taking the seat next to her.

"For your information, duke, not all women read Gothic romances." She looked up at him frowning.

"I beg your pardon," he drawled, "I didn't know you were a literary snob. If you aren't reading her, then what are you reading that interests you more than civility to your future bridegroom?"

"I am reading *The Wealth of Nations*, and you are not my future bridegroom." She snapped the book shut and started to rise.

His hand on her knee stopped her. "Don't be so huffy, sweetings. And why are you reading that tome?"

"Camber," she said wearily, "desist your pursuit. You have nothing to prove by it, and I have no intentions of marrying you, so you might as well take yourself off."

"You are becoming a bore, Lady Damaris. Not that I'm not aware of your leanings in that direction, but I am getting heartily tired of it." He crossed one leg so that it blocked her path. To get up she would have to step over it. Knowing she was trapped, he lounged back. "Isn't that book a little deep for you?"

She decided to humor him. "In places, but overall it seems a sensibly written book. I am only in book one, and his premise that labor is what provides us with our necessaries and conveniences is very apt when one thinks about managing a large estate such as Green Leaf."

He gazed at her with dawning respect. "You really do grasp the basis of his work. My compliments."

"Thank you," she said sarcastically. "I take that as a rare compliment."

He fell silent, but only for a moment. "Won't you play for us?" The devil leaped in his eyes as he watched her.

"You know I can't," she hissed.

"I thought that was just another one of your games to give me a disgust of Lady Damaris."

"So you figured that out," she purred.

"I would have to be a clod not to have, you played your hand so heavily. A little more finesse would have lent spice to the game."

"Well, it's too late to mend matters now, Your Grace. I have decided to show you my true colors, and I know that they will give you a distaste for me that my falseness never accomplished."

"Why do you say that?" He looked genuinely curious.

"Because what man wants a bluestocking for a wife—a woman who can't manage his homes, embroider, sing, play the pianoforte, or watercolor? What man wants a woman who is his intellectual equal, or, heaven forbid, superior? None that I have yet to meet." She met his gaze defiantly.

"You are so vehement that I must believe you when you say you possess none of the accepted accomplishments. Does that extend to riding, too?"

"You know it does," she snapped, turning away from his knowing eyes.

"I thought so, but I'm never sure of anything where you are concerned. You are like a chameleon, and it behooves me to be constantly alert and prepared for any contingency."

"Well, now you know my worst faults, and in plenty of time to retract your flattering offer of marriage."

"Is this what all this soul baring was leading to? I'm disappointed in you. I thought for sure you had more spunk than to try to worm your way out of a situation that has become touchy."

"If you are trying to say I'm a coward, then come out and say so. It doesn't matter."

"How convoluted this conversation has become, sweetings. Can I look forward to such stimulating repartee after our vows? Or will you turn into a dull matron with only her books to liven her existence?"

"You can look forward to the absence of my company if you continue to treat me as though I were a child."

"Then stop acting like one." His face was hard and

closed.

She was so furious that had they been alone she could have hissed and spit at him like an enraged cat. Instead she leaned forward and pushed his leg off his knee. Then she bounced up and stalked to the door.

Simon and Johnny looked up from their game of chess as she passed, and the dowager watched her with a smile before turning for Camber's reaction. Camber kept his face shuttered as he met Lady Cleve's glance.

Chapter Twenty-Four

The next morning Dami kept to her room, telling herself she had no wish to meet up with the duke and have him make a mockery of her. Last night he had taken her words and her thinking and twisted them until she sounded like a sapskull with more hair than wit. She wouldn't give him another opportunity.

She twitched the curtain aside to let in the warm August sunshine. He hadn't disagreed with her when she'd listed the accomplishments gentlemen wanted in their prospective mates, either. At the time, she had let her momentum carry her past the moment, but now, with all day to reflect on it, she admitted that deep down she had hoped he would assure her that they didn't matter to him.

She jumped off the windowseat and paced to the mirror. Looking herself up and down critically, she sighed. He was like all the rest. They wanted beauty, not brains. They wanted complacency and breeding, not love and passion. She turned her shoulder to the haggard-faced girl in the mirror. He had wanted passion from her when he thought her only good enough to be his mistress. Since finding out her true identity, he had barely laid a hand on her.

She returned to the window, drawn by the cheery sunshine. Looking down, she saw Camber and Simon headed for the stables. They were dressed in easy-fitting jackets, handkerchiefs tied around their necks, buckskins, and spotless top boots. Minutes later she saw them leave the stables on their mounts, headed for the duke's property line. She quickly left her room to replenish her books from the library while he was safely out of the house.

Meanwhile, Camber and Simon pulled their horses up to the stream that separated their lands.

"I have bad news," Camber started without preamble. "De Bourville eluded Perth."

"When?" Simon asked.

"Perth's letter, which I just received, since it chased me from my London residence to here, says it was the same night that the count abducted Dami." He beat his riding whip against his palm. "It doesn't sound good. Perth also said de Bourville has a hunting box somewhere in Yorkshire, and that his informants indicate the count has fled France."

Simon watched his friend's brow crease. "Do you think Dami is in danger?"

"I don't know. The man certainly acted demented about her." Camber stared at the horizon. "I just don't know, but I don't think we can take any chances. Yorkshire isn't so far that we would be out of his way if he is headed there."

"You're right. But let's not tell Dami yet," Simon said. "I don't want to worry her—or give her an opportunity to come up with another madcap scheme."

"I agree. I hope we are wrong, but I'm not willing to take a chance on it." Julian said, turning his attention back to Simon.

Dami looked belligerently at her mother, ignoring Lady Sebastian and Kit, who had just arrived. "I do not want to have a ball to announce my engagement. You are constantly harping at me to put the best face on the situation. I have tried. My face will crack if it is displayed for all to see at a ball."

"Don't be disrespectful, Damaris," the dowager reproved. "It is for your own good. I don't want any shabbiness to be connected with your engagement, and the best way to ensure that is to have a ball and treat the situation as though it isn't a nine days' wonder."

"She's quite right," Lady Sebastian interjected. Her eyes were understanding as she watched Damaris. "I know it goes against the grain to acknowledge something Camber so obviously wants, but I know my nephew. When he decides to have something, he won't be gainsaid, and the sooner you come to terms with that and learn to work around him, the sooner you will rule the roost."

"Mother," Kit said primly, "that isn't the proper advice to give a young woman. A wife ought to be demure, deferring in all things to her husband's superior judgment."

"Pshaw!" Lady Sebastian exclaimed, "such dullness. Unless I miss my guess, and I doubt very much that I do, Camber doesn't want a milktoast for a wife. He wants a spitfire, like that great brute of a stallion he rides, always snorting and raring to go."

Dami pretended to be scandalized. "Are you comparing me to a horse? If so, you're little better than your nephew."

"Doesn't surprise me," Lady Sebastian said. "We see eye to eye on most things."

Just then Julian entered the room. "Do I hear my praises being sung? Ah, Aunt and Kit," he said, taking their hands and kissing them each on the cheek.

"If you will excuse me," Dami said, leaving the room.

Camber shook his head. "I see more of her back than her lovely, er, front."

"And no wonder," said the dowager. "You are such a bold scamp that I think you frighten her as much as you attract her. My advice to you is to start wooing her in earnest and stop poking fun at her every chance you get."

"Lady Cleve, I never poke fun at her. But there are times when her pomposity lends itself to deflation."

"Exactly," the dowager, as she led her new guests out of the room.

That night after dinner, Lady Sebastian, Kit, Simon, and Johnny sat down to a game of whist while Lady Cleve embroidered. Dami had made her excuses and gone to bed. Julian had left shortly after.

Johnny sat up in his chair. "What is that caterwauling I hear?"

Lady Cleve raised her attention from the seat cover she was finishing and said complacently, "I believe it is Camber serenading Damaris. He took my advice without delay. I like to see that in a man."

Lady Sebastian winked at her, and the two matrons returned their attention to their pastimes.

What is that awful noise, Dami thought, going to her window. She pushed it open and leaned over to look down at the ground. One story below her Camber was on bent knees, and the excruciating sounds were coming from his throat.

"What are you doing?" she demanded. "You can't sing any better than I can."

He broke off to say, "I know. Does it bother you?"

"Only when you sing." She couldn't help smiling.

"My sentiments exactly," he said, rising and dusting off his buckskins. He looked back up at her and shrugged apologetically. "I'm sorry for my attire, but I didn't want to ruin a perfectly good pair of satin breeches by kneeling in the dirt."

"I understand. You are a dandy first and a lover second." She regretted the words immediately when he grinned wolfishly at her.

"I knew you would come around, sweetings," he said, going to a nearby bush and extracting a ladder, which he leaned up against the wall right under her window.

"What do you think you are doing?" She backed away from the window.

"Guess," he said, rapidly ascending the ladder.

"You can't do this," she said as his head appeared

373

in her window. "I shall scream."

"No, you won't. It will just put you in another compromising position with me, confirming the need for our immediate joining."

With a heave, he was in the open window.

She sidled around the table where her books were stacked. "Oh, my," she gasped, reaching for the ribbons that held her muslin nightgown together at the throat.

"I wondered when that would hit you," Julian said.

His eyes raked her. The white folds of the demure gown should have covered her like a tent, but the material was so thin he could see right through it. Her high breasts rose rapidly under the gown, their peaks pale pink in the dimly lit room. From there, the muslin fell in revealing folds around her waist and down to cup her slim hips. She had nothing on under the nightdress. Julian's teeth showed in a wide grin as he padded after her.

She circled the table and edged toward the far wall. "Let's talk about this," she managed to get out past the lump in her throat.

"I didn't come here to talk," he said, moving in on her. His eyes ate her. "You are beautiful, Dami, and tonight I intend to imprint myself so completely on all your senses that all thoughts of denying me will fade from your mind."

"Ha, ha," she said flatly. Her back met the wall. Her head whipped from side to side looking for an avenue of escape. "You are so amusing, duke." She didn't look amused.

"Come here," he commanded. "I want to see if

374

Lady Damaris is as abandoned as Amalie."

"No, you don't," she countered. "You just want to brand me." She took deep gulps of air. "Don't think I will let you have your way without a fight."

"You stimulate me, sweetings," he said, pinning her to the wall with his body and arms.

"Too bad you don't do the same to me," she said in a small, defiant voice. She wouldn't respond to him. She wouldn't show him how true his words were. Lady Damaris would be a cold fish. She would.

"Don't be a spoilsport," he whispered into her ear.

Dami cringed back from him, trying unsuccessfully to get her ear away from his teeth. Goose flesh broke out on her neck and shoulders. She twisted within the prison of his arms.

"Stop it, Camber. I don't like that," she snapped, turning her head again, trying to evade his tongue as it made its moist way from her ear to the hollow at her neck.

Excitement gripped her stomach and tensed her leg muscles as he pressed against her. His mouth sucked and nuzzled the rapidly beating pulse in her neck.

"Stop that!" She wiggled against him.

"Mmm, that feels nice. Yes, I do believe that Lady Damaris shall be every bit as much fun as Amalie was."

His mouth suckled her through the transparent muslin of her nightgown, making the material cling damply to her taut skin. He stood back to admire his handiwork, and the heat in his eyes made her weak.

He swooped her up in his arms, pressing her to his beating heart. Her hair fell out over his elbow and down to his knees like molten silver. She shivered as her body was removed from the warmth of his, and her nipples rose to hardened points. When she raised her eyes to his, the desire in his confused her at the same time it drew her.

He laid her on the bed. Not giving her a chance to demur he stripped and was beside her, his body burning hers through the muslin separating them.

He ran his hand up the nightgown, raising it until it bunched around her hips. "You may take this off and save it for another night, or I will rip it now."

For a second she failed to comprehend his words, they were said so lightly. When she understood, she couldn't decide whether to be angry or gratified that she affected him so strongly. It was her last coherent thought as she pulled off the nightgown and succumbed to his passion.

Many hours later she lay in the circle of his arm, her head pillowed on his shoulder. Warm lassitude engulfed her body, and the love she had denied for so long suffused her.

He repositioned them so that he could see her face. "I am gratified to have my Amalie back."

"Even though you refused to marry her?"

"I was a fool," he murmured, circling her swollen lips with his finger. He turned her to him and pulled her flush to his chest, crushing her breasts against him. This time their lovemaking was fire and ice as they melded their bodies and their souls. He left her sleeping.

Downstairs, Johnny looked up from his losing hand. "It's been quiet for quite some time. I guess Camber gave up and went to bed."

"It would seem that way," Lady Cleve said complacently.

Chapter Twenty-Five

The next morning Dami awoke and was immediately contrite that she had slept. There was still so much she and Julian had to discuss.

She allowed Suzy to dress her in a frosted grey morning dress. Silver braid rimmed the high collar and narrow sleeve cuffs, and matching braid was swirled into fleur-de-lis around the hem.

After she was dressed, she tripped out the door and down the stairs to the breakfast room. Without waiting for the footman to open the door, she burst into the bright yellow room. The pale yellow silk curtains were pulled back, letting in the early morning light to reflect off the cream-and-buttercup-flocked wallpaper.

Her eyes sought out Julian's. Rising from his seat, he came to her and took her hand in his, drawing her to the seat next to his.

"You look beautiful today, Lady Damaris," he said, ignoring the curious gazes of the other occupants of the room.

"Thank you, Julian. But I am sure you flatter me, since I got very little sleep last night, and must have dark circles under my eyes."

He shared her amusement. "Were you kept awake by the heat?"

"Heat?" Johnny interrupted, unable to listen quietly any longer. "It wasn't hot last night, but there was the damndest noise coming from right outside in the rose garden." He wagged his eyebrows at the duke.

"You don't say," Julian said suavely. "No doubt a tomcat calling for his mate."

"What a diverting conversation," Lady Sebastian said, entering the room in time to hear Julian's comment. "Are we discussing the mating habits of felines?"

"Mother, really," Kit scolded. "That's hardly a subject for polite company." Her fair skin was flushed to a charming peach shade.

Taking pity on her, Simon changed the subject. "Mother says the invitations for next week's ball have gone out and she has already received acceptances."

From the sideboard, where she was filling her plate with eggs and kidneys, Lady Sebastian said, "Did she doubt it? We all know that *no one* would miss the engagement party of the long-elusive duke of Camber. They shall all be here to see what pattern card of propriety has finally entrapped him."

"And have their preconceived notions turned on their heads by Dami," Julian teased.

The rest of the meal was spent joking and talking about the upcoming ball.

Afterward Dami and Julian lingered over their coffee.

"And what do you have planned for us today?"

Julian inquired.

She looked shyly at him. "Well, I thought . . . That is, I know it will be dreadfully boring for you. . . ." She flung her hands in the air. "I'm making a muddle of this."

"You are, aren't you," he smiled at her. "Come, I won't bite you. Tell me what you'd like to do."

She drew in a deep breath. "It's not much, but it is important to me. You see," she said earnestly, looking him in the eye, "I started a school here two years ago for the daughters of the workers." She looked at him expectantly, not sure what his reaction would be.

His eyes softened. "Very noble of you. How has it turned out?"

She watched him carefully. He didn't sound sarcastic and he looked genuinely interested. Her bowstring-tight nerves loosened. "I'm so glad you aren't shocked at my bold behavior. My family has always supported me, but the local gentry have made it plain that they consider it a waste of good money to educate laborers' children, particularly girl children."

"Then I would have to say they sound shortsighted."

"Do you really mean that? Does this mean that you won't object to my continuing after we are married?"

"What do you take me for? If I didn't know better, I would think you hold me in very low esteem." He tipped up her chin with his finger, since her face had dropped at his words. "And that isn't true, is it?"

"Well," she squirmed, "I did have my doubts, but I know now they were foolish," she concluded with a sunny smile.

"We won't argue the point," he said, kissing the tip of her nose. "I've had my fill of fighting with you. Now, when are we leaving, and how are we going?"

In a twinkling she had him in a small gig drawn by one stubborn donkey and they were on their way. They drove leisurely through the countryside, following the winding dirt roads that connected the small hamlets and isolated cottages. The summer sun warmed their backs and glinted off the small streams they crossed from time to time.

"I so much enjoy the countryside," Dami said impulsively. She could have bitten her tongue. Julian was never in the country. He kept his principle place of abode in London. How could she have been so stupid.

"Don't look so chagrined, I like the country, too. But up till now there has been more to do in the city." He put an arm around her shoulders and drew her to him. "When we are married, we will spend long months at my main estate. So many that you will wish heartily for town."

"Well," she began grudgingly, "I suppose there are many compensations in London that country life lacks."

"Of course, there are. There is the British Museum, the opera, more libraries than you can count on both hands, your papers and periodicals reach you the same day they hit the street instead of weeks later, and there are always art exhibits. A veritable smorgasbord of activities for a lady of intelligence."

"What about you, Julian? What will you be doing while I sample all these delights?" Doubt pricked at her. It seemed the ideal ending to a delightful fairy tale for her to marry him, but would they live happily ever after?

"I will be with you, sweetings. Or taking my seat in the Lords. I am not such a ne'er-do-well as you seem to think."

"I realize that, for I know you take your position in the Lords seriously." She gazed pensively in front of them. The narrow track was bumpy and constantly threw her against him. The solid strength of his thigh felt good along hers and his shoulder was a pillar of strength against hers, but was physical gratification enough to compensate her for a possibly turbulent marriage?

"There's a building off to our right," Julian said. "It appears to be swamped with young girls terrorizing one harassed-looking woman." He chuckled. "Is it your school?"

"Yes," Dami said, forcing her mind on the present. They pulled up in the dusty yard and climbed down. Before Dami's feet even touched the ground Miss Merriweather was upon her.

"Milady, it is so good to see you back." She curtsied to the younger woman. "Things don't seem to go as smoothly when you aren't about, and the girls miss you."

Dami took both the teacher's hands and drew the older woman forward to meet Camber. Julian shook hands with the woman, pleased that his betrothed had made an astute decision in hiring her. Miss Merriweather was tall and lean, past the first blush of youth, but with an air of authority about her that he was sure kept the girls she taught in line.

After a few moments of polite talk, Dami drew him into the one-room cottage. The walls were whitewashed and the windows were covered with red gingham curtains. Ten scaled-down desks, simply constructed of oak, filled the center space, and a large cubbyhole desk stood at the front of the room. He looked around and noticed there was a side table with a jug and eleven glasses on it, and a tray of macaroons.

He raised an eyebrow. "You even provide nourishment. Commendable."

Dami flushed, but bit back the sharp retort. He wasn't being sarcastic. "I've found that a break with some lemonade or cool water and a cookie or biscuit often revives flagging spirits."

"True. I found it to be so in the Peninsula. But our sustenance consisted of stronger drink and heartier fare." He winked at her. "Not the thing for young girls."

They spent a few minutes more, while Dami listened to Miss Merriweather's needs, and Julian complimented the teacher on her well-behaved pupils and orderly school.

"What do you think?" Dami asked afterward on the ride home.

"It is well planned and organized. You are to be commended. In fact, I think that your first task as my duchess shall be to start one on my land."

"Julian," she squealed, flinging her arms around him.

Unintentionally, he jerked at the reins, pulling the donkey's head sideways and driving them smack into a ditch. The right wheel of the gig stuck tight in the mud, causing the vehicle to jolt to a stop that sent both passengers careening to one side.

With a plop, Dami and Julian found themselves up to their bottoms in mud, with more mud splattered on their coats and faces. Dami's eyes rounded in surprise, before she burst into a peal of laughter.

"What's so funny?" Julian said awfully. "If you hadn't thrown yourself at me, I wouldn't have been so mutton-handed with the reins and we would still be on the road; dry, clean, and safe in the gig."

She smothered her giggles. "But you look so funny. The perfect Corinthian, sitting in the mud. It is too . . . much!" And she started laughing again.

"Come along, my girl," he said, standing and pulling her up with him. "You may have a fit of the giggles, and this may be hilarious, but I have no intentions of enjoying it with my backside in a mud puddle."

With no more ado he climbed out of the ditch, yanking her behind him. Once on dry land, he let out a loud guffaw.

"You should look at yourself," he said. "Your hat is hanging by mud-caked ribbons, and your hair is done à la mud. You even have a large beauty spot in the middle of your chin."

"You aren't much better," she retorted.

Wiping his eyes, he said, "No, I daresay I'm not." His eyes turned serious, and he grabbed her to him.

Her whole body thrilled to his touch. Her limbs heated even as they went limp with response.

It was Julian who pulled away first. "You make me forget everything," he said. "Even to the point of seducing you in the middle of a country lane where anyone might come by, and," he grimaced in distaste, "while covered with enough dried mud to thatch a cottage roof. Now we must see if our combined strength can free the wheel, or if we are doomed to walk home."

Dami grabbed the donkey's rein and pulled while Julian put his shoulder to the back of the gig's seat. Try as they might, they couldn't budge it. After working up a sweat, Julian finally called a halt.

"We will never move it," he said, wiping at his face with his hand. He left a streak of dirt behind him. "I will unharness the donkey and we shall walk back to Green Leaf." He looked at her and frowned. "Do you think you can make it, or should I leave you here and go for help on my own?"

"What kind of flat do you take me for? You will not leave me here alone, and I can walk as far as you, milord. We shall take turns riding the donkey."

His eyebrows rose. "Ride this beast? You must be joking."

"No, I'm not. Methuselah here is trained to hold a rider. He is a little slow, and a little bumpy, but he gets where he's going." At his continued astonishment, she added testily, "It is better than walking four miles without respite."

"We shall have to see about that."

They soon had the donkey freed and the three of them set off down the lane, Julian and Dami bickering over who would ride the animal first, Julian stating flatly that he would not ride the beast, and Dami telling he must learn to swallow his pride when situations were less than conducive to it.

It was a good hour later that the very bedraggled

pair presented themselves at Green Leaf to the scandalized, but long suffering Smithfield. The butler admitted them without blinking an eyelid.

His only words were, "The earl of Perth awaits your convenience in the library, Your Grace."

Chapter Twenty-Six

Every bone in her body ached as Dami stretched to the ceiling. She wasn't even sure she would be able to sit at the musical recital that night, so sore was her posterior from riding the donkey the day before.

"Milady," Suzy said, "His Grace requested through his valet that you wear the same red dress you wore to that ball you went to back in London."

Dami looked at the maid in surprise and saw the girl was agog with anticipation to hear her answer. Leave it to Julian to dress his respectable betrothed as a not-so-respectable lady of the night.

"Bring the dress here, Suzy, and we will see what can be done with the neckline. As much as the duke might enjoy seeing so much of me, you and I know it isn't the thing."

"Yes, ma'am." Suzy rushed into the dressing room and back out with the silk dress draped over her arms.

Dami donned the dress, then stood in front of the mirror. "Hmm, perhaps a discreetly placed black lace handkerchief? Do you think you can get it sewn into place in time?"

Suzy nodded enthusiastically.

Dami smiled her thanks at the maid, then wandered to the window. She felt restless, but didn't want to see Julian just yet. She would go to her "thinking tree."

Decided, she slinked down the hallway from her bedroom to the servants' stairs. Picking up her lemon-colored skirts, she made her way to the back door leading into the gardens.

The scent of honeysuckle and roses blended with the fresh smell of late autumn as she made her way through the garden to the stables. It had been a long time since she had escaped to her "thinking tree," but today she felt drawn to it. There were so many things she had to work out.

Why had Perth been here yesterday afternoon, and then gone before dinner? And why had Julian refused to discuss it? Particularly now, when things were going so well between her and him? Was there something he didn't want her to know? Obviously, but what? They would be married in two weeks; they should be telling each other everything.

Then there was his belief that she had aided de Bourville. Somehow, they had let the subject drop, by mutual agreement. She knew this was best, but there were times, like now, when it intruded on her happiness. Could that be why Perth had come? She shook her head in frustration.

Reaching the stables, she absentmindedly asked the groom to saddle her horse.

"Lady Damaris," the groom said a few moments later, "your mare is saddled now."

She focused her attention on the man. "Thank you, Tim. Please bring her over to the mounting block and give me a hand." She smiled. "As you can see, this is a spur-of-the-moment decision. I have no riding habit on."

"Yes, milady," he said, with a reproachful look at the immodest amount of ankle her seat on the horse showed.

"I know, Tim. It isn't done, but hopefully it is too early for anyone to be about to see me in this shockingly exposed position." She winked at the man and urged her horse into a walk.

Not paying attention to what she was doing, her mind chewed the most important thing bothering her at the moment, while her mare, Ginger, headed for the woods. The musical evening at the earl of Compton's. It was tonight, and everyone would be there. She would have given anything not to go, but there was no polite way to refuse. Especially, in light of the coup the earl had effected by getting Pavloti to sing. She was one of the most celebrated sopranos in Europe. She was also Camber's ex-mistress.

Dami put her horse into a canter, her absorption in her problems blanketing the unease she usually felt on a horse. What if Julian found he wanted to take up with the lovely singer again? What should she do? What would she be able to do? And the stares of curious people, some sympathetic, others greedy to see a rift between her and Julian.

She was in a quandary.

From his window overlooking the back of the Cleve estate, Julian saw Dami leave the stables. His forehead wrinkled as he realized she wasn't wearing a habit or boots. Her ankles protruded from the bottom of her dress by a good twelve inches. He shook his head, not sure whether he was angry with her flaunting of convention or amused by it.

Already dressed in a loose-fitting coat, starched shirt, and buckskins, he decided to follow her. The chit wasn't a good horsewoman, and if her state of dress was any indication of her state of mind, she wasn't even concentrating.

Entering the stables, he ordered his stallion to be saddled. Then turning to the groom he said, "Tim, where is Lady Damaris headed?"

Tim scratched his head before answering. "Don't rightly know, Your Grace, but if I was forced to guess, I'd say to her 'thinkin' tree.' "

"Her what?" Julian asked, swinging himself up into the saddle.

"It's a tree she goes to, along the stream that borders Your Grace's land. Hasn't been there in a while. Must be somethin' botherin' her."

"Hmmm," Julian said, guiding his horse into the yard. "Thank you, Tim."

He spurred Diablo into a trot. When they were clear of the formal grounds, he urged the stallion into a canter. The animal's stride ate the distance. Soon, Julian could just make out the figure of a horse and rider. They were moving slowly, so he had no worries about catching her or keeping her in sight.

He turned to look around him, memorizing landmarks so he would be able to find his way back if the occasion arose. When he looked for Dami again, she was gone. He touched his horse's flanks with his boots, putting Diablo into a gallop.

Seconds later he came upon a hedge fence, the gate open. He guided his mount over it. Now the ground was rocky, and in the distance was a copse of trees. He slowed the horse up on the uneven terrain. Entering the woods, he heard sounds of someone else passing through: the crackle of leaves being stepped on, the slap of branches being moved out of the way.

The sounds changed. A small army seemed to be crashing its way through the undergrowth. Fear gripped Julian, sent energy to his arms and legs. With no regard for the danger of moving quickly in nature's tangle, he spurred Diablo into a trot.

Dami must have lost control of her horse, he thought, urging his stallion on. He had to find her. The noise led him in her direction. Breaking through a massive barrier of leaves and brush, he saw her off to the right.

She was clinging to the mane of her horse, the reins flapping in the wind. Her hair had come loose from its pins and streamed out behind her. Even in the distance, he could see the tenseness of her body as she pressed along the neck of the horse.

"Infuriating chit," he cursed her, pushing Diablo on. "We will both break our necks," he muttered.

Dami held onto Ginger's mane with fear-strengthened fingers. She was so scared she felt sick. The wind rushed past her ears, laughing at her on its way. If only she could swing one leg over and ride like a man. If only she had put on a riding habit, instead of this confining dress. If only she had paid attention to what she was doing.

It was too late now. All she could do was ride it out. Either the mare would tire and stop or trip in a hole, sending them both to the ground. She squeezed her eyes shut. The crazy-quilt pattern of the woods as they zoomed through added to her queasiness. She prayed for a miracle.

Above the sounds of her racing heart and Ginger's plunging hooves, she heard another horse. She dared not look, for fear of loosing her grip.

A strong arm wrapped around her waist. She was lifted high in the air. She found herself perched on the pommel of a man's saddle, a solid chest holding her up.

She watched the man's forearms bunch into cords of muscle as he slowed his lathering horse. The fingers holding the leather reins looked familiar.

"Julian," she said thankfully.

When Diablo was finally stopped, Julian slid to the ground dragging her with him. She leaned against him, her body buckling from delayed reaction. His arms were the only things keeping her up.

She lifted a grateful face to his. His anger was like a slap. She cringed back from it.

"You crazy woman! You could have killed yourself!" He shook her like a mastiff shaking a bone. "Do I need to lock you in your room to keep you out of trouble? For if I do, I will start tonight." His shaking stopped as suddenly as it had started. He yanked her to him, his arms around her like bands of steel. One hand cupped her head and pushed it to his shoulder. His head bent to rest on the top of hers.

"Sweetings, don't scare me like this. All I could think of was losing you."

"I'm sorry, Julian," she said.

He put her from him, keeping his hands on her shoulders. "You look a veritable ragamuffin. Your hair is wild as a nymph's, and there is a smudge on your nose. As for your dress . . ." His eyes unfocused for a moment. "When have I seen you like this before?"

She blushed.

"I have it! You were that forward little girl I saved from a runaway horse years ago." He looked around them. "And it was near here, too." Looking back at her, he said, "I'm right, aren't I?"

She nodded.

"Well, I'll be. I might have never realized if it hadn't been for this. It was many years ago, and too much has happened." He shook his head. "I told you to find me when you got older, and you certainly did."

"Yes, and you said we might find we have some things in common, too." She looked prim and proper, adding, "At the time I had no idea just what sort of things you were talking about. Had I, I'm sure I would have been mortified and never looked for you."

"Minx," he said. "You would have hunted me down sooner. I remember that kiss." He moved her into the shade of a tree. "Do I need to wet my handkerchief in the stream this time to cool you off? Or are you going to faint away on me instead?"

She laughed with him. "If you remember, I didn't faint the last time, and I have no intentions of doing so now. I doubt if you are anymore in the habit of carrying smelling salts now than you were then."

"You're right, but," he said, getting serious, "what prompted you to take off today? I know you aren't comfortable on horses, and you certainly aren't dressed for the endeavor."

He pulled her down to the grass to sit by him, keeping one arm around her waist. When she didn't answer, he raised her chin so that he could look into her eyes.

Dami dropped her eyelashes. She couldn't tell him about her fears for tonight. If she knew nothing else, she knew one didn't question a man about his former mistresses.

"It was nothing. I only wanted a breath of fresh air."

"You could have gotten that in the garden. Look at me. The groom said you were going to your 'thinking tree,' and I got the impression that it is where you go when you are troubled." His eyes were tender and concerned as he said, "Trust me, sweetings. If something is bothering you, tell me about it. I may not be able to solve it, but I can listen."

She wanted to tell him, knew that if she didn't it would bother her until it became an obsession. She took a deep breath. "It's about Pavloti!"

Understanding cleared the surprise from his eyes. "There is nothing for you to worry about. That was over years ago."

Now it was her turn to look surprised, and she was getting mad. "Years ago? What kind of fool do you take me for? I *know* she was your mistress just eleven months ago! Deny it if you can."

He looked puzzled. "She is yesterday's mutton, several years aged."

She knocked him in the chest. His arm fell from her waist, and she tried to rise. He recovered and grabbed her around the ankles. She tumbled down on top of him. They lay spread-eagled in the fragrant grass, her face held defiantly above his.

"You lie," she hissed.

"Only with you," he murmured, "I wouldn't bed another woman when I have you to go to."

"Ohhh," she said. "Don't play games with me. You lie when you say Pavloti was your mistress years ago."

"Well, since you're so adamant, give me a minute to think about this."

While he thought, his hands wandered. They roamed over her back, moving with the sureness of familiarity down her spine to the flare of her buttocks, then back up to massage her shoulders, pressing her breasts against his chest.

She closed her eyes and tried to ignore his caresses. It was no use. She was a confused welter of tensed muscles and melting heat.

"This is more like it," he whispered into her ear. "I honestly had forgotten that Pavloti had been my mistress, and you are right, it was more recently than three years ago. But it could have been ages ago, so completely have I forgotten her."

She opened her eyes, wanted to say "I told you so," but the desire she saw in his face stopped the words better than any kiss.

It was hours later, the sun low in the sky, when they finally came to their senses. They lay in the lush grass with tree branches woven into a roof above them. Their arms and legs were tangled together. Their clothes were a pile of cloth shoved to one side.

"Oh, Julian," Dami said, realizing how late it was, "we must hurry or we won't have time to dress for tonight's musical." The words reminded her of her worries. Her mouth tightened and her eyes clouded over.

"Sweetings," Julian noticed the change in her, "I love you. Haven't I just proved it beyond a doubt?" He grinned wickedly. "It's not part of my repertoire to make love to a woman in the wild. I prefer scented sheets of silk next to my skin, not grass. The lovely soprano, by the way, was only my mistress a matter of weeks before she bored me, and there is nothing that makes me lose interest sooner than boredom. Now *you* have never bored me, and I doubt, sometimes with regret, that you ever will."

She smiled.

"That's better," he said.

He pulled her up and with each other's help they scrambled into their clothes, now quite wrinkled.

"It's a good thing you are to marry me," Julian said, "otherwise my reputation for suave seductions would be in jeopardy."

Dami twisted from side to side, taking one last look at herself in the mirror. Suzy had sewed the wisp of black lace just right. Now, instead of a brazen plunge between her breasts, there was just a hint of shadowed depths. The gown was also low in the back, something she knew Julian favored, so her hair was dressed with one ringlet falling down the indentation of her spine. It tickled when she moved, but not as much as she imagined Julian's finger would when he traced the curl.

A knock on the door made her turn around. She nodded to Suzy to answer it.

"Good evening," Julian said, his eyes raking over her appreciatively.

He dismissed Suzy, who looked rather scandalized at leaving her mistress alone with the duke in her bedchamber. Then he drew out a jeweler's box and flicked open the lid. Inside was a diamond necklace set in white gold. Next to it was a bracelet.

Dami sucked in her breath. "So you saved that bracelet. Did you intend to try and give it to Amalie again, or were you planning to give it to Lady Damaris?" A twinge of pain curled her fingers.

"I returned it to the jeweler, who is in London. But when we came back from France I decided to go back and get it, along with the necklace the proprietor had tried to sell me in the first place. Does that make you feel better?"

She looked sheepish. "It seems I always jump to conclusions where you are concerned."

"That's fine, as long as you always give me a chance to explain. It keeps things interesting. Now, turn around."

She did as bid. His fingers were like butterflies on the nape of her neck, sending little chills down her arms. Then he ran a finger around the outline of her curl.

"A beautiful ringlet, and placed at my favorite spot," he murmured against her skin where he placed a kiss.

"I thought you would appreciate it, Your Grace."

"Minx!" he said, turning her around. "Now your wrist, then we must go. I told your mother I wouldn't be longer than five minutes alone with you. Cagy woman, your dame. She understands me perfectly."

"So she says." Dami dimpled up at him. She picked up her black lace shawl and they went down to the foyer.

With a bustle of skirts and wraps, Lady Cleve, Lady Sebastian, Kit, Dami, and Julian fitted themselves into the traveling chaise. Lady Cleve and Lady Sebastian had a seat to themselves by virtue of their rank, while Dami sat between Kit and Julian. Simon and Johnny traveled in front in Simon's phaeton.

The moon was a burnished sliver in the black sky. The weather was good, so even the small amount of moonlight was sufficient for travel when combined with the light provided by their carriage lanterns.

"Why the Friday face, sweetings?" Julian said, intruding on Dami's thoughts.

"I was just thinking."

"Then we are in for trouble," he said.

"Camber," said Lady Cleve.

He gave a guilty start. "I know, madam, I shouldn't tease her so, but she will put herself in the spot."

"Yes, but you must learn self-control. It is the only way you shall manage to govern your household after the two of you are married."

"Well, I never!" Dami said. "My own mother conspiring against me."

"It's for you own good, Damaris," Lady Cleve said.

"I believe I've heard that line before." Dami bridled.

When they pulled up in front of the earl of Compton's great house they became lost in the crowd of carriages ahead of them. A full thirty minutes later they finally climbed down and entered the massive mahogany front door. Next they stood in the receiving line for another hour, until at last they were in the music room.

Dami, her perceptions heightened by the emotional strain she found herself under, examined the room she had spent many long hours in through new eyes. It was a long rectangular room, with slate-blue walls trimmed near the ceiling with embossed silver leaves. Hanging from the center was a large Waterford chandelier that cast its light directly on the floor below it like a spotlight. Normally a massive, double keyboard pianoforte resided in the light, but tonight the spot was bare. On either side of it were chairs arranged in spacious rows for the guests.

Dami's eyes were riveted to the spot where the soprano would give her performance. Her mouth tasted of bile. It seemed she would be forever running into Camber's discarded mistresses. How could she ever hope to deal with them with equanimity?

When the time came, Dami took a seat in the front row, Julian at her side. With a flourish of violins, Pavloti entered and made her regal way to her position under the chandelier. She flashed a smile of large white teeth and full red lips to her audience. For a flicker of an eyelash, she let her gaze linger on Camber. Then she was into her recital.

Dami sat transfixed. The woman was full-busted, with a narrow waist and full hips. Her hair was ebony and her eyes were sparkling sapphires. Her nose was small and straight and her cheekbones were prominent. She was dressed in a velvet dress the color of royal purple. It plunged almost to her navel, accurately portraying her charms.

Dami's evening soured beyond redemption. She couldn't compare to the rare creature who was singing her heart out, her eyes now locked on Julian. Somehow, Dami determined, she would get through the rest of the performance. She would go with Camber to compliment the soprano on her excellent singing. Then she would continue with him to make polite conversation. When it was time to leave, she would hold her head up proudly, and once safely in her room, she would cry her heart out.

At last, Pavloti stopped. There was thunderous applause. People stood up and continued to clap. Dami joined them, her movements like a wooden doll's. Dimly she was aware of Julian at her side, his hands moving.

The noise died down, and people began to mill around. She felt Julian's hand on her elbow steering her to where the Italian woman was graciously accepting her accolades. Dami didn't think she could bear to face the woman. Memories of the time in Covent Garden when she'd had to sit by and do nothing while Mrs. Smith fondled Julian ran amuck through her head. Her heart thumped, and her throat closed painfully.

Julian bent down and whispered, "She was the mistress of my lusts, you are the mistress of my heart."

Dami turned to look at him. She knew then that she would be able to greet the singer with grace, even feel pity for the woman who had lost Camber.

Chapter Twenty-Seven

Dami walked the early-morning gardens with a lightness of heart she hadn't felt in a long time. The light breeze rustling through the trees lifted tendrils of her hair and floated against her cheeks. She breathed deeply. The heady scent of roses and honeysuckle perfumed the air. She felt content to be by herself, savoring Julian's words of last night. He had introduced her to Pavloti and made it clear that the singer no longer had any ties with him. At the same time, he had ensured that everyone present understood that Dami was the only woman he was interested in now or in the future.

"Dami," Simon yelled from the nearby veranda, "I would like to speak with you."

"If you insist," she said grudgingly as Simon caught up with her.

"Beautiful here at this time of year, isn't it?" Simon asked conversationally.

"Yes, it is, but I doubt if the scenery is what you want to discuss."

"True. Let's go sit on the bench."

They sat on a white iron bench for two under an

apple tree. Dami arranged her skirts.

Clearing his throat, Simon said, "It's time I told you. De Bourville got away from Perth."

"Oh, no! How horrible. Not that I want to see him hang, but he can't be allowed to continue giving our secrets to Bonapartist sympathizers. What is being done?" Dami asked.

"It's worse than that. It seems that the count has left France." He watched for her reaction.

"But where could he go? Napoleon is on Elba, and I doubt if our agents would allow the count to pay a social call on the emperor, and the island is so small it would be difficult for him to hide out for long."

"There's the rub," Simon said. "All evidence indicates he fled here. He has a hunting box somewhere in Yorkshire. Perth knows the town it is near, but not the exact location."

"But Yorkshire is just a few days from here." She stopped, her eyes unfocusing as she thought. "He would go through, or near here, if he landed at Felixstowe. Is this why Perth was here the other day?"

"Yes. He intimated that de Bourville may have escaped on a smuggler's boat. That's what we're afraid of. Also, we half think he *will* pass by here, and in the passing contrive to pick up extra baggage."

She didn't say anything for a while. When she did, she looked worried. "You mean he might try to abduct me again."

"I'm afraid so." He sighed. "Julian and I have racked our brains for a way to foil de Bourville, but until he shows his face, or Perth tracks him to ground, there is nothing we can do, except be prepared for the worst."

"You and Julian weren't going to tell me, were you?" she asked, suspicion growing in her mind.

"No." Simon looked distracted and uncomfortable.

"Julian still thinks I'm in league with de Bourville. He was afraid that if I knew the count was near here that I would go to him." She let the bitterness she felt drip from each word.

"Nothing of the kind," Simon said forcefully. "He, we, were afraid that you would get some hare-brained idea that you must try to help smoke the man out. And that, let me tell you, is something neither of us relishes."

"That's almost as bad as thinking I was in league with the count, to think I'm muttonheaded enough to put myself in his clutches again." She jumped up, jerky in her agitation. "You are both insulting, as well as domineering. The least you could have done was credit me with enough common sense to know when things are beyond my ken."

Simon watched her huff back to the house. He had known his talk with her would end in an altercation, but it had been necessary for her own protection. He hadn't told her that Perth had located the smuggler who had transferred de Bourville. The man had said he had let the count off at Aldeburgh, which was only thirty miles east of them on the East Anglia coast.

With her independent ways, both he and Camber had been afraid she would take off on her own without notifying them or taking a groom. In which case, she would be the perfect target for the count if he were skulking in the area, waiting for an opportunity to grab her. That was why Camber had been at his window yesterday and seen Dami going to the stables. A good thing, too.

Meanwhile, Dami stormed into her room, slamming the door behind her. So! That was why Camber was sticking to her like a burr to a horse's coat. It also explained why he had taken up residence at Green Leaf instead of at his own place, just a few miles distant. Simon and he must have decided she would need to be watched like a child who might run from its nanny.

This situation had to be solved. She sat down in a Louis XV chair upholstered in green and pink chintz, her elbow on her knee, her fist under her chin. There had to be something she could do to bring this de Bourville matter to a head.

She sat up, a pleased look on her face. Her idea would take some time, and some judicious dropping of hints, but it might work.

Dami left the house without notifying Julian where she was going. She suppressed a twinge of guilt she felt over this by telling herself it had to be done this way. However, she did allow a groom to go with her on her walk to Framlingham.

It was barely a mile into the town. She stopped at the chemist, the butcher, the baker, and last, the local pub. Mr. Snopson, the pub owner, was a short, thin man with balding brown hair and bulging blue eyes. His nose was long and thin and constantly into other people's business.

"Mr. Snopson," Dami said, entering the tap room, "May I have a glass of lemonade?"

"Certainly, milady," he said. "Would you be wanting a private parlor?"

"No, thank you," she said. "I shall be perfectly fine

405

drinking it out on your little patio in the back. I fear these are the last peaceful moments I shall have for the next weeks." She watched him carefully to make sure he was listening to what she said. He was looking at her avidly. "This time next week is my betrothal ball." She sighed hugely. "There is so much fuss and bother, I'm sure that I shall be heartily sick of it by then. Not to mention the crush of people. I hear that there is a second ball for the servants and such to celebrate. I hope to see you there. Anyway, I shall be in need of fresh air before that evening is over, I'm sure." She let her shoulders slump as though exhaustion already overwhelmed her.

Mr. Snopson led her to a small wooden bench under a large apple tree.

"I'll be right back, milady," he said, scuttling away.

Dami grinned. Unless she misread her man, he would impart the information she had just given him before he even returned with her lemonade. She shuddered to think what her mama or Camber would say if they had heard her very vulgar words. True, there was to be a second ball for the servants and village folk in Green Leaf's smaller ballroom, but it wasn't something she should have prattled on about. Smithfield would already have taken care of the details and let everyone know.

It was a good fifteen minutes later when her lemonade arrived.

"Begging your pardon, Lady Damaris, but we had to squeeze some fresh lemons. Didn't want you to have yesterday's drink and such." He shuffled on his feet as he laid the small tray holding a glass of lemonade and a plate of crackers on the table.

"Thank you very much," she said. "Please see that my groom gets a pint of ale also."

After the thin man left, Dami quickly ate and drank her repast. She still had other areas to seed with her tale.

So went the next couple of days. Sometimes she took a groom with her on these jaunts, more often than not, Julian accompanied her. She even carried her charade of looking forward to some respite, possibly at some time during the night of the ball, into the parlors of the local gentry. She reasoned that one never knew who a spy's contacts were.

The day before the ball Perth returned.

Dami and Julian were in the drawing room when Smithfield announced the earl. They looked up together as Perth entered.

"Don't let me interrupt you," Perth said.

"Not at all," Dami said, rising and putting down her whist hand. "I was losing anyway."

"Well, I think you're dashed ill-timed, Perth," Julian said with a wolfish leer at Dami. "I almost had her where I wanted her."

Perth looked around the room. "Not here, Camber. That really is shockingly poor behavior."

All three laughed as Dami rang the bell for tea and wine.

"What brings you here, earl?" Dami asked.

"I was passing through the area and wanted to stop and see how you and Camber are doing." Perth's voice was nonchalant, and he studied his fingernails as though their condition was of the utmost importance.

"In that case," said Julian, "why don't you stay a while. I know this isn't my home, but I'm sure Lady Cleve and Simon won't mind your company. And we have a ball tomorrow night that promises to be a sadder crush than any London could boast."

Dami watched the two men, knowing they were telling each other more than their words implied, but uncertain just what. She looked at Perth again and noticed for the first time that he looked tired and wan, and his left shoulder seemed hitched higher than the right.

"Here we are," she interrupted them as Smithfield entered with a silver tray holding a Wedgewood teapot and matching cup, saucer, and plate, and a bottle of port and two cut crystal glasses. "Some refreshments. I hope you gentlemen don't mind, but I thought you would prefer wine with your cakes."

"Better than tea," Julian said. "But just the wine, sweetings. And not too much at a time, either. I learned the hard way with you not to drink indiscriminately when Perth is in the same room."

Both men chuckled, but Dami maintained a stony face. "Very funny, I'm sure," she said.

"As I was saying," Julian said again, "why don't you stay at least through the ball?"

"I should be glad to," Perth said.

After the refreshments, Julian went with Perth to show him his room. Dami followed discreetly behind them. She knew of a place in the wall of the room the earl would be staying in where putting a glass to the spot and then to one's ear enabled one to hear the conversation in the next room. She reasoned it would work in reverse. On her way, she stopped in the kitchen to pick up a plain glass, saying she had broken the one in her room.

She gave them ten minutes to get arranged in the room before she slipped into the adjacent room. Locating the spot, she positioned the glass and listened unabashedly to their talk.

The upstairs maid had already turned down the bed and lit a cozy fire in the grate of the Red Room, in which the men were. The mantelpiece was blood-red marble, and the walls flanking the fireplace were papered with red flocked roses. The furniture was heavy Elizabethan oak, stained almost black and intricately carved in fruits and flowers. The drapes, pulled against the evening sun, were thick red velvet trimmed with gold tassels.

"What really brings you here, Perth?" Julian said, sitting in a chair by the fire.

"My own folly. I underestimated my opponent— again. I continually forget the count is wily and desperate. This time it has proved to be a painful lesson." He eased out of his coat, then turned and laid it across the bed. When he faced Julian again he was wincing. "Moving my shoulder is almost as painful as the actual infliction of the wound." He collapsed into the chair across from Julian.

"Dammit," Julian said under his breath. "Who would have ever thought de Bourville capable? Did he shoot you or get you with a sword?"

"He got me with a knife as I was coming out of a tavern in Aldeburgh. I'd been there drinking, dressed like a fisherman, and trying to garner any new information on the man. I hadn't been able to trace him beyond Aldeburgh, and I was hoping to loosen some tongues of information that had no meaning for anyone unless they were looking for the count. As it was, when I left the place I had been drinking for some time, but I didn't think it would impair my reflexes. I was wrong. It slowed me just enough that when a man appeared out of a dark alley on my route home, I wasn't fast enough to avoid his plunging hand, which held a rather nasty little present."

"Here, let me ring for some more wine, Jason, you are looking as though you won't make it through the telling of your tale." Julian got up and went to the bell pull near the bed.

"To finish," Perth said, "I managed to deflect the knife from my heart and to get a grip on my assailant, thus allowing me a good look at his face. The count is thinner and his face shows more wrinkles, but by and large, his avoidance of justice doesn't seem to have seriously affected him physically."

"How long ago was this?" Julian asked, returning to his seat.

"The day after I left here last week. The wound became infected, and I was bedridden until yesterday. Otherwise I would have been here sooner to warn you that de Bourville is more dangerous that we originally thought." The earl slumped further down in his large red leather chair, his eyes closed.

To the knock on the door, Julian bade the footman enter. As soon as the servant left, he poured them each a glass.

Handing the glass to Perth, he said, "How bad is it now?"

Perth took a long sip of the burgundy. "I think I might have torn it open again. But it will heal again; it is no big matter."

"I'm not going to let you wither and die on me now," Julian said. "I'm going to get Williams. As you know, he was my batman in the Peninsula, and if anyone can fix you up right and tight it is he."

From her crouched position in the next room, Dami heard the door close behind Julian. She judged it time to make her escape to her room. She rose up, feeling the pricking in her feet and the ache in her knees from her prolonged listening. Going to the door, she opened it a crack and made sure there was no one in the hallway before slipping out. She rushed to her room. Once safely inside, she fell against the closed door.

Things were getting more complicated by the day — and de Bourville wasn't the harmless man she had thought him. He could strike out viciously at his enemies. Perhaps her plan wasn't so brilliant as she had originally thought. It was too late to change the rumors. She could fail to take the walk in the garden she'd been hinting at. Her head whirled in confusion.

She would decide what to do tomorrow.

Meanwhile, Julian returned to Perth's room with his valet.

"Milord," Williams said, "let's have a look at that cut."

With a grimace, Perth unbuttoned his shirt. The valet took one look at the blood-soaked bandage and said he would need a basin of hot water, fresh bandages, some basilica powder, cheap gin to sterilize the wound, and unless he missed his guess, a needle

411

and thread.

Julian went personally to procure the items. Passing the drawing room, he remembered the full bottle of brandy on a side table. He got it.

The rest of the house was in bed before Williams and Camber finally allowed Perth to sleep. The earl was sewn, powdered, bandaged, and drunk as a wheelbarrow.

Early the next morning, Dami donned a royal blue chintz day dress, with black ribbons banning the scooped neck and the stiffened skirt. Her hair twisted into a knot and secured with more black ribbons, she descended on the breakfast room, eager to see how the earl looked and to see if she could wheedle any information from the men while they drank their coffee and ate their kippers and eggs.

"Good morning," she said, entering the sunny room. She looked around expectantly. "Where is everyone?" she asked Julian, the only other occupant in the room.

"Is this how I can expect to be greeted every morning after we are married?"

She grinned at him. "You know different," she said, taking the place next to him. "I just thought there would be more people here."

"Perth?" Julian asked. "Is there something about Jason that interests you?"

"Me?" she said innocently. "Why, of course not. I merely wondered why he showed up here. His excuses last night didn't ring true."

"He merely came to pay his respects, coupled with needing rest."

She eyed him askance, hoping her acting was good

enough. "What does the renowned Earl of Perth need rest from? His bit-o-muslins? Really, Julian, there must be a better reason than that."

He was suddenly serious. "He needs recuperation time for his wound."

She tried to look surprised. "His wound? Whatever are you talking about? Has he had a hunting accident?"

"No, he hasn't. It seems de Bourville knifed him. Right now, Perth is upstairs in bed delirious from fever and infection. Simultaneously, de Bourville is somewhere in the vicinity or in Yorkshire, fleeing from the law." He wiped his mouth with his napkin, looking at her thoughtfully.

"Who is watching Perth?"

"Kit."

"What? Surely I heard incorrectly."

"No, you didn't. She found out from Smithfield that Perth arrived last night. Then she saw Williams entering the Red Room and demanded to know why he was going in. Williams let it slip that Perth was badly hurt. That was all it took." He shook his head wonderingly. "I've never known my prim cousin to defy convention before—except for that time with you in Paris—but before poor Williams knew what was about, she was in the room, and that is where she has been since."

Dami met his eyes boldly. "Perhaps it is time you reconsidered your refusal to let Perth court her."

"Sweetings, don't let our happiness color your thinking. Jason has not asked to renew his suit. But more important, the two of them don't suit. It would be like mating a tiger to a sheep. Perth is aggressive; a flaunter of convention. Kit is an avid participant of convention, following the crowd without uttering a protest. She even finds her mother's little acts of rebellion to be too much. How would she contrive married to someone of Perth's stamp? No, I should never have an easy conscience were I to countenance a match of such disparity."

"I hadn't thought of it that way," she said. "But," she wagged one finger at him, "it isn't so very different from us. I am a shy, retiring person who prefers books and the countryside, while you are aggressive and a flaunter of propriety."

He looked incredulous. "You—*shy*? You—a person who dare not fly in the face of society? Have you looked in the mirror lately, Lady Damaris? Have you given any thought to the life you have been living the last four or five months?"

She sniffed. "Well, that is merely an aberration."

He chuckled. "Yes, and I fear you are full of such aberrations. Life with you will not be dull. Thank God," he added.

Later in the day, Dami went to her room to rest before preparing for the ball. Suzy helped her take off her dress, and then Dami lay on the bed, closing her eyes.

Julian would be so proud of her when she captured de Bourville. Never again would he suspect her of treason. Her senses floated away on the most satisfying scene of her being accosted in the gardens by the count, then luring him to the library while everyone else danced at her ball. She would woo de Bourville with praise, allowing him a few judicious liberties. She would let him kiss her hand, perhaps. She would

414

tell him she would go away with him, but first she must pack a small portmanteau. Then she would rush to Julian and tell him everything, and he would return to the library with her and capture de Bourville. She could hardly wait to see the look on Julian's face.

She sighed contentedly in her sleep.

Chapter Twenty-Eight

The ball was mere hours away when Suzy woke Dami from her nap. Dami sat up yawning, wisps of her dream coming to her, awakening her completely. She had to dress just so, demure yet seductive, if she hoped to twist the count to her plan. And it wouldn't hurt to have Julian admire her a little, either.

"Is my gown ready?" she asked the maid, hopping out of bed and going to the window. She pulled back the curtain. "Oh, Suzy, have you seen the gardens? They are beautiful with the candles scattered along the paths."

Dami observed that there was one area where there were no lights. It was the folly her father had built for her mother when they were newly married. She smiled, imagining the way the thing looked. It was made of white wrought iron twisted into shapes of lovers kissing, with loveknots and roses all around them. It would be perfect for her scheme.

"Lady Dami," Suzy said, "I've got your gown ready."

Dami let the curtain go and turned to face Suzy. "Did you bring Julian's diamonds?"

The maid nodded.

"Good. They will go perfectly with the silver in the dress." She raised her arms to facilitate the dropping of a muslin slip over her head.

When they were done, Dami went to look at herself. "It's perfect," she breathed.

The dress was thin white muslin, heavily embroidered with roses in silver thread around the low square neck, tiny puff sleeves, and slim skirt. Long white gloves bunched at her elbows, and white satin pumps, trimmed with silver, added the finishing touches. Her hair was gathered in loose curls on top of her head and a silver ribbon was threaded through it. Tendrils were allowed to fall in the back, emphasizing the low cut that went almost to the swell of her hips. Last she put on the diamond necklace and bracelet.

Suzy stood speechless with admiration. Even Dami was awed. She must show Kit. She grabbed up the silver-spangled stole and headed for Kit's bedchamber.

To get to her room, she had to pass by Perth's room. The door was open, and she looked in, as much from habit as from curiosity.

Kit was in the arms of her patient. Dami stood stock still. The earl's arms were about Kit's waist and tangled in her hair, making her short curls come loose from their riband. Dami hurried away from the door. Neither one saw her, so engrossed were they in each other.

Should she tell Julian? No, she decided. She wanted to give Kit and Perth a chance before Julian became involved again.

Dami returned to her room, bursting with speculation.

Dami thought her feet would turn to stone before they could finally leave the receiving line. Everyone from miles around was there. It seemed that hundreds had gone by and, she craned her neck, hundreds were to come. Julian stood by her side, with Lady Cleve on his other side. Next to the dowager was Simon.

Finally, Dami greeted the last guest. Her smile seemed permanently etched in her face, making her muscles ache. She noticed that Julian looked much the way she felt.

"Thank goodness, we won't be having this type of thing once we are married," he whispered to her. "I don't think I can stand this on a regular basis."

"But, Julian, I particularly want to entertain when I am a duchess," she said, batting her lashes.

"Don't try to gammon me," he said, taking her arm. "Especially right now when it is our duty to open the ball with the first dance and the first waltz of the evening."

He put his arm around her waist, his left hand took her right one. They dipped and swirled to the music, their bodies closer than the regulation twelve inches.

All around them other couples began to join in, the formal black attire of the men set off by large pins in their cravats, and the rainbow-hued plumage of the women enhanced by the sparkle of myriad jewels. Overhead, four cut crystal chandeliers, each holding fifty candles, provided the light of day. Along the silver-flocked walls, chairs and refreshment tables were set. The large French doors on either end of the long rectangular room were draped in silver satin and open to the fragrant scents of the garden's blooming flowers.

When the dance ended, Julian led Dami off the dance floor. He went to fetch her a glass of champagne, and she immediately was besieged by well-wishers and gentlemen asking for a dance. She laughed her way through the congratulations and managed to fob off most of the dance requests. She didn't want anyone missing her later.

"Here you are," Julian said, making his way through the throng to her side. He turned good-naturedly to exchange banter with the local bucks.

A country dance was forming. Dami's partner claimed her and she went to take her place. She had told Julian her dance card was filled. In reality, this was the only dance taken.

When the dance was over, she made her excuses to her partner. She quickly slipped out of the room into the hall. Luckily, the servants were below stairs replenishing the punch bowls and food trays. She hurried down the hall and into the library.

She closed the door quietly behind her, then moved to the window. There were no lights in here, so she could look at the gardens without being seen. Her fingers trembled as she moved aside the burgundy velvet drapes. Outside the candles glowed like diamonds in the night. There was no moon. A light breeze moved the tree limbs and waved through the shrubs and plants. She shivered.

Taking a deep breath, she opened the window and climbed out, then quickly made her way down the path.

The wind picked up. It trailed past her, touching her face with moist fingers and catching up her dress to swirl it around her ankles. She looked up. The clouds were scudding across the sky, a patch of black on dark. Soon it would be raining.

She picked up her speed. Please let de Bourville be there, she said silently. All her plans and plotting had been to lure him to the gardens tonight. He had to be here.

Her skin rose in goose flesh in the damp breeze. A picture of Perth in bed, sick from the knife wound inflicted by the count, flashed through her mind. Why hadn't she thought to bring a weapon of some sort? In a panic she turned to go back and fetch something — anything —

"*Ma cherie.*"

The whisper came from the very edge of the lit path. Her breath caught in her throat, her heart pounding. He was here.

She turned in the direction of the sound. "Jacques? Is that you?" she asked softly.

"None other. Quickly, before someone comes."

She jumped when his hand grabbed her wrist. Calming herself, she allowed him to guide her further from the path.

"Oh, Jacques," she said, "I was afraid you wouldn't come. Quickly, let's go someplace where we can talk."

"My thoughts, exactly," he said, "but where? Everything is lit up like Covent Gardens before a fireworks display."

Did he sound irritated? Skeptical? She must be careful. "This way," she said, allowing her wrist to remain in his grip without a fight. "There is a folly further back that is in darkness."

They moved rapidly through the damp night. Soon the folly rose above them, its twisted iron casting grotesque pictures of men and women writhing in one another's hold. Gone from the design was the touch of love. It looked perverted.

"Well, *ma chérie*?"

She strained to see his expression, but the dark was complete in the summerhouse. Chills ran up her arm from his touch.

"I was afraid that you wouldn't come." Her voice was hoarser. "I've been working for weeks trying to get the information to you through local gossip. I heard that you had escaped from Perth and were on your way here." It was so hard to keep the loathing his spying engendered in her out of her voice.

"Why did you want to see me? You ran from me in France."

"I . . . I'm sorry I ran away in Paris. It was a mistake. You were right, Camber doesn't love me, and he will only make me miserable." She forced her breathing to slow down, felt sweat break out on her palm. "I want to be with you."

The next minutes seemed agonizingly long. Surely he would believe her. If not, she had thrown herself back into his clutches for no reason.

"Ah," he said at last, "you've discovered that the duke of Camber is not for you. But perhaps I no longer want you. A woman used by another man, who gave herself willingly to him. I have pride, too. What can you give me that another lover can't, if not your virginity?"

His voice lashed at her like a whip. So he wanted to humiliate her for having thwarted him before. So be it.

"Answer me," he said in a cold, flat voice.

"I can . . . pleasure you as no chaste maiden ever could," she managed. "Camber has taught me well." Bile rose in her throat at having to lure him by such means. Suppose he insisted on sampling her offering right here in the folly?

His laugh was low and menacing, with undertones of excitement. Her skin crawled. She could hear the first raindrops hitting the leaves. She shivered, from fear and cold. A drop of water landed on her wrist where his fingers still held her in a bruising grip.

"So, I have you where I have dreamed of all these weeks. Do you know what I have been through since you left me? No, I don't imagine you do. I will tell you."

He drew her to him, his free hand taking her curls and pulling her head back so that his hot breath hit her in the face. He smelled of tobacco and fish and mints.

"I managed to evade Perth in Paris, but only narrowly. I had to go out a window, much the same as you did, only I suffered a bad cut. It became infected and I had to hide in a small fishing town on the coast of France while it healed. Meanwhile the earl was sniffing around like a bloodhound on the trail of game. At last I was well enough to be smuggled into Aldeburgh, a filthy, fishy town, where I stayed for a week. Then rumors of your betrothal ball began to make their way there. Fool that I am, I couldn't stay away. At first I was undecided about what to do, but when gossip had it that you were tired of the fuss, possibly even taking a new lover—why else hint at walking in the gardens alone—I knew that I had to come. You see, *ma chérie*, you are like a drug to me. I must have you. And this time I will have you. You are going with me, tonight."

"Oh my darling," she said, "I have dreamed of hearing you speak those words. I have packed a portmanteau and am ready to go. It is in my room. I planned on having you come back to the library with me, it's dark and no one is in there. You can wait there while I fetch my bag."

His grip tightened as she took a step toward the path that led to the house. He jerked her so that her breasts pressed against his chest. Dami forced herself not to struggle as he bent her backwards, his lips crushing hers in a rough, hungry kiss. Savagely he forced her lips apart with his tongue and plundered the softness within. Dami couldn't stop her moan of dismay, but the count apparently took it as a sign of her pleasure, for he began to thrust his tongue rhythmically into her mouth until she thought she would gag.

His lips moved to the white column of her throat as Dami gasped for breath. Then, mercilessly, he moved to the valley of her cleavage. He pulled at the flimsy fabric of her bodice and lifted out the creamy white globes of her breasts, squeezing them cruelly together. Shock waves of revulsion passed through Dami as he nibbled first one tender nipple and then the other. She had to stop him; she couldn't bear such intimacy with him.

"Jacques," she said, trying to pull away. "You're

hurting me."

"Come, come," the count said thickly, "surely Camber has taught you that pain and pleasure are as one in the realm of love and lust. If not, then you have much to learn at my hands."

"Yes, of course," Dami said desperately, trying not to cry out as his fingers bit into her flesh. "He has taught me all of that and more, as you will soon find out — just as soon as we fetch my portmanteau and flee to more private quarters. My darling," she gritted out, "I am positively wild with anticipation. Shall we go in?"

He lifted his head, and she felt a wave of relief that she would finally triumph.

"Do you take me for a fool?" he hissed.

Her blood turned to ice.

"What do you mean?"

"I have traveled the last three weeks with no change of clothes, even now I am forced to wear these fisherman's rags that reek of fish and bag on me. Do you seriously think that I am going to meekly follow you into your house? Let you out of my sight again? No! You will come with me as you are."

"But, but . . ."

She tried to twist from his grip. He pushed her arm behind her back toward her shoulderblades. A stab of pain lanced through her. She thought she was going to faint. He steered her backwards. Her knees met a bench. Off balance, she fell onto it. The iron was bone chilling. Her back and neck shrank away from the cold wet that penetrated so deeply her whole body started shivering. His knee was over her stomach, preventing her from moving.

"It won't be long now, *chérie*," he crooned.

She heard a stopper being popped from a bottle. A smelly cloth was pushed to her nose and mouth. The wind seemed to be rushing past her ears. She flailed out, trying to find purchase. Her eyes widened, but her vision grew hazy. Her mind worked in incoherent snatches.

The smell of fish mingled with the new smell, one she couldn't identify. Her eyelids drooped. She tried to open them.

She mumbled into the cloth. "What are you . . . doing?"

"Merely drugging you so that you will be easier to handle. I don't have the time or the safety of distance to allow you to remain awake, possibly hampering me."

She felt the cloth move away. Tried to sit up. Couldn't. She heard his voice in the distance.

"It is only chloroform and will wear off in several hours."

Chapter Twenty-Nine

Julian glanced around the ballroom. Dami wasn't dancing. Nor could he find her talking with anyone. He looked around again, this time more slowly. The floor was full of couples dancing the waltz. He looked at the refreshment table on the opposite wall, thronged with guests. He scanned the chairs flanking the table.

His dark eyebrows drew together in a frown.

Maybe she was outside. He strode first to one door, then the other. She wasn't visible in the lighted areas outside the room. How stupid, he thought, she was very likely in the lady's retiring room. He walked quickly from the room, keeping his eyes straight ahead to deter anyone seeking to catch his attention.

He decided to wait at the foot of the stairs. Ladies going up the steps looked at him curiously, ladies coming down the steps looked at him with interest. The ladies returning from the retiring room who had seen him on their way up looked flustered. Julian increased their discomfiture by bowing gallantly offering his hand for the last steps down. He smiled and wished them a good evening. To a one, they stammered their pleasure and made their escape. It was the first time since he had been breeched that women ran from him.

Soon this diversion paled. There was still no Dami. He looked around the foyer until he spotted a maid.

"You," he waved imperiously, "please go up to the lady's retiring room and desire Lady Damaris to come down."

The maid hastened to do his bidding. Minutes later she was back. "Lady Damaris isn't there, Your Grace."

"Thank you," he said and pivoted on his heel. He headed for the library. Where could she have gone?

Entering the darkened room, he crossed to the window. The curtains were billowing into the room, and he could feel the damp air from outside. Scowling, he yanked the open windows shut. Then a thought struck him.

He turned to the mantel, grabbed the conveniently placed tinder box, and lit a candle. Returning to the window, he opened it again and leaned out. The wind blew out his candle.

Cursing, he lit the candle again. This time when he leaned out he was careful to keep the flame shielded with his hand. At the base of the window, up against the outside wall, was a small footprint. It was quickly becoming unrecognizable as water flooded it.

What had that little fool gotten herself into this time? He pulled his head back in, banged the window shut, and pondered the situation. He had thought it deuced odd that her dance card had been filled and no dance saved for him. It was their betrothal ball, after all.

He swore under his breath. He felt in his bones that de Bourville had something to do with Dami's disappearance. Damn the girl.

Spying Smithfield, he motioned to the butler. "Fetch Lord Cleve immediately. Tell him to meet me in Perth's room."

The butler lost no time.

Julian took the steps two at a time, ripping off his tight-fitting cravat as he went. Without knocking he barged into the room.

Perth was lying in bed, his eyes closed and his face flushed. Next to him, on a straight-backed chair, sat Kit. Her eyes glistened with moisture and she looked worried.

"Oh, Julian, I'm so glad you came," she said on a sob. "He's gotten worse. I've sent for Williams, but he hasn't come yet. We've got to do something. I thought his fever had broken earlier," she blushed rosily, "but then he fell asleep, and it seems to have come back. He's been tossing and turning, and there seems to be nothing I can do to lessen his discomfort."

He watched her dip a cloth in a nearby basin of water, wring it, and put it on the earl's brow. She wasn't going to like what he was about to do, but he didn't see any way around it.

"Kit," he said, approaching her and taking her free hand, "listen to me. Dami has disappeared. I fear she has gone to meet with the count." He allowed her time for all the ramifications to sink in. "Simon is due here shortly. I imagine he will start a discreet search of the grounds, but I doubt if he will find her. If she has met up with de Bourville, they are very likely already on their way to his hunting lodge in Yorkshire."

"Then why are you here?"

He could tell by the look on her face that she already knew, but didn't want to believe it. "I must get a coherent direction from Perth. He is the only one who knows where to find de Bourville's property. It may be for Dami's life, Kit."

"I see, cousin, but I fear you haven't an easy task."

Even as she said the words, Perth began to toss and turn, throwing the covers from himself and babbling an incoherent stream of words. Simon and Williams entered into this scene simultaneously.

"Julian, what is the matter?" Simon said, moving to look down at Perth. "Is he worse?"

"Your Grace," Williams said, "please move away and let me have a closer look at the earl."

Julian did as his valet asked. He took Simon to a corner and told him the situation. Immediately, Simon was out of the room to organize the servants. Julian turned back to Williams.

"How is he?" Julian asked.

"Not good, Your Grace, but he'll live. Right now we've to calm him before he tears open his shoulder again with all his activity." The valet reached for a glass and an open bottle.

"What are you doing?" Julian asked sharply.

"Givin' him some laudanum to calm him," Williams answered, pouring out the drug.

"No, not yet." Julian advanced on the bed and took the bottle from Williams's hand. "First, we must find out from him where the Count de Bourville's hunting box is." He explained again.

"Won't be easy, Your Grace," Williams said.

When Simon returned to tell them the search had

started, they still hadn't gotten the information. They had tried everything: sitting him up, shaking him, putting cool clothes on his neck and chest—nothing worked.

There was a knock on the door. Simon answered it. When he returned, he looked haggard.

"Bad news, Julian, it is as we feared. They just searched the folly, which wasn't lit, and found a scrap of silver-embroidered muslin, and a rag soaked with chloroform."

Julian looked fierce. "Perth has got to tell us." He bent over the earl and said loudly, "Where is de Bourville's hunting box? He has Lady Damaris and has taken her there drugged." He repeated himself, barely restraining his impulse to shake the earl.

Perth stirred, his eyes opened, unfocused, closed, opened again. "De Bourville? The scoundrel. I'll catch him even if I have to chase him to Marton."

"Marton? Where in blazes is that?" Simon asked.

"I don't know, and I don't care," Julian said, jumping up and tearing out of the room. Simon followed in time to hear Julian say, "Do you have a map?"

They plunged down the stairs.

"In the library," Simon said.

The two men burst into the library, calling to Snithfield to light all the candles in the room.

"Over here," Simon said, going to his desk and opening a drawer. It's not recent, but it should have most of the major towns on it."

They poured over it, starting at York and working outward in a circle.

"Here it is," Julian said. "Just northwest of York

and slightly northeast of Knaresborough. Won't be a comfortable journey, but I'll be on horseback."

He flung himself from the room, roaring for someone to see that his horse was saddled. Meanwhile, the guests in the ballroom were getting an inkling of excitement from people returning from the retiring rooms and commenting on His Grace's air of desperation.

"Simon," Julian turned at the front door, "you'd better try to calm the frisson I've caused. Don't worry, I'll bring her back safely. That scoundrel will pay."

It was late the next day, and Julian felt as if he had been on the road all his life. Leaving Green Leaf, he'd headed for Thetford and on to King's Lynn, going over mud-riddled country lanes, not even stopping at the small inns he passed to inquire for the count and Dami.

There was no way he could trail them in the continual downpour, and too many ways they could have gone. Instead he hoped that the fear of pursuit would keep the count moving too fast to take his pleasure with Dami. That was the only thought that kept his sanity for him, as he pulled into a small inn just outside of King's Lynn. He knew if he didn't rest soon, he would be in no shape to fight de Bourville.

Signing his name to the register, he noticed that a couple, Mr. and Mrs. Smith, had signed the line above his. He frowned.

"Innkeeper, when did Mr. and Mrs. Smith arrive?" Hope squared his shoulders when the proprietor said it had been just an hour before. "Describe them."

Disappointment let all his tired, aching cold settle back. The man had black hair, the woman's was tucked under a dirty handkerchief, and both smelled of the fields. He turned to mount the narrow stairs to his room for the night.

He put the key in the lock and twisted it, going into the small, dank room with a wrinkled nose. The accommodations were deplorable, but then so was he. Mud caked his evening clothes, which he hadn't taken the time to change. He had no cloak, either. Well, he would put that all to rights immediately.

Julian pulled the bell, calling the landlord. When a bootblacking boy arrived, he sent his message via him. Within minutes, there was a knock on his door.

"Landlord," Julian said, after bidding the man enter, "I want you to get me some clean clothes and a pair of boots, and I want a hot bath brought up."

"Milord, I don't have access to any clothes that would be acceptable to you."

"Get what you can." Julian turned his back on the man and heard the door close.

He had an idea. He had purposely signed the register with his least title, that of baron of Chesswick, and now he would carry the imposture further. He would disguise himself as an ordinary man traveling. The clothes wouldn't fit right, and he would undoubtedly get blisters on his feet from the boots, but it would allow him the anonymity he needed. This way, he stood a chance of sneaking up on the count and getting past any minions de Bourville might have working for him who would be on the lookout for pursuit.

A knock on the door heralded the entry of the

chambermaid with his wooden tub. She left and returned shortly with buckets of hot water.

Just as he was preparing to undress, he looked at the woman, who was still in the room. "Yes?" he said in his coldest voice.

"I was just thinkin', your lordship, you might be needin' someone to be rubbin' your back." She eyed him coquettishly through her lashes, and her buxom bosom threatened to overflow the material straining to keep it in bounds.

"No, thank you," he replied curtly. There had been a time when he might have welcomed such a diversion as the wench had offered. But at that moment only Dami could have satisfied him.

Next door, Mrs. Smith cringed in the mildewed sheets of her bed. Did Mr. Smith—better known as de Bourville—intend to leave her alone, as it seemed, or could she expect to be visited before the night was over?

Dami punched the pillow, then sneezed. She heard the noise of something large hitting the floor in the room next door and surmised it to be a tub. How she longed for a bath. She and the Count had been traveling since he had abducted her, he on horseback, she lying across a second horse until the effects of the chloroform wore off.

In the small hours of the night, de Bourville had stopped at a deserted hut and dragged her into it. He had closed the door and lit a rush light, then rummaged about in a corner until he came out holding a skirt and blouse for her that reeked of

433

manure. He had stripped her without ceremony of her torn gown and forced her into the clothes. The rest of the trip here had been a nightmare of cold and dread.

She tossed and turned, only falling into a light sleep as the sun came up. It seemed she had just dozed off when she heard the occupant of the room next door getting dressed. His heavy boots clumped across the floor. She heard his door slam behind him and then there was silence. She fell back asleep.

Groggily she became aware of a hand shaking her shoulder. She swatted it, mumbling, "Leave me alone. I need to sleep."

"You have had plenty of time already. It is half-past noon as it is, and we must be on our way. If you don't get up now, you will have to travel on an empty stomach."

It was de Bourville. She woke, then sat up, intending to tell him pithily not to enter her bedchamber, when she remembered she had only her chemise on. She fell back.

"The fight is hard to maintain when you aren't dressed for it," he said.

She glared at him. "I have no intentions of going on with you."

"Tut, tut, *chérie*. Just last night you assured me you had every intention of going with me. What a fickle female you are." He pulled back the covers. "Now get up and get dressed. You are embarrassed. I will leave, but only for five minutes. And don't think to go out the window. I have already checked it. There is no trellis and the drop is every bit of thirty feet. You would break your neck. Surely I am not a fate worse than death. Not yet." He grinned.

As soon as the door was shut behind him, she scampered out of bed and pulled on the smelly clothes. She didn't doubt he would be back in five minutes. He was.

They descended for cold porridge and kippers with weak coffee. Then it was onto the horses again. This morning Dami was more alert, and consequently, more nervous on her mount. Luckily, the count had picked endurance over highbred speed. The horse plodded along at a regular, bone-jarring pace that allowed her to keep her seat without much trouble.

Hours later the sun went down. The rain had stopped, and the roads they were traveling now were dry and dusty. Dami's mouth felt like a desert was growing in it, but she wouldn't complain.

Just out of Sleaford they stopped for supper, but were back on their horses within thirty minutes. She felt that she would fall off if de Bourville didn't let her rest.

"Are you tired, *chérie*?" he asked in a kind voice. "I am sorry, but there is no choice."

She turned gratefully to him. "Yes. Are we going to stop soon?"

"Not while there is light to travel by. I gauge we have four hours left. We should be able to make East Markham by then. There is a small inn there, and I know the proprietor."

"Is that near your hunting box?"

"About a day's ride. Actually, East Markham is southeast of Sheffield. We will be skirting all the large towns."

She nodded, exhaustion making her lose interest in something so abstract. When they finally stopped, she all but fell from the saddle. De Bourville had to support her with an arm around her waist. Entering the rundown inn, she saw the owner give them a knowing look. He handed the count the key to one room. She shoved viciously at the count's chest, making herself fall against the counter where she managed to regain her balance. De Bourville did some fancy stepping before he regained his balance.

"What was the cause of that?" he asked in an irate voice.

"Because I refuse to be treated like your doxy! That's what. I demand a separate room." She stood her ground against the fury that brewed in the count's eyes as he looked at her.

"So, you will let the duke use you like a plaything, but I must be prim and proper." He beckoned to the innkeeper. "Another key, Pierre. We will play it your way for now, Damaris, but don't get used to this."

She forced herself to stand without his aid as they followed the keeper up the cracked stairs. Pierre. He had called the man Pierre. She took a good look at the man. He was tall and must have been muscular when younger. Now his middle had gone to fat, and his chin was doubled. Dark beady eyes returned her gaze, and he broke into a toothless grin. He wore a white apron that was stained with blood and who knew what. He stank.

Was he another one of de Bourville's accomplices? That would explain how the count knew about this dilapidated inn. And what better place than this? Out of the way, where no one would want to come or even think of coming. And, if their time was any indication, it was within an easy day's ride of the coast.

"Here," the landlord said, opening a door a good foot shorter than Dami.

She went in, and before she could turn around, heard the key turn in the lock. Rushing to the door, she heard a mumble of voices and shuffling of feet as the men moved down the hall. Tears of frustration and exhaustion welled up in her eyes. She wanted to pound at the door, but she wouldn't give them the satisfaction. Instead she went to the single bed pushed up against the wall. It smelled so bad she decided to sleep on the floor with just the top blanket for cover.

The wooden planks of the floor were like rocks under her aching muscles. She tried lying on her side, but her hips hurt. Then her back, but the small of her back arched painfully unless she forced it down. Then her stomach, but her breasts flattened uncomfortably. She forgot how many times she rotated, like a roast on a spit, before she finally dozed.

The next day was much like the last, as Dami dragged herself out of bed, ate the miserly breakfast of hard toast and milk, then mounted the horse. Toward evening it began to rain again, a light drizzle that left diamond drops on the leaves of overhanging trees and a shimmer of silver across the fields as the sun began to set. Soon a full moon began to make its way across the night sky, lighting everything in its path. However, instead of clarifying what it touched, it turned the night to a mysterious pewter. The weather was getting colder, too, and Dami huddled into the meager warmth of her cloak.

Hours past they had gone by a sign post that said Harrogate to the left and York to the right. At the time, her heart had quickened, knowing they must be getting close to their destination. Now that organ had settled into a dull thump, despairing of ever stopping. All her hopes were pinned on Julian's being at the hunting box, or arriving there shortly after them.

Up ahead was another signpost. The letters were almost indistinguishable in the moonlight, for they had seen much weather. It indicated that the village of Marton was to their right. She expected they would go past it, too. They didn't.

She sat up straighter in the saddle. Were they finally nearing the end? She knew of a certainty that she wouldn't be able to hold de Bourville off much longer. She had noticed the glances he cast her way out of the corners of his eyes when he thought she wasn't looking.

While she knew she would survive any liberties he might take with her, she didn't know if her emotions would be able to handle them. But, she comforted herself, it wasn't as though she had been the only woman Julian had ever bedded. So it shouldn't make any difference if another man bedded her. It was all the same. He hadn't loved the other women; she didn't love the count. She wouldn't even be willing, as Julian had been. Somehow, though, the thoughts didn't comfort her.

The sounds of the horses' hooves changed. They were on gravel now. She looked inquiringly at her captor.

"Yes, we are almost there. It is just around this line of trees, but you won't be able to see it well because of the dark. It is only a single story and has massive oak trees overshadowing it. They block out any of the moon's light that might otherwise illuminate it."

She didn't answer.

At last they were in front of the single front door. It appeared to be made of oak and looked sturdy enough to keep an army out if the owner so intended. She looked further. There were two small windows in front, boarded up with wood thrown haphazardly across them and then nailed down in any old way. Once it must have been blue, but the elements had nearly stripped it of paint. It would be cold, too, with the fireplaces not having been used in a long time.

She sighed, knowing she was in for another very uncomfortable night.

"So eager, *ma chérie*," de Bourville taunted her.

He helped her from her horse and with his arm under her elbow guided her up the front steps to the door. From his coat pocket he took a large steel key, which he inserted into the lock. He had to let her go to turn it. Using both hands, he twisted. There was a crack and the door swung open.

The musty odor of disuse engulfed them. The count pulled her into the hall and shut the door behind them, locking it and then throwing the bolt across.

"Don't tell me you are afraid of burglars?" she said.

"I have learned from experience never to leave things to chance," he said, going to a small table pushed up against the wall.

From it he took a tinder box and a candle. Seconds later, the flickering light of a lone candle showed them a foyer inches deep in dust and with all its furniture covered by a mantle of dirt. The candlelight played against the walls, doing a macabre dance against cobwebs and a mirror that hung drunkenly.

"It's obvious you don't employ a housekeeper," she said waspishly.

"I have not been here in years. An emigré in England is careful not to show wealth, should he have it. Besides, I had no intentions of returning here. To have kept a servant would have been a waste of money."

She jumped at a sound. "Are there rats in this house of yours?" she asked, edging closer to the count.

"Really, sweetings," said a familiar voice, "you have called me many things, but I object to being mistaken for a rat!"

"Julian!" She turned to see him standing in a darkened doorway, a candle held under his face, casting his features into satanic relief. Her eyes traveled over his ill-fitting clothes and dusty boots. There was a tear in the jacket. Her eyes questioned him.

"I came in through a back window." He explained.

"Your Grace," said the count, "what an unpleasant, although not completely unexpected, visit."

Both men bowed in mock greeting. Dami lifted her skirts to flee to Julian. De Bourville grabbed her arm.

"Not so quickly," the count said. "It would appear that you are about to become the spoils of war."

The count reached into his coat pocket and drew out a pistol. Dami's eyes went large as saucers.

She twisted painfully in de Bourville's grasp, lunging onto him with all her might. They fell to the floor. Her skirts tangled their feet. The gun exploded.

Julian was on them. He grabbed the count's arm that held the pistol and banged it against his raised knee. De Bourville's hand opened. The gun fell to the floor.

Julian yanked the count to his feet and slammed him in the face with his fist. De Bourville folded.

Still sitting on the floor, Dami watched in awe. Then she was sobbing in Julian's arms.

"Hush, sweetings," he crooned, stroking her head. "It's all right. I am here, and you are safe. Shh."

"Oh, Julian, what will we do with him now?" she hiccupped.

"That's been taken care of." He smoothed the hair from her face and gave her a slow kiss. "I stopped in York and contacted the magistrate. He should be here soon."

Relief swept through her body.

Chapter Thirty

It was several weeks later at a small house in Kensington. The windows were dark, and the knocker was off the door, indicating that the owners were out of town. However, if one looked closely enough, a faint flicker of light could be seen in the largest upstair's window.

"Julian," Dami gasped, "do be still for just a minute."

"Must I, sweetings?" he answered in mock dismay.

"Yes. You are such a hardened rake," she sighed, relaxing against the pillows.

"Most perceptive of you, my darling wife." He kissed her, lingering at the hollow of her neck. "What is it you wish to discuss?"

"Oh, nothing serious . . ." she paused, pursed her kiss-ripened lips.

"Then back to business," he said.

"Rogue!" Her dimple peeked out at him. "It's just that I was hoping once Kit and Perth are married, she might put aside her scruples and have a mirror just like ours hung over her bed!"

He roared with laughter. "We shall make it our wedding present," he declared.

"Really, Julian," she began indignantly, before sighing again. "You make the most delicious movements when you laugh."

She forgot her original subject and succumbed to His Grace's ministrations. Later, in the light of a flickering candle, she lay looking back up at the mirror.

"Do you know," she said, snuggling into the warmth of his body, "this room positively terrified me the first time I saw it. All this red, and that mirror. It is decadent. Jaded." she made a moue. "No wonder you had such a shocking reputation. I'm sure all your ladybirds couldn't wait to tell their later protectors about how you set them up in debauched style."

"But that is all past." He ran a loving hand along her flank. "And if you insist, I will have this room redone, although," he said in regret, "I have always found it to be very stimulating."

"Julian!" She punched his chest.

He caught her hand and grinned wickedly at her. "You rise to the bait so readily. I really couldn't resist." He uncurled her fingers, kissing each one. "If you would rather, I will sell this house and we will build another."

"Oh no, I have nothing against this house. I have rather a fondness for it. After all, it is your Kensington residence, reserved expressly for your amorous liaisons."

"That is, reserved especially for you, sweetings." He

kissed her nose. "You are the only lady of the night I shall ever require."

Dami sighed with satisfaction and gave herself up to Julian's loving passion.

THE TIMELESS CHARM OF ZEBRA'S REGENCY ROMANCES

CHANGE OF HEART   (3278, $3.95)
by Julie Caille

For six years, Diana Farington had buried herself in the country, far from the gossip surrounding her ill-fated marriage and her late husband's demise. When she reluctantly returns to London to oversee her sister's debut, she vows to hold her head high. The behavior of the dangerously handsome Lord Lucan, was too much to bear. Diana knew that she could only expect an improper proposal from the rake, and she was determined that *no* man, let alone Lord Lucan, would turn her head again.

The Earl of Lucan knew that second chances were rare, so when he saw the golden-haired Diana again after so many years, he swore he would win her heart this time around. She had lost her innocence over the years, but he swore he could make her trust — and love — again.

THE HEART'S INTRIGUE   (3130, $2.95)
by Evelyn Bond

Lady Clarissa Tregallen preferred the solitude of Cornwall to the ballrooms and noisy routs of the London *ton,* but the future bride of the tediously respectable Duke of Mainwaring would soon be forced to enter Society. To this she was resigned — until her evening walk revealed a handsome, wounded stranger. Bryan Deverell was certainly a spy, but how could she turn over a wounded man to the local authorities?

Deverell planned to take advantage of the beauty's hospitality and be on his way once he recovered, yet he found himself reluctant to leave his charming hostess. He would prove to this very proper lady that she was also a very *passionate* one, and that a scoundrel such as he could win her heart.

SWEET PRETENDER   (3248, $3.95)
by Violet Hamilton

As the belle of Philadelphia, spirited Sarah Ravensham had no fondness for the hateful British. But as a patriotic American, it was her duty to convey a certain document safely into the hands of Britain's prime minister — even if it meant spending weeks aboard ship in the company of the infuriating Britisher of them all, the handsome Col. Lucien Valentine.

Sarah was unduly alarmed when her cabin had been searched. But when she found herself in the embrace of the arrogant Colonel — and responding to his touch — she realized the full extent of the dangers she was facing. Not the least of which was the danger to her own impetuous heart . . .

Available wherever paperbacks are sold, or order direct from the Publisher. Send cover price plus 50¢ per copy for mailing and handling to Zebra Books, Dept. 3426, 475 Park Avenue South, New York, N.Y. 10016. Residents of New York, New Jersey and Pennsylvania must include sales tax. DO NOT SEND CASH.

DISCOVER THE MAGIC OF REGENCY ROMANCES

ROMANTIC MASQUERADE   (3221, $3.95)
by Lois Stewart

Sabrina Latimer had come to London incognito on a fortune hunt. Disguised as a Hungarian countess, the young widow had to secure the ten thousand pounds her brother needed to pay a gambling debt. His debtor was the notorious ladies' man, Lord Jareth Tremayne. Her scheme would work if she did not fall prey to the charms of the devilish aristocrat. For Jareth was an expert at gambling and always played to win everything—and *everyone*—he could.

RETURN TO CHEYENNE SPA   (3247, $2.95)
by Daisy Vivian

Very poor but ever-virtuous Elinor Hardy had to become a dealer in a London gambling house to be able to pay her rent. Her future looked dismal until Lady Augusta invited her to be her guest at the exclusive resort, Cheyenne Spa. The one condition: Elinor must woo the unsuitable rogue who was in pursuit of the Duchess's pampered niece.

The unsuitable young man was enraptured with Elinor, but *she* had been struck by the devilishly handsome Tyger Dobyn. Elinor knew that Tyger was hardly the respectable, marrying kind, but unfortunately her heart did not agree!

A CRUEL DECEPTION   (3246, $3.95)
by Cathryn Huntington Chadwick

Lady Margaret Willoughby had resisted marriage for years, knowing that no man could replace her departed childhood love. But the time had come to produce an heir to the vast Willoughby holdings. First she would get her business affairs in order with the help of the new steward, the disturbingly attractive and infuriatingly capable Mr. Frank Watson; *then* she would begin the search for a man she could tolerate. If only she could find a mate with a *fraction* of the scandalously handsome Mr. Watson's appeal. . . .

ELEGANCE AND CHARM WITH ZEBRA'S REGENCY ROMANCES

A LOGICAL LADY   (3277, $3.95)
by Janice Bennett

When Mr. Frederick Ashfield arrived at Halliford Castle after two years on the continent, Elizabeth could not keep her heart from fluttering uncontrollably. But things were in a dreadful state. Frederick had come straight from the Grange, his ancestral home, where he argued with his cousin, Viscount St. Vincent. After his sudden departure, the Viscount had been found murdered.

After an attempt on his life Frederick knew what must be done: he must risk his very life, and Lizzie's dearest hopes, to trap a deadly killer!

AN UNQUESTIONABLE LADY   (3151, $3.95)
by Rosina Pyatt

Too proud to apply for financial assistance, Miss Claudia Tallon was desperate enough to answer the advertisement. But why would any man of wealth and position need to advertise for a wife? Then she saw his name and understood why. *Giles Veryland.* No decent lady would dream of associating with such a rake.

This was to be a marriage of convenience—Giles convenience. Claudia was hardly in a position to expect a love match, and Giles could not be bothered. The two were thus eminently suited to one another, if only they could stop arguing long enough to find out!

FOREVER IN TIME   (3129, $3.95)
by Janice Bennett

Erika Von Hamel had been living on a tiny British island for two years when the stranger Gilbert Randall was up on her shore after a boating accident. Erika had little patience for his game of pretending that the year was 1812 and he was somehow lost in time. But she found him examining in detail her models of the Napoleonic battles, and she wanted to believe that he really was from Regency England— a romantic hero that she thought only existed in romance books . . .

Gilbert Randall was quite sure the outcome of the war depended on information he was carrying—but he was no longer there to deliver it. He must get back to his own time to insure that history would not be irrevocably altered. And that meant he must take Erika with him, although he shuddered to think of the havoc she would cause in Regency England—and in his own heart!

Available wherever paperbacks are sold, or order direct from the Publisher. Send cover price plus 50¢ per copy for mailing and handling to Zebra Books, Dept. 3426, 475 Park Avenue South, New York, N.Y. 10016. Residents of New York, New Jersey and Pennsylvania must include sales tax. DO NOT SEND CASH.